TEDDY

TEDDY

A NOVEL

EMILY DUNLAY

HARPER

An Imprint of HarperCollins*Publishers*

HarperCollins books may be purchased for educational, business, or sales promotional use. For information, please email the Special Markets Department at SPsales@harpercollins.com.

Originally published in Great Britain in 2024 by 4th Estate, an imprint of HarperCollins Publishers.

FIRST U.S. EDITION

Library of Congress Cataloging-in-Publication Data

Names: Dunlay, Emily, author.
Title: Teddy : a novel / Emily Dunlay.
Description: First US edition. | New York, NY : Harper, 2024.
Identifiers: LCCN 2023055974 | ISBN 9780063354890 (hardcover) |
    ISBN 9780063354906 (trade paperback) | ISBN 9780063354913 (ebook)
Subjects: LCGFT: Political fiction. | Novels.
Classification: LCC PS3604.U553 T43 2024 | DDC 813/.6—dc23/eng/20231218
LC record available at https://lccn.loc.gov/2023055974

24 25 26 27 28 LBC 5 4 3 2 1

For Betty Louise; I'm sorry it took so long.
And for Mom and Dad, for everything.

She didn't understand that rain will gather in lakes on the roof of a house when the gutters are full, and she might have remained safe in her ignorance if she hadn't suddenly discovered a crack in the wall.
—Gustave Flaubert, *Madame Bovary*

Prologue

Early Morning, Wednesday, July 9, 1969

Tomorrow, or maybe the day after, everyone will know what I've done. Who I am.

The story will start in the Italian scandal sheets, in *Gente* and *L'Espresso*, then land in London at the *Mirror* and the *Sun*. It will crackle across the Atlantic on underwater cables—I imagine monstrous, bottom-feeding fish gaping snaggle-toothed, appalled, at the report of my depravity as it speeds past them—and by the time it crawls from the sea at New York Harbor or the Chesapeake Bay, my story will have evolved into something much more dangerous than mere gossip: it will be news.

The *New York Times*, the *Washington Post*; my tale will pick up stakes and head west to the *Dallas Morning News* and the *LA Times*. At dinner parties and after-work drinks, at industry events from DC to Hollywood, my name will be in everyone's mouths, crunched and swallowed between the crushed ice and maraschino cherries of their juleps and Manhattans.

And by the time it reaches Walter Cronkite's trusted lips on *Evening News*, someone will have come to get me.

I say all this, or some muddled, meandering version of it, to the men sitting across from me on my hideous terra-cotta velvet sofa.

It's not my sofa, actually—I would've done it in a nice, neutral bouclé, if it had been up to me. Or I might've had it reupholstered

1

in one of those satiny, mint-green Venetian damasks like they have at the Cipriani Hotel. David took me there for a night, once, at the end of our honeymoon. We had Bellinis overlooking the Venetian Lagoon and swam in the beautiful saltwater pool on the terrace; you can see all the way to St. Mark's Square from that hotel. The whole city smells like a swamp in the summer, though. We might as well have been in Houston on the Buffalo Bayou.

But it's not my sofa, and really, nothing in this apartment is mine—it was all here when I moved in. That was part of the problem, I think: this life, in Rome, has never fully felt like mine.

"Now," the shorter of the two men says, interrupting me—I've been speaking aloud, I realize; rambling—"Mrs. Shepard. Please try to remain calm. This is just a friendly conversation—in fact, there's no reason anything you tell us ever needs to leave this room. We're just trying to understand what happened tonight."

"This is a routine investigation—" the other, taller man begins, but his colleague interrupts him with what seems to me to be a warning look.

"Think of it like an interview," the short man says. "Like in a magazine. Like in *Ladies' Day*, or *Women's House Journal*."

"It's *Woman's Day*," I say, "and the *Ladies' Home Journal*," and both of my guests are silent for a spell.

It's hard to tell the men apart—they're both dressed in white shirts and black ties like David wears, though their Italian-cut suits are far slimmer than the boxy American styles David still insists on wearing; they both sport dark-rimmed eyeglasses perched on unremarkable noses, just like David does. They have the same short brown hair.

"It's just a formality," the tall man says, after a pause. "Paperwork. We're only trying to fill in the blanks, here. So please, Mrs. Shepard. Relax. Have a sip of your drink. This is just a friendly conversation."

It occurs to me that if I hadn't changed out of my party dress before they arrived, they would have seen the bloodstains. Then it might not be such a friendly conversation.

It took me a moment to realize what it was, when it happened: the spots blooming purple on my blue chiffon dress, a beautiful, rusted gold on the yellow beads around the sleeves and collar. Blood was supposed to be red, I knew, but it mixed like paint with the colors of my clothes. It wasn't until I saw the smears across my hands, undeniably a violent, bright crimson, that I understood.

I left the dress crumpled like a used tissue on the bedroom floor, changing into blue jeans (*dungarees*, my mother would have said, with disgust) and one of David's wrinkled white work shirts (wrinkled because I had failed to iron it, of course) as soon as I got home.

We're wearing the same type of shirt, I realize, these men and I.

If they go back to the bedroom and start digging around, lifting up dirty towels and old clothes and looking underneath, they'll find the bloody dress soon enough.

I've never been very good at covering my tracks. There has always been proof of my dissolution if anyone bothered to look.

They'll find all of it, eventually, because they will start searching now. David and his people, the State Department, my family—hell, even the damn Russians. And the reporters, too. I can already see some intrepid young journalist touching down in Dallas, in Washington, DC, and asking around. Peering under rocks and finding all my disgusting little worms.

These men in their suits would tell me not to be paranoid, if I said this out loud. They might say I sound like a nut, like one of those loonies shouting "Conspiracy!" after the Warren Report came out.

But the truth is, I haven't been paranoid enough. I've always had a nasty habit of taking other people at their word and assuming I'm the only wolf in sheep's clothing. It's something that has caused me no little fear and guilt, all my life. But I've seen beneath their skins, now, all those sheep in my flock, and I can say with some certainty that they're mostly wolves underneath, after all.

I take a sip of my drink—a few fingers of David's bourbon—as instructed. I offered to fix my inscrutable guests something, too, when they arrived at the door to our little flat—knocking softly and knowing I would answer, as late as it was, because what choice did I have?—but they turned me down. They probably think it will help them, to stay clearheaded.

The whiskey makes my eyes water, and I rub at them, then realize I'm smearing my eye makeup and crushing my false lashes, still glued on from the party. I pinch at their spidery edges, the Andrea-brand falsies in 100 percent European hair, and begin to peel.

"Child-at-heart," this model is called, and the ad I saw in *Woman's Day* showed a gallery of different lash lengths and shapes under bold black text, asking, *What kind of woman are you, anyway?*

I can feel the delicate skin of my lids lifting briefly away from my eyeballs as I pull at the adhesive strip, and one of the men—the taller of the two—gapes at me in horror. I probably look like something from *Night of the Living Dead*, like one of the cannibal corpses.

"Liz Taylor wears this kind," I volunteer in my defense.

The men only stare.

The phone on the wall in the kitchenette screams like a siren and I should have expected it, that someone would call, but still I jump and vibrate at the sound, and I can feel the men watching me, waiting to see what else I might inadvertently reveal, until the shorter one finally answers on the seventh ring.

My mother would have been horrified; she always said you should pick up the phone by the third ring, if you intend to answer it at all.

The man doesn't really answer, though—no "Shepard residence, Teddy speaking," as I used to chirp to my callers; not even a terse

"Hello." He just listens, silently, to whatever is coming through from the other end of the line.

"Who is that?" I ask.

The phone cord springs and swings like a lock of hair released from a curling iron, and the man watches me with the receiver pressed to his ear. From where I sit, I can only hear a muffled murmur, but I see the corners of his mouth flatten and then drift downward until finally, with a grimace, he says into the receiver, "Understood," and hangs up with the softest little click.

"Who is that?" I ask again. "Is everything all right?"

The man glances quickly, just once, to his right—something people do when they're about to lie, Eugene told me once—and says, "Of course, Mrs. Shepard. Everything is just fine. As we've said, this is simply a friendly conversation."

"Now," adds the taller man, "why don't you start at the beginning?"

"I didn't mean to do it," I say, and he tilts his head, curious.

"Didn't mean to do what?"

I hardly meant to do any of it—anything I ever did—all my life. So where do you start *that* kind of story?

1. Dallas

January–May 1969

David took me to Arthur's Prime Steaks & Seafood for our first date. I think about that night often, twisting it over in my mind like an oyster sucking on a speck of sand. Trying to pick out the warning signs.

But it was an ordinary evening, or at least not notably life-changing. I didn't even fall in love. I thought he was awkward and unattractive, at first, with his horn-rimmed glasses and his ears that stuck out like sails from the sides of his head. They were fat and puffy, almost cauliflower ears, but David was no boxer. I don't mean to say he wasn't dangerous, just that he had a particular way he liked to fight, and it wasn't with his hands.

I have to say I'm ashamed, now, of my first impression of him. That I judged him so harshly over something that wasn't his fault. There was plenty to judge him for, later, but I didn't know it at the time.

My cousin Marcia had convinced her husband, an old pal of David's from the University of Wisconsin, to give him my phone number. He was in Dallas on business for the government, apparently, having flown all the way from the American Embassy in Rome, and he didn't know anyone in town to have dinner with— or rather, didn't know anyone aside from Marcia's husband, and Marcia, as I learned much later, found David off-putting and cold

6

and didn't want to waste a babysitter on him. So, she thought of me instead.

Marcia was always trying to set me up. "You'll do great together," she said on the phone, when she told me to expect his call at any minute. "You're the two most eligible spinsters I know."

I was very beautiful—and I'm not being vain, you know; it's something people used to say to me. Still do, actually—so you might have thought dating would be easy for me. But everyone is beautiful in Dallas, and I was already thirty-four, and every other man Marcia had set me up with had apparently reported after the fact that he found me to be distant and aloof and strange—"a tough nut to crack," which was a characterization that always surprised me, given that I mostly felt like I was missing my shell, leaving the tender and rumpled meat of myself out in the open for any errant squirrel. Marcia was always free with these reviews, as if I could adjust my demeanor by committee. "Loosen up a little, Ted," she'd say. "Let your hair down."

I did, that night. I wore it long and loose, tousled at the top like Jean Shrimpton's on the cover of *Vogue*. I'd copied one of her ensembles, as well—a square-necked shantung cocktail sheath worn with enormous rhinestone earrings and silver pointed-toe pumps. I was six months away from thirty-five and I was determined to find a husband before then, a plan of which absolutely everyone approved.

"Some women age like fine wine, and some age like milk," my Uncle Hal was fond of saying, whenever someone asked me on a weekend at the ranch when I was finally going to find a man. He never followed the statement with the comforting clarification that I was one of the lucky ones, which I took to mean he thought I was already spoiling. "It's not too late," my mother liked to say, smiling benevolently at me. "And you're such a lovely girl."

"I'm going to take you to dinner," David had said on the phone, when he finally called on January the twenty-third after two days of meetings with Braniff Airways about their Italian expansion. "I'm going to take you," he said, as if he would come to collect me and then deposit me safely at the table. But then he told me a time and a place to be, and I realized I was meant to meet him there, and Daddy had taken my car to the shop earlier in the week and at that point in the month I barely had enough cash left for a cab. I couldn't reasonably ask my parents for more, and even though I wasn't getting paid for my work at the Huntley Foundation, it was the sort of job you only did if you already had money, so I couldn't plead poverty, either, like I was a secretary or a stewardess, and ask David to come get me instead.

There was no way for him to have known all of that, obviously, but it shouldn't have mattered. That wasn't how these things were supposed to work. Over time I would learn that David was always like this—overconfident, strangely so given the initial impression he made, and then stumbling, unsure, when it came to certain details.

It's frustrating: you want these men to be the masters of the universe they claim to be, you want them to be in complete control of the world they do such damage in, but then they don't know not to give their secretary roses for her birthday or how to pronounce *hors d'oeuvres*.

The only information I had about David when I met him at Arthur's was that he worked for the government and liked to drink bourbon, neither of which he had told me. I knew about the government from Marcia, and I knew about the bourbon from her husband, Roy, who'd grabbed the phone to tell me a disgusting story about a fraternity party that had taken place in Madison fifteen years earlier. I still spent hours getting ready, though, trying to be beautiful. I thought it was an issue of mathematics: if I accepted every date, if I presented myself perfectly, eventually one of them would want to keep me.

I was horrible at math, though. How else do you get to the end of every month without enough for a cab fare?

I remember crying in the bathroom of my little apartment, the one Daddy had bought for me after graduation and that Mama had furnished with silk curtains from Scalamandré and a bedroom set from Weir's, when my hair wouldn't go right. Considering canceling when I picked too hard at a spot on my cheek and it began to bleed, and then I had to put a little piece of tissue on it to absorb the blood, just like a man who'd cut himself shaving, to get it dry enough for my makeup to stay on. It eventually scabbed over and looked like a beauty mark for a few days, until it healed. I still have a scar.

In the end, I was half an hour late to dinner, and I'd had to take the city bus. I tried to play it off as something fashionable and fun, like I was independent and devil-may-care, but I could tell David was annoyed from the way he said he wasn't and how he smiled with his teeth closed, and it made me want to get up and walk right back out that door. I had already ruined it, this thing I didn't even think I wanted, and now it didn't matter if I sat through dinner or not, because at the end of the evening I would go back alone to the apartment on Turtle Creek, to my fancy floral curtains, knowing however many men I said yes to, or even if instead of going straight home I went to the French Room or the Library Bar or any of the other usual places, the nights of my life were always going to end this way, eventually, until everyone agreed there was no point in me trying to live on my own and I was reabsorbed by my family. I'd be returned to my childhood bedroom in the big house on Beverly Drive, where I would eventually, I supposed, die.

"I guess Huntley girls can't afford real jewelry," David said that night, pointing to my earrings after we'd ordered drinks. "Unless you've got real diamonds the size of pigeon's eggs. Or maybe you're the ones who bought the Hope Diamond. Any bad luck lately?"

So, Marcia had told him about the family. My mother's family, that is—Daddy had done well enough with cattle ranches up in

the panhandle, mostly because they turned out to have oil underneath, but Mama's family owned half of Dallas. Or had, in the
old days, before they sold it and invested the money. Now they
had the largest fine art collection in Texas—the foundation that
"employed" me—and Uncle Hal, my cousin Marcia's father, was
a senator.

Everyone knew he was going to be president one day, too, just
as soon as Dick Nixon's time was up. Grandpop had been the
governor, once upon a time, and after he died they named an
interchange down in Houston after him. Huntley money was behind
the most important Party victories in cities and states across the
nation, not to mention a men's dormitory at Texas A&M and the
new stadium at my own alma mater, SMU.

David's joke was outdated; the Hope Diamond wasn't for sale
anymore, and anyone who'd seen that *The Name's the Same* episode
with the Marx Brothers would've known the curse was just a rumor,
but David was always behind the times on things like that. The
only news he paid attention to was politics, his favorite music was
jazz from twenty years ago, and he didn't like going to the movies
or watching television.

I didn't know any of that at the time, of course, but I could see
that he was trying to charm me by insulting me and was failing
miserably at both. That endeared him to me. He got better at being
mean as he got to know me.

I laughed. And then when he asked me what I did with myself
all day, I told him about the Huntley Foundation, and instead of
saying something cutting about me staying so close to home, the
way a pilot from Braniff I'd been out with once had, he said, "So
you're a rare and beautiful thing who collects rare and beautiful
things." And that was enough.

Enough for four more cocktails, for the surf and turf special with
half a dozen baby Baltimore oysters each to start ("Oysters in Texas,"

David said. "Well. Let's see."), and for me to return to his hotel with him at the end of the evening, "for a nightcap."

And then, in the morning, when I woke in his room at the Statler Hilton in a panic, thinking, Marcia will hear about this, everyone will hear about this, and they'll learn what kind of girl I really am, it was enough for him to hold me and rub my back soothingly under the sheets and say, "I'm sorry, I shouldn't have asked you back here. I know you've never done this before."

So that was a lie I had told him, apparently, while letting my hair down.

I was always careful on my dates with friends of friends, friends of the family, but I wasn't always careful in general. I wasn't, as David seemed to think, inexperienced. But I decided to let myself be comforted, because I was already tingling with fear at the alternative, at the thought of everyone finding out and what they would say, and because time was bearing down on me and I could feel the weight of it, and because I did like him, in the end—the sweet way his cheeks flushed in bed, the way he shivered a little when I traced the tips of my fingers down his broad, sweaty back.

When we kissed goodbye in his room, after we'd had coffee sent up from the kitchen and had rinsed off together in the little shower cubicle, so strangely intimate, he told me that he was leaving for Rome in the evening but that he would be back in two weeks and wanted to take me to the Old Warsaw.

He called every other day in between, even though it was international and we didn't have that much to talk about, anyway. But he called at the same time every time and stayed on the line for five minutes or more, though at least one or two of those minutes was spent in long silence. Charges didn't apply to calls from the embassy, he explained, when I said it was too expensive to go on like this. He couldn't say much about his work over the phone, he also said, and I certainly didn't have anything to say that would amuse him about my own life, having already exhausted his limited interest in the foundation's primary collecting areas of Flemish Renaissance sculptors and French Impressionist painters, so we confined ourselves to discussing the weather (fine) and the news (bad—mudslides, fires, executions, Russians up to no good, Vietnam).

After two weeks of this he landed back at Love Field, came straight to my apartment building in a rented car, and told me he didn't actually have work in Dallas at all, this time, but had come just to see me. And to collect me and take me out for dinner, so it seemed the first date and the requirement that I arrive there under my own steam had been a fluke, or maybe he had just decided, as the constant telephone calls seemed to indicate, that I was his responsibility now.

I waited to tell my friends about David until after the second date, though even that seemed too soon to be sure that we were really going to amount to anything.

"Yes, but what does he *look* like?" my friend Eleanor asked, when I explained how reliable he had turned out to be, how punctual. "How does he make you *feel?*"

I told her how his skin was surprisingly soft for a man's, and how he blinked like a kitten when I took his glasses off to kiss him. Then I tried to describe his ears, which I had already come to think of as something that I loved about him especially much, and Eleanor said, "You sound like you're describing a cat you found."

After our third date and another two weeks of phone calls, he asked me if I thought I could live in Rome. It was getting expensive, David explained, to switch continents for every date. I suppose, looking back, that up to that point he'd thought of it as an investment.

"You can't just move to Italy," Eleanor said.

"And certainly not without a ring," said Marcia.

So, on our fourth date, which was just to El Fenix for enchiladas and then back to his hotel room to make love, I told David as much, and a few weeks after that, we were married at City Hall.

It all happened so fast that there wasn't time for a big celebration or a church wedding. That's what Mama said, but I know that really, she thought I was too old.

All my friends' weddings had been in the *Dallas Morning News*, the photos of them in white dresses printed alongside formal announcements of their new, married names. But nobody gets excited when you're thirty-four; my mother would have been embarrassed to have it in the papers. It would have been a farce, me in an enormous white dress and veil marching down the aisle of Highland Park Methodist, everyone bringing wrapped gifts, matching dishes and punchbowls and silver samovars, to a reception at the country club.

It wasn't done, Mama said, to wear a full wedding dress after thirty, and the white dress from my debut didn't fit me anymore, so she bought me a boxy Oleg Cassini suit in a pale gold that washed me out, what with my coloring, and shoes to match in a shade the saleswoman at Neiman's called buttercup but that I overheard Uncle Hal describe as cat-piss yellow. I might have laughed at poor David's bewildered expression when he saw what passed for his bride walking down the hallway on the second floor of City Hall, which was all we had for an aisle, but he never liked it when I laughed if he hadn't been the one to make the joke, so I didn't.

David and I had decided, or it had been decided for us, that since we were moving abroad to his posting in Rome to start our new life, the rest of it—the gifts and the luncheons and crossing the threshold of a new home—wasn't necessary. So, there was a little party at the Beverly house after City Hall, and that was enough to formally signify that David and I were joined together, now, and let no man tear us asunder.

I would have liked the gifts, if I'm honest. I would have liked a matching set of tumblers from Baccarat, like Eleanor got for her wedding. I would have liked to go with Mama and pick out my silver pattern, adding spoons and oyster forks and a cake knife at each special occasion over the years. But we couldn't take anything with us, and we didn't have anywhere to put it.

It was fine, of course. I didn't need all those dishes and decorations. But I think maybe it would have felt more real, if we'd bought a house and filled it with things. Maybe it all wouldn't have ended up the way it did, if we'd had the trappings of a marriage, and not just the title.

When I was little, my Aunt Sister—Cecilia, as she was baptized, but everyone called her Sister—liked to quote Henry David Thoreau: "All good things are wild and free."

Sister was my mother's youngest sibling, Hal the oldest, and Cecilia Huntley had a quintessential baby-of-the-family's lack of interest in convention. She never married or settled down; when someone would ask her at Thanksgiving or Easter if she'd met a nice man, or if she had been seeing anyone recently, she would say, "Oh, no one in particular," and my mother would shake her head and mutter over the implication that Sister was thus seeing a lot of people in general.

She lived out of hotels in Biarritz or on yachts in the Aegean or stayed with rich friends at their apartments on the rue de la Paix. She told me once, "They want to tie you down with refrigerators and good china, with your silverware set as an anchor around your ankle." She never specified who "they" were, but she said marriage and domestic life was a trap for women, and whenever Mama caught her talking like that she would try to hush her, but it was hard to disagree, sometimes, when I looked at Mama's life compared to Aunt Sister's.

Aunt Sister used to come and stay with us for a few days here and there—"Any longer in Dallas," she would say, "and I'll break out in hives"—and every time she would appear on the doorstep of the Beverly house with stacks of photographs and a bag of souvenirs from her most recent trips. Everything seemed brighter and more chaotic when she was in town; the grownups would stay up later than usual after dinner, laughing and talking, and even Hal would make time to stop by and see her.

The only person who never seemed to enjoy these visits was Mama—Sister was always doing something to disrupt the order of the house, and it drove my mother to distraction. I remember one summer Sister came back from France with beautiful printed silk scarves for me and Mama—"She's twelve years old, Cecilia, she doesn't need a silk scarf," Mama said before she confiscated mine—and a recipe for a soufflé flavored with candied violets ("You can only buy them in Toulouse") and served with champagne crème, and Sister said that when you cut into it, you could see the colors of a sunset inside. The soft golden brown of the eggs and flour and butter once baked, Sister said, mixed with the melting purple violets and the pale, milky peach of the champagne. I'd never heard of anything so lovely; I'd never even heard words like that together before. Candied violets sounded like food for fairies, not for earthly beings.

Mama never let us have dessert except on special occasions, and she hardly ever ate any herself, except on the third Saturday of every month, when she would allow herself a single scoop of vanilla ice cream after dinner. I used to hate that day, watching her get more and more agitated as it got closer to evening time, to ice cream time, like a little dog dancing around the dinner table on its clickety-clacking toenails. Begging for scraps.

She tried to object to Aunt Sister's grand culinary plan on those grounds—that it was indulgent, unnecessary—but Daddy heard, and said, "Let the girl make her fancy cake." And so that Saturday,

Aunt Sister and I spent all afternoon in the kitchen preparing and then baking the soufflé, although we had a few unsuccessful attempts, collapsed constructions, piles of purple goo that we hid from sight, laughing as we did so.

But in the end, she was right, it looked just like a sunset when you cut into it, such a beautiful soft lilac color fading into orange and gold, and even Daddy and Uncle Hal noticed at dinner how lovely it was, and how interesting and strange it tasted.

"Like a mouthful of perfume," Daddy said, "but you know what? I think I kind of like it."

And Mama sat through all of this and said, "No, thank you," when we offered her a slice of the soufflé, and she let the whole table be cleared with her portion still left in the pot, and I forgot all about it for a while after that, because it was time for me to go to bed and Daddy and Uncle Hal went off to have their cigars and tell dirty jokes and funny stories, as they always did on such evenings. Aunt Sister had some magazines she wanted to read on the porch, she said, and Mama said she wasn't feeling too well and would go to bed early.

I didn't fall asleep for a while after I got into bed, though, and I thought perhaps the rest of the soufflé was still in its ramekin—perhaps it had been put away for tomorrow. So I snuck downstairs knowing the grownups would still be doing whatever it was they did after bedtime for hours, and therefore would be unlikely to catch me prowling around, but then there was already a light on in the butler's pantry when I got there, and I saw Mama in her stuffy quilted housecoat, which she wore year round despite the summer heat, standing over the soufflé bowl and shoveling chunks into her mouth with her hands. Licking her fingers.

I remembered it was ice cream night, and realized we must have interrupted her scheduled treat with our fancy soufflé, and I felt that I was witnessing something I shouldn't be seeing, and I couldn't quite identify the feeling at the time, but I think I was a little disgusted, too.

I went to find Aunt Sister on the porch with her magazines, with her dark hair ("The color of a crow's breast," Daddy had said once, remarking on how different her coloring was from Mama's; "Don't say breast," Mama had responded) already in curlers, and she showed me in her *Harper's Bazaar* (*Harper's Brassiere*, Daddy liked to call it, to Mama's dismay) the nine-page spread of summer fashions— "ageless, easy evening dresses that can be worn in all kinds of company." And then we marveled at the incomparable Dorian Leigh on the cover of *Vogue*.

"What an elegant woman," Sister said. And then, conspiratorially, "You know, she's from Texas, too. And you kind of have her nose."

Aunt Sister told me about other pastries we could try, and perfumes and clothes she would bring back from abroad. She said there were all kinds of things you could find in France, even after the war. I wanted to go to Paris to taste them. I wanted to try the delicacies she had described on other visits, things that felt so far away from me—the sweet, burning sour taste of limoncello, stews and spices she'd had in Morocco and Egypt that I couldn't even name. And more than flavors and scents: the pyramids, the Sphinx. The souks of Morocco, the stone cathedrals of Italy and France. The museums and parks and palaces of the old world.

I admired her for a long time, when I was younger, and for a while I dreamed of a carefree, unbounded life like hers. But by the time I met David, I wanted to be weighed down. I wanted a houseful of things to keep me tethered, lest I float away entirely. The way Aunt Sister had, in the end.

Still. A small, dangerous part of me thought, when David decided to take me with him to Rome, that this was it. My chance to see and touch and taste the world—to understand it and take it in—the way Aunt Sister had. I was playing with fire, and I knew it, but I couldn't quite stamp out the feeling, thrumming thrillingly and treacherously in the back of my mind as I packed bags full of everything I would need for my new life as David's wife—the silky nightgowns with matching peignoirs in pastel colors, the bright spring dresses for garden parties and ladies' luncheons, the varnishes and curlers and creams— that I was preparing, too, for some other adventurous, electrifying Teddy who would reveal herself to me in due course.

But this was a thought to be tamped down rather than entertained, so I mostly tried to ignore it. I did allow myself to be excited, at least, for the sea—for our honeymoon, David and I were going to Capri and then driving up that beautiful coastline to our new lives in Rome.

I had been to Sea Island and Palm Beach before, but Aunt Sister had said once that the water was different, *abroad*. No country clubs or golf courses just past the beach. No summer vacation with your parents in pastels. Aunt Sister had spoken of blue waves crashing on rocky shores where Caesar and Antony and Cleopatra had once walked. She said she had read that in ancient times you could see all the way to the bottom of the seabed, to shipwrecks from the days of the *Odyssey* and the *Iliad*.

On a trip to Palm Beach, once, we went down to put our feet in the water, even though it was early spring and too cold to get all the way in, and Sister said that the ocean connected all members of mankind to one another, and that it turned and turned around the world, touching everyone, and you could stand on the shore and know you were at the edge of something connecting you to your brothers and sisters, and whoever you were in that moment was eternal, and you weren't alone.

I later established that this was a philosophy she had cobbled together from various transcendentalist authors she'd picked up during her rushed wartime college education, mostly Emerson and Thoreau, plus a few days she once spent visiting a red-and-gold-painted Buddhist monastery on a hill in Tibet. Mama and Daddy used to roll their eyes when she talked like this, and of course, later, we all thought maybe she was just crazy. Maybe she believed that a person's life was contained in moments because anything longer tended to slip through her fingers.

After the wedding, at the party, my Uncle Hal wrote us a check for twenty thousand dollars to start us out, winking all the while at David, saying, "Boy, you just let me know if you ever get tired of being a pencil-pusher and want to have a little fun. I could make you a state senator in two years, congressman in five."

Then, reconsidering, "Maybe not in Texas, not with those ears. But we'll move you to Montana, somewhere like that. Teddy won't mind, even if there's no Neiman Marcus. Five years, I swear it."

David smiled with his teeth closed, and I rubbed his arm thinking the comment about his ears was what was bothering him, and we took the money and had a wonderful time in Capri, or at least I did, at least for the first few days, and we put the rest of it in a joint bank account with David's name on it for our future. And my mother and Hal promised, too, that in a few more months, once I was thirty-five, they could release the rest of my inheritance from Grandpop, now that there was nothing to worry about. I had a stable future established, I had proven I wasn't spoiled milk, I had a man to help me manage myself, and I wasn't too old, still, to have children. They didn't like David as a dinner guest (Uncle Hal told Daddy "The boy looks like a kicked dog when he smiles"), but they thought he had a promising future in the Party if he would ever just be sensible and give up on the State Department.

"We can go look at houses in Georgetown," Mama said while she helped me pack my bags, "when David's posting is up."

Now

Early Morning, Wednesday, July 9, 1969

"Sorry, Mrs. Shepard—"

"Teddy, please," I say. "And you haven't told me your names, yet."

These are my guests, after all. I have a social obligation to get to know them.

"Mrs. Shepard," the shorter man goes on determinedly, and still he doesn't tell me his name, "could you pause for a moment, please? You say Senator Huntley—your uncle—provided David Shepard with a check totaling twenty thousand dollars?"

"Yes," I say, and I take another sip of my bourbon, but then I realize the glass is empty.

I stand up and pad on bare feet—a bit rude, I suppose, for a hostess to be shoeless; Mama would never have approved—over to David's liquor cabinet.

"Are y'all sure you don't want anything?"

They don't answer, but the taller man makes a few scratches on a yellow notepad and then looks up at me.

"And did you happen to overhear, in any conversation between the senator and your husband, what the reason was for this payment?"

"Oh," I say, returning to the threadbare love seat opposite my interviewers, "it was a gift."

"And is your family in the habit of making such extravagant

gifts?" the shorter man asks, and I think I can detect a hint of something ugly. A sneer, perhaps.

Real emotion—that's good. That's useful.

"Sure," I say, "and it was supposed to be a gift for me, too. That's what I thought, anyway. It was supposed to be for both of us. For our new life."

"And this was a source of some discord between the two of you?"

"Well, I've always been bad with money, I guess. So you could say that had something to do with it."

I expect one of them, maybe the taller man, to crack some kind of a joke, probably about women and math, but the two of them only exchange a glance, and I can't quite read between the lines.

"Moving on, then," the short man says. "When did you first arrive in Rome?"

"I'm getting to that," I say.

They're very impatient, these men.

"It's my birthday today, by the way," I say.

Then I look at the clock and see that the minutes have ticked over past midnight, and actually it isn't, anymore.

"We didn't go straight to Rome," I add. "First, we went on our honeymoon."

I might be wrong, but I think the taller man sighs.

They don't stop me, though, so I carry on.

2. Capri

May 1969

It only rained one day on our honeymoon. It started out sunny; we'd gone to La Canzone del Mare for the day as usual, because our hotel didn't have a beach or pool. The Gatto Bianco was a lovely little inn in town—Ingrid Bergman and Roberto Rossellini had stayed there on a lost weekend during their affair, apparently, and I'd read in an interview that it was Sophia Loren's favorite spot on Capri—but it was inland on the island, so David and I went to the lido at the Canzone beach club most days to get some sun.

I loved walking through the little town to and from the hotel; the low, whitewashed villas and hotels, some colorfully painted, with little balconies covered in vines or edged in boxed flowers. There were apartment buildings along the harbor, no more than a few stories high, and I imagined how happy I would be to live in a little flat in one of those, just a few simple rooms by the water, waking up every morning to the sunrise, and at night watching the fairy lights of ships in the distance going by.

I used to do that a lot; see a little house or someone else's flat when I was walking around or driving, and imagine myself in it. I came by this type of reverie honestly, I believe; my granny—my daddy's mother, not a Huntley relative—had a collection of little ceramic houses that she kept on the windowsill over her sink. The

Victorian, the Cape Cod, the Hacienda, the Cottage. I never knew where she got them, or what they meant to her, but from the reverent way she said their names, and how she looked at them when she washed the dishes, I suspect they represented other lives she imagined for herself.

My Carlyle granny washed her own dishes: she was a tough East Texas woman who didn't come from money like Mama's parents did. She wore little lace-up black boots every day of her life, and she lived, until her death, when I was still pretty small, in the dog-run house she was born in, feeding chickens in the yard and planting pumpkins and tomatoes all the way up to the end. She was mostly a practical woman, from the stories I've been told, but she did love her little houses.

I noticed right away that Aunt Sister had been telling the truth about the water in Capri: it felt different from Palm Beach or Sea Island. The twisting, ancient rocks offshore, the arches and columns naturally carved into them over thousands, probably millions, of years of turning, churning seas. The waves were much wilder than in Florida or Georgia; I had the feeling, as Aunt Sister had described it, that the earth really was moving all around us. That this island was an outpost in a larger world, not a sheltered inlet populated by bankers and automotive heirs.

Which isn't to say there weren't plenty of the beautiful people there: you could find a host of them at the Canzone del Mare, slim, long-legged, bronzed women in whisper-thin red one-piece swimsuits, the kind I never could have worn. Not with my chest. Others in impossibly tiny bikinis, looking so confident and glamorous, so comfortable with the sun warming their flat bellies. I would never have been allowed to wear something like that to the pool at our country club in Dallas, or to the beach in Sea Island. I would never have even tried. But the way the women stood with their perfect bodies, the way their long, loose hair swished around their shoulders when they stood from their lounge chairs to sway for a moment to the music or walk over to a husband or boyfriend or lover—men who looked like Alain Delon, who smoked and wore Persol sunglasses like Steve McQueen—to place a hand on his sun-warmed shoulder, to lean down to kiss him . . . Well, I was impossibly, achingly jealous.

That day, David was laid out by the pool, squinting at his newspaper through the tinted lenses he clipped to his glasses, and I went down to the beach to be alone for a while. You could see starfish in rocky pools along the jetty. I never saw an octopus, to my regret, but I'd heard they gathered there sometimes, too. People even spoke of dolphins dancing on the waves, but I never saw them, either.

I spread my striped towel out on the warm wood of the deck just at the water's edge, and I lay there for hours. There was a breeze, and I felt wrapped in it, cocooned. I couldn't hear what was happening up by the pool aside from faint strains of music and an occasional loud laugh; it was a muffled, peaceful feeling, like the world was far away. Like it couldn't touch me.

And then the clouds rolled in, gray and soft overhead, and it started to rain, so I held my towel over my hair and ran back up to the pool where David was waiting. He had his newspaper over his head, and we laughed the way people do when they run from the rain, because there's something childlike in it, and because no matter how many times it happens it still seems strange and absurd and miraculous, water falling from the sky, at least if you're from certain parts of Texas, where you can have a thunder and lightning storm without ever seeing a drop of rain, and we hopped and skipped over to the club's restaurant, to sit under the overhang and have espresso and rich, chocolaty *torta caprese* and watch the rain come down over the palms, their fronds like spiders stretching against the gray sky in the villa gardens along the cliffside.

David kept his thick, wavy hair cut short, but wet as it was from the rain, it stuck out in all directions and down at the edges of his forehead like a fringe. He looked so young, and sweet. We sat there with our cake and our espresso, smiling at each other, chatting about nothing, and he took my hand during a lull in our conversation and said, "Teddy, I think we could actually be happy together."

And at the time I thought, of course, we already are, that's why we're doing this. I didn't realize that for David, it wasn't obvious. For David, there was still a decision to be made.

I was too blinded by my own success, though, to know that anything was wrong—at least at first. Things hadn't always been easy for me, in Dallas. I'd had a few bad habits. A few tendencies that occasionally got me into trouble—things that I could mostly hide from my family, but that a husband would have eventually started to notice.

But somehow, now that I was married, all my troubles had miraculously, conveniently, disappeared. There was still the past, of course, and some things David didn't need to know about, but the future was well within my grasp. Our whole honeymoon, I woke up early and walked on the beach in the fresh air, I ate when David ate, no more and no less, I had a glass of wine or two with dinner, and that was all. I read Muriel Spark in the sun, I did almost everything right, and I felt like I was finally one of them, those married women whose lives were in order, who seemed to have it all figured out. I could look down the road and see children, see a house in Georgetown, see myself in a skirt suit from Chanel at David's side. I could see safety.

I did almost everything right, just up until the last day. I'd bought a bikini in one of the shops on the island, a little Pucci two-piece number printed in pastel pink and lavender and sherbet orange. I was going to wear it at the Canzone with high-heeled sandals the way the other girls did, and slather myself in baby oil to work on my tan. I didn't look exactly like the thin, athletic Italian women who lounged around the pool in their flimsy maillots, with their gold jewelry and Forte dei Marmi tans, but I thought, observing myself in the cabana's mirror, that I still looked pretty good. A little softer, maybe, a little paler, but close enough. I looked like I belonged, or would soon, in that poolside tableau of warm, confident European women and their handsome lovers. Of people who relaxed and enjoyed things, moment to moment—people who sucked the marrow out of life, as Aunt Sister might have said, quoting Thoreau again.

David didn't say anything, at first, when I came out of the dressing room, which perturbed me—no whistle of appreciation, no randy comment—but I didn't realize anything was actually wrong until an hour or so later by the pool, when he took a sip of his Aperol while looking at me, and finally said, "That sure is a lot of chest, Teddy."

I didn't know his habits, then; I didn't know what that meant.

"Do you like it?" I asked, in a tone I thought might be sultry. I wanted to be flirtatious. Charming and adventurous.

"I just don't know that every man in here needs to be seeing that much of you," he said. He was looking off into the distance, now, at the other people by the pool. Or at least, I could tell he wasn't looking at me anymore, even through those clip-on lenses.

"I don't know what you were thinking," he went on, "or whether you were inclined to wear that sort of thing before, but you're married now. You're my wife."

Before I go on, I don't want to give the wrong impression of David. I don't want anyone to get the wrong idea. He was mostly very sweet and patient with me, at first. And he never touched me in anger, not once.

In fact, the only time I ever saw him cry was also on our honeymoon. We'd been in bed for most of the morning before breakfast, rustling around in the sheets. I wanted to please him, my new husband, and so I'd done my best to be pliant, flexible. I mean that literally—I was arching my back and moving my hips in a way that no one but a Rockette should ever attempt. I felt something like a rubber band snapping in the meat just above my rump, just as he was finding his rhythm, and I winced a little, I'm sure, but didn't say anything, and David was too far gone to notice. But then after another hour—we spent so much time in bed, those first few weeks, that I didn't realize he would mind so much how sleepy I was, how slow-moving, once we got to Rome—he reached for me again and I said, as sweetly as I could, "Let's go gently, this time. I think I hurt my back."

He stopped and pulled away and then questioned me until I admitted it had happened that morning, it had happened while we made love, and then he said, "Teddy, you have to tell me these things!" and I thought he was angry until he put his head in his hands and said, "I don't want to hurt you, Teddy. I never want to hurt you. I want the opposite."

When he lifted his head again, I could see his eyes glistening and full. He went out onto the balcony after that for his coffee, and I didn't know what to do, really, and we never spoke about it again except that he was unusually tender with me for the next few days, and then he seemed to forget about it altogether. He never did hurt me, though, not on purpose. As I said, he was always very careful with his hands.

A woman in my apartment building in Dallas ended up at Parkland Hospital once, when the Cowboys lost to Green Bay. It wasn't that her husband cared so much about football, she explained, when I saw her in the elevator coming home with her bandaged eye and her fingers taped together. It wasn't that he was so obsessed with the team, she'd said, as if that would have been embarrassing. It was just that people drank so much for those big games. All

27

those men together, and tensions running high. Her husband always smiled at me in the elevator when I saw him, and even after that, I didn't know what to do but smile back.

The men in my family never hit women; Uncle Hal used to joke that it showed a lack of creativity.

So it's easy for me to remember David's colder moments, now, but perhaps it isn't fair. He could be sensitive and tender, sometimes, too. I collected the little cruelties later, though. They comforted me.

That day, in Capri, I went back to the cabana and changed. I put my dress back on and waited for David to finish at the pool while I sat alone at one of the café tables by the clubhouse. I ordered an Aperol of my own, though I'd avoided drinking anything but a little wine with dinner up to that point on our trip. The herbal, bitter taste reminded me of medicine. It tasted like a thick orange cough syrup my mother used to give me when I was little; it tasted like the promise that you'll be better soon.

Now

Early Morning, Wednesday, July 9, 1969

"Have you ever been to Capri?" I ask the men. "To the coast? You really ought to go, if you haven't yet. It's stunning."

"Haven't had the pleasure," the short man says, while the taller one taps his pen against his yellow notepad.

"You should take your wives," I observe, looking down at my glass of bourbon. At my long, pink claws around it. "They might enjoy it."

Neither man responds, this time, so I suppose this conversation, this getting-to-know-you, really is intended to be one-sided.

"Where did you say you gentlemen were from, again?" I ask.

"The Foreign Buildings Office," the short man answers, just as the tall one says, at the same time, "Don't worry about it."

"Oh, so you're just here about the damage to the embassy building, are you?" I ask. "I suppose it is historical, after all."

"Mrs. Shepard, please," the shorter man says, very slowly, because he thinks I'm stupid. "Would you mind telling us *when* you arrived in Rome?"

I think I can see a bit of a reddish tinge to his hair, maybe, and a few freckles—not unlike my David's—across his nose.

I'm getting to know them, my inquisitors, whether they like it or not.

I decide, in the absence of a given name, to call this one Archie, after the character from the comics. The taller one should naturally

29

thus be Jughead, but there's a bit of a menacing, bullyish air about him, so I settle on Reggie, instead.

"And describe your first contact with the ambassador," Reggie orders.

"Well, first I have to get to Rome," I say. "So, let's go."

3. Rome

May–Early June 1969

When we finally made it to Rome, after spending a night, first, at the Cipriani Hotel in Venice, I really started to slip.

I didn't seem to fit into David's life there, and I mean that literally; he was still in a bachelor's apartment that the State Department had provided, a little flat in an old building in out-of-the-way Trastevere. The married couples and families all had places closer to the embassy, David said.

Nicer, newer, bigger places, he didn't say, but I knew. One day I had wandered through the residential streets in Ludovisi, the neighborhood where David spent most of his days, and saw just how far removed our crowded, narrow street was from the wide boulevards, lush gardens, and enormous palazzos by the embassy. Our street, though home to a lovely basilica—one of the oldest churches in Rome, in fact—was otherwise populated primarily by greengrocers and a few dingy cafés, a far cry from the Alta Moda ateliers and celebrity haunts of the via Veneto. There were always a few stray cats lurking around the shop entrances and alleys in our neighborhood, and children running unattended in the street, making a racket or kicking a ball around. I actually liked the children and the cats, but they drove David mad. He hated noise.

He said we didn't need any more space, though. He said it would only be a few years, anyway, and it was just the two of us in the flat.

No need for another bedroom. I told him I'd like for it to be more than just the two of us in the flat, and he stared at me uncomprehending until I explained that I meant I wanted a baby.

This was, he said, once he understood, a topic for a later discussion.

"Let's get to know each other, Teddy," David said, in those first few days. "We have plenty of time."

I wasn't sure we had enough space even for just the two of us, though. There was one bedroom, a single bathroom that we shared, a little sitting room with an even littler kitchenette, and not nearly enough room in the wardrobes—even the few suitcases of clothing and beauty products and various knickknacks I'd brought seemed to tip the apartment over the edge of slight disorder into a state of permanent disarray, no matter how hard I tried to hang things up and fold them and tuck them away. David objected to the number of perfumes and lipsticks and lotions I had set up in the bathroom; the last straw seemed to be when he found a row of nail polishes I'd lined up atop the toilet tank, lacking anywhere else to put them. After that, he gave me a few empty boxes to fill with my things, to keep in one of the kitchen cupboards.

"I don't care how many syrups and oils you have, Teddy," he said, and he was smiling a bit, so I knew he wasn't really mad. "Just keep them off the toilet, please. Keep them out of the sink."

The embassy apartments came furnished, which had horrified my mother when I told her on the phone.

"Someone else's chairs—someone else's *bed?*"

She wasn't a fan of antiques, unless they were art. I was glad, at least, that she never saw the flat; she and Daddy had considered coming to visit me once I settled in, but then I never settled in, after all, and anyway, Daddy hadn't really wanted to go. He always said he wasn't interested in traveling anywhere he couldn't drive to.

David was gone a lot, those first few weeks—he left for a work trip to Naples the day after we arrived. I tried not to complain too much, at first. I knew it was important, the work he did. Or at least, I'd been told (by him) that even if his job seemed simple— smoothing the way for American companies to put down roots in Italy, and vice versa—it was part of a bigger plan. A larger front in a cold war. David had explained what he called "the geopolitical situation" to me, in terms he thought I would be able to understand.

"It's like checkers, Bear," he'd said. "Us against the Reds. We have to keep them from taking every square."

I've never heard of anyone else playing checkers that way, before or since, but I never told him that.

For David, the fight against Communism involved facilitating the sale of American-made refrigerators and rubber tires to the Italians, setting up deals with companies like Texas Instruments and Nabisco for distribution overseas. Which was why, David said, he had to take so many last-minute trips to Naples and Verona and Milan and back to the States, staying for days at a time, sometimes, leaving me alone in the apartment in Rome.

"Encouraging economic cooperation," he called it. "Spreading prosperity to dull the shine on the Iron Curtain."

I really didn't think there was any more to it than that. Why should there be? David liked to talk about how his work was confidential— as if there was something particularly secret about selling Pepto-Bismol and Singer sewing machines to upwardly mobile Italians—but there was no reason to suspect him of anything beyond the exaggerated sense of self-importance that everyone's husbands, I had been led to believe, exhibited sometimes.

I can be awfully naive for such a practiced liar.

David never wanted to talk much about work—about the actual details of what he did—but he was always ready to talk (or, more often, complain) about the Wolf.

The Wolf was what they called the ambassador, the men who worked for him at the embassy, when they wanted to flatter him in person or mock him behind his back. He had been an actor before he entered politics, and "the Wolf" was the name of his character in *One Week on the Rio Grande*, a flinty, blue-eyed cowboy who claimed to pick no side in any fight except the open road, but could always be counted on to do the right thing, in the end. And the ambassador had bought into this idea of himself, which his voters had loved during his congressional run but which his employees couldn't forgive him for.

I had yet to meet him, but had heard that in honor of his character, the ambassador kept the corpse of a wolf, stuffed and mounted, on the wall of his office, and everyone said it looked ready to pounce from above his head when he sat back, legs crossed, behind his desk. David had heard that the ambassador took particular delight in this effect when a bunch of tree-huggers came to petition him about something or other at his office back in California.

"Imagine it," David had said, laughing. "They came in with their hair and their signs, their beads and what have you, saw that dead thing on the wall, and still had to finish their presentation about logging. Against logging, I think it was. Knowing from the second they walked in and caught sight of that dead animal that they didn't stand a chance."

If that wasn't enough, there was always the gun. Hanging next to the wolf on the wall was a Nambu pistol that the Wolf—the human one—had taken off a Japanese soldier he'd killed at Rendova. It still had the bullets in it, apparently. The Wolf was known to say that he kept the bullets meant for him as a reminder. Not of humility in the face of death—not that anyone would have thought that was the reason—but as a reminder that he couldn't be killed. It was a version of one of his lines from *One Week on the Rio Grande*: "Well, darlin'," I've been shot at before, but unless this is heaven, I ain't dead yet."

David said the Wolf claimed to have gotten his taxidermy name-sake the same way he got the gun: pitched battle, man against man.

Teddy

Or beast, in this case. It attacked him one night as he was out riding on his land in Northern California, according to the Wolf, according to David. But David also said that there were no wolves in California anymore, that in fact this was probably one of the things the hippies had come to complain about, the lack of wolves, and that actually, the Wolf bought the thing off an antiques dealer in New York and had it shipped over. David said he heard this from someone who saw the receipt on the crate when it arrived.

He wasn't sure about the gun, though. Whether that story was true or not. But the purpose was clear: "The Wolf likes to keep his enemies close," David said. "He tells us all the time."

In any case, the Wolf was a decent marksman, according to David, who had gone hunting with him in the Apennines on the weekend a few times here and there. He thought the Wolf was soft, a Hollywood lightweight, a movie cowboy. Not the real thing. But even so, he had good enough aim as a hunting partner, and David's career depended on making nice with him.

The Wolf had been appointed to his post by the president back in January. Some people said this was because the Wolf was the most prominent Italian American in the Party (he'd been born Venanzio Caruso in Brooklyn in 1918, but Warren Carey worked better on the marquee), but others, including David, thought it was because certain prominent people in the Party wanted him out of the way for the time being. Voters were clamoring, apparently, for the Wolf to run after a second Nixon term in '76. They liked his Hollywood glitz, his (relatively) youthful and attractive image. The Party'd had a devil of a time getting any good stars or singers on board for Nixon's most recent campaign, and they were already dreading '72, so a movie cowboy was starting to look pretty appealing for the nomination after that.

I knew this part, at least, because it was hardly a secret that my Uncle Hal had also wanted to run in '76, and he made no bones

35

about how little he'd liked the idea of having to go up against a man who'd worn makeup for a living. Hal had been planning his offensive for years, because whatever David said about checkers against the Russians, Hal played chess, and he played against everyone. He always said he liked to get as many pieces off the board and out of his way as he could, long before anyone even knew for themselves that they were in the game.

Hal thought the Wolf was just an opportunist who didn't really care about the Party's policies; he'd been a liberal, in the old days, and then made a name for himself denouncing other actors as Communists back in the '50s. His political career took off after that, right as he was aging out of the cowboy role, but Uncle Hal could never, he said, respect someone who switched sides. Even if they'd been wrong and switched to the right one. The Huntleys still donated to the Wolf's early campaigns, though, wherever it would put him over the edge in a state as godless as California. "California," Hal used to say, "is a problem."

Despite his misgivings about the Wolf, David still went off with him every now and then to shoot deer or some sort of wild pig or whatever was to be found in the mountains of Italy. It sounded medieval, boar hunting in the Apennines: I always pictured David and the Wolf as the men in feathered hats and velvet shirts and gilded vests in *The Hunt of the Unicorn*, those famous medieval tapestries. I pictured them pointing long spears at a pale unicorn on its knees.

I'd studied the artworks in school. They were at the Cloisters museum in Manhattan, but I'd never made it to New York to see them; other girls' mothers took them to the city on shopping trips, but Mama never would. "New York is no place for good people," she used to say, and left it at that.

Daddy and Hal had taken me hunting a few times when I was little—"a girl from Texas needs to know her guns"—so I learned how to shoot on the Hill Country ranch when I was only ten, and

Daddy said I was almost as good as he was by the time I was twelve. Kids are better with guns, he used to say, because they don't over-think it.

But I hated the actual hunting, and cried so much every time, even though I never shot anything bigger than a squirrel, that eventually they gave up. It made me so sad to see them—the little critters with their bright eyes, so light on their feet, suddenly falling heavy and fat to the ground, sacks of guts like a bag of beans spilling into the grass. It scared me, too, the rapid cracking of the guns firing all at once—it wasn't anything like using a pistol or a rifle, one shot at a time on a target, and getting a pat on the back after.

Mama had a cookbook from her mother's mother that had specialties in it for people who had to work with what they could get, in the old days, in Texas, and so she had our cook make my victims into squirrel pot pie. I got so sick afterward, though the food seemed to settle just fine in everyone else's stomachs, that nobody made me shoot or eat a squirrel ever again.

"If you'd had a brother," Daddy said, "I would tell him to toughen the hell up."

I complained the first time David went on one of his hunting excursions with the Wolf. He had only just gotten home from a work trip, the one for which he'd left right after our honeymoon, and there he was taking off again.

"Why are you stomping around the mountains with other men, David," I asked, "when you should be spending time with me?"

I wanted him to take me down to Ischia to go sailing and see the ruins of the Castello Aragonese, or on a weekend trip to Florence, or even to dinner in Rome at Giggi Fazi, just the two of us, together. But in those early days he was always somewhere I couldn't go, shaking hands and smiling with those big, white teeth of his—I loved his smile when he meant it, when he grinned with his mouth open, like he couldn't help it—and performing the business, apparently, of placing American checkers on every square of the board.

David said all of these outings were necessary for work, as if Uncle Sam had personally come down from his poster to ask the men of the embassy to go hunting, and golfing, and drinking in particular types of bars where one might meet particular types of women.

Where, once upon a time, on a night out in Dallas or DC, one might have met me.

David didn't know that part, though. Not yet.

I asked him to at least not bring home any animals he might happen to kill; I asked him not to stuff them and mount them on the walls of our little flat on the via della Scala. I could imagine them there, all of David's victims staring down at me while I tried to eat my tuna fish sandwich or read my magazines.

To this, David said, "Well, but how is my hunting any different from you eating your osso buco or veal Milanese for dinner? I've seen you enjoy it. It's just another kind of dead animal. Don't you think you're being a little bit silly, Teddy?"

Always this—"Don't you think you're being a little bit silly, Teddy?"

And what could I answer to that? How could I prove, under the circumstances, that no, David, sometimes I mean what I've said?

After the first few times he left me alone in Rome, I asked David if there was anyone he could introduce me to, maybe the wife of a colleague or even one of the secretaries at the embassy, but he said people mostly just got on with their jobs, here, and there wasn't a lot of socializing outside of work hours. The trips and dinners David went to were *work*, he explained, and nobody brought their spouses.

Marcia and Eleanor had told me before the wedding how envious they were of all the fabulous parties I'd be attending in Rome—we'd all seen photos in the scandal sheets of stars on the via Veneto;

we'd all seen *La Dolce Vita* and *Roman Holiday*, and we'd read about Liz Taylor and Richard Burton getting up to no good on the set of *Cleopatra*—but for the first few weeks, I mostly wandered around the city alone. When I wasn't out walking, I stayed in the flat, and it didn't take long for me to start to unravel.

I'd watch the television as late as it was on, even though I couldn't understand what they were saying on any of the Italian shows, then stay up the rest of the night reading magazines, pulp novels, anything I could get my hands on, and then I'd be too tired to do anything but sleep during the day, until I was so disoriented that David would come home from a trip to find me in bed at three in the afternoon. Or I'd let the laundry pile up—David had been sending his shirts out to a laundress who pressed them and delivered them back to him stacked neatly and wrapped in paper, but he happily informed me that there was no need for that service anymore, now that he had me.

It was a shame, and not just because I had no idea how to iron—I loved the sound of the crinkle of paper in the mornings, when my husband—so strange to have a *husband*, I still felt, in those first weeks—unwrapped his crisp white shirts to dress and go to work. I loved how smooth his cheek was, freshly shaven, and the spicy scent of his cologne when he kissed me where I lay, still in bed, before he left.

I loved this until I understood that it was a problem, me being in bed. David having to unwrap his own shirts. I half wondered if I was supposed to shave him, too, but that was something men liked to do themselves, apparently. It was hard to know which things were, and why.

I didn't want to seem entirely useless, so I made a few feeble efforts at the laundry those first weeks, but I always seemed to fall behind, until one Friday David came home to find that he had run out of clean shirts altogether, and there was no time to send them out to be washed and wrapped in paper, so he had to wear a dirty one from his suitcase to the office, at which point he finally asked one of his colleagues for a recommendation for a housemaid. He hired a middle-aged Puglian woman named Teresa to come in every few days to restore some semblance of order to the place, though when David was out of town, I told her not to bother.

I didn't like her being in the apartment, moving my things around. Watching me; judging me.

She would come on the last day before he returned, though, just to undo all the damage I'd done while he was away. Fold the clothes I'd left draped on chairs and tables and on the floor, put everything back together again like all the king's horses and all the king's men, because somehow it all always got away from me.

Every now and then I would try to make some grand gesture, just to show that I could be a good wife even though I couldn't do laundry or wake up early. I would spend all afternoon preparing an elaborate meal that inevitably took longer than I'd expected, and David would be drunk from his evening bourbon on an empty stomach by the time it was ready to be served. Or I would buy bunches of fresh flowers to liven up the apartment, then forget to change the water and fail to throw them away before they moldered and smelled. Or I'd make a pineapple upside-down cake for after dinner and it would come out beautifully, really impressive, but then I would eat all the leftovers the next day while David was at work, and he'd come home and say, "Really, Teddy? The whole thing?"

Little problems, I suppose, on the scale, but they piled up, and David started to notice. I could tell he was thinking: perhaps we can't be happy together, after all.

One Thursday in June, after we'd been in Rome nearly a month, an envelope was slid under the door of our flat while David was away. It was heavy cream cardstock, addressed to a Mr. and

Mrs. David Shepard. I forgot who Mrs. David Shepard was, for a moment, and then remembered that she was me, and opened it.

The envelope was lined with a beautiful Florentine marbled paper in green and gold, and the card, in hand-lettered calligraphy, invited us to dinner the following evening at the Villa Taverna. The ambassador's residence.

He and his wife were hosting a dinner, and I was finally going to meet them.

I called David at his hotel in Milan in a panic.

"It's nothing too fancy," David said. "Don't worry about it."

"It says black tie, David. I don't have anything to wear."

"Anything will be fine," he said, "they're just inviting us to be nice. We'll be seated at the opposite end of the room from them, with the other grunts. No one will be paying attention to what you wear."

"It says it's a dinner in honor of the Aga Khan," I said. "And his fiancée, formerly Lady James Charles Crichton-Stuart."

I'd seen photos of the beautiful couple in a copy of *Elle* magazine. She was a fashion model; he was royalty.

"How about that blue dress you wore in Capri?" David asked.

I was surprised that he even remembered it, but I didn't bother explaining to him that it was a daytime dress in a casual fabric—in chambray, of all things! Clearly, I would need to handle this myself. I didn't know how to properly wash or iron a shirt, or keep a house, but I knew how to dress for a black-tie event. This was an opportunity, I realized, to show him the kind of wife I could be.

"I'll find something," I said, already calculating how many hours more the shops on the via Condotti might be open, so I could try to get an appointment with one of the couture houses there. "It's awfully short notice, though. I'm surprised they didn't send the invitations out earlier."

"Oh, they did," David said absently. "But the invitation was just to me. I guess I forgot to tell everyone at the embassy that I'd gotten married, and then I said something about my wife the other day and the ambassador asked where I'd been hiding you. Antonella said she would drop the corrected invitation off at home."

Antonella was David's secretary; I'd never met her, either. I'd never met anyone, and I was mortified, because now I realized that was because David had never told them about me at all, and David didn't seem to have any idea what he'd done. The ambassador's wife must have gone to so much trouble to add me to the guest list at the last minute, adding an entire place setting, probably having to rearrange seating charts that had been planned weeks, maybe months in advance. I'd already caused a problem, already made a bad impression, before I'd even met them.

David's colleagues, his boss—these were supposed to be the people in my new life. This was supposed to be my chance to be someone different. Someone better. And who knew what stars and luminaries would be there? There might be all kinds of celebrities in attendance, Hollywood people from the Wolf's past, and of course, the Aga Khan himself. David didn't understand, but that was all right—I knew the right thing to do, the right kind of dress to wear.

David promised to be back in Rome the next day in time to collect me from the flat and take me to the party, and when I fretted over whether his tuxedo was clean, he said not to worry, he had it with him. I didn't have time to wonder what kind of Milanese trade meetings required a tuxedo; it was a relief, really, that he wouldn't be coming home to change before dinner. I'd let the apartment get away from me, in his absence, and I didn't have time to call Teresa in to clean it, now that I had a party to prepare for. And anyway, I didn't want her sighing over the dishes and dirty laundry while I was practicing my makeup looks, testing out different accessories.

I hung up the phone and got to work. It would be difficult to find something that fit at such short notice, and there wasn't time to have it tailored much. But this was Rome! Surely one of the designers on the via Condotti, one of the most famous shopping streets in the entire world, would have something for me. I had a little book with a watercolor foldout map that Eleanor had given me, a shopping guide she'd picked up a few years ago that listed all of the designers and luggage shops and jewelers of note to be found in Rome: Angeletti, Battistoni, Buccellati, Bulgari, Castellano, Fornari, Gucci, Polidori.

Plenty of options, but I knew where I wanted to go first: Valentino of Rome. If he was good enough to design Jackie Kennedy's wedding dress for her marriage to Ari Onassis, he was good enough for me. And in some ways, this was more important than a wedding dress, wasn't it? Or at least equivalent: this was the first outfit of my new life.

I called the number in Eleanor's little guidebook and made an appointment for noon the next day at the Valentino atelier. I was lucky to get it—I had to mention Stanley Marcus, and that I knew him, to get a spot at such short notice. I tried to make one for even earlier—I wanted everything to be resolved *now*— but noon was the first available. That was fine, though. It wasn't too, too long to wait, after all, to meet her. The person I was going to become.

I woke up early for maybe the first time since I'd moved to Rome, and not long after the sun rose, I left our little flat on foot. I was too impatient to wait in the apartment, and it would take me a while to reach Valentino's atelier, anyway. There were plenty of places to visit on the way, to pass the time before my appointment at midday.

I stopped outside our building first, as I always did, to feed the stray cat who lingered around the doorstep. He was black and dirty white, with a crusty pink eye, and I thought of him as mine, though I'm sure he would have disagreed. Beppo, I called him.

David hated that I fed him; he said it made him hang around. Sometimes David would kick at Beppo as we left the apartment—

it was just pretend, he would say, when I protested. He was only kicking at the air, I suppose, and he never actually hit the kitten with his foot, but he would say, "Scram!" in a loud voice, and I hated that he did it, but what was I going to do, really, to stop him?

David didn't realize that I was restraining myself, feeding only Beppo; there were cats all over the city that I wanted to take in. There were too many of them, though. You would cry all the time, for strays on every corner, if you let yourself.

"I wish you wouldn't do that, Bear," David would say, whenever he saw me setting down an opened can of tuna for Beppo, watching him lap at the juices with his little pink tongue. "Before you know it, you'll be surrounded. And anyway, it makes you smell like fish."

I strolled through the little streets of Trastevere, and then over the Ponte Garibaldi, enjoying the morning in spite of the minor apparel emergency I was faced with. The air was still cool from the night before, but the sun was shining, warming my shoulders. I hadn't bothered with a sweater today; sometimes if I went out bare-armed, I caught a look from David—he said he didn't want men shouting at me on the street, though so far I'd largely been left alone aside from the odd *"Ciao, bella,"* which struck me as mostly nice. But he was in Milan, so I didn't really care.

I loved walking through Rome, seeing the layers of the city, one on top of the other. Early on, I had journeyed to each of the seven hills of Rome, the foundations of the ancient city: Aventine, Caelian, Capitoline, Esquiline, Palatine, Quirinal, Viminal. The site of the legendary beginning of Rome, where Romulus slew his brother Remus over auguries. The place the Senate used to meet; temples in which ancient supplicants made offerings to their gods.

There was an eighth mound in Rome that I had visited, too. This was Monte Testaccio, the Mountain of Shards. It was located in a neighborhood seldom visited by tourists, or really anyone who didn't live there or have specific business in the area: Testaccio was best known for its butcher's shops, and the "mountain" from which the neighborhood took its name. Monte Testaccio was an ancient trash heap of broken amphorae from thousands of years ago that had grown over with grass and now housed a little park. You could still see the broken shards of terra-cotta layered atop each other under the grass of this man-made mountain, created out of the refuse of the ancient Romans. This was my favorite, the eighth hill of Rome.

I'd spent a lot of time in those first few weeks wandering around, when I wasn't sleeping or reading or watching television. It's something you can always do if you're lonely—it feels good to be moving. It feels good to be going somewhere. I used to do the same thing in Dallas, though you have to drive everywhere there. I used to spend hours on the highways going nowhere in particular, just speeding up and down the wide concrete interstate that snaked over the flat Texas landscape, cruising in the white Thunderbird Daddy had bought me, a convertible with special-order red leather seats, driving as far out of the city as I dared to go until I passed fields and dilapidated farmhouses and knew it was time to turn back.

I made my way past the Pantheon, that ancient pagan temple. Stopped at Tazza d'Oro for one of their sweetened espressos with thick, snowy crema, sipping it from a marigold-colored cup at the glossy wooden bar. I passed the Largo di Torre Argentina, a grass-covered square of Roman ruins under medieval ones. I left two cans of tuna as an offering by one of the broken columns; there were dozens of cats living in the stone shells of the older city. They were just some of the ones I would have taken in, if David had let me. And, I suppose, if they had even wanted it: they seemed pretty happy coming and going and bearing their litters on the mosaic floors of ancient temples to Venus, to Mars, to Jupiter.

I had a good idea of how I wanted to spend the rest of the morning while I waited for my appointment. I had worked my way through some of Rome's best museums in the early days: the

Vatican, the Borghese Gallery, the Museo Nazionale. I'd seen some of the works to be found there on slides before, in school; I'd seen photos in books. And I'd had access to the best art collection in Texas on a daily basis, back in Dallas. But what was the Huntley Foundation and its holdings, rich as they were, compared to the Vatican Museums? Compared to Michelangelo's *Pietà*, with its delicate, perfect depiction of grief, or Bernini's sculpture of *Apollo and Daphne*, with its frantic movement ending in the grotesque transformation of a woman into a tree?

The next museum on my list was the Palazzo Barberini, so I ambled over to Trevi. That part of town was crawling with tourists in the summer, making wishes in the fountain and climbing up and down the steps, and I felt like one of them that day, though at another time I might have found them foolish. But that Friday, I watched everyone throwing their coins in the fountain and laughing and taking photos, and I tossed a quarter I'd found in my purse into the Trevi Fountain, too. A bit much to throw in with all the pennies and lire, but it was no use to me in Italy, and anyway, greater sacrifice brought greater reward, didn't it? It was an investment in the new me. I don't remember exactly what I wished that day, but I can say with reasonable certainty that it didn't come true.

There were palm trees, stately and tall, standing at the entrance to the Palazzo Barberini, and they seemed to me a good sign, proof of the power of my wish in the fountain. They reminded me of that day in Capri, the palms against the cloud-covered sky, and David saying he thought we could be happy. And now I had a chance to make it so. The right dress, the right hairstyle and accessories, and I knew I could be perfect at the party. That was one thing I knew: how to dress up, how to look just right. How to speak to the wealthy and powerful, how to behave at a formal dinner, how to make my husband look impressive to his colleagues because of how brilliant and beautiful and charming I was.

The Barberini Museum was in a stunning old palace: three stories of ornate, columned stone, with enormous latticed windows all across the front. I dug a few coins for a ticket from the layer of debris at the bottom of my bag, handed them to the old man at the front desk, and wandered through the gilded, frescoed hallways of the palace, walked its winding marble staircases, checking my watch every so often to be sure I was making good time, but mostly entranced by all of the paintings I had seen in books suddenly there before me, on the wall. Caravaggio's *Judith Beheading Holofernes* was there, as was one of Holbein's portraits of Henry VIII, who was, I suppose one might say, a sort of reverse Judith.

There was a portrait of a lady by a minor Renaissance artist, Jacopo Zucchi, that I found particularly enchanting when I stumbled upon it in a small gallery, though according to the label, she had no name. It's not unusual to have a portrait of a particular woman, a real one who existed but whose painting is unnamed aside from *Portrait of a Lady*; there are thousands of them, maybe more. A near-infinite number of nameless ladies and portraits thereof, and you can try to guess at who they were, but all you really need to know is, it doesn't matter. Here she is, isn't she lovely, she doesn't need a name.

This one was a beauty, even by modern standards. You can usually see from the old portraits how the faces we find appealing change over time; the high hairlines and wan complexions of the great medieval beauties would read as tragic and milquetoast in 1969. The Huntley Foundation bought an early Renaissance *Portrait of a Lady*, once, by a Dutch painter, and when Daddy saw the pale woman with her high, veiled headdress and her plucked forehead, he said she looked like a hall-of-fame grump, and like she'd been rode hard and put away wet. He would have liked this one, though. She looked lively. She would have been gorgeous even walking around Highland Park Village with the best of the oil and gas executives' wives. She wouldn't have looked out of place at Arthur's Prime Steaks and Seafood, or at the Old Warsaw, on a date.

She had big, dark eyes like a cow's that turned downward at the corners in a teardrop, the edges dark like she'd been at them with a Max Factor pencil. Her skin was pale, her cheeks were flushed, and she had a hint of a smile on her coral lips. The color, I thought, was almost exactly Coty 24 in Resort to Coral. I knew because it was one of my favorite shades for summer. But there was something else there, too, in her eyes and around her mouth. Something like laughter, but also disdain. Like she knew something you didn't. Like she was in complete control. She wore jewels in her ears, diamonds and pearls around her collar, and flowers, little pansies and violets and fairy roses, in her coiffure, and I thought she must have been perfect, in life. This was the sort of woman I wanted, I needed, to be that night. The knowing, self-contained lady; bejeweled, flawless.

At a quarter past eleven, I left the museum. I was still early for my appointment, so I decided to do some window shopping. It was a quarter to noon by the time I made it to the via Condotti, and the Spanish Steps at the end of the street were already packed with tourists. The cafés were crowded with beautiful people having leisurely lunches, sipping chilled white wine, eating their antipasti. I would have liked to sit in a café like that, laughing with friends. But of course, I didn't have any, yet, and David was never around to take me anywhere. I didn't know anyone in the city aside from David, but I hoped that would change after the ambassador's party. I had the sense that if I wore the right thing, if I presented myself just so, it could be the beginning of something, for me. In just a few days, I could be one of them, those happy, chatting, polished people. I felt that they were smiling at me, like they recognized that I was soon to be part of their world. That I deserved to be.

I turned onto the via Gregoriana, just a few streets over, where Valentino's famed atelier lived in a sixteenth-century palazzo. I hit the buzzer, and went inside, and it looked just how I had imagined it: big, bright windows letting the sunlight in, black-and-white tiled floors, high ceilings ornately decorated. It smelled rich, in there, a sort of powdery, sweet scent like a lipstick, or a peony.

There's something calming about walking into a luxury store, knowing they're going to help you. If you can pay for it, they'll be your best friends in the world, at least while you're in there. I used to love going to Neiman Marcus back in Dallas, trying on dresses and chatting with the girls, drinking the complimentary champagne they brought. You have to buy something, though—you can't just try it on, not if they're being so helpful and kind. I've ended up with more than a few blouses I didn't need that way.

An older woman who introduced herself as Vanessa, immaculately dressed in a tailored black skirt suit, with her hair in a sleek bun, welcomed me and asked how she could help, and when I explained what I needed—a dress in my size for a dinner tonight—she blanched. "For tonight? But *signora* . . ." She eyed me skeptically for a moment, then sighed. "I will see what we have."

I was going about this all wrong, I knew, and it was all David's fault. For couture, you have to make an appointment to see the season's designs on a model—this is when they bring you the champagne, to sip while you watch—and then you tell them which dresses you like, and they're made in your size. Just for you. It takes at least a week, often longer, and we had about five hours.

I waited on a gilded Regency chair, sipping a champagne cocktail that one of the salesgirls had brought me, until Vanessa reappeared, followed by a gorgeous young woman in a loose-fitting velvet dress. Vanessa explained that she had gathered all of the samples she thought could be made to fit me, and would now show me on the model.

"These should really be made for you, *signora*," she said, shaking her head, "but let's try."

There were only three dresses, it transpired, from the last few

49

seasons that might fit me in the sample size: a chiffon gown from the current season in Valentino's signature red, an embroidered dress in green velvet from the Autumn/Winter '68 collection, and a short-sleeved white silk sheath with swirl patterns in metallic sequins, also from this season. I knew the velvet wouldn't work for June, and the sequined dress looked heavy and uncomfortable, so I went straight for the red chiffon, to try it on in the curtained fitting room.

I don't think I'll ever be tired of the rustle of fabric, the sound of the zipper, the way it feels to try on a new dress for the first time. The way the lining caresses your skin; the little details, like lace along the edge of the underskirt, that nobody will see but you; the tiny stitches at the seams bringing the pieces of the dress together to fit you so perfectly. The person you'll become when you wear it. The red dress fit like it was made for me, sample size be damned; the full skirt and the gathered waist flattered my figure. The fabric was loose and flowing in the right places, but tight through the bust and waist—my best features, I've always thought. It had a sweetheart neckline, and I admired the hint of cleavage you could see. I looked sophisticated; I could imagine myself with my hair piled atop my head, sweeping into the ambassador's residence in my flowing crimson chiffon, making delightful conversation, charming everyone.

And then I remembered how upset David had been when I tried to wear the two-piece in Capri. We hadn't even known anyone there, and he'd said they didn't need to see that much of me; how much more would it bother him if I wore a dress that showed my décolletage in front of his colleagues, his boss?

It pained me, almost physically, though perhaps that sounds like an exaggeration, but I took the red dress off and hung it on the rack. The green velvet was a winter fabric, so I knew there was no point in bothering with that one. That left the white sheath.

I asked Vanessa if the model could bring it out again, for a second look, and I walked back out into the entry room to wait. The atelier had been empty when I came in, but now there was a beautiful young Italian woman, probably some countess or the wife of a wealthy industrialist, seated on the same little chair I had occupied, flipping through a book of sketches while a bored-looking child played around her feet.

When the model walked out again in the white dress, the little girl glanced up at the rustle of the sequins, and then gasped. She tugged at her mother's skirt and pointed.

"*Che brillante!*" she whispered, and the woman smiled and patted her daughter's head and said, "*Si, Antonia, come una principessa.*"

"I'll take it," I told Vanessa, and went to the fitting room to try it on for myself.

It took some wriggling, but I managed to squeeze myself into it. I knew it was meant to hang loose on the body, as it had on the model; that's how this style looked in the magazines, too, or on sylphlike socialites like Jackie and Slim Keith. On me, though, it fit like a glove.

I actually thought it looked all right—a bit like something Marilyn might have worn, perhaps, or Jayne Mansfield—but that wasn't how it was intended to fit. Still, the neckline was high enough—there was a sort of beaded collar around the top, and the swirled patterns of plastic sequins and bugle beads covered the areas where the fabric strained at the seams. It was beautiful, even if I wasn't quite as comfortable as I'd been in the red. The sequins shimmered like scales, paillettes and spangles in pale gold and pearlescent white and silver. They reminded me of the jewels on the Lady's collar—the one in the portrait. If I wore the right girdle, and held my stomach in, it would be fine.

The dress had mashed my breasts down into a lump, though, so when Vanessa came to check on me and hmmed and humphed over the way it fit (I could see her considering, and then deciding not to mention, that it wasn't supposed to fit like this at all), I asked if they could at least let it out a bit in the bust. There wasn't much time, she protested, but agreed that if I came back in a few hours, they could add maybe a few centimeters on either side, under the arms.

I wrote Vanessa a check for the dress—a bit expensive, but it was important, and such short notice, and anyway, we had the money for it from Uncle Hal. What was it for, if not our new lives? And wasn't my first impression on David's boss part of that?

I had been worried about the dress—the seamstress, when she came out to consult, wasn't sure she would be able to add enough room in the bust—but I felt better after I'd paid for it. I always loved writing checks; I had paid extra for a custom set, had gotten my full name embossed on them. It irritated David that I hadn't updated my nameplate since the wedding, but it had all happened so fast, there wasn't time to have a new one engraved. This one had been a gift from my mother: after my debut, she'd taken me to the stationer's to have the plate designed. Every woman was supposed to have one; you could use it to print stationery, envelopes, calling cards, too, so that all your correspondence would match. It was one of those things you had to have, like an add-a-charm bracelet or a silver pattern. It would show people who you were.

The checks were a color called Nile blue, a dusky, powdery shade, with my name written in ornate cursive, embossed in silver: Teddy Huntley Carlyle. When we went back to Dallas at Christmas, I would go by the stationer's and have them add "Shepard" to the end, just so David would settle down. I loved those checks; I loved paying for things with them. I had a silver Montblanc fountain pen to write on them, too, and ink to fill it that I ordered specially from a French company that came in colors like Perle Noire and Cyclamen and Ambre de Birmanie.

I left Vanessa and the panicked seamstress with the task of expanding my new dress, and returned to the via Condotti where I found a salon, all plate glass and potted ferns and enormous photos of fashion models on the wall, and managed to convince Sergio, the master stylist, to refresh my color with no appointment. I'm naturally blond, but nobody is naturally *blond*, and from the signed photos on the wall, I could see that he had done the hair of several Italian screen stars, including Virna Lisi herself, which meant I could rest assured he'd give me the perfect silvery strands I craved, with no risk of brassy yellow. I've been coloring my hair since I was in high school; as I got older and the shade began to darken, my mother took me to her colorist along with a lock of my baby hair that she'd saved "for just this occasion," she said, and showed the colorist the fine golden curls as a reference to turn my hair back into what it had once been. She also told me I was never to tell anyone it wasn't natural, but that nobody with any manners would ever ask.

I'd been anxious about the party, and about the dress, which was beautiful but still not quite right, but I've always found that a visit to the salon has the potential to cheer me up, no matter what. It's the possibility of being new, and better. An hour or two in the chair and suddenly your hair is brighter and your nails are glossy, and you look like the person you wanted to be when you woke up. I liked the sound of the hairdryers, too, and the way it muffled the chattering voices of the other ladies in the salon.

After Sergio had painted on the peroxide and left it for a while, his assistant washed my hair with shampoo that smelled like cut pears, lathering it twice to make sure it was clean enough. They always did it so much better than I could on my own. And then she combed it out, and rinsed it, and Sergio himself trimmed the split ends, and it all felt so neat and tidy. Precision, organization; I envied them their ability to set things right. The ladies dried my hair and sprayed it up into a pillowy bouffant that would have been at home on the great Brigitte herself.

No touching, Teddy, I thought to myself, knowing how hard it would be to fix if I did mess it up. I had let the nail girls give me long, opal-colored acrylic claws while Sergio worked on my hair, and in the end I could barely get my checkbook out to pay at the register. I thought David would probably hate the nails, and I knew if my mother could see them, she certainly would, but I couldn't help it. They looked just like in the magazines. They shimmered like pearls.

When I collected my dress from Valentino's atelier, a dismayed Vanessa showed me how they'd managed to add a few extra centimeters on either side of the bust, but this had been taken from the inside seam, which was sequinless, so it had created the effect of bald patches on the gown under either arm.

"Fine," I said, "I'll just keep my arms down."

There simply wasn't time to do anything about it, though I hated the sight of the broken spots in the beautiful, shimmering fish-scale swirls. I had taken too long at the salon, and David would be home in an hour or so, and I still needed to bathe and do my makeup and get dressed. Finding the right undergarments would take some time, too. I didn't have shoes that matched, either, but there was no time to buy any from a shop, so my wedding heels would have to work.

The dress looked damaged, a little bit dead, now, but I tried not to think too much about it. About how it reminded me of the rainbow trout Uncle Hal liked to stock in the pond at the Hill Country house, and the way they would flop around on the dock with the hooks pierced through the sides of their mouths when he fished them out, and the way the beautiful pink shimmering scales on their sides, the pearly ones of their bellies, would be crushed and bruised in patches, once they had finally gone still.

I took a taxi back to the flat, now too weighed down with the garment bag to walk, ran a bath, splashed around for five minutes, then dried off and managed to strap myself into a tight-enough girdle that the altered gown glided on over it. You couldn't see any lumps or bumps as long as I stood very, very still. The beaded fabric felt heavy, substantial. I thought perhaps it might keep me steady at the party; between that and the girdle, I couldn't move all that quickly, anyway. It was like a suit of armor. I would be tethered to the ground, which seemed like a safe place to be. But most importantly, I shone: I was beautiful.

When I was thirteen, Aunt Sister came for her usual whirlwind week-long tour through Dallas, not unlike a tornado blowing through in the summer and tearing the windows out of buildings, scattering papers and uprooting trees.

That's an exaggeration, obviously, but sometimes it felt that way.

She liked to come in summer, despite the heat; she said it was good for her—"It reminds me why I don't live here anymore." It was just a few days after my birthday in July, so it must have been the tenth or eleventh or so. I remember running excitedly from the telephone to tell Mama and Daddy that Aunt Sister had called from California and was on her way over.

"That's our Cecilia," Daddy said, smiling, "coming to town to shake the hat again," and Mama shot him a look I couldn't read. I remember being puzzled because Sister didn't often wear a hat—she'd told me she thought they were stuffy. And I'm sure she had trouble keeping them on when she laughed the way she did, with her head thrown back. Still when I think of her, sometimes, I picture a laughing mouth—red lipstick, perfectly outlined, and bright teeth. She loved to laugh. Mama didn't laugh much, and she only wore the palest lipstick—she refused any blush at all, and told me I wasn't ever to wear it, either. That did change, of course, as the fashions did, but at least until I was fully grown and out of the house, it was no blush or lipstick allowed.

Soon enough, Aunt Sister was settled in the guest room on the third floor, although it was so hot that summer, and especially in the stuffy little guest room, even with the attic fans open, that we slept on the second-floor porch most nights with the windows cracked to the cooler air outside. You could hear cicadas droning all day and crickets and katydids singing at night, and see fireflies sparkling around the trees, and sometimes toads would hop up to the backyard from the creek down the street where they'd been tadpoles, and they would croak from the grass while the sprinklers made a shushing sound in the dark. If it was so hot we couldn't sleep, even on the porch, Aunt Sister and I would run out into the backyard and through the sprinklers to get our hair and nightgowns wet, so that we could cool off under the fans enough to finally get some shut-eye. That was how she talked—every word was a more casual, fun version of the thing it represented, like "shut-eye" for sleep or "duds" for clothes.

I remember one night I had been sent to bed already and Sister was staying up with the grownups as she often did—I suppose she was one of them, though I often forgot—so I decided to sneak out onto the lawn by myself. I knew they would be busy in the sitting room or on the front porch, which is where they usually had their after-dinner drinks or played a game of canasta, so they wouldn't even notice that I was gone. I wanted to find a toad; occasionally I would manage to catch one and keep it for a little while, in one of Daddy's old King Edward cigar boxes, feeding it little bugs I found in the yard for a few days and then eventually setting it free again—usually when Mama found it in my dresser drawer and said that she was going to step on it and kill it if I didn't get it out of there. "Aren't you too old for this, Teddy?" she would say.

The grass was damp from the sprinklers, which weren't running anymore, and my toes squished in the mud, and I had a pretty good haul right away: a fat little toad that I tucked into my cigar box, which encouraged me to keep looking for more. The droning of the crickets and katydids was so loud that I was pretty sure nobody would be able to hear me rustling around, hunting among the trees. And the grownups were on the other side of the house, anyway—or so I thought, until I noticed that the big French doors leading into Daddy's study were open, and the lights were on inside, and I could hear voices escalating and then falling again out into the night air, so I tiptoed over, as close as I could get, close enough to hear from behind the low brick wall that ran around the gardener's shed. The study, with its warm lights flooding out into the night, shone like a beacon of secret grownup things, and I knew whatever I was liable to hear would be boring, but it would be something I could know, that they wouldn't know I did.

"But Alice," I could hear Aunt Sister saying, in a whining, pleading tone I'd never heard from her before, "why not? It's only a little, and you know I'll pay you back!"

"With what?" Mama's voice was cool, and calm. It was her "you're in trouble, but it is uncouth to raise one's voice" tone.

"You've spent everything they left you," Mama went on, "everything Mother and Papa worked so hard to save for you, so you would be protected. So you would have a good start in life."

"Oh, please, Alice!" Sister was angry, now, and she sounded a bit more like her usual self. "Don't pretend to be so naive. You know they didn't do that for *me*."

"Cecilia—" Mama's voice came out strangled, and then I heard the door from the hallway open and close loudly—as near as Mama ever came to slamming something.

There was silence for a moment, and I thought perhaps they'd both left the room and had forgotten to turn out the lights, but then I heard Aunt Sister's voice again.

"It's not like there isn't plenty of money left," she said, "and I'm hardly asking for anything. She's such a miser; good Lord!"

And then I heard Daddy's laugh and realized he had been in the room the whole time, too.

"Is there something you want to ask me, Cecilia?" he drawled.

"Why don't you freshen my drink, Stan?" Aunt Sister answered, and it was another tone I'd never heard before. She sounded like a woman in the movies; she sounded so much older. Serious, but playful, too—it worried me.

I heard the sound of liquid pouring into a glass, and then nothing for a while, so I crept over closer to be able to see into the study, thinking perhaps they had left again, but then I saw Aunt Sister sitting on a chair and Daddy standing over her, with a hand on her cheek tilting it up toward him, and I heard him say, "You're lucky you're so beautiful," and it made me feel sick and ashamed to see this, and I had my toad in his box and suddenly I hated myself.

I thought of how it would feel, to be in that dry, cramped space. Longing for the night air on your rumpled warty skin, wishing you could go thumping through the wet grass, and I couldn't believe I had been the one to trap him, my toad, in his prison, and I backed away from the window and released him again down where it was safe, in the moist earth of a flowerbed under the hydrangeas and caladiums, and then I tried to drag my muddy feet clean across the grass, and I went back into the house.

I was as silent as could be, so silent that my mother didn't even hear me, or turn to see me from where I saw her, crouched by the door to Daddy's study with the side of her face up against it, one hand over her other ear, trying to hear through the mahogany.

And the next day, when Aunt Sister took off for Istanbul, to meet some friends at the Pera Palace hotel for a while, to drink sidecars in their fabulous little bar, which was where Agatha Christie had worked out the draft for *Murder on the Orient Express*, if you can believe it—the next day, Mama didn't make a single comment, as she usually did when Sister told us one of these fantastical tales; she didn't ask, "And how are you going to pay for that, Cecilia?"

David arrived at half past five and I ran out to the sitting room, spangles rustling, to meet him.

"Look what I found!" I told him, turning so he could see the dress from every angle, its gold and silver swirls.

"What am I looking at?" David asked.

"For tonight!" I said. "I bought it. It was tricky at such short notice, but it should do, don't you think?"

"Well, it certainly fits you," he said, and I could see him eyeing my rear, which was eminently visible in the dress.

"They didn't have anything else," I said defensively, thinking longingly of the red dress. "There wasn't enough time to have it tailored much."

"I'm sure it will be fine," David said, putting a hand on my shoulder.

All I wanted, I suppose, was for him to tell me I looked beautiful.

"How much did it cost?" David asked.

"Well, it isn't all *that* much, if you think about it, for couture," I said, but then I told him the number and he pulled his hand away from me like I had burned him. Like I was radioactive.

"Goddammit, Teddy! That's more than a car!"

"Well, it depends what kind of car, doesn't it?" I tried.

I thought he might laugh—I thought maybe this was something husbands and wives did, playful bickering about the cost of things—but then I saw him staring at me, like he didn't recognize me, and his eyes were cold. They were a pale, muddy green, and it really did, as they say, send a chill down my spine, the way he said nothing but just watched me with his cloudy eyes under their heavy lids, and they looked like lake water, like there was something moving beneath the surface that you couldn't see, and wouldn't be able to see until it was right up on you and it was far, far too late. It wasn't just that he didn't think I was funny, it wasn't just that he didn't laugh. It was the absence of a laugh; it was the opposite.

"How did you pay for it?" he asked.

"I wrote a check."

"You wrote a—" He stopped and pressed a hand to his forehead. "You know what? Take it back. There's still an hour before we need to be there. You have time."

"I can't," I said, "I had it altered."

And the thought of going back to the atelier with the dress, handing it over and saying it didn't work, and everyone there thinking maybe she was too fat after all, or worse, knowing that my husband had made me return it, made my cheeks flush hot with shame. And I felt a little chill, a little sweat of dread, beginning under my arms. My arms that I couldn't move because then he would see the bald patches down the sides of the dress, and know that I had paid that much for a dress that didn't even fit, and that I had destroyed it a little, actually, to make it work.

David never raised his voice, not really. Mama would have liked that about him, if we'd ever bothered to talk about such things. He hardly even reacted to my transgressions, at least not right away. But he watched me silently, waiting. For floods of tears, for an apology, for me to do something else stupid and rash—I never knew. I didn't want to cry just then, because I'd spent half an hour on my eye makeup alone, but I could feel tears in the corners of my eyes. I pressed the tips of my fingers into them and pinched the bridge of my nose. The long acrylic nails dug into my tear ducts and made my eyes water even more.

"I'm really sorry, David," I said. "I just wanted to look nice for the party. For you."

Some bubble of tension burst in the room—David gave up on his anger, I believe, and realized he needed to spell it out for me.

"You can't do things like this, Teddy," he said, in a gentler tone now. "You can't be spending my money like this without asking me."

It was *my* money, too, I thought, and it was from *my* uncle, but I knew that wasn't really how it worked. Mama's money had been hers, after all, along with her name, but once she and Daddy were married, she couldn't spend much of it without his permission. She couldn't even sign her own checks, at least not until they finally changed that law in '68. I'd grown too used to living alone, I supposed. To paying my own bills with my allowance, as poorly as I managed them.

And anyway, I didn't want to argue. I wanted to show David. I wanted him to see what he'd seen that day in Capri: that we could actually be happy together. I hated the dress, in that moment. I would have given anything to take it back. To not have bought it in the first place.

"I know. I'm sorry."

"When we get home from the party tonight, we'll talk about an allowance. I'll give you money at the start of every month, and if you need to spend anything more than that, we'll have a conversation about it." David sighed, and added, "This can't happen again. You can't just—you're like a child, sometimes, chasing after shiny things. Like a magpie."

He was right, probably. I was always good at hoarding glittering bits and pieces, dragging tinfoil and chewing-gum wrappers back to my nest. But I suppose if we were birds, he was a crow, or maybe a parrot. Something smart, something that could mimic human speech.

David went to the bar cabinet for a bourbon, and then he went outside to start the car, and he drove us in silence along the river and over the Ponte Umberto and past the Borghese park to the Villa Taverna, to the den of the Wolf.

4. Villa Taverna

Friday and Saturday, June 6–7, 1969

The ambassador's residence was a cream-colored stucco palace set on seven acres of manicured lawns, encompassing lush gardens and fountains—and, I had heard, an enormous, blue-tiled swimming pool. It was, David explained, one of the best addresses in Rome. And the guests would be the best company in Rome, so I should be sure not to approach anyone without being introduced, or speak too loudly, or, really, speak unless spoken to.

He said all of this as if I had no idea how to act at a formal party. As if he, not I, was the one who'd taken ten years of etiquette classes and executed a flawless Texas dip at my debut, from the opening Idlewild ball all the way to Terpsichorean at the end of the '53 season. He didn't have any reason to doubt my ability to behave properly in polite society; there *were* reasons, of course, but he didn't know them.

And as I walked up the driveway to the ambassador's house in my cat-piss yellow shoes and my dress that didn't fit, the one I wasn't supposed to have bought but couldn't resist because I was like a child, a stupid, impulsive child, I almost believed it. Who was I to think I deserved to be there, among the rich and famous?

You could find the most interesting people in the world in Rome. Actors and actresses and famous directors, writers and artists and English aristocrats. Princess Margaret was known to appear every now and then. Heiresses with more liberal families than mine, ones that let them go running off to Marrakech and Monaco. Various sons and daughters of minor and major nobility from all over Europe, racing-car drivers and professional gamblers and the lead singers of rock bands with their socialite wives. Aunt Sister would have loved it; she was always telling stories about the people she'd met on her adventures: the young Dalai Lama at Potala Palace in Lhasa, so-and-so de Rothschild at a famous hotel in Cap d'Antibes.

She would have made the most of a party like that, but I just felt like I didn't belong. What was I going to say to Catherine Deneuve or Gloria Guinness? I'd never been farther from Dallas than Washington, DC, where I used to tag along, sometimes, with Uncle Hal; I'd never had a job that wasn't handed to me, just to keep me busy.

I listened to the sound of my beads rustling as I stepped over the threshold of the Villa Taverna and remembered the little girl's expression of wonder in Valentino's atelier. *Che brillante!* How shiny! And that had been enough to make me buy the dress, one that cost more than most people made in months, one that didn't even fit. I was just a little girl playing dress-up. David was right to treat me like a child; I acted like one.

There was a flash of light as soon as we stepped inside the door, and I raised a hand to shield my eyes.

"Don't worry, Bear." David laughed. "It's only a camera."

He made a joke to someone I couldn't see, as spots still danced in my eyes, who stood beyond the entry. He said, still laughing, that I was a little gun-shy.

"You should see her when there's fireworks," David said, "she hits the deck!"

I supposed it was fine to be the butt of the joke. As long as David was laughing instead of still angry with me.

I'd thought, from the way David had so quickly jumped to joviality, to deference, that he might have been speaking to the ambassador himself, but when my eyes finally cleared I saw that this humor was for the benefit of a man a bit older than him, with newly graying hair, who stood next to a carved walnut cabinet inside the foyer. I would've recognized the Wolf; this man wasn't a movie star.

"Arthur," David said to the man, and put a hand behind me to usher me forward, "this is my wife."

Then, to me, "Teddy, this is Arthur Hildebrand."

The man shook my hand and gave me a vague smile, and I asked him, "And what do you do?"

David should already have told me that. You're supposed to inform someone of how you know a person, or who they are, when you introduce them, but David always got things like that wrong.

"Oh, I'm an architect," he said, and made a face that I couldn't quite read—surprise, perhaps, at how little David's wife knew of his colleagues. "I'm here with the Foreign Buildings Office."

"Of course," I said, and smiled, though I had no idea what that meant.

I had thought David would introduce me to his boss—to the Wolf—soon after that, but he guided me with a firm hand on my waist through the entryway and into a hall, explaining as we walked that he had forgotten to warn me about the flash, but that the ambassador and his wife, a former actress herself, always hired professional photographers for their parties.

"To document all the bright and beautiful people they hobnob with," he said with some disdain, then added, in a slightly more respectful tone, "and because it keeps the paparazzi away. If there are enough photos from the parties in the society pages, there's less of a market for pictures taken sneakily outside the gate."

The interior of the Villa Taverna, which I mostly saw in passing as David shuffled me onward, was beautiful—high, coffered ceilings, tiled floors, brocade curtains. And I could see paintings on every wall, sculptures in nooks and alcoves. I wanted to look, but David steered me briskly past it all. I grabbed a glass of champagne from a tray, at least, when one orbited within my reach.

David finally stopped in a sort of conservatory, a room far less ornate than the ones we had passed, populated by a few small clusters of people. I scanned their faces, looking for anyone famous, but came up empty. Based on their attire, these were the "other grunts" David had said we would be sitting with. I didn't think anyone else in this room was wearing Valentino, to put it mildly. I felt a momentary flush of pride at my outfit, as ill-thought-out as it was. I, at least, was dressed appropriately to meet heads of state and celebrities.

David led me over to two women standing by an enormous potted palm.

"Teddy," he said, "this is Margot," gesturing to the shorter of the two, a delicate-looking brunette with a sharp jaw and enormous dark eyes, "and Anna," nodding toward the taller woman, a giantess with hair the color that mine might have been, if left to nature.

"Ladies," he continued, "this is Teddy. My wife."

"The elusive Teddy!" Margot cried, and clutched my hand. "I'm so glad you finally had the time to join us!"

I looked to David for clarification, but didn't even know what question to ask him. What had he told his colleagues about me, once he *had* finally told them about me? Had he said I was staying away because I wanted to? Because I thought I was too busy, or too good, for them? Not because he refused to invite me?

"And you both work with David?" I asked.

Again, David had forgotten to tell me how he knew them. It was almost like he was doing it on purpose.

"I don't," the one David had identified as Anna said. "I'm a hanger-on."

65

"Journalist," Margot clarified. "So we try to keep her on our side. Anna and I went to school together, ages ago, at Bryn Mawr."

"Not that long ago, I'm sure," David said, and winked at Margot. To me, he said, "They're barely out of school, these young things," and somehow my strange, immovable husband was flirtatious and charming as I had never seen him before. I began to think I hardly knew him at all.

"Well," Margot smiled, "anyway, Anna and I just happened to cross paths here in Rome! You know how it happens."

I didn't. Or at least, nothing like that had ever happened to me.

"And Anna writes for *Vogue*, can you believe it?" Margot trilled.

"Sometimes," Anna said. "When they'll have me. Other times, not so much."

"So we love to have her around," Margot went on, "but yes, *I* work with David," she said, finishing her thought. She patted his arm.

"Margot is a protocol officer," David explained, "which means a lot of these parties are her doing."

"Oh, I can't take credit for all this," Margot said, sweeping her hand out across the room, "I just handle the briefing books."

"Briefing books?" I asked.

"For guests," David said. "Usually a visiting congressman, or someone, but anyone the Wolf is hosting will do. Dossiers on rich people, basically, so that everyone knows how to talk to them at events. What to get out of them."

Margot nodded. "You know, 'Mrs. David Shepard is an avid gardener. Education: Southern Methodist University, degree in Art History. Mr. Shepard enjoys watching college football. They have two children—Alice, twelve, likes to read, and James, nine, wants to be a professional baseball player. They have a Labrador.'"

"None of that is true," I said. "Except the degree."

"Not yet, anyway," David said, and he took my hand and smiled at me.

I wanted that smile. I wanted what it promised. I wanted to go home together after the party and wrap my arms around him, I wanted to stay up all night telling each other everything. I wanted to confess and be absolved, I wanted him to take care of me, I wanted to feel safe and petted and loved. In that moment, I wanted to smile back at him, but I was too shocked; the idea that he wanted me in a house somewhere, gardening, with a Labrador and two children, was impossible to believe. He'd told me that we should wait a while before we tried for a baby, and he'd changed the subject every time I'd brought it up since.

And the Labrador? He wouldn't even let me get a cat to keep in the flat. "It's a lot of work, Teddy," he'd said, when I asked. As if it would be too much for me to remember to feed a cat a few times a day. As if Beppo wasn't living proof that I could manage at least that much.

My surprise must have shown on my face because Anna laughed and said to David, "Your wife looks like she's seen a ghost. The ghost of Christmas yet to come!"

And David smiled again, but with his teeth closed this time, and he let go of my hand, and I felt like something had slipped out of the window. Something caught out of the corner of my eye and then gone; a shooting star dissolving mid-flight.

When I was nine or ten or so, Aunt Sister took me outside at the ranch in West Texas one night to look for shooting stars. We stood in the sagebrush wrapped in blankets and looked up at the inky sky; the trick was to unfocus your eyes, she said, so you could catch the stars moving at the edge of your vision. The first one I saw, a streak of white light barely there, like a floater in my eye, I made a wish on, but soon there were too many to count. I turned my head faster and faster, trying to catch them all, and I thought it must be a good omen to have so many wishes at once. I didn't learn until much later, when I read it in a magazine, that what we were watching was a meteor shower. That what I'd wished on was a meteor burning up, dying.

David must have thought I'd made a face at the idea of a family, of a life with him. I was only surprised, that was all, but he thought I was mocking him, and I didn't know how to fix it, and I thought if I reached for his hand again, he would pull it away.

"Let me know if you ever need help!" I offered, falsely cheerful. "I've organized a party or two in my time—I used to set up charity galas for an art foundation."

I wanted David to see that I cared about his work; I wanted to be useful.

Margot exhaled; if I were to interpret it uncharitably, I would say it was more like a snort. "It's not just party planning. It's important to know these things; it's politics. Not so much for the Hollywood types, maybe, but when a senator visits, for example, for the meetings. Especially if the family comes along: is Mrs. so-and-so going to get along with Leone's wife if they're seated together at a luncheon at the Quirinale? Don't have to worry about the prime minister's wife, since he hasn't got one, but what about the other leaders of the Christian Democrats? What if Mrs. so-and-so is known to be shy? Leone's wife is famously social, always listed as one of the best-dressed women in Rome."

"Plus," David added, "if there's anything else—any scandal, any rumor—that goes in there, too."

"Hey, tell me something." This was Anna. "What about the pope's wife?"

She was already grinning gleefully as she followed up, "An accomplished pianist? Prefers the French designers over the Italians? You need to know. For the *meetings*."

David answered, without missing a beat, "Oh, I wouldn't sweat it. He's divorced."

We all laughed, me harder than anyone. I was relieved that he'd made a joke: he couldn't be that upset with me, then, and it diffused the tension after Margot had obviously taken offense at my offer to help. And I was proud of him. Look at my David, how clever he was. It bothered me a little, how much livelier he seemed with his colleagues than he did with me. But mostly, it was a relief: here he was, making everyone else laugh. Joining in the fun.

I got about fifteen seconds, maybe thirty, of pleasure out of that before I began to worry. Because then I wondered what was in my briefing book, if there was one.

Surely the government knew about Aunt Sister. About what had happened to her. Then again, perhaps Uncle Hal had made it all go away, as he was wont to do.

And I wondered what else they might know. Had David been told about all those nights in Dallas and in Washington when I wasn't where I was supposed to be? How deep did they go, these briefing books?

Margot had known that I went to SMU. Was that because David had told her? Or because there was a file on me, too?

"Do you have them on everyone?" I asked her. Trying to sound casual. Teddy is just curious; she finds her husband's work fascinating. What a good wife.

"Everyone?" Margot repeated.

"The briefing books. Do you just do them for visitors, or is it for everyone?"

She laughed; pointed at me. "Teddy wants to know what's in her file!"

David shook his head. "No, Teddy, there's no file on you, if that's what you're worried about."

"I'm not," I said, but I don't know if he believed me.

"Anyway, what would it say?" Margot added. The implication very obviously being: there's nothing much to say about you. It was rude, but it was also a relief. I would have loved to be someone with nothing to hide.

Then Anna said, raising her eyebrows, "The Russians probably have one on you, though."

"The—what do you mean, the Russians?"

"Oh, they're a people who live in the north of Europe," David said, "and Asia, too."

"Don't be nasty, David," Anna said, and smiling at me, explained: "They keep tabs on everyone. Everyone at the embassy, everyone even remotely connected. Delivery boys, gardeners. Names and whatever else they can get their hands on through their informants."

"Anna doesn't know what she's talking about," David said mildly, and she shrugged. To me, David said, "Don't worry about it. It's not a big deal."

"I wasn't worried," I lied.

"All I'm saying is what I've heard," Anna said. "I heard that a secretary at the US Embassy in Berlin fell in love with a man who turned out to be an East German operative. He tricked her into handing over all kinds of files. Apparently, they keep lists of lonely, older women. People who would do anything for love."

"We don't need to be discussing this," David said, and put a hand on my shoulder. "Really, Teddy, there's nothing to be afraid of."

I had a moment, just a moment, of panic—Anna's words had raised something half remembered, from years ago—but then there wasn't time to let it surface: I had more immediate concerns, like showing David that I could be the wife from Margot's hypothetical briefing, the avid gardener who was a loving mother to two children, and a Labrador.

In retrospect, perhaps I should've paid more attention to what Anna said, and what it dragged up in my memory. It might have saved me some grief, later on. But at the time, I mostly thought it was the saddest thing I'd ever heard. Not the deception, or the state secrets being spilled. But the idea that someone had sat in an office somewhere—I pictured someone like David, or Margot—and made a list of lonely people, well, that just about broke my heart.

"So," Margot raised her eyebrows at David, "will you be staying long after dinner?"

"Oh, not a chance," he said, and squeezed my arm. "Teddy and I will be leaving as soon as we can do so without being rude."

"Why?" I asked. "What happens after dinner?"

"Oh, the ambassador's parties are famous," Anna said, "for . . . devolving, somewhat, as the evening wears on. Personally, I think it's more fun when everyone relaxes a bit."

"That's because being here isn't your job," David said.

"Isn't it?"

Anna, I would learn, was never without a retort. She always knew exactly what to say.

I met a few more of David's colleagues over the next hour or so, though he kept us secreted away in the conservatory right up until dinner was announced. I thought I could hear laughter and lively chatter from elsewhere in the residence as we conversed with his coworkers, and outside, too, through a set of open French doors, but there was no sign of our host or hostess and David made no move to follow the sounds of the party. Waiters continually circulated through with bottles of champagne, at least, and I let them refill my glass every time. David didn't seem to notice; he might have had something to say by the third or fourth glass, if he'd been paying any attention. But he was standing with a group of other officers, angling his back toward me and talking to them about the situation in Berlin.

The situation—my situation, not the one with the damned Wall—hardly improved when we finally took our seats at the table. There were a few dozen other guests, and we were so far away from the main table that I couldn't even make out the Aga Khan or his bride-to-be, which was a shame, as I was dying to know what she was wearing. And I couldn't see the Wolf or his wife, either, from where I sat, but it would have been rude to stand up and gawk at them.

Of course, it was also rude that neither of them had been waiting in the foyer to greet each guest as they came in—at least, Mama would have said so. She would have been shocked, really, by the general disorder of the party, the way different groups of people were siloed away from each other, the shabbiness of David's introductions. Perhaps it was just what these Californians were like; I'd heard things were more "relaxed" there. If relaxed can be taken to mean careless.

I was squeezed in at the end of our table, in a place so obviously added at the last minute that I expected David to apologize, or at least say something to acknowledge this indignity, but he spent most of the dinner yammering on about air pollution or some other boring thing in Berlin with an attaché from the West German Embassy. He was just getting started on the subject of fuel standards in the GDR when the dessert course—a lovely molded blancmange, perfectly refreshing for a hot June evening; the menu had been well chosen, at least—was cleared. I found a lot of his conversation tedious, but even so, I could tell that David was very smart. I don't know if I've mentioned that yet—whatever else, he was sharp as a needle.

It can be a dangerous thing, to show that you're the smartest person in the room; I've often found it safer to seem stupid.

People began to rise from the table and migrate out over the lawn, where a string quartet accompanied by an Italian guitar had been playing all through dinner. I stood from my seat and pulled the skirt of my dress out as much as I could, trying to keep the straining silk from bunching around my behind and my belly—too full; I'd eaten far more than I'd meant to, but the food was so good, I couldn't stop—then prepared to join the crowd across the grass. I wanted to meet the Wolf and his wife, and the Aga Khan and his soon-to-be bride, and I wanted to sparkle. I'd had just about enough of being ignored all dinner, and I'd also had just about enough champagne that I was ready to do something about it.

David and Udo, the West German attaché, stood with me and regarded the groups of revelers drifting over toward the band, and then Udo said, "My God! I really was not expecting to see *them* here," and nodded his head in the direction of a group of men who looked the same as every other, to me.

"Who?" I asked. "Who are they?"

I was getting tired of not being properly introduced to anyone.

"They're from the Russian Embassy," Udo said, with a dramatic drop to his tone that suggested he expected me to shiver, or something.

It wasn't obvious that there was anything unusual about them, though. One of the men was facing away, but from what I could see of the rest of them, they could've been anyone's husbands, anyone's colleagues. I expected them to look different, somehow. Deprived, maybe, or sad. But they wore the same suits as everyone else, the same Ferragamo ties and shiny loafers, and they had the same haircuts, too. Perhaps there was something a bit more closed about their faces, but then again, that could've just been because everyone looked like that, to me. Inaccessible. Treacherous.

The Russian diplomats could've been any group of men from New York or Chicago, at least until they all grinned, apparently at a joke one of them had made. Then I could see that their teeth were mostly small, and some crooked or chipped. They didn't have American smiles.

"I'm surprised they were invited," Udo went on. "Though I suppose it's fine as long as they are here, outdoors, instead of in the embassy."

"Why can't they go to a party at the embassy?" I asked. "Why do they need to be outdoors?"

"Because of Moscow," Udo said, and when he saw my blank face, explained, "here is the short version: the Reds gave your ambassador in Moscow an enormous, carved wooden United States seal, the one with the eagle and all, just after the war, as a gift, to hang on the wall. Only for the ambassador to find out, about seven years later, there was a bug hidden in it, and the Russians had been listening to him—to everything—the whole time!"

"A bug?"

"A covert listening device," Udo answered. "It's famous, now. In the industry, they call it 'The Thing,'" and David, who'd been eyeing the men, distracted, finally jumped in to say, "But that doesn't matter, because these gentlemen are just diplomats. Right, Udo?"

"Might as well be," Udo answered. "Aksakov and Pavlenko are old drunks, and the young one, the new one—Larin's the surname— is a buffoon."

David was watching me, I realized, when I asked, "A buffoon?" and I wondered if he wanted to see if I was frightened by the idea of these supposedly shadowy men. I was craning over Udo's shoulder, trying to put faces to names. The "young one" was looking away, but from what I could see, he was tall, with a shock of blond hair.

"His father's high up in the Party," Udo explained. "He's just another one of these feckless papa's boys with important connections. He's the cultural attaché, which is hardly even a real job. Of course, we didn't know that right away. So we looked into him, a bit, when he first appeared in a posting, in Berlin."

He winked at David. "You did, too, I think, in Washington—"

"Let's go find the ambassador," David interrupted. "It's about time you met him, don't you think, Teddy?"

The tall, blond man—the feckless buffoon, the appointee— turned, just then, and as soon as I saw him—the long face, the round eyeglasses (why can't any of the men in my life see?)—I knew. I recognized those brown eyes behind the lenses, which were like a puppy's or a rabbit's, wholly trusting, almost blankly affectionate, and . . .

Well, there's a roller coaster at Six Flags Over Texas, the amusement park, called the Runaway Mine Train. Near the end, after you've already been through two peaks and two drops, you chug up to the Ace Hotel and Saloon and stop there for a while. There are animatronic miners, so eerily lifelike, sitting in the saloon chairs, at the tables with their glasses of Plasticine whiskey, and it seems like you're going to stay there with them. Like maybe the ride is over, and this is the fun bit at the end.

And then suddenly, without warning, you drop all the way down into a tunnel under Caddo Lake.

I'd thought I was on my way up to the Saloon, in Rome, with my new life and my new husband—at the party, in my Valentino dress and my shiny nails, with my hair up like I thought I was someone, like I was Brigitte Bardot or Sophia Loren—and I had fooled myself into thinking I could stay.

But now here I was, falling down under the water.

Now

Early Morning, Wednesday, July 9, 1969

"Let's pause for a moment, Mrs. Shepard," Archie says, and he's already standing from the couch. He heads for the kitchen, and the phone.

"Larin. Is he one of ours?" Reggie calls after Archie, who promptly shushes him and gestures in my direction.

"Oh, she won't be talking to anyone," Reggie says, and he says it calmly, like it's a fact, and I know there's a threat contained within.

Even so, they ask me to leave the room for a moment while Archie makes his call, and why shouldn't I comply?

I walk down the narrow hallway to our bedroom, mine and David's, and I think about tidying up—about hiding the bloody dress better, or putting all my purses back on the shelf where they belong, but really, why bother?

I'm in there half an hour, maybe more, and I consider lying down on the bed to take a nap, but despite all the bourbon I've had, I'm too agitated to sleep. I think about taking one of my pills, too, but I can't decide which one the situation calls for, so I abstain.

Archie finally comes to get me, and I return to the sitting room to find a third man on the not-mine rust-colored sofa.

This man, I know: it's Arthur Hildebrand, the architect. David's graying colleague from the Foreign Buildings Office.

Well. I should have guessed.

76

It's a shame, though, that I know his name—he would have made a pretty good Jughead, with his eccentric, distracted air and his long nose.

I offer him a beverage—bourbon, or I could make coffee, I say—but he declines. In fact, Arthur Hildebrand doesn't say much beyond, "Mrs. Shepard. Nice to see you again."

"Now," says Reggie, "why don't you continue where you left off, Teddy?"

It isn't lost on me that he's using my given name, now.

"Tell us how you know Yevgeny Larin, please."

5. Washington

February 1963

It was wintertime. I was in Washington, DC with my Uncle Hal, and I didn't have a coat that was warm enough for the cold. Another girl from Dallas might've just worn her furs, but Mama had never bought me any. She said they were vulgar.

I used to go along with Hal, sometimes, when he was in DC for a vote or something. It was a good place to meet with art dealers, to keep them from having to go all the way from London or New York to Dallas. And we were planning to have a few items on loan to the National Gallery, that year, for an exhibition.

Hal liked to have our pieces on display in Washington. It had something to do with taxes, first of all, but he also said it let everyone know he didn't only care about oil. About money.

"I like art and all that shit, too," Hal used to say.

I don't know if very many of his colleagues in Congress believed him on that score; he'd been invited by a senator from New York to go see Rudolf Nureyev dance a couple of years earlier, right after he defected, and Hal laughed for about ten minutes straight at the idea of a man ballerina.

We stayed at the Mayflower, as always, and I went window shopping at the luxury stores over by Embassy Row the first day while Uncle Hal took meetings. He was in town because the current president—Hal didn't even like to say his name, but it was Kennedy, obviously—had finally introduced his Equal Pay Act into Congress, and Hal and his people were so mad they could spit. He was posted up in the hotel's restaurant with senators from Georgia and Alabama and Arizona, plus representatives of the Chamber of Commerce and the Retail Merchants Association, trying to figure out how to respond to the absurd, impossible imposition, which frankly, Hal said, the federal government did not have the *mandate* for, that the businessmen of America, the backbone of the country's economy, be required to pay their female workers equal wages, even though everyone knew women were already more expensive to employ.

There was a furrier between Garfinckel's and the hotel that I passed coming and going, and there was a long fox-fur coat in the window, russet and caramel-colored and impossibly soft-looking— it looked like it would be as soft as a cat, though I hadn't had much opportunity to pet one, since Mama had never allowed pets, and we weren't supposed to touch the barn cats at the ranch, likely as they were to have fleas and God knows what else. I thought about buying it, I was so cold, but I knew Mama would be angry if she saw it, and Hal would tell Mama, anyway, and I didn't have much money left in my account until March, and I still needed to pay for my meals for the next few days, unless I ate at the hotel, in which case it would just go on Uncle Hal's tab. He always checked the bill at the end, and would say things like, "Well, Teddy Bear, an entire vol-au-vent, all to yourself? Better watch your figure, or we'll never manage to marry you off!"

I was already twenty-eight, and it wasn't looking good.

I skipped dinner that night when I got back to the hotel, and the next morning I had a single deviled egg and black coffee for breakfast, so I was really doing quite well by the time I went to my meetings at the National Gallery around noon. I had to rush back to the hotel after lunch, though—Hal wanted me to meet him in the private dining room at the Mayflower's restaurant, because he and his cohort were meeting with the lady senator (senatress, Hal and his friends liked to say) from Minnesota, to try to get her on their side, and they thought she might appreciate another female face in the room.

Rebecca Niebuhr ("May I call you Becky?" Hal asked, when she walked into the room, and she smiled at him and said, "No.") was a formidable presence. She was the only woman in the entire Senate at that time, though there was another handful in the House, and she was nearly six feet tall in flat shoes. She had a strong jaw and a helmet of graying hair, which was probably normal for her age but which none of the women in their fifties that I knew, including my mother, would ever have allowed to happen to them. Hal called her the Hausfrau from Duluth.

She came into the room and took a seat, and she swatted away all of Hal's little jokes and barbs like they were flies. I thought she was magnificent, and frightening, and when Hal explained what he wanted, which was for her to come out against the Equal Pay Act, and indeed, to help them draft a response, because it would be irrefutable, their position, if they had the lone woman in the Senate on their side, she said, "Now why would I want to do that?"

"Because it's bad for business," Hal said, and then the fellow from the Chamber of Commerce went into a long explanation of how it would harm Senator Niebuhr's constituents, and the union voters she depended on for her post, and she listened intently and then said, "But on the other hand, half of my constituents are women. As they are in any population."

"Yes," Hal said, and he was grinning wickedly, "a grave error, giving them the vote."

Senator Niebuhr didn't smile. I thought perhaps she might seek me out to make sympathetic eye contact—"These men!" our expressions might say. But she never looked at me, not even once, the entire time she was in the room. I don't think, in her eyes, I was much of a compatriot.

"I fail to see," she said, and her voice was quiet, but in the way a schoolteacher's is when they'll brook no dissent, "why a woman ought not to earn the same wage for the same work as a man."

"Well," Hal said, and he had pulled a cigar out and was clipping the tip, which struck me as disrespectful, somehow, though I couldn't put my finger on why, "setting aside the fact that it ain't ever equal work, is it, when we're talking about a factory or a farm, they just don't need the money. They have their husbands to provide for them. And they should be at home with their children."

"Not all women are married," the senator said. "And not all married women want children."

Hal laughed at that.

"I'm not sure I see how they're gonna stop it, if they're married."

Senator Niebuhr looked down her nose at Hal, and the skin below her neck formed a sort of layered jowl that I knew Hal was taking note of, to laugh about later.

"Contraception, Senator Huntley," she said.

I could already hear Hal's voice in my head, what he would say after she left the room: he would joke that she'd surely never needed to worry about birth control, because who would ever want to mount *that*.

And I was right, by the way—he said it later almost word for word.

"Or failing that," she went on, "abortion."

He restrained himself from speaking in the moment, though I had no doubt he had plenty to say, and he puffed slowly at his cigar instead. I knew him well enough to see that he was trying to intimidate Senator Niebuhr.

"Well," he said, finally. "I *fail to see*," he began, and we all knew he was mimicking her, mocking her prim patterns of speech, "why the honest business owners of the United States are required to subsidize women who make such unnatural choices. Who are, let us assume, so *disagreeable* as to be unable or unwilling to find a man to take care of them. In fact, we're doing these women a disservice by telling them that they can and should live on their own, when time has proven the exact opposite to be true."

Senator Niebuhr wanted to know what he meant by that, and what statistics he had to support it—she'd been a math teacher, it transpired, at a girls' academy in Duluth before she felt called to politics—and Hal said he didn't have any ready to hand, but that he knew this to be true, that women left alone in the world inevitably came to tragic ends.

And the senatress from Minnesota didn't know, but I did, that there was another woman in the room with us just then, and she was Aunt Sister, who had, Hal was right, come to a tragic end; and I suppose he was right, too, that no act drafted by Jack Kennedy or concession by the Chamber of Commerce would have been enough to save her.

Rebecca Niebuhr left the room a bit angrier, probably, and more convinced than ever of the need for her presence in the Senate, but with no progress on either side toward a resolution. And Hal and his buddies made all the jokes I'd expected, and then some, about how fat she was, how old and ugly, and there was a discussion of that word she'd used—contraception—and the kinds of women who employed it.

"If we're paying women more so they don't have to get married, and they don't have children—they're using the 'contraception' they would need in order to live that way—then aren't we just making them into whores?" Hal said. "Aren't we paying them, ultimately, to let every Tom, Dick, and Harry between their legs?"

Hal eventually remembered I was in the room and told me I could go, and to have a nice dinner—"but not *too* nice!"—and to charge it to the room, and it was hard to imagine what else they had to say, once I left, that would be even more vulgar, but I had confidence they would come up with something. My mother would have been horrified to know they spoke that way in front of me. About things like sex, I mean, not about the senatress from Minnesota and her jowls, but I never wanted to tell her, to have her put a stop to it. It was a kind of privilege, I imagined, to be included. To be in the room with these powerful men, and to hear what was in their minds.

I didn't go back to my room, or to one of the other restaurants in the hotel to have that nice, but not too nice, dinner.

I went back to the shopping streets over by Embassy Row, and I went straight to the furrier, and I bought the fox-fur coat without even trying it on. I paid in cash, and I suppose the salesman thought I was some filthy rich and uncouth oil executive's wife, because he treated me politely, solicitously.

There's a kind of power in it, to have a man at your beck and call that way; I asked him to bring me a glass of champagne while I waited for him to package the coat, and he did, and when he offered to have it sent on later to my hotel because it was too heavy for me to carry, all alone, in its garment bag, I asked him just to pay for my cab, instead, and he had to do it, because the customer is always right. The customer is king.

That was good, because I hardly had any money left, anyway.

As soon as I got back to my room I unwrapped the coat, and I put it on inside out so I could feel the softness against my skin, and it was so warm and luxurious and I felt enveloped, and calm, but then pretty quickly I started to notice that it smelled like death. It smelled like roadkill in the heat, and I thought of dozens of little foxes without their skins, and I hardly even had time to realize there was a roiling in my belly before I was retching, I was on the floor of the bathroom still in the inside-out fur, vomiting and weeping into the toilet, strings of saliva catching on my hands when I tried to brush the tears away from my eyes.

When I finally felt better, I rinsed my mouth and took the coat off, and shoved it back into its garment bag. I put on a black dress, a nice one for night—an old pleated silk one from Madame Grès that had belonged to Aunt Sister, and which I would never have worn around Uncle Hal—and fixed my hair and makeup, and I walked out of the room with what little cash I had left.

I knew Hal and his people would be in the Mayflower's bar or the Round Robin at the Willard until the early hours, plotting and complaining about the Act and smoking their cigars, so as long as I avoided those places, I figured I'd be fine. I could go to any other bar in DC, really—nobody knew me here, aside from a few people at the National Gallery, so even the most connected of political players wouldn't recognize me on sight. Really, if you thought about it, the whole city was open to me, so I decided to go to the bar at the Hay-Adams Hotel, which everyone always said was the place to be if you wanted to meet someone discreetly. Senators' staffers and higher-ups at various agencies would go there, sometimes, to meet journalists, if there was a story they wanted, unofficially, to get out.

I wasn't going to meet anyone, though. I wasn't going to spill any secrets. What happened next was entirely coincidence; an unfortunate one, though at the time it seemed like nothing at all.

The bar was in the basement, snugly furnished and upholstered and painted in oranges and reds so that it seemed like the inside of an organ, perhaps a womb. The lights were low, and everyone looked up as I descended into the room, then just as swiftly looked away—not for lack of interest, necessarily, but because it was part of the code.

There were tables and booth seats in alcoves all along the walls, but I took a spot at the bar. I had enough money left to reasonably swing a couple of drinks, and then I would return to the Mayflower and be safely in bed before Hal ever even stumbled back into the lobby.

There was no one else sitting on my side of the bar—it was a varnished wooden hexagon, with the bartender trapped in the middle—but a trio of women in heavy makeup and tight dresses sat laughing across from me. I didn't know much about such things, but I was fairly certain they were what my mother might have referred to as "working girls," and what Hal would have called something much ruder. They looked like they were having fun, though. And at least they weren't alone. One of them had her hair done high up on her head and it looked soft, cloudlike—I used to wear my hair very straight and sensible, back then—and in the moments since I'd begun observing them, a man had come over from a nearby booth to speak to her, and she put a manicured hand out to rest briefly on his chest, and I wondered what it would feel like. To be able to reach out and touch, like that.

"Are you waiting for someone?"

The bartender leered at me, interrupting.

"My husband died last week," I said, without thinking. It wasn't an answer to his question, and I didn't mean to say it, but I wanted him to stop looking at me like that. Like I was one of them.

The bartender's face fell, and he brought me a martini on the house after that, and then another. He left me alone, too, which was good—I wouldn't have been able to come up with more to that story, if pressed. I had no idea what it would feel like, to lose a husband. Or to have one.

It might've been a bit much on an empty stomach, but I felt like the vodka was burning through me, cleaning out the rot and rust and smell of death, of old blood, from the fur coat.

After a while I began to enjoy looking around the room, the feeling of the crooning music in my shoulders, the scent of smoke in my hair, and I suppose I was acting not so much like a woman whose husband had died last week, but the bartender had never met one of those, probably, so how would he know?

If I could have seen myself from somewhere else in the room, in the warm, low lights of the bar, I might have thought, look at that woman. She knows what she wants. Sitting there alone, so confident. There's a woman in control of herself; there's a woman on her own.

I saw him walk in the door. I saw him walk right past me, then take a seat on one of the velvet-covered stools a few places down. He seemed nervous, hesitant, which made me like him. He seemed like he wasn't sure he should be there, and neither was I. And I was so used to men who swaggered into rooms half-cocked, who sat with their legs spread wide, who took up all the air in whatever space they entered.

He didn't say anything to me, but when that snide bartender came over to ask for his order, he fumbled with the menu card and stuttered out a word.

"Whiskey," he eventually managed, and then the bartender asked him what kind and he floundered again, and finally said, "Anything."

That was the wrong answer—everyone who came here had their preference. It would have signaled that he was an outsider even without the foreign accent, which I couldn't place but thought was something European. German, maybe, or Polish.

He unfolded a pack of cigarettes, a label I didn't recognize with words I couldn't read, and pulled one out. It was a delicate movement for big, clumsy hands, and he pinched the cigarette a bit, wrinkling the paper. The skin on his hands looked soft, and smooth. Unused. He took out a box of matches, not a lighter, lit the cigarette, and pulled hard on it, like he'd had a long day. I don't think he was trembling, exactly, but I had the sense of vibrations coming off him. Like an animal that's overtired, or a little scared.

I thought he might say something—he kept glancing over at me—but he stayed silent through his first drink, and then his second. I'd reached the end of the two I'd initially decided to allow myself, and I knew it was time to go back to my hotel, but I couldn't seem to find my pocketbook in my purse, and I couldn't get the bartender's attention to close out and leave, and also I didn't want to. I think I would've stayed there until the bar closed, that night, waiting.

Eventually, after I'd switched to a standard old-fashioned and the bartender had begun to leer a bit again, thinking perhaps I was no widow after all, the man two seats down from me spoke.

"Are you waiting for someone?"

He furrowed his brow as he said it, like he wasn't sure it was the right question. It was the same thing the bartender had asked me, but the meaning felt different.

"No," I said, "just killing time."

"Killing time," he said, and smiled. "I like that."

I still couldn't tell much about him from the accent, which was sometimes almost German, sometimes a bit English, so finally I asked where he was from and he said Russia, but he said it like Raw-shuh. Moss-koh, he said, which was funny, because I had always thought it would be pronounced the way it was spelled, like Moss-cow.

I knew the Russians were our enemies, but I reasoned that if he was here, in this bar, in this country, he must be all right—I imagined a tragic, romantic background for him, like the defecting dancer Nureyev, the one my uncle had found so absurd. He probably wouldn't want to talk about it, or it would be rude to ask, so I didn't.

He moved the two seats over to sit directly next to me, and I could tell that I had been right, there was a kind of brightness, an intensity about him like an animal in flight—like a deer just before it runs, or a squirrel when it hears the crack of a hunter's gun. We clinked glasses and spoke of the usual things people say when they first meet and aren't destined to ever know each other very well; I talked about how cold it was in Washington, and Eugene laughed— he told me his name was Eugene, or rather he said something else, first, but then suggested it might be easier for me to pronounce "Eugene"—and said if I thought it was cold here, I should never go to Moscow.

"No problem," I said, "done deal," and he laughed.

It was like that: flirtatious, fun. I felt powerful, and beautiful, and desirable, and he seemed to, as well—the lack of confidence he'd displayed when he walked in, the sense that he was trembling, seemed to thin and fade with every drink, with every peal of laughter, and soon enough he had a hand on my arm, then on my knee. He'd been brushing them every now and again as we talked—a touch here and there, just punctuation. Nothing identifiable, nothing I could say for sure was anything.

But eventually that hand was heavy on my thigh, and it wasn't moving. And he was looking at me, really watching with those sweet brown animal eyes, and then he asked me if I wanted to come back to his hotel room with him and I said no, and that's when he told me how to spot a liar, because he said I looked away when I refused him, and so he knew I didn't mean it.

He was right.

It was enough; I could feel myself slipping that easily. I wanted to feel my fingers on his skin. I wanted that mouth, so timid and unsure with his words at first, on mine. I wanted to run my fingers through his golden hair.

So I let him pay for the rest of my bill—the free widow's martinis had ended when my conversation with Eugene began, and the bartender could tell at that point that I wasn't exactly in mourning—and we went upstairs in the hotel's wood-paneled elevator to his room.

He was nervous, and so he didn't touch me at first when we got into the room, but instead invited me to look at all the lovely things around us, the television set and the view of the city's monuments from the window, and he brought me the little soaps and shampoos from the bathroom and asked if I'd like to keep them, as if they were great offerings, luxurious gifts, and it was sweet and strange, and then finally he did come closer, and he kissed me.

There were moments, lying on the bed, on the mattress with no top sheet—which he later explained he had removed because he didn't know what to do with it, they didn't have those at home, and he felt stuck in it, trapped—when I felt like I must be someone else. Here was my body, here was what it was doing, and feeling, but I was up above it, or outside it. I realized at one point that I was staring out of the window, at the lights of the monuments shining brightly against the night sky.

Afterward, I stood up from the bed, clutching a stray blanket from the floor around myself to wear to the bathroom. I would rinse off, I thought, and get dressed, and it was late but hopefully not too late for a taxi, and the driver might judge me but I would never see him again. It would be all right.

And I knew Uncle Hal was probably still out somewhere, so as long as I was back at the hotel in time for breakfast in the morning, he would never even know that I'd been gone.

If I left now, I would wake up in my room at the Mayflower and hopefully wouldn't remember how I had gotten there, or that I'd ever left, and I would feel okay. At least until the fog cleared.

So I stood, wrapped in the blanket, but Eugene just started to laugh.

"Why are you running away?" he asked.

He reached for me and pulled me close, back into his long, awkward arms. Kissed the back of my head three times, loudly, like

89

you'd kiss something small and sweet, a puppy, a kitten. It was so tender, my heart hurt.

And even though I was afraid, and I thought I would be in trouble soon, and I knew what it might cost me—or at least I thought I did, though really I had no idea—I stayed.

I let him wrap his arms around me and hold me the way a child holds a teddy bear, for comfort, and I let him breathe loudly into my neck as he slept, and I stayed. I looked out of the window at the sodium vapor lamps on the street, gold against the blue night, and at the monuments, and finally, I didn't mean to, but I slept too.

I woke before him when the yellow light of early morning came shading through the window, falling in beautiful angles on the bare bed, on our bodies.

I knew I needed to leave, but I didn't; I stayed, and I lay there listening to his quiet breathing—I'd never spent a full night in bed beside a man before, but I'd expected them to be noisier—and I waited for him to wake up. Hoped he would pull me close again with warm hands and kiss me on the shoulder and play with my hair. Tell me not to worry, and that he was glad I was there.

I drifted away again. Even though I knew I had somewhere I needed to be. And when I woke up the second time he was still sleeping but had rolled over so that his face was buried again, still softly breathing, in the back of my neck, on my hair, and his body was shaped to mine. It felt so impossibly intimate—two bodies, as close as they could be. Nothing, not even clothes, not even sheets, between us.

And then I knew he was awake because his breathing changed, and his warm hands were on my sides, drifting over my form.

"Good morning," I said. Whispered.

"Good morning," he said into my neck, and then he turned me over.

I expected to find him on top of me again—was waiting for it, even—but he sat back and stared down at me.

"I want to look at you," he said.

But it seemed he wanted to touch, too, because he caressed my ankles, then calves, then knees, moving his hands up my body and stopping every so often to ask, "What's this?" at a freckle or a mole.

He said I was flawless; he said he'd never seen a woman like me before. And as he kissed his way up my frame, I was relieved he couldn't see it—everything that was there, spoiling, beneath the skin.

And I began to believe—foolish, stupid Teddy—that perhaps he was right. That maybe everything underneath was the same as it looked on the outside. That maybe I was just, and only, beautiful.

So when he asked later, as I dressed and prepared to leave, if he could see me again, if maybe I would meet him again, for dinner that night, I agreed. I wish I hadn't, all things considered—I wish I'd done something, *anything*, else—but I said yes.

6. Washington

February 1963

Hal was in fine fettle that morning when I met him in the Mayflower's restaurant for breakfast; he was ranting about Kennedy again. Apparently, the damn fool was talking behind closed doors about going to Berlin himself, to smile with his horse teeth and his haircut, to shake hands and pal around and try to lift everyone's spirits, as if that was all they needed, and not military intervention.

I was in the mood to eat something more substantial than my usual dry toast and deviled egg that morning, so I ordered pancakes and bacon, and Hal took a moment out of his monologue about what Kennedy had gone and done now to joke that if I wasn't careful, I'd end up as big as a house, as big as the Hausfrau.

So I didn't feel too bad, after that, telling him I wasn't going to be able to join him for the reception that evening—a dinner for some special interest group or other that had donated to his campaign—because I wasn't feeling well. Hal said I sure had an appetite for someone who was sick, and I said it was a migraine headache coming on, not my stomach, and he said well all right, Teddy Bear, I hope you feel better.

So then I had to go up to my room and stay there and pretend to be sick for the rest of the day, which was actually pretty easy, as I hadn't slept as much as I would have liked the night before. I napped and spent hours bathing and styling my hair and doing my makeup, and once I was sure Hal had gone to his reception, I left the hotel down the back staircase, not in the elevator, and snuck away to meet Eugene.

I couldn't very well wear what I'd been planning to sport at Hal's reception; it was far too frumpy for an assignation with your lover. And I didn't have anything more seductive left to wear; I'd only brought Aunt Sister's pleated silk, the one I'd worn the night before, on a whim. So I ended up wearing that again, and in retrospect it's possible that it contributed some to the later misunderstanding. And I still couldn't stand to wear the fox-fur coat, so I layered up against the cold, wearing a hooded velvet evening cloak—also once Aunt Sister's, also from Madame Grès in Paris—and my boring old wool coat on top of that.

Not, perhaps, the exact picture of the daring, sophisticated woman I wanted to be, sneaking off to meet my Russian lover, but not too far away. I would just take the wool coat off as soon as I walked in the door of the restaurant, so all he would see was the velvet. I was going to meet Eugene there—he hadn't offered to pick me up, but that was actually for the best, as I had to do a bit of skulking around to get out, and that way his first impression of me wouldn't be all buttoned up in conservative wool.

I met him at Rive Gauche in Georgetown, which was very popular in Washington but only with the other team—the Kennedys were said to love it—so I didn't have to worry that Hal or anyone who knew me would be there. And it was a younger crowd: beautiful, well-dressed women and their handsome husbands, so I didn't think we would look altogether out of place.

He was waiting for me at the entrance, my date, and I thought as we walked together over to our seat in a red velvet–covered booth, at a table set with white linen, that everyone who saw the two of us together, tall Gene with his golden hair, and me with mine, probably thought, there's a couple of young movers and shakers, there's an elegant, connected couple out on a date. Maybe we'd left the children with a sitter. Maybe Eugene was some European official, and our children went to the Lycée Rochambeau with all the other diplomats' kids, and we took them home to the Continent in the summer for the climate, and the culture.

I hadn't been on many second dates in those days, so the whole routine was a bit unfamiliar to me. I knew, though, that the conversation should be deeper, more personal than the playful banter of the night before—at least it should if this was going to go anywhere. Eugene didn't ask me many questions about my life to start with, but when I asked about his family as we waited for our cocktails, he did tell me how strict his father had been, how high his expectations. This was something I felt we had in common, and he nodded his head like he understood it, had been waiting to hear it, when I mentioned that I had always felt the weight of expectations, too. I couldn't tell you exactly what else I said about my family—and believe me, that was something I would try very hard to remember, later—but I know I didn't talk about money, at least, or power, because that would have been tacky. I spoke mostly in vague terms, without much detail, but I thought he would understand the feelings I described; I had the sense that we were kindred spirits.

I was surprised at how bewildered he was by the menu, though, and by the restaurant's table settings, and when I offered to order for us, he smiled with relief and said, "Yes, thank you, it wasn't like this in Berlin."

He'd been in Berlin for work, he explained, before Washington, and when I asked what he did for a living—it hadn't come up the night before, somehow—he said "cultural affairs." So I'd been right, apparently, that this was a tragic, exiled Russian artist, and I was all the more determined to help him out by ordering a perfect dinner.

First, two glasses of champagne. Brut for him, rosé for me. Cut-crystal glasses and bubbles like pearls shimmying to the top of the gorgeous liquid, the color of a blush. A lip.

Then a bottle of white wine to share for the first courses. Scallops sliced so thin as to be nearly translucent, escargots in garlic butter, tiny puff pastries filled with cheese, and an entire small squid for each of us, stuffed with herbs and breadcrumbs.

I was already full to bursting after all of that, but I wanted Eugene to see how lovely a meal with me could be—I wanted to show him the flavors. And, too, this was the first time I'd ever dined in such a nice restaurant with someone who wasn't keeping an eye on me. Eugene wasn't going to tell Mama or Hal or my cousin Marcia or anyone who knew me that I'd stuffed myself to the gills. He wasn't going to report back to anyone on my behavior.

That's what I thought, anyway.

So we kept eating and drinking, all the way through several more courses and a bottle of burgundy. I had *fricassée de poulet à la savoyarde* in a beautiful cream sauce, and tasted some of the *coq au vin* that I ordered for Eugene, too. Scalloped potatoes with Gruyère and nutmeg, green beans with almonds and tomatoes, and endless warm, soft bread with salted butter.

I spoke to Eugene almost constantly, soothingly, as you might speak to a frightened animal. He didn't ask me many questions, but that was fine. I was more than happy to talk his ear off, telling him things I'd felt deeply, things I thought he would understand. About art, about a sense of being alone, sometimes, in the world. Asking him about Berlin—I didn't ask about Russia, as I was certain it would make him too sad. I told him I'd like to go one day, to Berlin, and then laughed and remembered what Hal had said that morning—that Kennedy was planning to go with his haircut, to rally the poor divided Berliners. Eugene laughed, too, when I told him I'd heard that, though I didn't say anything about it coming from Uncle Hal. Gene perked up a bit after that joke.

For the most part, though, he was quiet, taking everything in, and I found it refreshing. There was no performance to this dinner together, I realized. He wasn't like other men I'd been out with; there was no "look what I'm giving you," cat dragging home a dead mouse to deposit at your doorstep and expect a scratch under the chin.

Actually, when I noticed that he wasn't showing off, I began to worry a bit. If there wasn't a point to this—if this wasn't a performance, if there was no expectation—perhaps it wasn't a date at all. He hadn't "brought" me here, had he? I'd brought myself. Perhaps he was lonely and just wanted someone to talk to. And what had I heard about Soviet women? People always said that they were forced to work in factories and fields alongside their men. Did they pay their own way at dinner, too?

I sat sweating, trying to carry on a conversation while doing the figures in my head, tallying all the food I'd ordered. I had no credit, and certainly not enough cash. And Hal didn't have an account here, and even if he did, I couldn't exactly charge it. Not on my secret date with my Russian refugee. Could I somehow speak to the manager without Eugene knowing? Offer to come back later, offer to wash dishes? Should I say I was going to the ladies' room and just leave?

When the bill came and Eugene paid without even looking at it, setting down far too much cash, so much that the waiter seemed irritated that he had to go for change, I was so relieved and grateful that of course I was going to go with him back to his hotel again, even though this was supposed to be the getting-to-know-you date. It was too late to play hard to get, at that point, anyway.

He opened the door for me as we left Rive Gauche, and people did this all the time for me, every man I'd ever met did, but it had never felt like this. They did it in a general way, for all women, and because it was polite, but this time I felt that Eugene was opening the door especially for me, because he cared about me. Because he understood me, I could just tell, and he wanted to take care of me.

And back at the Hay Adams, in his room, I didn't feel as far away from myself as I had the night before. I was with someone familiar; someone I liked—could even love.

"Do you like it?" he asked me, kissing up and down the side of my neck as we moved together. "Is this good?"

No one had ever asked me that before. I didn't like it, I had always assumed, or in any case I wasn't supposed to. It was something I suffered to happen to me, for some dark unknown reason. It was something I had to do.

But when he asked me, I realized that I did. For once, in that moment, it felt the way it was supposed to. Like you read about in books, or saw in certain movies.

"Yes," I said to him. Opened my mouth to him. "Yes. I like it."

Afterward, he got up to take a shower, and I stayed in the bed just a moment longer, luxuriating in this newfound feeling, this realization, while he rustled around with his clothes on a chair nearby.

I didn't realize what he was doing until he returned to the bedside and set a roll of bills down on the nightstand, then turned to walk away.

"What's this?" I asked, and he turned toward me again, and shrugged.

"It is customary, no?"

And then I understood.

It didn't feel like I was drawing a line in my life, when I took that money. It didn't feel like it mattered. I could forget exactly what had happened as soon as I left the room, forget the foolish idea I had entertained that this could be my life—it had only lived for a second, anyway, so it was easy enough to stamp out—except that now, at least, I had the money; money that nobody knew about. Something that was entirely mine, in the absence of anything greater, like love.

That was the first time something like that happened, with the money and the nightstand, but not the last. But I suppose, after everything else, it was the most important instance.

I suppose I thought if I'd done something wrong, it was only against myself, and it was mostly sheer stupidity. It was mostly the mistaken belief, however brief, that I deserved something more. I didn't think it was any bigger than that, and I certainly didn't think anyone would ever find out, though I guess I should have known better.

David told me much later on that they used to keep track of all the girls coming in and out of the hotels where foreign diplomats stayed in DC. You never knew who might be useful one day. You never knew what piece of information would help.

Now

Early Morning, Wednesday, July 9, 1969

Archie has the tips of his fingers pressed to his forehead. Reggie's lips have disappeared into a thin, white line.

"Okay," Arthur Hildebrand says slowly, finally. "Okay, Mrs. Shepard. Can you recall, very carefully, please, the amount of money Mr. Larin left on the—ah, on the nightstand?"

"Well, I don't know," I say, equally slowly, "I don't remember exactly. But I can tell you I used some of it to buy myself a bottle of champagne when I was back in Dallas, and a pair of little gold earrings shaped like knots, and a pink clambroth milk-glass jug and matching platter to serve things, you know, like shortbreads on. So about that much, I guess."

Arthur Hildebrand isn't as easily perturbed as the other two. He continues to regard me calmly, in a sort of unfocused way.

"And so how much is that?" he asks.

"A few hundred dollars, maybe? It seemed like a lot."

"What would the going rate be for—" Reggie begins, but goes quiet when Hildebrand turns to look at him.

"And there was never," Hildebrand continues, "any sense—*any* sense—that any . . . additional services were required? For that amount of money?"

"Like what kind of thing?" I ask, acting like I think maybe he means something dirty.

99

"Information, for example," he says. "About your husband, maybe, or Ambassador Carey."

"Haven't you been listening?" I ask. "I hadn't even met David yet. Or the ambassador, for that matter."

Arthur Hildebrand smiles at me.

"Information about your uncle, perhaps? About his position on the Committee on Foreign Relations, maybe?"

"I actually didn't know Uncle Hal had anything to do with that," I say, "at the time."

"But you did know," Arthur Hildebrand continues, "that President Kennedy was planning a visit to Berlin, long before the formal announcement. And you shared that with Larin."

"I didn't think it was important," I say, and shrug. "I just thought Hal was being funny, with the line about the haircut."

"The East German agencies knew about that visit well before it was announced," Reggie says, sneering at me. "You certainly gave them plenty of time to prepare."

"But nothing bad happened on that visit," I say, and Reggie hits right back with, "That you know of."

I don't admit that I've had cause to wonder the same thing pretty recently. To wonder exactly how much damage I am capable of.

Now I know, though.

"Moving on," Arthur Hildebrand says, though I don't get the sense he's finished with this subject for good, "you were going to tell us about the first time you met the ambassador."

"We're almost there," I say, and smile. I no longer have my lashes on to bat coquettishly at him, but I hope my tone is convincing. Stupid Teddy. Sad, stupid, pretty, silly Teddy.

7. Villa Taverna

Friday and Saturday, June 6–7, 1969

I needed to get away from the party. From the Russians, feckless and buffoonish or otherwise.

David wasn't watching me, anymore, because Udo had asked him another question about fuel standards, but I still thought he would probably notice if I threw up, or cried, or any of the reactions that felt imminent and possible the moment I saw Eugene—or Yevgeny, I guess—there at the US ambassador's house, trailing the muck of my old life on his stupid Ferragamo loafers into what had once been the shiny, pristine, freshly mopped expanse of my new one.

Enough people had risen from their seats at that point that I thought my departure wouldn't be too obvious, so I told David I was off to find the powder room and walked as quickly as I could without appearing to be running back into the house through the French doors.

I actually did need to find the powder room, or at least somewhere I could be alone for a little while—I needed to find somewhere to learn to breathe again. To lean on the wall until my body stopped shaking, until the cold sweat now soaking my too-tight dress began to dissipate.

When I got like this, as I sometimes did, my heart would start pounding, racing, and I'd think it might finally give out. And I would feel like I was floating, and my whole body would tingle, would be pins and needles all over, and I would get the sense that it wasn't my body, at all. Then the squeezing in my stomach, the cold feeling in my chest, which I had recently begun to imagine as an octopus trapped in the cage under my clavicle, wrapping its tentacles around my ribs. Strangling my heart.

The first night Teresa worked for us, she made us dinner. All of her favorite recipes from home, and so we dined on dish after dish of fresh fish in sauces of lemons and white wine and bright tomatoes, and there was an octopus, too, cut into two- and three-inch segments so that it appeared before us as a plate of disembodied tentacles resting wetly among sliced carrots and celery, still with suckers on, the purple color of a bruise.

It was those tentacles I imagined invading my chest, curled around my organs until I couldn't breathe, until my heart stopped beating. I was a little silver fish caught in the grip of a strong, suckered arm, and it dragged me down to the bottom of the sea and held me there, drowning.

I stumbled through the villa, which was somehow empty now—I didn't even pass a maid or footman on my flight, or an errant partygoer—and eventually found myself alone in the long hallway that David had rushed me through earlier. I pressed a hand against the wall, and my forehead on that—I didn't want to get my makeup on the beautiful paint.

The hall was a soft powder blue, decorated with gilded moldings and trompe l'oeil medallions between each pillar. Even the coffered wooden ceilings and the tile floors were ornately decorated, and the walls were lined, too, with paintings in baroque gilt frames.

I needed to put Eugene out of my mind. I needed all of the thoughts gone—I needed to forget he even existed. Actually, I needed to forget that I existed, too, and so, since I couldn't see any leftover glasses of champagne or half-drunk cocktails left behind on a credenza or a coffee table that might do the job for me, I decided to distract myself, instead.

I took my time moving slowly down the hall, stopping at each painting. I wanted to wait until I could be sure I wouldn't melt, dissolve, die, when I went back out to the party and saw Gene again, or, God forbid, had to talk to him.

I stood blindly before several artworks, portraits of wealthy Romans and pastoral scenes, my mind still running too fast to really see them, until I finally began to feel myself grow calm in front of a painting of the sea. There was a signature in the corner reading "Signorini"; I'd heard of him—he was an Italian artist from a school known as the Macchiaioli, who painted in a style akin to the Impressionists. I knew them well, because we'd bought a small painting by a similar artist from a very rude dealer, a hirsute man with sweat stains under the arms of his Oxford shirt who'd remarked how shocked and pleased he was to see that Texas was finally coming around to culture.

"You're really quite knowledgeable," he'd said, with his brow furrowed, watching me like I might perform some additional trick to surprise and amuse him. I learned much later, from Her Majesty's ambassador to Italy, that sometimes when the English say "quite," they mean, "not very."

The painting on the wall at the Villa Taverna was a view of a town on the coast, somewhere near the Cinque Terre, perhaps, I thought. White houses on a green hill running down to the pale sea below, which started in cerulean at the bottom of the frame but faded to white, like the sun was glinting off it, in the distance. I lingered at this one; something about its faded waters, and the town in white lines high above the sea, on the cliffside, calmed me.

I thought of Capri, and the way the sound of the waves rolling made everything feel softer, and safer. Like a shushing sound, or the beating of a heart. I remembered the little apartments I'd seen in the buildings by the harbor, and to soothe myself in the moment, I imagined my life there—a new one, anonymous, alone. How I would grow beautiful flowers in the window boxes on my little balcony. How I would sit out there on a rickety little wrought-iron stool in the evenings, smoking my Nazionales and watching the container ships glittering on the horizon like dying embers, on their way to Naples bringing all of David's goods from far away, his rubber tires and radios and cases of Coca-Cola, to the Italians, so they would need us.

I thought of what Aunt Sister had said, about the ocean. About how it meant something—something she could only vocalize vaguely—about my place in the world, something eternal, and that I wasn't entirely, exactly, alone.

I'm not sure how long I stood there, staring at that painting. Imagining myself inside of it. How quiet it would be, how calm. No David or Eugene or Margot or Mama or Hal. No Teddy.

But after a certain point, I realized I had been gone for a significant enough stretch of time that someone at the party might reasonably come looking for me, though I doubted anyone actually would. And it felt like the octopus had begun to shrink away from the lattice of my rib cage, had gone from constricting and clogging my chest to a softly throbbing little presence curled just above my pelvis, something I knew was in there hidden behind a rock or reef, waiting to strike, but that was, for now, no threat.

So I decided to be brave, and also it had occurred to me, once I was calm enough to think through it, that Eugene—no, he needed to be Yevgeny Larin to me, now—probably wouldn't even recognize me as the new Teddy I was trying to be, the one who lived in Rome with her diplomat husband. So I made my way back through the villa and this time I did find a few stray glasses of champagne on my route, and I returned to the tables under the portico, only to find that the party had migrated farther out on the lawn.

I walked across the grass to where I thought David might be; I passed Margot in conversation with a group of women I hadn't met, and I waved. When she thought I was out of earshot, or maybe she didn't think that at all, she said to the slender woman beside her, "She looks like a stuffed sausage in that dress. It's ridiculous."

"Hush," the other woman said, but she was smiling.

I could have gotten angry, but I always seemed to find it easier to feel hurt, instead, and anyway, I didn't think it would make a difference if I turned around and shouted, "It's Valentino!" at Margot's smug, skinny face, because she clearly didn't know a thing about couture; she didn't need to. She would've looked fine in anything she grabbed off the rack at a department store, with her little Hepburn doe eyes and her baby-deer legs. I was pretty sure the dress she had on was polyester and I doubted it had been tailored, even frantically in a few hours, as mine had been, but she still looked lovely and elegant and trim.

I also didn't have too much time to wallow, because I was trying as hard as I could to look out for Yevgeny Larin without seeing him—to make sure I didn't make eye contact, or accidentally bump into him. And I needed to find my husband, too. I thought perhaps it was time for us to leave.

I had an image in my mind that I would go to find David and trail a hand down his back, and tell him I'd been looking for him, and that I wanted him to take me home, now. And maybe he would think that I meant I wanted to make love, I couldn't wait, or he would at least be delighted that I was ready for bed. That I was a responsible Teddy who didn't want to stay too late at a party. I thought he would understand all of that, when I found him, and then he would take me home and protect me and I would feel safe; I did often feel safe with David. Sometimes, when he held me, enveloped in his solid bulk, I felt like I could disappear.

I realized this night wasn't going to end just yet, though, when I finally spotted David up ahead near a line of cypress trees. Because he was deep in conversation with the ambassador—the Wolf himself—and his wife, Lina.

Lina Montgomery, as she was known in her Hollywood days. There was no mistaking them: I'd seen them both in the movies before, though it didn't make me feel more like I knew them. It made them stranger to me, not more familiar, that I'd once seen their faces projected on a screen like one of my paintings in school.

"My wife," David announced, as I walked over to join them.

I have a little trick I use sometimes, when I need to come back from far away. When I need to stay alert or not dissolve completely—I clench my fists as tight as I can, digging my fingernails into the fat of my hand. It worked especially well, this time, with the long, artificial pearl-colored nails from the salon. By the time I made it over to David and the ambassador and his wife, I thought I was mostly back in the present. As much as I ever am, I suppose.

When I reached them, I stretched out a hand, still smarting.

"Teddy Huntley Carlyle," I said, and then, because I had forgotten, and it was the right thing to do, added, "Shepard."

I knew David would be upset at the delay, considering how much he hated that I hadn't changed my name on my correspondence yet. But I couldn't help it; I had forgotten who I was supposed to be.

The ambassador—the Wolf—stuck his hand out and grabbed mine. "Huntley!" he said, and his voice was as dry and soft as his cowboy character's. "Now that's a name I know. Your daddy?"

"My grandpa. Uncle Hal, too."

"Hal Huntley! You thank him, next time you see him. That thirty thousand got me over the hump in San Bernardino in '62."

"Warren never forgets a name, or a dollar amount," his wife said, and held out a hand to take mine.

106

Her voice was the same as it was in the movies, too. The low purr of a woman in black and white, the femme fatale of a dozen detective films. I don't think I had ever seen her in color, even in a photograph, until that moment; pink blush on the long cheek-bones instead of gray shadows beneath, pale red hair instead of silver. The Wolf's face was as tanned as it was in the full-color *Rio Grande*, his eyes as blue.

"Look how gorgeous you are," Lina said, kissing each of my cheeks, then holding me at arm's length. "Look at your beautiful blond hair."

"That's a Texas woman if ever I saw one," the Wolf said, and I could tell from his tone he meant "Texas-sized." My height, my figure.

David smiled with his teeth closed.

They were so kind, and I had been so agitated, and I couldn't very well apologize for the thing I wanted to apologize for, which was everything, and beg them to understand or to please not notice, or find out, about Yevgeny Larin, so instead I heard myself babbling, pleading: "I'm so sorry," I said, stumbling over the words a bit, "so sorry you had to make room for me at such short notice—"

"Oh, not at all," Lina said, interrupting me. Rescuing me. "No, we were just so delighted to hear our David had gotten married! Though of course he didn't tell us for weeks afterward, did you, you naughty man?"

She wagged a finger at him, but there was nothing censorious in it; other women seemed to always be flirting with my husband, I was learning.

The Wolf narrowed his famous eyes at me. I got the sense he was trying to affect his character's steely gaze, and I worried for a moment that he was looking into my soul, and he would see—he would ask about—Yevgeny.

"Now, Miss Huntley—I mean Mrs. Shepard—" he nodded to David, "was your husband here hiding you away from me because of all those nasty rumors that your uncle and I might be fighting each other for the nomination in '76?"

Relief—the intensity of his focus wasn't on me, and my past, after all. And who cared, really, about '76? Not me—not then. Not now, even. Hal was always up to something, at any given time—it was hard to keep track of his specific schemes.

"If I were to run," the Wolf added, grinning, "but of course, I have not said so, one way or the other."

"Seven years is a long way away," Lina said gently. "We certainly don't need to be discussing it right now."

The Wolf laughed. "You think Hal Huntley hasn't been planning this for longer than that? Seven years is nothing to the eternal demon that lives inside that man, and if he dies before he makes president it will just go on and inhabit a new host. Tell me I'm wrong, Mrs. Shepard."

The Wolf's final big film had been a horror flick in which he'd played a Catholic priest, which I assumed was where the demon talk had come from. My brain wasn't moving fast enough to concoct an answer to this, though.

"Oh, I . . ." I looked helplessly to David.

"I'm only teasing," the Wolf said, and his eyes crinkled at the corners when he smiled. "I may not always play nicely with your uncle, but I won't hold it against you."

"You really are so gorgeous," Lina said, putting a firm hand on her husband's shoulder to steer him out of dangerous waters. "You should have been an actress."

She turned to her husband. "Shouldn't she, Warren? They would have loved her at Paramount. A blond bombshell."

"Teddy studied art, actually," David said. "She has a degree from SMU."

It wasn't like him to brag about that—he had taken to referring to my work at the Huntley Foundation as a hobby, after the wedding—but I suppose he wanted to say, my wife would never be an actress. Fine art wasn't serious, to him, but it meant more than Hollywood.

"An artist!" the Wolf said. "Well, how about that?"

"Not an artist," I said. "Art history. I worked for a museum, before."

"Her family's museum," David added, "in Dallas."

I couldn't tell if he was clarifying that it wasn't a job I'd had to apply for, so don't be too impressed, or if he was pointing out that my family was *that* wealthy, so we were people the Wolf should pay attention to.

It was exhausting, always trying to guess what David meant. You might say, maybe he meant exactly what he said. You would be wrong. There was always something behind the words, with David.

"Then you should take a look at all the art we have in the residence," Lina said, "it's absolutely stuffed with it! The embassy, too."

"I know," I said. "You have the sea on your wall."

"The what, Teddy?" David chuckled nervously.

He had a hand on my waist, and he pinched softly at my side, shaking the chunk of fabric and beads and flesh in his hand a little. I don't think he even realized he was doing it.

I knew I was being stupid; sometimes my words fail me, and particularly when I've had a nasty shock and about five too many drinks.

"Sorry. I mean a painting of the sea. By Signorini. It's beautiful."

My feet were really hurting, and the dress was beginning to strain. I imagined my stomach inflated full of all the decadent food from dinner, with a foam of champagne bubbles at the top, threatening to rise up through my throat at any moment.

Lina smiled benevolently at me.

"So you already know more about our art than I do! There's all kinds of things around here, and I have no idea what any of them are. You know," and now she was looking at her husband, who was looking at me, "perhaps we could use your help. Apparently, they've been meaning to catalogue and restore everything in the residence and at the embassy, but there just isn't the time. Or the money, really. Perhaps that's something we could get your help on."

"Oh," I said, and I was preparing a more intelligent answer than that, when David said, "Teddy will think about it, won't you?"

This last bit he said with his opaque lake-eyes on me, and it felt like a warning. Pull yourself together, Teddy.

I could feel the ambassador watching me, too, and I wondered if he could tell that I'd lost count of how many glasses of champagne I'd had, plus the wine with dinner, of course.

My feet were on fire; those cat-piss yellow shoes weren't meant to be stood in for this long. They were only ever supposed to get me down the aisle at my wedding to the doorstep of the New Me, which I guess one could argue they ended up doing even more that night at the ambassador's house than they ever did at Dallas City Hall.

I was beginning to feel lightheaded. I was beginning to feel removed from the world, or at least a step back. It was like being on the beach, or in the hair salon under the dryer. I liked it. And I began to feel brave.

And the attention on me was so beautiful—or rather, they kept saying I was so beautiful—and they were interested, really interested in me, the Wolf and his wife, these Hollywood people, and I could still feel in the back of my head, probably somewhere just under the beautiful cottony cloud of my hairdo, the fear that there was someone at this party I wasn't supposed to have seen, or wasn't supposed to know. But they were so kind to me, these beautiful, important people, that I thought surely I would be fine. I would be perfectly safe, and fine.

And that's one of the last things I remember clearly. Feeling like I couldn't be touched. I've tried to recall more of the night after that, for obvious reasons, but I only have bits and pieces. Images; snippets of sound.

I remember seeing the glowing red tip of a cigarette making arcs of light in the dark, casting sparks like fireworks or fireflies when I blew on it. Holding it in my elegant hands with their long, pearlescent nails.

David hated smoking. I remember the ambassador cupping his hands around the end of my cigarette to light it.

I remember asking the Wolf about the swimming pool I'd heard so much of; we had one at the country club in Dallas, I believe I explained, and I missed it. I'm fairly certain he invited me to use the one at the Villa Taverna any time I liked.

"Let's go look at it," I recall the Wolf saying, or maybe it was me—maybe I invited myself—and I remember him taking my arm.

"It's not as big as the one we have in Montecito," I think he said, or maybe that was another time, later, "but it's not too bad. A goddamn lifesaver when it's this hot out."

I know, or think, I looked at David for a signal, and he said go ahead, though I doubt he was pleased about it. He wouldn't have undermined the ambassador, no matter how much he hated the idea of me making a spectacle of myself. I know David came with us, too, because he told me all about it later; how I leaned on the ambassador for support, how I took my shoes off to walk over the lawn.

The grass was damp with night dew, perhaps, or maybe from sprinklers, and I could feel mud between my toes, and I thought I could hear frogs croaking and calling, or maybe cicadas, droning at some lower level somewhere under the clinking glasses and laughing and singing and shivery guitar strumming sounds of the party.

I remember looping through clusters of people all over the Villa Taverna's grounds on the way to the pool, stopping every few feet to greet people that the Wolf said I had to meet, absolutely *had* to, and every so often I thought I saw someone who looked familiar, a bright red-lipsticked mouth laughing with a head thrown back, with glossy black-brown crow-colored curls, but of course, I don't know for sure. I only know about the people I did meet that evening, the princesses and counts and sirs and movie stars, because I saw many of them at later functions, and without exception they told me how delightful I was that night, how sweet and bubbly.

They would say that, wouldn't they, was David's feeling. They didn't want to be rude, afterward, about me making a fool of myself.

I don't know if I met the Aga Khan. I don't know if he was even still at the party, at that point. I don't know if I met his beautiful, aristocratic fiancée. I doubt she was as drunk as I was.

There was a lot of talk about the Wolf's famously wild parties, the whole time I was in Rome. There were rumors that people used to swim naked in his pool, after the more conservative dinner guests went home. But I only put my feet in the water, that night, I swear it. I only put my feet in, and I had unzipped my dress just a bit, just in the back, because it had grown too tight after all the champagne I'd been served. Or guzzled, to use David's word. I didn't get undressed any more than that; I don't remember much, but I'm sure that much is true.

That blue pool, and the lights around it, are the last things I remember. My feet in the cool water, and the beautiful color of it, little ripples, and everyone being so kind to me at that party; everyone around the pool with the music, the Italian guitar, and their laughter, and grins. They were so kind, so friendly, in Rome. I don't think anyone would have expected what happened next.

Now

Early Morning, Wednesday, July 9, 1969

"And if you ever hear anything to the contrary, people saying I swam naked in the ambassador's pool that night, in full view of the assembled dignitaries and so-and-sos, you should know it was completely fabricated," I say.

"That's not—nobody is saying—" Archie begins, and then Reggie interrupts, close to shouting.

"Mrs. Shepard! That's just about enough of this. If you won't tell us, we can make your—"

Arthur Hildebrand shoots him a look of reproach, and I'm grateful, for the first time in a while, that Uncle Hal is such a shark. That's the only reason I can think of that they aren't tightening the screws a bit more. They're worried he might object to poor treatment of his niece, from his lofty position on Foreign Relations.

He wouldn't, actually; he would probably encourage it at this point, but they have no way of finding that out for at least a few more hours, until they can get him on the horn.

"I don't know if I saw Yevgeny Larin again that night," I say, "if that's what you wanted to know. Or any of the Russians. Or if I talked about him, either, to anyone I met that night. I suppose that's what you're getting ready to ask me, now?"

Reggie seems unable to speak. I wouldn't say he's apoplectic with

113

rage exactly—he's too professional for that. But he's certainly not doing well.

Arthur Hildebrand is silent. I don't like silence so much.

"Hmm," I say, and look down at my nails. I can hear Archie sighing, probably with exasperation. It sounds like a noise my husband would make.

"So?" I say, picking at my cuticles. There's a little edge loose under the acrylic on my left pinky finger, and I slide a nail from the other hand underneath and begin to peel.

"So?" Reggie echoes.

"So, I've told you how I met the Wolf. What else do you want to know?"

Archie sighs again, and asks, "How many times did you have access to the ambassador's residence after that? Or to the embassy itself?"

"Oh, a million," I say.

"Why don't you tell us about that," Archie says, and smiles encouragingly at me.

I don't need Eugene's—Yevgeny's—expertise on liars to know the smile isn't real.

8. Via della Scala

Saturday, June 7, 1969

I woke with a splitting headache and David rubbing my shoulder. A warm hand, a rustling sound from the sheets.

I didn't remember where I'd been the night before, and even once I recalled the party, I couldn't remember the car ride home. I didn't remember falling asleep, either, but then suddenly I was awake and there he was, reaching for me.

The blinds were closed, the bedroom dim and stuffy even though I could see from the clock on the nightstand that it was well past ten and the sun was probably high in the sky. I wondered how long David had been awake. I wondered if he'd had time to see what a mess I'd left the apartment while he was away. On the chair under the window, which was the only pile of my debris I could see from the bed, there was a particularly egregious heap of clothes. A brassiere hung over the back of the chair, straps dangling like tentacles. David hated messes.

He didn't say anything, just reached for me. I was facing away, and he held me like that, sliding a hand quickly down over my chest, then slower across my hips, my thighs. He never liked to touch my breasts; he thought they were too big, I think.

After he'd finished with me, he whispered, "Good morning, Teddy," into my ear, and then when I turned to look at him added, sniffing my hair, "Why don't you go clean yourself up?"

"We were out late," I said, as if he hadn't been there, too. "The party, and everything. You know."

"Well, it was work," David said. "For me."

"Sorry," I said. "I meant to have a bath before bed. I probably smell like an ashtray."

"More like a brewery," David said. "I'll go make some coffee," he added, standing and beginning to dress himself. "Would you like it in bed?"

This was something he'd done in the first few weeks, bringing me coffee in bed, as if I was delicate, someone to be taken care of. I hadn't understood at first that I was supposed to refuse. That I was supposed to be the one in the kitchen making his coffee, making his breakfast, and that I was supposed to have known that. He never demanded. He never punished. He just let you know, eventually, how you'd fallen short.

"No, that's okay," I said, "I'll join you in the kitchen."

I wanted to say yes, bring me coffee, take care of me, let me stay in bed.

I didn't. Flashes of my night were coming back to me, already—a glimpse of a placid blue pool, cypress trees against the night sky. A plume of smoke from my mouth, the Wolf's wicked grin. A vision of David's disapproving face, pale under his freckles, staring.

And a man's liquid brown eyes, eyes like a prey animal, ones I had seen before.

"It's a little dark in here, Teddy," David said. "Let's get some light in."

He raised the Venetian blinds with a sound like a zipper, and I pulled the sheet up over my head to shield my eyes from the light pouring in through the window.

I recalled a flash of brightness the previous night—the photographs taken when we first entered the ambassador's residence. It occurred to me that there might have been other photos taken,

116

later on—I thought if I could see them, I might be able to piece more of my night together; but also, the thought of remembering, of proof, made me feel ill.

"Oh, she's still tired, then," David observed, apparently to no one in particular. "She had plenty of energy last night, though, dancing on the lawn and talking the ambassador's ear off."

I don't think I need to mention that his tone was sarcastic.

When I lowered the sheet, finally, David was standing by the window, holding a dress shirt out in front of him like it was a dirty rag, letting it dangle off one finger.

"Are any of my other shirts clean?" he asked. "I'm going into the office, and I can't wear this one."

"Why, what's wrong with it?" I was still drowsy. "And isn't it Saturday?"

"I set it on the chair on top of the towel you left there. I didn't realize it was still wet."

I tried to recall—yes, I'd forgotten to hang the towel up after my bath before the party.

"I'm sorry, I don't know how that happened," I lied. I often settled on seeming stupid over careless. It was safer. "I don't think any of the other ones are clean, though."

I knew they weren't, because I hadn't washed them, and Teresa hadn't been in for days.

"It's okay," David said, pulling the shirt on and buttoning it back up. "It has a nice dampness to it. It's refreshing."

I laughed, and finally stood up from the bed. Went over to my husband and helped him with the rest of his buttons. Kissed him.

He was funny sometimes, my David. I ignored, for a moment, the cramping, burning feeling in my stomach that had returned as soon as I remembered another scene from the night before—David, steering me with a firm grip barefoot through the Villa Taverna, whispering, "Teddy, you're making a fool of yourself," and the ambassador calling out from behind us, "Aw, let her stay!"

I ignored, too, the other thing I knew from last night. I wouldn't be able to avoid it forever, but my head was thick and dull and painful enough to let it lie, for now.

"Why don't you go take a bath, Teddy?" David suggested, putting his hands on my hips and pushing me toward the bathroom. Slapping me lightly on the rear. It was the way you would get a horse to move along, though David didn't know a thing about horses. It was a quality Uncle Hal distrusted in him, I'd overheard him telling my father.

Once I'd drawn the bath and finally gotten into it, I felt much better. It was one of those easy fixes I could never remember when I needed to.

Sometimes when David made a comment, if he hadn't seen me take a bath on a particular day or he thought it was time for me to wash my hair, I would go into the bathroom and run the water so he would hear it, then sit on the side of the tub picking at my fingernails until I thought enough time had passed. I don't know why I did that. It just felt like so much work, sometimes, to take my makeup off and wash my hair and then put it all back together. I always smelled more or less fine, I thought, but I suppose he wanted me to smell like soap. He always wanted me to be cleaner.

Still, I usually did feel better when I actually took a bath. I would lie in bed for days, sometimes, when David was gone in Milan or Naples or wherever he'd disappeared to, and think I would never get up again, but as soon as I finally dragged myself up from the mattress, took a bath, and had my coffee in the morning—or, more often, early afternoon—everything felt manageable again, at least for a little while.

I agonized for a bit over my wardrobe, once I was clean, and all the rumpled clothes therein. I needed to find something appropriate, something penitent. I finally settled on a black-and-white houndstooth dress in a lightweight poplin. It was clean and not that wrinkled, and it was calf-length and had a high neck, and with a short-sleeved black cardigan over it, even David would have to approve.

No chance I would look like someone who had been out too late and left damp towels, dirty dishes, all over her apartment. No chance I would look like someone who'd taken her shoes off and put her bare feet in the ambassador's pool. If I wore it with sandals and my hair pulled back, and the gold-filled hoop earrings that Daddy got me for my birthday last year, and the straw purse with the leather strap I'd bought in Capri, I would be unimpeachably appropriate.

It's funny how just getting dressed can feel like a start, some days. How it can feel like fixing something.

When I finally made it into the kitchen, David came over to me, sniffed my clean hair, and said, "Good girl."

I'd been right about the dress, too, based on the way he patted my shoulder, which was safely encased in its cashmere-blend knit. It would be hot today, and if I started sweating I would end up with the pungent odor of wet wool hanging around me, but at least David wouldn't be able to complain that I was showing too much skin. Not when there was so much else to complain about.

I poured myself an espresso from the stovetop, while at the breakfast table David buttered his toast and unfolded his newspaper. Before we met, he'd spent two years in Washington learning Italian in preparation for this posting, he'd told me, but he still struggled with the language, so every morning he looked through the paper, trying to see how far he could get before he found a word he didn't know.

I never even tried.

Teresa was in the kitchen, too, muttering over the piled-up dishes. I hadn't heard her come into the flat; I wondered if she had been out there all morning. Basically, I wondered if she had been out there while David and I made love, and if she had heard it, as silent as we usually were, or if she'd at least guessed what we were up to.

The dishes: my own personal mountain of shards. I felt a sudden affinity for the Roman housewives who'd tossed their amphorae into that ditch in Testaccio, so many of them and so often that they'd built an entire peak. It wouldn't have solved all my problems, but if I could have thrown the dishes out the window, that would have been a start.

I realized that Teresa had been the one to put the coffee on, this morning, so David's martyr's offer to bring me coffee in bed had been theater, after all.

"Don't worry about the dishes," I told Teresa, "I'll get them."

I pictured myself pulling up the window sash and dropping them into the street, the chipped blue willow plates that had come with the apartment, the mismatched rose-patterned mugs: one, *crash*, two, *crash*, three.

Teresa smiled for David's benefit and said, "*Grazie, signora,*" but she and I both knew it was an act. When David wasn't home, I would let the dishes stack up, days' worth at a time, enormous heaps.

I gave Teresa extra on top of her salary when David was gone. I didn't bother believing myself to be generous; we both knew it was because Teresa helped me play pretend. And I did think that David was too stingy with her, when it came down to it; when we hired her, David had asked the other officers at the embassy what they paid their girls, and then he settled on the lowest amount. It was half what I would've paid someone back in Dallas, and I tried telling him as much. "We're not in Dallas, Teddy," he'd said to that. "And you don't want to falsely inflate the market, now, do you?" So I secretly inflated it behind his back.

I was standing at the sink, vaguely scrubbing at some plates as if this was what I always did in the morning, as if I always woke up and cleaned things and put them in place, and David was seated at the table, the newspaper unfolded in front of his face. It was something his father used to do, I think, sit at the breakfast table with the newspaper spread out before him, so David did it, too.

Even when all other signs of fatherhood were absent—the child-sized cups and saucers and forks and spoons, the soft scrambled eggs. The child.

"So, did you enjoy it?" he finally asked. "The Wolf's big Hollywood bash?"

David said this last part with some sarcasm.

"The party was fine," I said. "Really nice."

"Glad to hear it," David said, without looking up from his paper.

By this point, obviously, I knew something was coming.

Teresa had serendipitously removed herself from the kitchen, probably to the bedroom to hang up the damp towels I'd left all around, to wash them, to try to return some sense of order to the place, out of earshot of whatever fight we were about to have.

I leaned against the counter with my coffee, waiting. My head was still pounding, so I couldn't quite muster the energy to be anxious, but there was a swirling sensation in my belly that I knew was probably fear. Topped with champagne, maybe, and the sickness it inspires the next day, but mostly fear. Yevgeny Larin—Washington—I couldn't even let my slow, stupid brain form the full thought.

Finally, David folded the paper closed, and then in half again. He set it at an exact angle to the table's edge. He sipped his coffee, then his orange juice. And then he looked up at me.

"Teddy," he began. "Teddy, I don't know what to do with you."

I thought I was about to be sick. I waited, silently.

"To be honest with you," he said, and I was ready for it, I thought, at least for a moment, for him to say he knew it all. About Yevgeny, about what I was actually like, under the clean hair and cashmere sweater.

"You embarrassed me," he finished, and I was relieved.

He listed, very clearly and calmly, all his evidence. And it wasn't just the previous night; I'd been right to think he was watching, and weighing. He had a catalogue of indiscretions going back to the night we'd met—because "*really*, Teddy, you shouldn't go home with a man the first time you meet him, as glad as I am that you chose me."

But nothing in his list really got to the heart of it. The things that were truly embarrassing about me, the things that made me truly bad. He didn't know about Yevgeny Larin—that much was clear. And it didn't help much, because the Russian still existed, but it helped a little.

My behavior displayed a level of impulsivity, I learned, that was troubling. David wasn't sure, he said, what kind of values I'd been raised with—and for the first time since realizing he didn't know about my ex-lover, at least not yet, I began to worry. I suddenly became afraid that he would tell my mother, somehow, or Uncle Hal, what I'd been up to. About the night we'd met. About all of it, at least the parts he knew.

Now I was his wife, David explained, and I represented him, and if I wanted this marriage to work, I needed to start acting like it. Like his wife or like I wanted it to work, it didn't matter which he meant. Both.

No more spending money on things like Valentino dresses, David said. Or, rather, I could spend my money however I liked, but I was only getting fifteen hundred dollars a month, which he would give me in cash out of the joint account, and which was more than most men made at their jobs to support entire families, actually, and in fact he thought less than half of that would be more than enough for household expenses and for my own needs, but he had promised my family that he would keep me more or less in the style to which I was accustomed.

"You need to learn to control yourself, Teddy," he explained. "I shouldn't have to do it for you."

He wanted me to be grateful, ultimately—he was trying to help me. I needed to behave like an adult. I needed to learn how to take care of myself, or I would never be able to take care of a family.

So there it was—there would be no baby. Not until I managed to grow up.

"We can talk about it again," he explained, "in a few months. Let's see how you do."

I probably would have tried to trick him, if I'm honest, and say it was an accident, the way a girl I'd known in school had done with her beau when he hadn't procured a ring within a year of graduation, but David was always very careful. He didn't leave it entirely up to me, if you know what I mean; I won't be indelicate and describe his particular methods any more vividly than that.

I really did want to be her: a woman he could trust, and love; a companion; a helpmeet. I imagined her—David's wife. The woman I'd been briefly on my honeymoon, who woke up to see the sunrise, completely content in each moment. In the magic of each day, in a walk on a little cobblestone street with her husband, with the lemons fat on the trees and the warm sun and the feeling that the world was ripe for her. That it was something bountiful and open, not a battlefield, or a trap.

And so I vowed to do better, there in the kitchen, in my appropriate, modest clothing with my clean and shiny hair. And I cried a bit, which was expected, I'm sure, and we hugged and he kissed me on the forehead but not on the mouth, and he left for work in his still-damp white shirt.

And then, as I was pacing back and forth in the kitchen, trying to think of a plan to be better, I came to understand that I could never actually be that woman. And so instead I fantasized about running away, hightailing it out of there in a taxi or hitching a ride with a stranger, and riding all the way down the coast back to Capri or one of the little towns on the way—perhaps the one from the painting, if I could figure out where it was—and living in a little flat just like I had imagined . . .

Well, while I was in the middle of all of that, the phone rang, and I picked up immediately, even before the second tone, and it was Lina Montgomery inviting me to lunch.

"How are you feeling, darling?" she asked, and when I said, "I'm okay," she laughed.

"Just okay? Come for lunch, have a little vino, and we'll get you patched up in no time. You were such a hoot last night, dear; everyone's talking about it!"

In my experience, it's never good if everyone is talking about you, even if they're saying nice things.

But I didn't know what else to do, and I didn't want to be alone in the apartment—Teresa had already left—and I couldn't really say no to the ambassador's wife, anyway, so I went to the Villa Taverna again, this time in a taxi, because David wasn't around to drive me and I didn't have time to get there on foot.

9. Villa Taverna

Saturday, June 7, 1969

The villa was even more beautiful during the day, the soft peach color of the main building's walls more inviting under the light of the clear summer sun. I'd been so nervous hobbling up the long driveway with my angry husband beside me the night before that I hadn't been able to appreciate it—the thick thatch of ivy over the entry, the bougainvillea with its tissuey blossoms in hot pinks and fuchsias climbing the façade. Sculpted boxwoods rested in stone planters next to Corinthian columns holding up the entry portico, wisteria dripping down over its sides. It was impossible to know, as with most things in Rome, whether the stone planters and columns were two thousand years old, or twenty.

A man in tails and white gloves opened the door—I suppose he must have been a sort of butler—and he escorted me, on polished shoes that tapped across the villa's painted tiles, through the entrance hall and out to the back garden, where I'd sat beneath the stars just a few hours earlier. And then, according to David, taken my shoes off and woven unsteadily over the lawn, and danced, and made a spectacle of myself. I felt a flush of hot shame, but then recovered—after all, hadn't Lina said I was fun?

There was no sign of last night's long tables with their formal settings, the sterling silver cutlery and crystal, the dozens of gilded Chiavari chairs. And there wasn't a single stray cigarette butt or

125

crumpled napkin to be seen on the lawn; there must have been an army of staff somewhere out of sight.

Lina sat at a small, round four-top table covered in a simple printed linen cloth, with just two places set. She stood to greet me, and I could see that she wore a long, diaphanous white kaftan, with her hair in a sleek chignon and golden tassels for earrings. She looked sophisticated but relaxed, the epitome of California cool, at least according to what I'd seen in magazines and movies, and I felt like a child in my checkered dress with my stupid sweater, which was already beginning to smell like a goat after it rains.

"*Benvenuta!*" Lina cried as I reached her, and she kissed me again on both cheeks as she had when we met the night before, and told me to sit.

"Warren is sorry he couldn't join us," she began, as soon as we sat down, "but he likes to go to the embassy on weekends, in the morning, to be alone. None of the other staff comes in, so he can, as he says, 'really get some thinking done.'"

She laughed as she said this last part, forming quotation marks in the air with her fingers.

I noticed an enormous yellow diamond on the index finger of her right hand; I wondered if it was real. Then thought, of course it was. I was the only rich woman that I knew of who couldn't afford more than rhinestones.

I noticed, too, that her nails were long, like mine, though she had them painted a soft, powdery pink. Mama would have disapproved of Lina, I thought.

"I like your ring," I said, and she smiled.

"If my husband wasn't so good," she whispered, though it was only the two of us there on the lawn, "you'd think he must have done something very, very bad. For a ring like this."

I must have looked puzzled, because she laughed again and said, louder this time, "Don't worry. It was an anniversary present. Bulgari."

"Oh, how wonderful," I said, and meant it.

"Never say no when a man offers you jewelry," Lina advised, as if this was a situation that often came up for me. "No matter who it's from, or why. Think of it as an insurance policy."

A waiter appeared, crossing the lawn with a bottle of Franciacorta and a white linen napkin over his arm, and while Lina was momentarily distracted with him, conversing in flawless Italian, presumably making some additional request, at least based on her gesture, I thought how perfect it must be to live this life. This gorgeous setting, with your husband, the ambassador, who buys you beautiful diamond rings. David would never do a thing like that—certainly not after the way he'd reacted to the price of my dress. Even my wedding ring was just a simple band he'd bought, and not from any of the major jewelers; there was no stamp from Tiffany or Cartier on it.

I recalled that Lina had said the Wolf was at the embassy today because he liked to be alone; I hoped he wouldn't mind that David was there. I imagined the Wolf in his office—which I had only heard about, at that point, and not seen—in that mythical space, with his vanquished foes on the wall, standing tall and handsome, squinting with his brilliant blue eyes at the taxidermy wolf, his old enemy, and thinking about the problems of the world and how to solve them.

And then being interrupted by David in his damp, wrinkled shirt, pushing his spectacles up on his nose, wanting to discuss some arcane detail in an economic report.

No, it wouldn't do; I hoped David would keep to himself.

Lina chatted away gaily all afternoon, telling me stories of her Hollywood days while servers brought out grilled whitefish in a lemon sauce, asparagus and artichokes and other simple fare, all of it so beautifully presented.

She ate the asparagus with her hands, holding a stalk and taking bites from the tip like it was a celery stick, and when she caught me staring she tossed off another of her brilliant little laughs and said, "Oh, Teddy, it's nice to eat with your hands, isn't it? It's good to get a little messy."

She was clearly a capable formal hostess when she needed to be—I'd seen it the evening before. Of course, she and the Wolf had been less traditional than Mama and Daddy were at their parties—no reception line, no one to greet guests at the door. But then again, Mama and Daddy had never hosted royalty before. Perhaps when you had the Aga Khan over, you spent most of the evening with him and let the rest of the guests fend for themselves.

In any case, the place settings and the courses last night had all been done correctly, elegant but exciting, and the drinks had been plentiful—too plentiful—and the company had been glittering, and I had felt so entirely welcome, in the end, in spite of David's admonishments, and I realized I felt that same sense of belonging today, too.

Lina's easy amiability, her confidence, was no doubt how she was able to help the Wolf turn all that MGM money, those rugged good looks, into a political career. That was why she lunched regularly with Lady Bird Johnson and Pat Nixon and Jackie herself. And here, in her own home, with an audience of only one, she was so relaxed. And I wondered if, in her position, I would ever be able to feel that way. To think that everything wasn't so dire; that I didn't need to be flawless.

At one point I tried to apologize for my antics the previous evening, and Lina wouldn't hear of it.

"So what? You put your feet in the pool? Please. One night at Clark Gable's ranch in Encino, Warren and I went swimming in our evening clothes when we lost at cards, even though nobody thought we would really do it. You're just a baby, Teddy, what damage could you possibly do? Don't listen to your husband, he's an old grump."

Lina told me how it was one of the things she liked about Rome, that the Italians were so much more relaxed in matters of manners, in affairs of the heart—sure, there were the frigid old families, the aristocrats and what have you, but people in general, in this part of Europe, were alive to possibility. To pleasure. In most of Europe, really, Lina said, minus the English and most of the Germans.

I didn't know what she meant then, about affairs of the heart.

"Anyway," Lina said, "you really have nothing to worry about. You made a splash last night, and I don't just mean in the pool."

I could feel my cheeks flushing with some residual shame, but also with a hint of pleasure when she added, "If I were you, I'd make sure my wardrobe is up to snuff. A few really good formal gowns, tennis whites, and maybe something to ride in. I expect you'll be receiving a lot of invitations. And, of course, Warren was completely smitten."

I really didn't know what to make of that.

After lunch she invited me for a walk through the gardens; there were some Roman statues and a few Renaissance replicas that she wanted to show me.

We followed the gravel path through the estate's acres, and I enjoyed the warmth of the Roman sun on my shoulders (the wet, barnyard-smelling sweater having been left at the table long before, with no David nearby to object). I felt myself finally breathing, relaxing, as we walked through the manicured gardens, past classical statues the likes of which I'd only seen in photographs before, with birds chirping in the trees, the beautiful cypress trees, and flowers—roses and marigolds and four-o'clocks—in bloom everywhere around us.

And immersed in all that sheer gorgeousness, I found the courage to pose the question I had been wanting to ask Lina ever since meeting her the night before.

Which was, what is it like—to be so beautiful? To be famously flawless; to have photos and films of yourself at the height of your power? To have people around the world see you, perfectly poised and made up, in magazines? To have them see you and think, what a perfect woman?

Lina laughed loudly at that, and I thought she was laughing at me, for a moment, at my stupid question, but then she said, "Oh, I'd hate to think that was the height of my power. And not all of my photos have been so nice, especially not in my younger days—but that's another story. The point is, and you'll need to remember this . . ."

She dipped her head to look at me; she was even taller than I was, and she slid the violet-tinted bug-eye sunglasses she was wearing—so chic and fresh and modern—down her perfect nose so that I could see her brilliant, silver screen eyes, and she said, "It's all a lie, and they hate you if they ever learn the truth."

I was thrilled to be spoken to like this, to be let in on such a secret—it was the way Aunt Sister used to talk to me. As if we were confidantes and compatriots, even though she was so much older and wiser.

But I didn't quite understand what Lina meant, and, newly emboldened at my inclusion in a sisterhood I hadn't known about, I said as much.

"They want you to be the woman in the photo," Lina explained, in answer to my question, and it sounded sad, but she was smiling at me. "When you're beautiful; when you're still young. Everyone wants you to be that perfect image, and they don't want to know the living, breathing woman behind it."

"Oh," I said.

I hadn't quite been prepared for the way they talked, these Californians. These stars. Nobody I knew would ever say such a thing so openly.

"It's something your mother really should have taught you," she said, frowning now. "And you're so lovely. No one ever tried to get you to model?"

"No," I said, and that was mostly true.

I'd dreamed of it, though, when I was younger. Of being so static and flawless, of existing forever elegantly in black and white—no red spots or visible veins or freckles or *flesh*—with my only purpose to be observed and adored. Of having professional photographs of myself in a single perfect moment, preserved on the Wall.

The Wall was the portrait wall in the formal sitting room at the Beverly house, the one we used only for guests and at Thanksgiving and Christmas. An entire gallery of Huntleys: old tintypes of the first of the family to cross into the Republic of Texas, oil paintings of Mama and Uncle Hal as children—anachronistic even when Grandpop had them done, but he was making a point with them, and it stuck. Look at the little dauphin and dauphine. Look at the Huntley dynasty.

Aunt Sister hadn't been born yet when he commissioned them; she had been a late-in-life miracle, according to Grandma, to which Sister had always said it was a miracle that she'd managed to escape having a spooky, haunted portrait of herself as a child put up on the Wall.

Also on the Wall: my mother's wedding photo, as well as a portrait of Aunt Sister taken by a famous artist in Paris before the war. Her debutante portrait had been up there, too, but that had been taken down and removed to an attic somewhere, either at the Beverly house, or the ranch near Fredericksburg, or, if they really wanted to hide it, the ranch out near Alpine. They would have removed the portrait by the famous artist, too, but it was too valuable. It was real art.

The portrait of me taken at my debut was up there, as well, but I didn't care for it, and always avoided making eye contact with my younger self in my white dress, with my pearls, when we opened presents on Christmas or bowed our heads to pray before Thanksgiving dinner.

My debutante portrait embarrassed me: a young Teddy, looking up at the camera from below, her head tucked down and to the side like a little dove. I must have imagined it to be a seductive, sophisticated pose at the time, which mortified me now. In the photo, too, I have one hand placed delicately on a strand of pearls at my neck—a gift from Aunt Sister.

Even now, I can remember how cool they felt, despite the heat of the photographer's lamps. How smooth. That photo has always struck me as proof of some deep, innate foolishness—of forgery. There's a girl who thinks she knows a thing or two. There's a girl who's faking it.

I can remember, too, the white dress I wore for the portrait, the sweetheart neckline barely visible below the pearls in the frame. Neiman Marcus had brought Christian Dior over from Paris to design it: white silk faille, in the New Look silhouette. Dior did dresses for all the debutantes in '53, or at least everyone I knew, mainly because Uncle Hal played golf with Stanley Marcus and got him to set it up for us. Everyone said I looked lovely in mine; the white set off my tennis tan, the neckline flattered my perfect décolletage.

That's what the photographer had said, anyway. Daddy had driven me to the Neiman's portrait studio, promising to take me to lunch at the Zodiac Room after. It was a milestone, everyone said, to have earned the white dress. It was important.

I wished I was wearing something else, though. *Bourgeois*, Aunt Sister had called the tradition. Ordinary. "Stifling and antiquated." The reason for the white dress, she'd told me once, was originally, in the old days, so you could wear it to your wedding as soon as your deb season ended, though no one did that anymore. Two for the price of one, she said. They'll let you have a party, as long as they can prop you up for sale on the marriage market after.

She wasn't wrong, exactly. About the double-header, at least. The *-eens* were all getting married a few months after they came out:

Eileen Walters, Maureen Davidson, Pauline Atkins, Tina James. Eileen was marrying Tina's brother, who worked at Bell Helicopter; Maureen, her boyfriend who was down in Austin at UT; Pauline was marrying Neil Arcenaux from the year above us at SMU; and Tina's groom, Don, had come back from Korea for the wedding.

I was sure I wasn't like them, but how could you tell? All in the same white, bourgeois, ordinary dresses.

The photographer at Neiman's said I looked like Grace Kelly and gave me his business card. Asked if I'd ever considered modeling. I had, of course. Considered it, obsessed over it, the idea that I might be so beautiful that someone would pay to take pictures of me. That something about me was so extraordinary as to be visible on film.

We never got the magazines at home; Aunt Sister used to lend me old copies of *Vogue* and *Harper's Bazaar*, but my mother detested them. This was a woman who still wore the same style of navy blue wool coat she was wearing before the war, even to the Music Hall at Fair Park, even while everyone else was sweating through the mild Dallas winters in new furs.

I wanted to be one of the perfectly polished creatures in the photographs I saw in those magazines. I wanted to be fixed on the pages of a fashion spread standing confidently in a black silk dinner dress, like Dovima in her beautiful gown posing with elephants, not wearing a debutante's white wedding gown. I wanted to be a woman of the world like Aunt Sister, not just another wife. And I wanted it to be permanent—I wanted people to see my picture and know instantly, no matter what else happened or changed or came later, that Teddy Carlyle was someone to reckon with.

I could get used to being photographed, I thought, that day in the portrait studio. The heat of the lamps overhead, the flash of the bulb, knowing that with every bath of light you're being stored away, perfectly made up, elegant, poised.

I was good at posing.

"Like a statue," the photographer had said. "Like a china doll."

"Don't let them do it to you," Lina said, as we continued down the garden path. "Don't let them trap you."

I was silent, considering this as we passed through a little court-yard with travertine benches that looked at least a few hundred years old, and the scent of lavender rising from the flowerbeds, and then she added, "But if you need a little help—just a little pick-me-up, to be a bit shinier, sometimes? There's a doctor you should visit. Dr. D'Abruzzo, over by the Sapienza. He'll set you up. Just for days when you're feeling a bit sluggish, you know," and when I asked what she meant, she said, "Pills, darling."

We passed another immaculately sculpted hedge and turned the corner and suddenly were in a clearing at that beautiful blue swim-ming pool, which I did somehow remember from the night before. A row of cypress trees along with another hedge created a sense of privacy around it, which seemed necessary, because there, in only a pair of nylon knitted swimming shorts, with the sun on his bare chest, was the Wolf.

"Well, look at these two beauties!" the Wolf drawled, sliding his sunglasses—Persols, just like the playboys in Capri—down his long, patrician nose. The better to see us with.

"I almost thought you were a pair of statues from the garden come to life," he said, and winked at his wife, who said, "Hush," and rolled her eyes.

"How was the office, darling?" Lina asked, walking over to the Wolf and placing a manicured, bejeweled hand on his back. Droplets of water from the pool ran down his chest and caught in the patch of hair there, which was mostly gray; but the muscles, I couldn't help observing, were still very well defined.

"Perfect," the Wolf said, and planted a kiss on his wife's pastel pink lips. "Perfectly empty."

I noticed that he'd gotten water all over Lina's white kaftan, and also that she didn't seem to mind.

"David wasn't there?" I asked, without thinking, and the Wolf shook his head.

"No, just me and the Marines at the door. A few of the office gals, too, but that's it. Just the way I like it."

"You do like your office gals, don't you?" Lina said, and laughed.

"I told the young fellas early on not to come in on weekends," the Wolf went on. "It's unsettling—they should be taking their wives to the beach, or strolling in the park. They really don't know how to enjoy themselves, these young men."

Then, "Speaking of—where is your David?"

I mumbled something that hopefully didn't sound too much like, "I don't know." Because if David hadn't been at the embassy this morning, where was he?

And, more importantly (or at least it seemed so to me at the time), would he return to our flat in Trastevere to find me gone? I'd left a note that I was going out for lunch, but I doubted that would pacify him. Not after our conversation this morning.

The Wolf lifted his arms over his head to stretch, the droplets on his tanned torso catching the sun, glinting, then pulled on a cabana shirt from a heap of clothing and towels on a daybed nearby and slipped a pair of flip-flops onto his feet. I wondered if this was what every day had been like, for Lina and the Wolf, back at their home in Montecito. The one he'd said had a nicer pool than this—I remembered that from last night, too.

David never tanned. He hadn't really enjoyed Capri that much, in the end; he thought sunbathing was basically a waste of time, which was sort of true, for him—he only ever burned. Our whole honeymoon, he was a soft shade of pink, and since returning to Rome he had resumed his usual pale hue, though he had retained a scattering of freckles across his nose and shoulders, which I loved.

"So did you ask her?"

This, from the Wolf, was directed at his wife.

"Not yet," she said, and then they were both facing me.

"So, you've seen the art we have around the house," Lina observed, and I nodded.

"It's a very robust collection," I began, and the Wolf laughed.

"Robust! I like that."

"Well, there's even more at the embassy," Lina went on. "All kinds of things—paintings, sculptures, whatever other kind of art you can have. Antiques, maybe? Dressers and tables and things. And we simply don't have the resources in the office—or, I suppose, Warren, it's *your* office, after all . . ." She looked over at her husband, encouraging him to continue.

"Nobody has any damned idea what's in there," the Wolf explained, "and they won't give us any money to hire someone to go through it all. But my beautiful wife, here," he pinched at Lina's arm, "thinks it would be a good thing—a good *public relations* idea, if we could figure out what all is in there and let people know."

"Put on an exhibition or something," Lina added, and I could see the logic of it.

And then she said, "And, well, you and I discussed this last night, but I thought perhaps you didn't remember—"

Another flash of shame, because of course, I didn't.

"—so," Lina went on, "since you have experience working with your family's collection, and you're already here in Rome, we thought—why not Teddy?"

I could feel the shame dissolving into an excitement that bubbled up under my collarbone, but I wanted to make sure I deserved it, and that it would last, before I let it through. And I had a sudden recollection, too, of Margot last night speaking of briefing books and secret files, and so I had to ask, "And there's no issue with me—no security issue—if I'm in the building?"

136

Because I had also remembered the thing I had been trying to avoid all day, and which had momentarily seemed so far away as I strolled in these perfect gardens with perfect Lina, and thought for a false moment that perhaps my life could be like this. Perhaps this was a possibility for me.

I remembered that Yevgeny Larin, that ghost from my past, had come haunting here in Rome, and he wasn't some romantic Russian defector, as I'd told myself at the time, but in fact a Soviet diplomat, and potentially a spy. And I'd told him all kinds of things at dinner, I couldn't remember exactly what, and worst of all, I was the wife of a man who worked at the American Embassy, and was now being offered a job there myself—surely this wasn't allowed. More than that—surely this was a crime.

It wasn't even that it would be bad if David knew, if Hal and my family knew, about some of my more significant indiscretions—what they would decide that meant about me. It was that I had done something dangerous.

"Well, I wouldn't think so," Lina said, "and, in fact, it's perfect. Since your husband already works for Warren, nobody has to worry!"

"And why would there be any security risk?" the Wolf asked, with his head tilted. "You're not hiding nukes under your skirt, are you?"

"Warren!" Lina scolded, but she was laughing, too.

And I began to grow calm again. Because after all, I wasn't hiding nukes under my skirt, was I? How big of a risk could I possibly be? The thing I'd been worried about, before—it was nothing, really. Right?

And anyway, even if the Russian had come sneaking back into my orbit, in the shade of these powerful, beautiful, wealthy, important people, what could harm me?

"We'll get someone at the embassy to help you get situated," Lina said. "Margot, probably. And I've made sure everyone who needs it has your phone number. For parties and such? Barb—her husband is the legal adviser, you'll love her—will give you a call sometime today or tomorrow, I'd imagine. I'm sorry I can't do more to help you adjust in Rome, especially after David kept you hidden away for so long—"

And I flushed again with shame but also with anger, at David, for keeping me away from all of this. From the life I was supposed to be living in Rome.

"—but I'm afraid I'm off to the coast tomorrow to visit friends for a few weeks."

"The Gettys," the Wolf said. "Hoity-toity."

As if he, too, wasn't one of them.

That was always his appeal—he made his voters think he was their friend. Someone just like them. They got confused, David always said, because they'd seen the Wolf in their homes. He'd been on a popular comedy show before *Rio Grande*—*Goodnight, Bobo*, it was called. Something about a zookeeper in Pittsburgh, I think, who lived with some of the animals in his charge. Giraffes poking their long necks through the window over the kitchen sink, apes tucked into bunk beds wearing pajamas, that sort of thing. I'd never watched it, but people had loved it. They thought the Wolf had been over for dinner at their houses because he'd been on their televisions, and so they would vote him into any office in the land over a cold and distant politician's politician.

I thought I was different, of course. I thought, after that day, that I really was their friend.

10. Rome

Week of June 9, 1969

"I'm happy for you, Teddy Bear. Really, I am," David said, when I got home from the Villa Taverna that afternoon and told him my news.

Unlike me, he had remembered Lina's offer from the previous night for me to work on the embassy's art collection, but I suppose he had thought of it as a throwaway comment—just cocktail chatter. He really did seem pleased, if cautiously so, and said, "Maybe this will be good for you, Teddy. To learn some discipline. Have a job."

It wasn't a job, exactly, because nobody had said anything about paying me, and I do wonder if David might have objected more strenuously had it been paid work. For all his anger at my spending habits, I think he liked that my work at the embassy was ultimately an indulgence—I think it would have bothered him, the proposition of me tagging along with him every morning to work at the same place, for a salary.

I forgot, in all the excitement about my news, and in my relief at the change to my circumstances in David's eyes, to ask David where he'd been all day. Since, according to the Wolf, he hadn't been at the embassy.

The following Monday, Margot sent David home from work with forms for me to fill out—routine personnel details, he explained, for the pass I would need to access the building. I worried and then talked myself down, unclenched, over and over again in waves while I waited for my approval to go through. Every evening for those first few days, when David and I sat down to dinner or when he first came in and took off his jacket and shoes to sit on the old terra-cotta-colored sofa for a while, I imagined the phone in the kitchen ringing, and his slow footsteps across the sitting room's parquet floor to pick it up, and then his voice murmuring assent and understanding—"Uh-huh, uh-huh, uh-huh"—until he came back into the sitting room to say to me, "Teddy, we need to talk."

But it never came. He never walked in the front door after a long day at work with accusations on his lips, or came home early to confront me, or any of the ugly scenes I had become convinced were only a matter of minutes, hours, days away, and so it occurred to me, once I had my embassy personnel badge in my hands, and I had been vetted and cleared, that perhaps everything I had ever done was in my file and nobody cared—or perhaps, more likely, nobody had bothered to find out. The truth about me—what kind of woman I really was, I mean. What kind of people I'd known.

In fact, the closer I got to the Wolf, to his orbit, to the embassy, the safer I began to feel. The less I believed that anyone would ever find out my secrets, or if they did, I thought perhaps I had friends in high enough places to keep me safe. I began to feel untouchable. If I was clean enough to work at the American Embassy in Rome, I really couldn't have done anything so wrong, right?

I was always bad at knowing which cans that I'd kicked down the road might trip me up later. I couldn't seem to see them coming, even though I was the one to have placed them in my path.

I hardly slept at all, the night before my first day at the embassy. I was so afraid that I would sleep through my alarm and David would have to wake me up—and he would say something, I was certain, about how I must not care very much about this new job, after all, or maybe he would say I'd better develop some kind of work ethic if I wanted this to be a success. He'd already given me a speech about not embarrassing him, a variation on the one he'd given the night after the party at the Villa Taverna. This was his career, his place of work, his employer (although he got pretty annoyed when I referred to the Wolf as his "boss"—"I work for the Foreign Service, Teddy," he said, "not any one man or party"), and any *shenanigans* from me would reflect poorly on him. And so on.

To be honest, I wasn't worried about embarrassing David. I was worried I had committed treason six years ago and was about to be found out, although as I've said, once they gave me the access badge, I thought maybe I had managed to fool everyone.

But still, I *was* worried, so I stayed up all night lying very still so as not to wake David, wondering whether all of this, the new position and the invitation to the embassy, had actually been part of some elaborate trap to force me to admit to my crimes. I went around and around like this for hours and didn't get anywhere, so in the end I did what I always did in situations like this, and focused on looking my best. They might be less inclined to arrest me if I looked the part, I reasoned, of the brilliant art curatress. And if someone did grab me and haul me away to a dark room to interrogate me—and I would tell them everything immediately— they might treat me more gently if I looked like I needed to be handled with care.

I'd selected my outfit after hours of trial and error the night before, and I'd skipped lunch and dinner, sticking to espresso without even a little milk, to make sure my figure would be trim and my belly deflated. I had finally settled on a Schiaparelli suit that had been Aunt Sister's, which I had rescued from among the things left in the Beverly house after she stopped coming around for her annual visit. It was beautifully constructed, a crisp skirt suit in lightweight charcoal-gray wool with the wide shoulders and nipped waist of those '30s and '40s silhouettes. It would be warm for June, but I knew I would feel brave in it. I knew the strong shoulders, the way it displayed and enhanced my figure, would make me feel powerful.

When the morning light began to slip under and around the curtains and into our bedroom, I left David snuffling and snoring in bed and went to get ready. I bathed quietly, so as not to wake him. I'd already washed and dried my hair the night before, so all I had to do was fix it into something a bit sleeker than my usual style, inspired by Lina's chignon on Saturday. I dressed in a silk slip to do my makeup—lighter on the eyes than usual, inspired by Lina, as well. And then I put my suit on with some low, sensible heels, and I looked like I was ready to go into battle. I looked like a woman to be reckoned with.

I was already sipping my espresso and reading David's newspaper by the time he woke up and came to find me, and even though I was feeling a bit tired and shaky, it was all worth it to see the genuine smile on his face.

"Look at you, Teddy!" he said. "You look like a lady lawyer, or something."

I took this as a statement of approval.

He kissed my temple and poured himself a cup of coffee, ate the toast I had prepared for him, dressed in his usual suit. And then he drove us to work.

As strong and powerful as I felt in my suit, I noticed that the espresso I'd had seemed to be doing funny things to my stomach, the closer we got to the via Veneto and the embassy. But I smiled for David every time he asked if I was nervous, and said, no, of course not, I'm just excited. And it wasn't a lie—I was that, too.

The American Embassy was in a pink brick palace in Ludovisi, the chicest, most exclusive neighborhood in Rome, right on the via

Veneto. It was a Renaissance Revival wedding cake of a building that had been purchased, along with all of the antiques and frescoes and statuary inside it, by the United States after the war. Queen Margherita of Savoy had lived there for twenty years earlier in the century, and the Palazzo Margherita, as it was called, had briefly served as office space for Mussolini's government. But now it belonged to America, and the art contained inside had been grandfathered in.

It wasn't, I suppose, so different from my life in Rome; I had signed on to David, and all of the objects in his apartment, in his life, and the flat itself, were suddenly mine, too, whether I liked it or not.

There were palms out in front of the embassy, inside the high wall that surrounded it, and I liked to imagine when I passed them, as I had outside the Barberini Museum, that they were a good sign. And it felt that way, walking into the American Embassy with my husband. I wanted to hold his hand, but I thought he might find it unprofessional; he did guide me some of the way with his hand at my back, though.

We passed the guards, the same Marines as at the Villa Taverna (or not the same ones, perhaps, but in the same uniforms), and David and I both displayed our identification badges at the gate. And then he took me inside the doors of the main building—the chancery—where he bade me goodbye, said he would head home around five if I wanted to hitch a ride, and kissed me once on the cheek for good luck. He said Margot would come to get me, and left me to wait there while he ascended the grand staircase to the *piano nobile*, where all the staff offices were.

Margot appeared after a few minutes, descending the staircase David had just climbed, and she was wearing a brightly patterned, tightly fitted summer dress with a little jacket over it.

"You're certainly dressed up!" she said, in a cheerful tone that made it difficult to know whether she was insulting me on purpose when she added, "How funny; I think my grandmother has a suit just like that."

Oh, really? I wanted to say but didn't. *Your grandmother from Burlington, Vermont, or wherever, has a 1940 Schiaparelli suit from Paris?*

"Aren't you a little bit warm?" she added.

I was, actually, I was already beginning to sweat, and occasionally had to lift a hand to my upper lip to make sure my makeup wasn't beaded with droplets of moisture. But all I had on underneath was a silk slip, so I couldn't take the jacket off, and anyway, it was part of the look. It was a whole ensemble.

Margot took me on a tour of the rest of the chancery—or most of it, anyway, the things that were all right for "civilians" to see, which seemed like a bit of a grandiose term in this context, but what did I know? The more important thing was that every other woman we passed, from the girls in the typing pool to the small number of female officers, was wearing some version of what Margot had on. Bright colors, light fabrics, casual silhouettes. She kept looking at me as she made these introductions; I think she wanted to see if I was embarrassed. If I had noticed it—that I was dressed all wrong. That I was out of place.

Most of my work, Margot told me, would be wandering the corridors of the embassy and photographing and making notes on the various lampshades and credenzas and paintings and sculptures—I noticed she listed the furniture first, just to make it all sound a little more frivolous. She gave me a Polaroid camera for this purpose, just to speed things along, so I could take references of each item back to my office with me. I wasn't to actually move anything, she explained, but they had dedicated a space for me to store any research materials I needed, and drafts of the enormous catalogue I was going to eventually compile. She said this as if she was giving me an assignment, not as if I was the expert who knew what needed to be done.

Margot set me up in an empty room, not in the main beautiful building, the chancery, but in an outbuilding they called the New Wing. The New Wing looked like any office building, really, inside, and was a far cry from the chancery building's ornate splendor. My office was on the third floor, about as far out of the way of the daily business of the embassy as you could be. The only other room in use on that floor was full of whirring electronic machines and men wearing headsets, whom David later told me not to ask about but the Wolf, in his cavalier way, referred to when he came to visit that afternoon as "the Pointdexters."

I eventually learned that he loved cartoons, the ambassador. He called the French ambassador Pepé Le Pew behind his back. I waved to the men inside when I passed the Pointdexter room—it was secret, apparently, but had to have its door left open to keep its machines from overheating—but they didn't wave back.

The Wolf came by about an hour or so after Margot had deposited me; I was sitting at one of the old metal desks in the room—my new "office" seemed to primarily be storage for surplus furniture—and I was sweating through my stupid suit, trying to make sense of the last short-lived attempt anyone had made to catalogue the embassy's contents, just after the war.

"There she is!" he cried. "The artist at work!"

He never did quite manage the distinction between artist and art historian, but it seemed pointless and rude to correct him.

I rose from my seat as he approached, and he whistled.

"Is that Joan Crawford?" he asked, and studied me with an appraising eye. "She used to wear suits just like that, if I recall. Gosh, you look stunning."

And even though I was still sweating, I loved the suit again. It had been the right thing, hadn't it? The Wolf and I, we knew better than all these secretaries and stuck-up Seven Sisters graduates. This was fashion; this was what people at the top of the heap were wearing.

Things got better from there. The Wolf invited me to his office—"to see where the sausage is made"—and as we walked through the floor where David and all of the other men worked, my husband came out with a few of his colleagues—officers of something or other, I never found out what—to say hello, and ask me how my day was.

I think he was a bit surprised to see me over there, in the company of the Wolf; I found out later that visits to the ambassador's office were an honor usually only reserved for the most senior of staffers.

"You're a lucky man," one of the men said to David, when he saw me, and at first I thought it was a compliment on my appearance, even if my hair had gotten a bit bedraggled around my temples from the heat, and my makeup was splotched with sweat, but then he added, "I wish my wife would work. The way she spends my money . . ."

David didn't correct him to say that I was doing this for free, I noticed, but he did grin and say, "Sure. I'm proud of my Teddy. She's a sharp little thing."

And then the Wolf took me into his office and closed the door behind us.

It was all as David had said: the enormous, ornate wooden desk. The wolf on the wall, and below that, the gun. To me, the taxidermy was the more alarming of the two deadly decorations—something about the way it had been done made the gums and the inside of its open, snarling mouth look red, as if it was filled with blood. I thought of a painting I'd seen in the collection of a family friend, a work by Gustave Courbet that showed a fox gnashing a rat with its teeth in a winter forest. The rat's red blood dripping onto the snow.

The Wolf had already asked me the usual questions when he appeared at my "office," things like, "How's the first day going?" (great) and "How's our Margot treating you?" (terribly, but I wouldn't admit it), and I realized when he closed his own office door that he seemed to have something in particular he wanted to speak to me about.

Once we'd settled in on the enormous antique sofa opposite his desk ("Hideous, isn't it? I prefer a more minimal style, myself—you should see our place in Montecito, hardly any furniture at all!"), he turned to me and put a hand down on the sofa between us, and it was as if he had put it on my knee, it felt that intimate, and he said, "You know, Teddy, I realized why your name seemed so familiar to me on Friday, and it's not just because of your incorrigible old Uncle Hal."

And my heart fell into the bottom of my empty stomach, and bucked and rolled around in there with the espresso that was all I'd consumed so far that day. Like a ship tossed on tidal waves, battered and crushed in the surf. The fearsome octopus was in there, too, of course—he never really left me, and he wound a sinewy purple tentacle through the slats of my rib cage, snatching at my organs.

This was it. This was what I'd been afraid of, turning it over and over in my mind all night instead of sleeping. This was the part where the Wolf told me he knew exactly who I was, had known all along, because he'd heard of a night I'd spent once with a Russian spy in Washington, DC, and I waited to hear the door slam open, for the handsome young Marines to come bursting in, weapons drawn, to take me away.

"Cecilia," the Wolf said. "Cecilia Huntley, that was her name. A relative of yours, I think?"

"My aunt," I said, and was surprised how well the words came out. And I wasn't even able to enjoy the relief that this wasn't going to be the moment they dragged me off to some dingy basement jail cell, after all, because here was another secret—one I had forgotten to worry about, like the fool that I am.

You have to keep track of these things. You're supposed to keep a catalogue of your other shoes, the ones that haven't dropped, yet.

"I thought so!" he cried. "I used to know her, back when. How the hell is she? What's she been up to lately?"

"Oh," I said, "she's in Texas," and that wasn't exactly a lie.

This answer seemed to satisfy him, and he began to reminisce about Aunt Sister in the old days, and I felt my heart inflating again and rising back up to where it was supposed to sit at the top of my chest, and the octopus retreated.

The Wolf explained that Aunt Sister had been in and out of Los Angeles right around the time his acting career took off after the war, and he regaled me with stories of what a live one she'd been, what fun. They hadn't been close, just occasionally orbited the same debauched parties, but he told me how everyone always wanted her around, and whoever sat next to her at dinner was the luckiest fellow in the room, would be laughing all the way through the meal to whiskey and cigars.

I suppose it's possible, looking back, that he made all of it up, but I hope not. I like to think a version of Aunt Sister is still out there in their memories, all the men and women who attended those Hollywood parties, all the people she knew. She's still telling stories at dinner somewhere, making everyone laugh, dancing with the fellas in her sequins and pearls. Most people never found out what happened to her, and I believe it's better that way; let her be alive as she once was, to them. Maybe there's a man somewhere in California, still, who recalls her only as the young woman who spent a night in his arms after a party; maybe all he remembers is the golden glow of the morning sun illuminating the soft curve of her cheek.

Let her stay there, forever alive in that moment, eternally connected to the world she so loved.

II. Rome

June–Early July 1969

Lina was as good as her word. Suddenly all of Rome was open to us, or more specifically, to me—I don't know how many invitations David used to receive before my arrival, since he had kept me hidden from everyone at first, and everyone from me. But after that night at the Villa Taverna, our presence was requested at dinners and cocktail receptions and evenings at the opera.

We were invited to these events because I was charming and made the most of myself and everyone loved an American, and especially a Texan, in Italy that summer, or at least all the other Americans did, but also, it became clear to me through comments made here and there in passing, because of my background. Because of my family and their money. And I have no doubt that this annoyed David, and I think I knew it at the time, but I also knew he didn't dare interfere, because it was good for him, too, and for his career, for us to be invited to an evening at the opera with the Duchess of whatever, or to a performance by the Cambridge Madrigal Choir, with a whiskey tasting after, at the British Embassy in the Villa Wolkonsky.

Someone at David's level would never normally socialize with the ambassador himself most nights, but suddenly we were everywhere, and we were seated at dinners at the main table, not all the way across the lawn.

I was invited, now, to the embassy wives' luncheons and game nights and horseback riding in the Villa Borghese, though of course I only knew Western riding and struggled to keep up with all the Vassar and Barnard and Bryn Mawr girls in their jodhpurs and smooth leather boots, with their helmets and perfect poise.

One of the personnel officers at the embassy helped me to find an Italian tutor, too. Signora Falasca was a retired schoolteacher with a Roman nose and a tangle of iron-colored hair whose husband, a poet, had died in '43 during the first wave of bombings. She bore no ill will toward Americans, she said, and was grateful for the liberation, but she also told me I had a lazy tongue and lacked passion in my speech. She came to the flat every other afternoon to engage me in imaginary scenarios: she would play the chef and I would have to explain in Italian that one of our guests was, if you can believe it, a vegetarian; she would play the valet and I would need to communicate that this evening, my husband was to be dressed in white tie; she would play a dinner guest dissatisfied with the seating arrangement because she had been assigned a spot next to a political opponent, and I was supposed to placate her. She may have been right about the lack of conviction in my Italian, but I think you'll agree that in the end, she was wrong about what it would have been useful for me to know. I gave up after a few weeks, right around the time everything fell apart, anyway.

I really did enjoy my work at the embassy. Not just the satisfaction of investigating each work of art, of organizing the pieces into categories and lists—actually, the organizing part was always a bit tricky for me—but also coming to an office. Feeling like I was part of something.

I started my investigations with a series of marble statues set in alcoves along the chancery's grand staircase, analyzing each one in turn from atop a stepladder (from which I would occasionally catch the Wolf's famous blue eyes, as blue as the sea in Capri, roving over my figure; at least, I thought so).

There was one sculpture in particular, a Renaissance statue of Venus, that enchanted me. She stood curled forward slightly, her left foot on a pedestal. She appeared to have been caught mid-bath—in her left hand was a stone sponge, which she held near one small breast; in her right she held a marble cloth draped across her lap. It was a variation on a common pose for statues of Venus, and perhaps for naked women everywhere: one hand over the breasts, one hand over what I once heard Uncle Hal refer to as the "sugar bowl." The *Venus pudica*, this type of statue is called. It means "modest Venus," according to what I've read on the subject, and was a favorite form of sculptors of the Roman Empire. It was a way to depict the beauty of the female nude without revealing too much; the statues are often draped with a marble towel where it counts, or else depicted as surprised, shielding their bodies with their hands as any righteous Roman woman would do. This type of Venus was popular with later Renaissance sculptors for the same reason—you would never find stone fig leaves added after the fact to cover the naughty bits; they weren't needed. When I checked my Latin dictionary, once, I learned that *pudica* also means ashamed.

The Wolf came to visit me sometimes over those weeks in June that I worked at the embassy, especially if David was out of town and the ambassador thought I might be lonely. I would be squirreled away on the third floor of the New Wing, poring over old sale catalogues and registers of the art collections of the wealthiest families in Rome from centuries before, and the Wolf would stop by to see what progress I was making, perching on an old office chair or leaning against the edge of a coated metal desk to ask me all about it.

It was nice, in my office—it had that quality of the seashore and the salon that I so enjoyed, the fuzzy sort of silence. There was always the background hum of the machines in the Pointdexter room, and so it felt like we had a bit of privacy, cocooned in my office by that electronic thrum, and we could actually speak openly, and get to know each other.

I learned that he and Lina had never had children—"Never wanted 'em," he said, "and anyway, Lina can't," and I sensed a story there, perhaps some private sorrow, that I didn't think I should ask about. I learned that his mother was still alive, installed in a widow's apartment over the guest house at the mansion in Montecito, having refused any plusher accommodations, and that she had also refused to come to visit him in Italy—and in fact was a bit annoyed, really, that he had gone to Rome, of all places, instead of Sicily. I learned that the Wolf found politics far more stimulating than he ever had acting, although there were, in his estimation, some similarities.

"But it's real," he said, when he explained his love of government to me. I asked if he meant because he could make a real difference, and he answered, "That, and you can have a real fight."

One night at a party at the Villa Wolkonsky—after the Cambridge choir was done and the whiskey had been tasted—the Wolf insisted on playing the Rolling Stones' latest record for the British ambassador, who just smiled and said yes, he was familiar. There was one song in particular the Wolf liked, playing it over and over at the party despite groans from the company by the third time he moved the needle. *You can't always get what you want*, the chorus went, and then repeated.

"An American would never sing that," the Wolf said to Sir Anthony, and Her Majesty's ambassador laughed politely, but I could tell he didn't like the Wolf.

"You can get everything you want," the Wolf said, that night.

The Wolf was flirtatious on his visits to my office, and irreverent, even vulgar—he once asked me how come Renaissance statues had such small nipples on their tits—but it felt warmer than David's vague and very occasional expressions of interest in my work. I began to think of us as friends, and when he found out that my birthday was coming up, less than a month away, he insisted that he would host the party—that in fact, he had a few old friends who were filming at Cinecittà and planning to come by the evening of July 8 for a little soiree, and they would just tweak the invitations to make me the guest of honor. It was more than I had ever imagined, the idea that my thirty-fifth birthday might be attended by a host of Hollywood stars.

If it was late enough in the day and most everyone else had gone home, the Wolf would invite me down to his office for a drink. He would ask me questions about art, he would ask me questions about my life, and he would say such kind things to me about how brilliant I was, how interesting, that I began to believe him. I thought perhaps I could be the person he described, the Teddy he saw when he visited the third floor or came across me studying a painting or a sculpture in a hallway of the chancery, lost in my work. I was enchanted by her, the Teddy the Wolf offered to me: Teddy with a purpose, Teddy the expert. Brilliant, funny, glossy, grown-up Teddy.

Those weeks at the embassy, with my fresh start and my newfound purpose, were some of the happiest, for me. And David was happy, too. Every morning, I met him at the door to the flat as he was leaving for the embassy, his briefcase in his hand.

"Oh, you're coming too?" he would ask.

"Well, yes," I would say, "I'm on my way to work."

"Oh, *work*," David would say, and there was some sarcasm in it, perhaps, but he would also kiss me on the cheek or on the top of my head, or pat me on the rear as I walked past him to the door. He would even tell me, occasionally, that he was proud of me, as he held the door open for me to walk out in front of him.

I went to see Lina's doctor, too, since occasionally I did feel, as she'd suggested, that I needed to be just a little bit shinier.

Doctor D'Abruzzo's office was located on a tree-lined street over by the Sapienza that I thought in another life would have been a nice place to live in an empty little flat, alone, and the good doctor gave me pills to help me sleep at night and pills to keep me awake, plus some to take when I felt sad or nervous, and armed with these and my brand-new job I managed to make it through a few weeks in fine fettle, at least as far as David could see.

Most days I stayed away from the sleeping pills because if anything, I was inclined by nature to sleep too much, but sometimes I would take the others, the stay-awakes, if I hadn't fallen asleep by three or four in the morning. And then I would lie in bed next to David for the rest of the night, listening to the rapid beating of my heart until it was time for me to start getting dressed at five thirty, and by the time he woke at a quarter to seven I was already glowing, shining blondly all scrubbed and dressed in the kitchen with espresso on the stove and eggs in a pan, his shirts pressed and ready on a hanger over the back of one of the dining chairs. Those were good days.

And sometimes David would take me out, if we didn't have another social engagement, and it was exactly what I had dreamed of those first lonely weeks in Rome, when all I wanted was for my husband to take me to Cesarina or Giggi Fazi or George's.

I remember one night in particular, at the beginning of July, when he took me to a restaurant in the Villa Borghese, and it truly did feel like the rest of my life had begun.

Casina Valadier was a place to see and be seen. That's what it said in the Alitalia ads, which featured black-and-white photos of revelers on the restaurant's scenic patio as an example of the kind of continental decadence you could expect if you took one of their Caravelles from JFK or Dulles to Ciampino. *See—and be seen.* There was another ad with the same photo that said, in a bold Roman typeface, *Let yourself go.*

The restaurant was housed in a centuries-old castle on a hill in the park; the terrace boasted a view of all of Rome. When the weather was nice, as it was the day we went, you could find the most beautiful people in the city on that terrace. Wealthy Italian women wearing sculptural gold jewelry, actors and actresses on a break from filming at Cinecittà, all impeccably dressed, laughing in groups, sipping their afternoon cocktails, looking down at their city.

David ordered pasta *all'amatriciana* for us, that evening, and I admired how crisp the bacon looked, the tomato sauce pooled around it. The grease was gorgeous, orange on the Casina's monogrammed white plates, but I was happy just to look at it. The stay-awake pills killed my appetite, and that made the whole evening so much more delicious—there was nothing else I needed to consume. I was lighter than air.

Armando Zingone's orchestra struck up at sunset, but David hated dancing, so he and I sat at the table for the rest of the evening, discussing possible futures—what if he was posted to Paris, next? Or Hong Kong? If we had a boy and a girl, what would we name them? What kind of dog would we get, when we eventually settled back in the States and bought a house with a yard? And even though we didn't dance, David did reach for my hand, and in the moment, that was enough. That was all I wanted, and I had it. I could enjoy myself on an evening out with my husband. I could have a nice dinner on the patio at an old palace in Rome. I could absorb everything around me, take it all in and make it mine. This was a life I could keep.

On the way home that evening, I reached over in the car to put a hand on David's knee. He met my eye and smiled. I wanted to show him that I needed him, that I wanted to keep him. That I was going to do whatever it took to make this life work. He didn't know what it meant, my hand on his knee, my smile, but I did.

When we got back to the apartment, I went to the bathroom to check my makeup and hair, to freshen up a bit. Even at night, it was so hot in Rome that summer, my hair and face were always in some kind of disarray by the end of an evening. I didn't want it to end, you see—I wanted to sit with David in the living room, him with a bourbon and myself with some tea, maybe, and talk about our future, and be completely in love.

When I came back out into the living room, David was standing by the door with his suitcase.

"I'm on the late train to Milan tonight," he said, "but I'll be back the day before your birthday. Give me a kiss."

So that was the other thing. I could go on with my prim and perfect Teddy routine, my stay-awake pills and my diet and my excellent new work ethic for a few days at a time, sometimes a full week, and David would be so proud and pleased and take me out to dinner or maybe window shopping on the via Condotti—though he blanched when we looked at the prices on a gorgeous double strand of pearls in the window at Bulgari that I itched to get my hands on—and he would call me his "good girl," and talk about our future family, but then he'd be off to Milan or Naples or farther afield, and I would take a bunch of the third type of pill, the ones to help me relax, all at once, and listen to music, David's old jazz records, and lie on my back on the sitting-room rug and stare up at the ceiling.

Those were also good days, as long as I stayed up there on the ceiling, but once I came down, I would be so ashamed that I'd drag myself from the carpet to the bed and remain there until he got home again, at which point I would take enough stay-awakes to whisk all the dust under the carpet and hide my dirty clothes for Teresa to deal with later, and the whole charade would start all over.

But mostly, for the rest of June and into the first days of July, we were really very happy, David and I. Mostly, we couldn't have been happier.

Now

Early Morning, Wednesday, July 9, 1969

"The, ah, the 'Pointdexters,'" Archie says, and then stops. He seems to be at a loss.

"They never talked to me," I offer. "They never even said hello back to me. It was actually kind of rude."

"Mm-hmm," he mutters, and then makes a note of something.

"Mrs. Shepard," Arthur Hildebrand says, and I notice, for the first time, how dark and yet bright his eyes are. "Mrs. Shepard, I feel that you're not being entirely honest with us."

I've been picking at my nails this whole time, peeling the pink acrylic off one by one, and now I have a little pile of plastic shards sitting on the coffee table in front of me. It tugs at the nail below, a bit, to try to take them off without acetone, and there's a crust of blood, now, around my nail beds.

Though I suppose that it could have been there before. That it might not be mine, at all.

"We need exact dates and times," Reggie says, "of every instance you had access to the chancery and associated buildings."

"Well," I say, "that's easy. Every day, during normal working hours, from June ninth just up until today."

Arthur Hildebrand is not amused.

"What happened on the Fourth of July?" he asks, and I begin to wonder just how much he already knows about what comes next.

12. Rome

Friday, July 4, 1969

As I've mentioned, David left again for an extended trip to Milan on Wednesday, July 2, which wouldn't have been a big deal except the ambassador was hosting an enormous Fourth of July party at the residence that Friday.

I would've liked for David to go with me; it was fixing to be the biggest event we'd been invited to since that first party in honor of the Aga Khan. But he said there was no way around it, "and anyway, Bear, you have so many friends now. You'll do great, all on your own."

Everything, even the way he spoke to me, had changed in just a few short weeks. I didn't know if it was the pills, or the job, or the fact that we were suddenly at the center of things in Rome—even though David didn't always love parties, he did like to be invited to them—but David was pleased with me, and for a time, at least, that was all that mattered.

He told me, too, on his way out the door, that when he returned, we should start thinking about when we might want to start a family. He said he thought I could be a wonderful mother, one day.

He also said that I should get myself something nice for the party—nothing too extravagant, he said, but something festive. Patriotic. This was the American century, after all. This was our year—we were on our way to the moon, weren't we? He even gave me an extra hundred dollars on top of the money that was supposed to be my allowance for July.

I probably should have viewed this as a test. I should have saved the money, along with what he'd already given me that month. But Lina had told me to make sure my wardrobe was up to snuff for the social world I was entering, and I'd already worked my way through most of the nice dresses I'd brought with me from Dallas. And I had been feeling better, lately, and David was happy with me, now, and I was well on my way to being the woman I wanted to be.

And that woman—well, I couldn't help picturing her in a long chiffon dress in Valentino red, one that fit perfectly through the waist. Nobody would say that woman looked like a stuffed sausage.

So, I bought the red dress, the one I had wanted before—the one that had felt just right. It didn't even need to be tailored, which Vanessa and the other women at the atelier seemed to find a relief. And I didn't have a purse to match it, not one for evening, not one that would look as modern and shiny as the future felt to me at that moment, but Paco Rabanne had recently debuted a silver chainmail purse that would match a pair of silver Dior pumps I already owned just perfectly, so I bought that, too.

I deserved those things, didn't I? I had been so good, and I had been working hard at the embassy, and wasn't this the lesson David had wanted me to learn? I wasn't getting paid, obviously, at my job, but wasn't this what people meant, about working hard for the things you wanted? There wasn't much left of my allowance after my purchases, but I didn't really need to pay for much else besides hair and nails, anyway. I wasn't too worried about groceries or any of that—David was gone, so no need to pretend to do the shopping or cook, and I had been eating for free, lately, at dinners and luncheons and cocktail receptions.

The day of the party, I went back to the via Condotti to have my hair and nails done again with Sergio; this time I asked the girls to make the long, false nails a shade of petal pink, just like the color I'd seen on Lina before she left for the summer.

Afterward, I went to meet Anna, Margot's journalist friend, at L'Antico Caffè Greco, which was right by the Bulgari store, so I snuck a look at those pearls I'd had my eye on, too, though they were far more expensive than anything I could manage with my allowance.

Anna and I had become something like friends in recent weeks, or at least, we had been to lunch and dinner a few times. I liked her matter-of-fact manner and that she had a job—I liked to think of us as two working women, out for a casual lunch. It occurred to me, as I sat there with her in the famous old dining room at Caffè Greco, that I was one of them, now. The happy, laughing people I had so envied when I first walked down this street.

Anna arrived with wet hair—she was running late, she explained, and hadn't had time to dry it, and her little studio flat was just a few blocks over, off the via Veneto. I found myself kind of envious of this—not just the fact that it didn't worry her to go out with wet hair, but that she lived so close to the heart of things; despite our sudden rise in fortune, at least socially, David and I were still stuck in his bachelor's apartment in crowded little Trastevere.

Anna was always good for gossip or news; she told me she'd heard that all kinds of celebrities would be at the Wolf's Fourth of July party, and that there would likely be paparazzi crowded around the gate. "Think of it—we might end up in one of the scandal sheets, or the society pages!"

In the background, most likely, behind Claudia Cardinale or some Italian socialite, but still—it was exhilarating. Anna had heard a rumor that Charles Bronson and Telly Savalas were in town filming something, which I realized, with a flutter, meant they might be among the Wolf's friends expected to appear at my birthday party the following week.

Anna wanted to talk about Harriet Pilpel's piece from last month's issue of *The Atlantic*, which was arguing for laxer abortion laws. I hadn't read it, but Anna summarized it for me. And she said that of course she, too, was in favor of more liberal laws, because she'd had to fly to Europe for her abortion and it wasn't fair to women who couldn't afford to.

She revealed this about herself so casually, like it wasn't even the point, and when I asked if she regretted it she just said, "No, Ted," and left it at that.

One thing I can say about Anna: she never seemed to carry things around with her. The details of her life were just facts, to her, which she related with a kind of neutral finality that I envied. I saw my past as a series of secrets and mistakes requiring penance, regret, obfuscation—I could hardly imagine how it would feel to speak about these things as if they were simply events in the course of a life. Not evidence.

When we paid the bill (Anna's treat, thank God, given my allowance situation), Anna bade me farewell until the evening.

"Why are you all buttoned up, Ted?" Anna asked, picking at my sweater after we hugged goodbye outside Caffè Greco. "It's a million degrees out and you look like a nun."

She was right—I was beginning to sweat in my cardigan. I had been wearing them out of habit, even when David wasn't in town, since I'd managed to turn things around with him. But this time I took it off and let the sun caress my shoulders as I walked back to Trastevere.

I got back to the flat with plenty of time to dress and do my makeup, which was good; I labored over the eyes, painting the liner heavy over my lids, and attaching my favorite false lashes, "Child-at-heart," from Andrea.

And I stocked my shiny new bag with everything I would need for the night, my tissues and lipsticks and powder; the chain mail was heavy, and the strap began to dig into the soft flesh of my shoulder the moment I put it on, but I liked how substantial it was. Like a weapon. It was iconic; all the magazines agreed it was the bag of the moment. I could imagine David saying the links of the bag looked like soda-pop tabs all stapled together, if he saw it; but he would never see it, at least not until I could truthfully say, "Oh, this? I've had it forever!"

I would bury it in the wardrobe before he got back, just so he wouldn't know I'd been shopping—and anyway, he didn't understand fashion. The power of these things—clothes, bags, shoes. Nails and lashes.

When I looked at myself in the long mirror beside the wardrobe, I thought I looked perfect. There was no sign of her—the old Teddy.

I called a taxi to take me to the Villa Taverna; when David was traveling, I didn't use the car. I had driven everywhere, in Dallas, in my custom Thunderbird, but David didn't trust me to use his precious little Fiat in Rome, not with all the crazy drivers barreling down ancient, winding streets. I wouldn't have minded walking, but the ambassador's residence was over an hour on foot, and it was hot out. And I was wearing heels, those Dior pumps, and I needed to look perfect when I arrived.

I suppose I might as well admit that even with my red dress, and even though I finally had friends in Rome, I was nervous. I was afraid to go to that party alone, without David to serve as a guide for me. As a bumper, or a curb.

The taxi dropped me outside the gates of the Villa Taverna, and as I exited the car, I pressed a finger to my upper lip—I was sweating, and what if it ruined my makeup? How was it still so hot outside, at well past seven in the evening?

Paparazzi, as promised, congregated all around the gate. Handsome men with a hungry look, jackals in suits holding silver accordion cameras, looking for a familiar face. They all turned at my approach, the click-clack of my heels like a rabbit rustling through the brush to them, and in a moment of panic I lifted my hands to shield my face. Scurried through the gate, past the broad-shouldered young Marines in their beautiful bright uniforms and into the front garden of the Villa Taverna.

The photographers were already looking elsewhere, anyway—they didn't call out, "*Signora, signora,*" as I walked past the way they did when Sophia Loren or Anita Ekberg or someone else like that was leaving a bar over on the via Veneto. Harry's, usually, or the Café de Paris.

When I walked around to the garden, I had to stop for a moment, just to take it all in. Lights were strung from the trees, and a twenty-eight-piece brass band played under garlands of fresh flowers in red, white, and blue. They must have cost a fortune, those flowers. Red roses and pillowy blue and white hydrangeas. And electric fans set up in glowing white tents, cooling the humid evening air into something more bearable.

I scanned the crowd for a familiar face and saw a group of women I knew, including Margot and Anna, in the nearest tent, so I made a beeline for them.

That's the key to going to a party alone—as soon as you get there, you have to find a friend.

I greeted them all with a kiss once on each cheek—Margot and Anna, then Barb, the Resident Legal Advisor's wife; Esther, whose husband was the president's representative to the Holy See; Kitty, whose husband didn't work at the embassy at all, but was an American film producer on a project at Cinecittà, and she had followed him all the way to Rome and left the kids back in Los Angeles with her mother because she didn't trust him further than she could throw him, she said—which was probably pretty far, actually, Calvin being on the slighter side. She preferred to spend her days with the officers' wives, women who had gone to the same girls' schools and women's colleges as she had, rather than the starlets who congregated on her husband's film sets.

"I prefer to socialize with women of substance," she said once, "over some bottle blond from Muncie, Indiana."

This was specific enough that we had to assume there was a particular bottle blond of concern on the set, but nobody had wanted to ask her about it.

"And where is David, tonight?" Barb asked me, once we'd all been supplied with fresh drinks by a wandering waiter. Her Jim was over at the edge of the tent, in close conversation with the Wolf.

"He couldn't make it," I answered. "He's in Milan—you know how it is, with these men. Always traveling, always working." I laughed.

Barb laughed too, then said, "You know, I think I have the opposite problem. Mine is always around, always home saying, 'Barb, what are you doing?' Always following me."

Margot had a small smile playing across her thin lips when she said, "But really, Barb, I'm sure you're grateful. That he gets to spend time at home with you. That you know where he is."

She turned to me. "You must worry, Teddy, mustn't you, with David traveling the way he does?"

"Well, he's only in Milan," I said. "Though I wish he would take me, next time. I'd love to do some shopping!"

I laughed again, inviting them all to join me. But the other women were mostly silent, though Anna chuckled a bit.

So then I began to wonder what I was supposed to be worrying about, with David, but I couldn't very well ask Margot and let her have the satisfaction of my ignorance. Or let any of them, my newfound friends with their collegiate confidence, their Radcliffe degrees, their brusque New England competence, know that I hardly understood my husband at all. That I had no idea what he did all day, even though I'd been working just a single building away for the past few weeks.

"Oh, look," Kitty said in an excited whisper, and I was grateful for the interruption until I saw what she was pointing at.

A group of men had joined Barb's Jim and the ambassador, with handshakes all around.

"They're here!" Barb said, equally thrilled.

I was back on the Mine Train at Six Flags Over Texas, with the bottom dropping out of the Ace Hotel and Saloon once again.

Because of course—how had I thought I would be able to avoid this moment? Stupid Teddy, naive Teddy. The new arrivals were from the Russian Embassy, and among them was a tall, blond man, with eyes as dark as a rabbit's.

The Wolf turned his sharp blue eyes on us, and smiled—it felt, in the moment, that this was specifically for me, and I began to wonder once again if he *knew*—and ambled over with Jim at his side, leaving the Russians to stand awkwardly by a tent pole.

"Have I got something exciting for you, ladies!" the Wolf crowed, though he kept his voice low. He was smiling like it was Christmas morning and there was a brand-new Buick with a bow on it, with our names on it, on the driveway outside.

"Want to meet some real, live, bona fide Reds?" he asked.

"Is it safe?" Barb asked. "I mean, aren't they all spies? Darling, you said—" She stopped herself at a look from her husband.

The Wolf just laughed. "Well, we had to invite 'em, didn't we? They let us come to their thing, their national what have you. Their holiday. What's it called?"

"May Day," Jim said. "It's like Labor Day."

"Strange party," the Wolf said. "Really strange—the music."

He scratched at his chin with a long-fingered hand, lost in thought for a moment. "Lots of shouting, but then a bit like church music. Kind of ominous."

He brightened again. "So we had to invite 'em—show 'em what a real party looks like."

"Now," the Wolf said, and this was what I had been dreading, "do you ladies want to meet the Russkies, or not?"

We all nodded—I'm sure I must have, as it was expected of me—and the Wolf put a hand at the back of my arm to guide me forward, which I thought was surely only because I was standing closest to him, and not because he knew that there was any specific reason for my reluctance to meet these men, and Jim and the ambassador escorted us toward the edge of the tent, and the Wolf whispered in my ear as we walked, "We'll show them what a real American beauty looks like; show 'em what they're missing, with their babushkas. The big ladies on their propaganda posters with hands the size of ham hocks."

I don't think I would have been able to make my legs move, to carry myself forward, if I hadn't still had the frantic thought, in the seconds it took us to reach the Russians, that Eugene— Yevgeny—might not remember me. Maybe all he would see was the new, polished, more perfect Teddy—a complete stranger. Maybe the sad, sick, desperate Teddy of six years earlier was nowhere to be found.

This was all I could think about as we approached and introductions were made, each wife to each Red, in turn, and then:

"It's nice to meet you, Mr. Larin," I said, when it was my turn, and I saw the lights come on behind his animal eyes, the spark of recognition, and I thought my voice sounded light, easy, like his was just another face. It was strange to be drowning, in the murky water under Caddo Lake, and for no one to hear it, at all.

13. Villa Taverna

Friday, July 4, 1969

I set off over the lawn at almost a run, down the garden path I'd walked only a few weeks earlier with Lina, as soon as I could reasonably excuse myself. Probably sooner, actually, and it had been rude—but I'd had to run, because I simply couldn't keep it up. I needed to be alone before I lost control and revealed too much; I knew my hands would start shaking any minute. I thought perhaps I might vomit.

He'd pretended to be meeting me for the first time, but I could tell. He saw me. He saw who I was, had been, underneath the Valentino and the shine of my stupid little pills and all my lies.

The path went a long way over the grounds and I walked briskly, winding past statues and fountains previously unseen, all centuries old. I decided to go as far as I could, trying to focus on the satisfying sound of my footsteps on the gravel, and the thought that maybe by the time I made it back to the party, something would be different. Maybe everyone would be gone. Maybe the world would be different; maybe my past would somehow have come undone.

I used to think like that, kicking the can down the road, living moment to moment. As I've mentioned before, it's one of the things that has always gotten me into trouble.

I still had a glass of champagne in my hand and it was sweating, dripping condensation that fell on my dress, darkening the bright

167

fabric to a deeper crimson as I passed a fountain, a statue of Neptune, a bust of some Caesar.

It was dark out under the canopy of trees beyond the party, but the statues along the path were illuminated from below, which cast a strange glow around their forms. I stopped for a moment before a bronze atop a column, a statue of *la Lupa Capitolina*—the Capitoline Wolf. The she-wolf who suckled Romulus and Remus, the founders of Rome, when they were abandoned as infants by the banks of the Tiber. I imagined finding a baby and feeling the animal instinct to nurture it. I wondered what it would be like, to be a mother.

I was beginning to understand that I would never find out. Not now. Not if this was going to keep happening to me, every time— if everywhere I went, the bodies I thought I'd buried kept popping back up.

Rome was supposed to be different. It was supposed to be a chance for me to be somebody better, and new, and now I understood that version of me didn't exist, and never would.

And it didn't matter how safe I'd thought I was, tucked between the paws of the Wolf—that had been only a fantasy. He might have invited Russian diplomats to his parties, but there was no way anyone would tolerate the wife of an American official having a past relationship with one of them. I thought about what Barb had said, that everyone knew they were all spies, and I thought about Anna's story from the first night we met, about the woman in Berlin passing secrets to her Soviet lover. I didn't think it would matter that I hadn't meant to—I didn't think anyone would believe me.

And then I heard gravel crunching behind me and turned to see the figure of a man approaching. Not just a man—the Wolf. I would have recognized his cowboy swagger anywhere. He looked like he was on his way to a shootout, and I was his foe. I was sure that Yevgeny had told them everything, and the Wolf had come to get me.

"Creepy, isn't it?" he asked as he settled at my side, looking up at the statue of the Capitoline Wolf with her engorged teats, the strange human children lit eerily from below.

"You all right?" he asked when I didn't respond.

I nodded—I didn't feel able to speak—and then he said, "Now, everyone back at the party is saying what a good American you are—'That Teddy Shepard, she must really hate the Reds,' they're saying, the way you went running. We thought you were gonna be sick!"

I think I managed a weak laugh, and then the Wolf added, "Either that, or you're sick for another reason."

He was eyeing me with his steely blue gaze, and I felt something curdling inside me, the deep fear that he had found me out, until he asked, "You're not pregnant, are you? It'd be a shame to lose you just when we found you—don't know who else we could get to do such a good job with the art, you know."

When I shook my head and said, "No, not pregnant," he grinned, and reached a hand out to touch my arm, letting it slide down to my side, and said, "You know, I think I would miss having you around the place."

And then I heard the popping sound of gunfire, of shots fired all in a row, and the sky above the trees was suddenly ablaze and the cracking, booming sound grew louder, closer, and I must have jumped, and maybe screamed, because the Wolf had his arms around me then, rubbing my back, saying, "Fireworks, darling, it's only fireworks."

I wanted to say I knew that, and I was startled, that was all, but I couldn't, because then his mouth was on mine, and I was folding backward, and his hand was on my leg, under my dress, and the lights in the sky were blinding. The flash of the fireworks was too close—I couldn't see—and I felt that I wasn't the Teddy I was supposed to be, at all, and that something else had taken over.

"Happy Fourth, Teddy," the Wolf whispered into my ear as he held me, and then he was gone again, walking away, saying, "I need to go make an appearance; they keep telling me I'm the man of the hour."

He turned back to face me when he was a bit farther down the path and said, "We'll finish this later," grinning, and I shivered a little, even though it was sweltering. Even with the sweat pooling under the arms of my once-perfect red dress, darkening half-moons of fabric to the color of old blood.

And then he was gone, back to the colder air of the electric fans by the glowing white tents, to the crowd of revelers now smiling, applauding, at the flashes in the sky.

It was dark out there in the garden, with only the faint, eerie lights below the statues to guide my way, so I might have missed the man behind the cypress trees if it hadn't been for the occasional illumination from the fireworks.

But I managed to see, in a burst of blue and red light, a slim figure in a dark suit sneaking toward the villa's front gate, tiptoeing over the grass away from the gravel path.

Around his neck, a silver accordion camera glinted, catching light from the sky.

And I was back on the Mine Train roller coaster once again. But I hadn't been at the Ace Hotel and Saloon, at that final drop before the finish, after all. I'd only been at the second peak, the Rock Crusher. I'd only felt the second drop, and now here was the third.

14. Villa Borghese

Friday, July 4, 1969

I followed the photographer all the way to the Villa Taverna's front gate, avoiding the party with its brass band and tents lest someone see me and call out, or wonder where I was going.

There wasn't time to bid anyone farewell—I would have to tell them, later, that I'd been sick. That this was the reason I'd run away to begin with, not that I had seen a man from my past—and, well actually, I didn't have time to worry about him now.

Anyway, it wasn't necessarily a lie that I was sick—there was a rising panic in my belly that felt like nausea threatening to erupt.

Because there was no way to know if the man had gotten us on film or not—I wasn't certain, after all, that the blinding flash had been his camera as opposed to one of the fireworks—and now I would only find out after it was too late. Tomorrow, or in two days, maybe three, there it would be in the papers and the tabloids. *Ecco*, the American ambassador with an unidentified woman. Only I wouldn't be unidentified for long, and then what?

I followed the man with his dark suit and camera out through the Villa Taverna's front gate and thought for a moment that the Marines would stop him before I realized that of course, they didn't know.

We walked at a brisk pace, my photographer and I, down the viale Gioacchino Rossini to the gates of the Villa Borghese, and then into the park.

171

We walked past the entrance to the Bioparco, the famous zoo with its miserable, ailing elephants that you could pay to let your children ride on a Saturday, with its mangy wolves and listless llamas—their enormous dark eyes always looked wet, to me, like they were holding back tears.

If it had been a normal evening, I might have found the beauty of the Borghese park at night to be soothing. The plane trees and laurels and holly oaks, the canopy of green against the depth of the dark sky, the sheer scale of such a lush and living space. The way it smelled so sweet, like pine needles; the color of it. I knew people in Dallas who used to spray-paint the dead, bleached grass of their lawns green in the summer, it got so hot and dry. Compared to that, the Borghese in July was a miracle. But that night, the sight of all that foliage—it felt like the green was closing in on me, and the air seemed to me to be full of the sicklier sweetness of decay. I thought of the forest of angry trees in *The Wizard of Oz*, which had been my favorite movie for a while, when I was small. I imagined the gnarled old oaks of the Borghese watching me, hating me.

I followed my photographer, staying several paces behind, going as quietly as I could in my silver Dior heels, onward through the park. Trying to walk silently over the grass instead of on the pavement, trying not to stumble over the rolling terrain. We passed Casina Valadier, which was still alive with revelers and glowing like a fairy-tale cottage in the dark forest, beckoning me. All I wanted was to be one of them, the people on the terrace of that beautiful place, listening to the music of Armando Zingone's orchestra, with a husband's loving hand on my arm.

I knew if I couldn't fix this tonight, right now, that the night David and I had spent together on that terrace was the only time we would ever be happy. It spurred me onward to think of the loss of it—the life I wanted, the one that was nearly within my grasp.

I didn't understand then that it never would be. That there would always be something behind me, some secret barreling down the road to knock me flat. In that moment, I thought if I could just take back the previous half-hour or so, if I could just keep going as I had been and convince David I deserved children, a house, a Labrador, then even if one of the cans I'd kicked down the road did come back to get me, I would be heavy enough that it wouldn't be able to bowl me over. Aunt Sister's problem had always been that she didn't have enough tethering her to the ground.

I tracked the photographer all the way through the park and down the precarious, worn stone steps that led into the piazza del Popolo, nearly falling a number of times in my efforts to do so quickly, quietly.

An Egyptian obelisk sat puncturing the sky from the center of the piazza, brought back to the city by Caesar Augustus two thousand years earlier, along with the corpse of Cleopatra, which he paraded through the streets. They used to hold public executions there, in the old days.

I began to feel that the city was taunting me; the Borghese gardens, of course, had once been the Gardens of Lucullus, in ancient days, and it was hard not to think of Messalina, the wife of Claudius, who was executed there among the greenery on her husband's orders. She was said to have taken whole hosts of senators and soldiers as her lovers, poisoning the ones who refused her. Her name was chiseled from history after her murder, her sculptures reduced to marble shards.

It may seem convenient that I passed through those places on that particular day, those monuments to the deaths of wicked women, but it would have been the same if I'd followed the photographer on any other route through Rome. The city has always been strewn with them, poisoners and seductresses, witches. And now I had joined that ill-fated sisterhood.

173

In another part of the city, I might have walked by the Vatican with its Borgia apartments, where the infamous Lucrezia used to visit her father while he was pope. They said Lucrezia had a little diamond ring, one she could slide the top from to deftly dump poison powder into a rival's glass unseen. I could have passed a statue of Livia Drusilla, the overbearing, scheming, prosecco-swilling wife of Augustus—at least if you believed Tacitus's account of her. Livia and Lucrezia died natural deaths, but their legacies lumped them firmly in with Messalina and Cleopatra and all of the other hags and sorceresses and succubi who had walked—or been carted—through these streets.

With all the carvings and paintings and statuary in Rome, it's easy to become convinced, if you're already so inclined, that signs are everywhere. That the city has something to tell you. You could begin to believe, if you wanted to, that Neptune or satyrs or eagles—or, like me, lucky palm trees—had become a kind of totem for you, and every time you passed a statue of one or a fresco or a fountain, you would think that some day of destiny was getting closer, either the day that your life would change for the better, if you believed in good luck, or the day of your doom, if you were like me. Which is to say, I wanted to see evil women brought low in every corner, just then. I wanted to see the wages of my sin, and so I did.

We passed Bar Rosati at the edge of the piazza and the sight of more people enjoying their evening, dining on *fritto misto* and caprese salad under bright awnings, conversing with their friends, tormented me; but not for long, because I had to keep moving. My photographer was striding onward.

I never approached him, not once, on our flight through the city; I had it in my mind that if I tried, he would run away. As I followed him through the streets of Rome, first tiptoeing in my heels and then, when they became too painful, barefoot, I thought he would be afraid of me, for some reason, if he saw me. By the time we reached his doorstep an hour and a half later, when he finally stopped walking at an old apartment block in Testaccio, I was breathless and sweating, with bleeding, bare feet, and when I confronted him, he very nearly was afraid.

He couldn't place me right away; I suppose if you take photos all day long, the faces start to blur together. I recognized him, though—I'd only seen the back of him as I rushed after him across Rome, this shadowy figure I was doomed to chase, but as soon as he turned, I knew it was the same man I'd seen by the light of the fireworks. The same handsome face; the narrow cheekbones, the soft mouth.

When I explained the situation to him—that I thought he might accidentally have taken a photo of me, and that I'd very much like to see it—and when it dawned on him that he'd seen me in the garden at the Villa Taverna, and further, when he took in my Valentino dress and my Paco Rabanne purse (which had left a red welt on my shoulder where the strap had dug in; the bag was meant to be left on the table at a party while you danced with your husband, not dragged all over Rome in pursuit of the man who'd caught your infidelity on camera) and, despite their sorry state, the Dior shoes in my hand, he invited me in. He could already see the dollar signs, I suppose.

He let me wash my feet with a towel and soap from his sink, and then he poured me a little glass of Amaro del Capo and gave me an espresso cup for an ashtray and went to work, talking all the while, sometimes in English, sometimes in Italian. He told me his name was Mauro, and that he would be happy to help me.

15. Testaccio

Early Morning, Saturday, July 5, 1969

It smelled like hell in Mauro's apartment, and it looked like it, too. I mean that literally: he was fussing around at the sink with whatever sulfurous chemicals he used for developing photographs, and the only light in the whole flat came from a single bulb covered in red cellophane. Mauro had explained that this was necessary to process the film, but as far as I could tell it served mainly to cast a satanic glow all around the room. He had enormous, blown-up photos of nude women on all the walls—I assumed he had taken them himself, I assumed it was "art"—and their bodies looked grotesque, demonic in that dim, stinking cave of an apartment.

He was taking his time with the negatives, really dragging his feet, so I sat there for hours in the dark at his little café table, sipping Amaro until I felt sick and chain-smoking and listening to him talk about the art of photography in his emphatic, accented English.

The Huntley Foundation was once offered a minor work by Hieronymus Bosch depicting Jesus Christ's descent into hell; I'd lobbied for it, but the family had ultimately rejected it, on account of how bizarre and profane it was. Uncle Hal had called it Catholic nonsense and said we could never invite anyone from Highland Park Methodist over again if we had a painting like that on the wall. I could picture the strange headless monsters and ghostly creepy-crawlies that populated its oily black rivers and flaming pits; I could imagine them prodding at me with their pitchforks and horns, here in Mauro's awful red room.

Up until the very moment that he turned the lights back on and hung the finished photos to dry on the line, I was hoping that it might all still be fine. I might walk away from this disgusting flat never to return, I might go home and take off my makeup with Pond's cold cream, apply my Hungarian serums—the same ones Marilyn Monroe used to use, I'd read in *Woman's Day*—and get some rest. I might tidy the apartment over the weekend and be ready for David when he returned from his trip on Monday in time for my birthday party on Tuesday, and he would come back and be so pleased with my progress that he would agree it was time to finally start a family, and I would then be so immersed in a real life, my own life, that they couldn't take me out of it the way they had Aunt Sister.

Of course, I had conveniently forgotten about Yevgeny Larin, for the moment, or at least I understood instinctively that the threat of his presence in Rome was of a lower order of magnitude than a potential photo of me with the Wolf.

That's what I thought, anyway.

"Well," Mauro finally said, quietly, and I stood from the table to join him in front of the photographs dripping from their clips.

"Here you are," he said.

He was perfectly polite about it; I'll give him that. He sounded as if he, too, wished it wasn't so.

There, in between snapshots of various glossy so-and-so's leaving Harry's Bar or sitting with aperitivos at outdoor tables on the via Veneto, and a few pictures of the revelers at the Villa Taverna party, was a photo of the American ambassador with his hand up the skirt of a thirtysomething blonde, his mouth on hers.

The blonde, of course, was me. Mauro could guess, I think, from my reaction, that the ambassador was not my husband, and that I was not his wife.

I felt a familiar sharpness in my chest, and saliva pooling in the back corners of my mouth, and my head began to feel like it was vibrating, flashbulbs going off in front of my eyes. I barely made it to the shared lavatory in the hall in time to vomit into the toilet and not on myself. On my stupid red party dress, the one I'd bought specially for tonight because I'd thought it looked like the woman I wanted to be. Or like the future, I suppose, elegant and refined and promising, which is how it had felt for me, at least for a little while.

When all the canapés from the party at the residence, and the Amaro and the champagne, had been ejected from my person, I stood and wiped my mouth and examined my face in the cracked, spotted mirror. I looked as I should, I thought. The way they would all see me once the photo came out. Dark hollows around my eyes, makeup smeared beneath. Eyelids sticking when I blinked, the lashes gunked together. New creases at the edges signaling that I was too old for youthful indiscretions, too old to pretend this was just an adventure. Everything else pale, dry, flaking away, except the wet pink mouth like a gash across my face. If I breathed through my nose, I knew I would vomit again, so I let my jaw hang open. They would see this, all of it, and they would hate me.

They would be right. What could I say to defend myself when they would see the truth on my face? I could already picture them before me, bearing down on me, and how could I argue with them? David's face, his anger. My mother on the phone, saying, Teddy, what a disgrace. Teddy, you're *ugly*. Uncle Hal wouldn't even speak to me, probably, but I could imagine him with my mother on the back porch of the house on Beverly, discussing what was to be done about me.

And no matter what came next—though I could see it, David kicking me out of the apartment, the sad, sweaty flight home from Ciampino, the silence and shame from my family, the inevitable hiding away—no matter what, there would also, always, be this photo. For the rest of my life, for anyone who wanted to see, proof pinned and labeled of a wanton woman with her fat thigh exposed in the middle of Rome.

I returned to Mauro's flat, to the rickety little table where he'd now laid the incriminating photo out for me to study, and swished some more Amaro around in my mouth. Swallowed it—why not?

"Don't worry," Mauro said, as I wiped away the makeup that had crusted under my watering eyes, "you look beautiful."

The funny thing is, he was right. Even on a bad day, the structure of my face was that of a beauty. The planes of my cheekbones, the arch of my brow. My jaw was a bit big for a woman's, maybe, and the dimpled chin could've read as masculine, but it had worked on Marilyn, hadn't it? And wasn't it lovely on Brigitte? I had the scaffolding of elegance; it was only the flesh—aging, beginning to sag, and now peppered around the eyes with burst blood vessels from being sick—that proved the lie. That revealed what I really was.

I eyed Mauro to see if there was anything behind his comment, to see if maybe he was offering a way out of this. Something I could trade. But as far as I could tell he'd meant it only as a kindness, and, perhaps secondarily, as a fact. He was watching me passively, waiting.

"What are you going to do with it?" I asked hoarsely. My throat raw, acidic. I thought I tasted blood.

"Well," Mauro said slowly, pushing the photo around the table with the tips of his fingers, straightening it and then mussing it again, not looking at me now. "It's a beautiful photo, you know. Such passion. Like a dance."

When I didn't say anything, he went on. "*Gente* will pay three hundred thousand for a photo like this."

Even knowing he meant lira, not dollars, I gasped. I couldn't help it. That was almost five hundred US.

"Why, though? There's no one famous in it. Who would care?"

179

He laughed at that.

"Oh, everyone knows Warren Carey. *One Week on the Rio Grande?*" He whistled a series of low, eerie notes—the theme from the film.

Mauro's reaction didn't surprise me, though I'd harbored some hope he somehow wouldn't know. Ambassador Carey hadn't acted in over a decade—at least not in the movies, as he liked to joke—so I'd thought there was a chance. But of course, Mauro knew the whole story: Warren Carey, Hollywood star turned politician. The silver screen cowboy gone to Washington. And the Italians loved cowboys—I'd gone to see *Once Upon a Time in the West* at the Inwood Theater alone in the days before my wedding, and you'd be forgiven if you couldn't believe that the director was born in Rome, not South Dakota or somewhere.

"Maybe I could buy the photo from you," I suggested, as if it had only just occurred to me. As if I didn't already know exactly what was about to happen here.

"Maybe so," he said, still not meeting my eyes. "But it might be expensive."

"How much?"

"As I said, *Gente* will pay three hundred thousand, and I think this is more important to you. One million."

The number was enough to make me feel ill again. In dollars, it was only about sixteen hundred, but that was still all the money David gave me in a month, and then some, and anyway, I was already through July's. He'd even given me extra, and still, I'd spent it. I'd spent most of it on this stupid dress, and the damn chainmail bag, and now there was no way to get more before August without asking David. Or my mother, or Uncle Hal, but I couldn't do that without them calling David, and he would know there was nothing I really needed that cost that much, and the whole thing would unravel. It wasn't even a lot of money, when you thought about it, for someone like me, to solve a problem like this, but somehow, I still didn't have it. Frivolous Teddy, stupid Teddy, with her expensive clothes, her couture dress, and no way to pay the piper.

Even after we finally got my inheritance after my birthday on Tuesday (and it would take quite a while after that, anyway—"An unbelievable amount of paperwork," Daddy had said), everything would have David's name on it. I might as well not have it at all, for all that I'd be able to spend it without his knowing.

"Could I write you a check?" I asked. "Make it out to cash?"

David would notice the withdrawal eventually, but maybe I could come up with something before then. Some reason for the missing money that didn't involve buying a photo of myself getting fondled by David's boss, for example. Or maybe I could find money to cover it some other way in the time between now and then. It wouldn't be stealing, exactly; it was the account we'd put Uncle Hal's check into, so it was partly mine, anyway, even if David's name was on it. I could figure it out, I just needed Mauro to agree to take the check right now and let me leave with the photo.

And the negative—if I'd learned anything from mysteries and spy films, and you might not agree that I had if you'd seen the clumsy way I tailed Mauro to his flat from the Villa Taverna, it was that you always needed the negatives. I could already picture myself returning triumphantly home with that terrible glossy photo, with the strip of negatives clutched in my fist. The crisp edges cutting into my hand, drawing blood, but I wouldn't care. I'd light them both on fire and make a wish, and then be done with it, and nobody would ever have to know.

I already had my checkbook out on the table. It usually pleased me to see it—the powder blue paper, my name in silver. The heavy fountain pen and the way it rested on the flesh between my long, elegant forefinger and my thumb. The weight of it in my hand.

Mauro shook his head at me. He didn't care how beautiful the checks were, how beautifully I could write them.

"No, I won't go to a bank," he said. "One million in bills, please."

Please, he said. He really was very polite. It was one of the things that made him frightening: he knew he had me by the neck, the whole time, so there was never any need to be rude.

"I'll need a day or two to get the money."

He sighed. "*Gente* pays in cash, on the spot. You can have until Sunday, then I have to sell it. You understand. You'll find a way to get the money. You're very . . . determined."

I suppose I had made him a little nervous, arriving at his doorstep like that. Stalking him through the city.

I pretty much knew, at that point, what I would have to do to get the money, though I hated the thought of it, and I still held out hope that some other idea would come to me. I didn't spend too much time, in the moment, mourning the person I had thought just that morning I was going to be. That strong, confident woman. Now I just wanted to go back to normal, to being David's wife and whatever was required of her. Waking up early, watching her figure, taking her pills. I would leave parties early for the rest of my life if I could get through this. I would wear sweaters when it was a hundred degrees in the shade.

"All right," I told him. "One million."

I stood from the table, lightheaded. I hadn't eaten in hours, just drunk the Amaro, and most of that was in the bowl of the toilet in the foul, green-tiled lavatory now.

"Who are they?" I asked, gesturing at the nude women on the walls. I had forgotten to ask earlier.

"Eh?" He seemed startled by the question. "Oh, *le mie signore*. They're just models," he said, after a pause, "artist's models." Then added, "I don't only photograph movie stars, you know. But it pays the bills."

"Just until you make it as a famous artist," I said, and it sounded as cruel as I'd meant it to be.

He only shrugged. "Something like that. You'll come back Sunday with the money? At night. Nine o'clock, maybe."

"I will."

Mauro walked me to the door, gave me a piece of paper with his address on it in case I forgot, and a phone number I could reach him at, he said, if I left a message. There wasn't a phone in the flat, but he didn't bother explaining whose phone the number would connect me to. He handed me the photo, too.

"Keep it," he said. "A memento."

I was shaking as I walked down the stairs of the apartment building, still woozy from the dark red room, from the smell of sulfur, from being sick.

At first, the cooler air of the world outside soothed me, and I drank in the comforting scent of exhaust from delivery trucks trundling around the corners. The sound of birdsong. But then I remembered that these were signs of morning, and it was already starting to grow light. I hadn't slept, and I needed a bath, and there were no taxis out at this hour, so I'd have to walk all the way to Trastevere, back to our little flat. I'd have to do it in my shoes the whole way, this time, because there were people out and about now who would see me if I went barefoot. Bad enough that they would catch me in last night's dress, my silly scarlet chiffon, now sweat-stained and reeking of sulfur and smoke. They wouldn't know the details, but they'd be able to see it, that I hadn't been home. They would be able to infer a number of possibilities for what that meant, none of them good.

I stopped for another cigarette by the meat market further down Mauro's street, standing on a raised cobblestone to avoid the puddles of water that stood red and rancid from the butchers sluicing down their storefronts. Flies buzzed hideously, waiting for more. The smoke burned my throat and I coughed but kept sucking at it, all the way down to the filter.

I walked past the famous mountain of shards, Monte Testaccio. I passed the remains of the Porticus Aemilia, those ancient arches that stood crumbling in the middle of modern Rome like bones, like the fossil of some great dinosaur's spine. I passed the old walls that used to mark the edge of the city, fortified by Pope Paul III in the sixteenth century, the same pope who'd hired Michelangelo to finish painting the Sistine Chapel and take over the design of St. Peter's. I walked all the way home, stopping once to vomit again at the edge of the piazza dell'Emporio, arriving outside our flat just as the sky turned the cold blue color it does right before the sun begins to rise.

My Aunt Sister used to have a perfume named after that time of morning. Or night, depending on who you were asking. L'Heure Bleue, by Guerlain. Sad violets, as she described it, and she said she still wore it even though it was almost discontinued and you could only buy it in Paris, because it reminded her of a night she spent at Vaux-le-Vicomte with some OSS boys after the war, when they lined the gardens of the ruined château with white candles in tins and stayed up all night working through the wine cellar until dawn. It's hard to know if that was one of the true ones or not, or somewhere in between. Uncle Hal used to call them Sissy Stories, before she disappeared. Before he and my mother stopped talking about their little sister entirely.

I only saw her once after that, and only because my mother wanted to make a point. This is what can happen. This is how it ends if you're not careful. The room smelling of bleach and bad breath, the sticky surface of the card table. Aunt Sister's vacant eyes, the slack mouth gaping toothless—the removal of molars an intervention, the doctors had explained, to preempt later decay.

That time of morning always made me nervous. It was the color of not being where you're supposed to be. Of being out in the world when you should be tucked safely in bed. It inspired in me that old child's fear that you're about to be caught.

There was no one home in our flat, and David wouldn't be back for days, I knew, but still I thought, I'm about to be in trouble.

When I got to our street in Trastevere, I stopped at the apartment building's entrance like I always did, to give Beppo a little scratch. I would bring him some tuna later when I thought of it. I wondered who would feed him when I was gone. When I couldn't find the money, and Mauro sold the picture to *Gente* and they published it, and then the American papers picked it up, and David left me, and I had no job and no money, so I had to go home, and then I didn't know what my mother and Uncle Hal would do, but it seemed inevitable that I would be sitting there with Aunt Sister, in the end.

I had only been gone since six the evening before, but the apartment seemed musty when I opened the door, as if it had been shut up and the furniture draped in sheets for months, maybe years. I remembered reading something about Egyptian tombs in a *National Geographic* or a *Reader's Digest*, about how the explorers who opened them said they contained the air of the old world, air that hadn't been tasted since the pharaohs. The little flat was full of it, the scent of the world before: a world where I was getting ready for my party and doing my makeup, a world in which I thought things were going to be easy, and that I would have fun.

I managed to brush my teeth and throw my dirty dress on a pile of laundry on the floor before I crawled into the unmade bed. At least I managed that. I'd planned to get up early and get some laundry done. I'd planned to organize the apartment over the weekend before David came home on Monday.

But of course I forgot to set an alarm, and anyway, it didn't matter. It wouldn't make a difference if I cleaned the place top to bottom, hung all my dresses in the wardrobe where they belonged, folded my nightgowns, and ironed my underwear. David would be able to smell it, I knew. The air in the apartment. That everything had changed.

Now

Early Morning, Wednesday, July 9, 1969

"Now, hold on a second," Reggie says, and has his hand out in a gesture that means "Stop."

I do as I'm told. My glass is empty again, but I make no move to refill it.

Arthur Hildebrand shakes his gray head at Reggie and says, "Evans, just let her tell it. Let her go."

Hildebrand unscrews the cap from the bourbon bottle and pours more in my glass.

"Do you want any ice?" he asks, and I nod.

Archie brings a handful back from the kitchen and drops the cubes one, two, three into my glass, where they crackle and hiss in the amber liquid.

"Go on, now, Teddy," Arthur Hildebrand says, and so I do.

16. Trastevere, Ludovisi

Saturday, July 5, 1969

I didn't sleep for long; in fact, I'm not sure I really slept at all. But the clatter of pots and pans in the kitchen—Teresa; I had forgotten she was coming to prepare everything for David's return—finally roused me around eight, and I went out in my dressing gown to ask her to leave. David was still gone, there was no point in cleaning, now, and I needed to be alone.

Teresa looked at me and muttered something in Italian that I didn't understand, maybe because I gave up on my lessons too early or, more likely, because Signora Falasca would never have taught me whatever derogatory comments about slothful sluts Teresa was whispering; I didn't need to check a mirror to know that there was makeup all over my face, bags under my eyes, and a rat's nest in my hair.

I asked her to leave, and she asked for her salary, and I knew she meant the extra money I customarily paid her to stay away, but I didn't have it. I was sitting at the kitchen table by then, with my pounding head propped up in my hands, and so I said, "I'll pay you later," and added Teresa to my running list of creditors to account for. As soon as she shut—maybe slammed would be more accurate—the front door, I found a pack of cigarettes I'd hidden in a cupboard and lit one. David hated smoking, hated the smell of it, but I really didn't think, under the circumstances, that it was the worst thing I could do.

I knew, obviously, that I needed to tell the Wolf about the photograph. I needed to ask him for help. But I spent hours that morning trying to think if there was another way out. I didn't want him to see me as someone weak and small; I wanted to be in command of myself.

I had already spent July's money, but I thought perhaps I could borrow from someone, maybe several someones, to pay Mauro, but then of course I would have to hand everything David gave me next month over to everyone I needed to pay back.

It made me sick to think about it—to figure out how I would have to move things around to make this work, how I would get through the month without anyone realizing how little I had left. If they did, it was only a hop, skip, and a jump to everyone finding out about the photo of me and the ambassador, and from there it was just a slip and a fall to all the way down. I could tell Anna and the officers' wives that I was doing my own hair because I enjoyed it, or because I didn't have time to go to the salon. I could skip luncheons and say I was watching my figure.

Maybe I could borrow from Anna, or Kitty, and somehow manage to pay them back when I finally got my inheritance. Maybe somehow when that happened, I'd be able to use some of it without David watching me. Maybe something else would happen, and it would all be fine. Maybe tomorrow will be different, maybe a miracle will come if I just make it through a few more hours, another day, another week. This kind of thinking is, I suppose, how I made it all the way to thirty-four without even coming close to marriage, until I finally met someone as determined as David.

I considered for a moment that maybe I could ask David for an advance on next month's allowance. It would be mortifying, and he might say no, and at best he would sigh and say I was spoiled, I was childish, and where does it all go, Teddy, really, despite your upbringing you must know that money doesn't grow on trees, but at least if I asked him, it would still just be that I had spent too much that month because I was foolish, not because anything was really wrong. If I asked my family before David, they would investigate, and start pulling on threads, and the fragile filaments of my life as a real person, the delicate lace of it, would come undone completely. Anything, even David's disdain, was better than asking Mama or Uncle Hal. Anything was better than that picture in the tabloids, in the papers.

I finished another cigarette and left my head in my hands for a while, thinking about nothing at all because it was all too much, and then eventually, because I had no choice, I started my day.

Sort of: I didn't bathe, just took one of the stay-awake pills, washed it down with tepid water from the toothbrush mug, and got dressed.

I found something in my wardrobe that I could wear to the embassy, because of course that was always, ultimately, where I was going to go, to try to catch the Wolf in his lair, alone in the office on a Saturday because he liked the peace and quiet. I settled on a blue dress—the one I'd worn in Capri, actually, that clueless David had suggested I wear to that first dinner at the residence. It had been all wrong for that party, but I had looked nice in it, and I needed to, today. I paired it with sandals and my straw purse from Capri, and I thought I looked about as good as could be expected, under the circumstances.

I moved the incriminating photo from last night's chainmail bag (and felt a lurch of shame at how flamboyant the bag was, how expensive, how much of my monthly allowance had gone toward it) to the straw one. It seemed safer than leaving it in the other bag or hiding it somewhere in the apartment; at least this way, I would know where it was, even if it meant walking around all day with my albatross around my neck. Or over my shoulder, rather.

And then I left for the embassy on foot. I always liked walking in Rome, when it wasn't at dawn with a salacious photo in my pocket and a sword hanging over my head. When I wasn't in my party dress from the night before walking on bloody, aching feet. They were still raw and red from the previous evening, but I had picked at the bubbled-up blisters until their clear fluid was released, so it wasn't that painful to walk in my sandals. The straps rubbed at the raw flesh, sometimes, but it wasn't so bad, all things considered.

The Marines let me past when I reached the Palazzo Margherita, and I wondered again at the fact that this could be happening to me, to the Wolf, and they simply didn't know. That we, the Wolf and I, were in danger.

I went to the chancery building first, to try to find the Wolf, but George (or more properly, Giorgio), the guard at the desk in the main hall, said he'd stepped out. I said thank you, I'll wait in my office in the New Wing, but then I noticed that George was reading the newspaper, and I felt my stomach lurch as I recalled that David read the paper every day, religiously, and so the second something scandalous appeared about me, the moment Mauro gave up on me and took the photo to *Gente*, David would find out.

George flicked his newspaper out with a sound like thunder, like a gunshot, and said, "Hey, Teddy, look!"

He spread the open pages over his desk, and I walked with a stone in my heart to where he sat, to see what I was certain would be Mauro's photo of me with the ambassador. I didn't need to check the photo in my purse to remember what it looked like; I would have seen it in my sleep, if I'd had time to really sleep.

The ambassador leaning down toward me. My head back, eyes closed, as if in ecstasy. It was only a moment—it hadn't really been like that at all, not that anyone would believe me. The ambassador's hand never made it past mid-thigh, the kiss was only a few seconds, but none of that would matter once everyone saw it. "It wasn't really like that" doesn't hold a lot of water, you know.

In the paper, though, there was just a photo of my Uncle Hal standing on the steps of the Capitol building, alongside an article about how Senator Huntley of Texas objected to President Nixon's withdrawal of troops from Vietnam, calling it cowardly and suggesting that he would fix it, if he were in the president's shoes. That he would not abandon the brave people of Vietnam to their fate at the hands of the Communists.

"Oh," I said. "Uncle Hal."

I doubted Hal cared one way or the other about what happened to the people of Vietnam, but he would never miss an opportunity to get attention, and approval, if he sensed one. Even if it meant taking a swing at the president, a member of his own party.

Uncle Hal fought dirty, and he was proud of it. I once heard a girl at school say her father had told her that my uncle couldn't take a single step without spittin' in your eye, and when I asked Hal about it, he laughed.

He laughed at Strom Thurmond, too, when he filibustered the Civil Rights Act in '57. "Look at him, shooting from the hip," Hal said. Hal never shouted out loud about desegregation, or about anything else, but then when the act passed even though Hal had quietly voted against it, Pastor Carson was suddenly sporting a shiny new watch and preaching at First Baptist about how the apocalypse was upon us, and the editor of the *Dallas Morning News* just happened to buy a new house the week after he ran an opinion piece about the government overstepping its bounds.

Hal didn't go to meet Lyndon B. Johnson in Dallas on the campaign trail in 1960, but a lot of people on his payroll were there with signs saying LBJ had sold his soul to the devil. I didn't think Hal had anything to do with Kennedy's assassination, but I wouldn't have put it past him. He hated Jack, and his brother Robert. He never believed the rumors that Kennedy had slept with Marilyn Monroe: "A woman like that? That boy wouldn't know what to do with her."

In '58, a liberal lawyer named George Powell gave Hal a run for his money for the Senate seat—the Democrats were gaining every year—and then somehow, suddenly, there was talk in the city that Powell was a known philanderer.

He was probably never unfaithful a day in his life, everyone knew his wife ran roughshod over him, but there was a story going around that Powell had been seen at the Petroleum Club with a Braniff stewardess, a redhead, getting far too friendly for a married man.

I knew that redhead; she was one of Uncle Hal's. She eventually married a plastic surgeon who worked over on Knox and moved into a duplex in Highland Park; she's still there, as far as I know, with a couple of redheaded kids, though I think the surgeon was eventually lost to a younger nurse.

Once my initial panic had passed, I realized it wasn't even possible for Mauro's photo to be in today's paper—it had only been developed a few hours ago. It felt like a stay of execution to see Uncle Hal's frowning face there, instead, and I dug my fingernails into my palms and said a little prayer, and renewed my commitment to fixing things. To keeping everything as normal and as pleasant as possible, just until I could get Mauro his money and then everything could actually *be* normal and pleasant again, and David would never come home to a messy apartment, and I would never do anything, ever again, that could be considered less than upstanding. I would never do anything, I decided, that I wouldn't want the whole world to see.

I had made some version of these vows before, but this time, with so much more on the line than David's general displeasure at my sloppiness, I really meant it. I meant it so much I went to the ladies' room and took another stay-awake, just to make sure I had enough pep in my step to keep everything bright and cheery while I saw it all through.

When I passed George's desk again, I asked if he was finished with his paper and he said, "Sure, go ahead," so I grabbed it and flipped through as I walked over to the New Wing, just to make sure. But there was nothing there. No photos of me. Just a frowning Uncle Hal and what I assumed, based on the photo and a headline about "*la luna*," to be an article about the upcoming mission to the moon.

I smiled at the men in the Pointdexter Room as I walked by; they ignored me.

I walked the rest of the way down the hall and unlocked the door to 33-B, my cave of wonders, of old file boxes and abandoned office furniture. I had no plan for what to do once I was in my office; I suppose I'd thought I could just sit and wait, and let my mind run. I knew there was no way I'd be able to focus on actual work.

It was too cluttered in there, anyway; there were stacks of documents and books all around the room that seemed to grow by the day as my initial research missives to various libraries and museums around Italy were answered, and though I had attacked the first to arrive with gusto, it became difficult to keep up with all the information coming in. I had catalogues of gifts received by every cardinal in Rome from the seventeenth century onward; I had inventories of art collections belonging to all the first families of Italy. Eventually, I would have to sit down and scan through every page, looking for any mention of the artworks in the building, but I never seemed to find the time. It wasn't that I didn't want to do the work, or that I didn't care about finding answers—I don't know what it was, actually.

It looked a bit disorderly, having those stacks of papers and piles of books. It looked careless. I supposed that was something else they would write, in the articles on how horrid I was, the ones that would eventually sit next to articles about Uncle Hal and the moon, once the photo was published if I couldn't get the money from the Wolf. Or once they found out about Yevgeny Larin—I didn't know who "they" were, or in which order these revelations would occur, but all my fears had compounded, and all I could think was that they were going to have plenty to say, the tabloids and newspapers, and none of it would be good.

Perhaps that sounds grandiose—who cares, after all, about a housewife from Dallas? But the Wolf mattered, and while we weren't the Kennedys, people did pay attention to what the Huntleys did. I imagined hungry reporters flying to Texas to speak to everyone who ever knew me, to learn just how rotten I really was. Would they speak to girls at grade school I'd been cruel to? Would they interview a professor whose class I had barely passed? Would they find men I'd known before David, men I'd spent a furtive night with and then never seen again, thinking that once they were out of my sight, they would be out of my life, forever?

I couldn't imagine a single person who would have anything good to say about me. Or they might say, "She was generally very polite," or "She was mostly a dedicated student," but it would be in the past tense, because everyone would believe I was the woman in that photo, nothing more, and it wouldn't matter what was real or had been, before. I'd seen it with Aunt Sister, after she fell apart. Suddenly everyone in the family had seen it coming, had said that she had always been out of control, and the smallest moments were picked apart as proof of her inevitable doom. The hungry journalists would find out about her, too, even though Uncle Hal had kept it out of the papers at the time, and they would write that I was just like her: mad, sick.

"There she is," I heard from the doorway, and I was relieved at the sight of the Wolf, in spite of all the trouble he had gotten me into, or that we had gotten into together, because I knew that soon

I wouldn't be alone in this. As embarrassing as it would be to ask for help, I had the feeling that out of anyone, the Wolf would be able to fix this. I could hear the twanging theme music of *One Week on the Rio Grande* in my head as he crossed the room, my cowboy, my savior.

But then he slipped a hand around my waist, and I yanked my body away from his grip, stepping quickly around a stack of file boxes to put them between us.

"Whoa, there!"

The Wolf talked like a cowboy, sometimes. It was one of the things that caused David and the other officers to roll their eyes, but I didn't mind it. I understood it; if I had played a hero in the movies, I would want to be him in real life, too. I needed him now, anyway. The Wolf from the movies. The cowboy. The priest to exorcise my demons.

"What's going on?" he asked.

"I can't . . ." I began, and then tried, "Well, last night—"

"Teddy," the Wolf interrupted. Stepped forward, bypassing the boxes and taking each of my hands into one of his. They were long-fingered, the skin dry and delicate for a man's. David's hands were wide and damp, the nails thick in their beds.

"It's all right. No one can see us."

He leaned toward me for a kiss, but I pulled back once again.

"That's not it. We can't—"

"Can't what? This is nothing. It's less than nothing. I'll be back in Washington soon enough, and you're young, you'll start a family soon, and we'll both forget it as soon as it's over. We'll hardly even notice it happened. So, let's just *enjoy* each other."

He was wheedling, pleading, speaking in that soft, low voice of his, the way you'd talk to a nervous horse. If they hadn't been political enemies, I remember thinking, Uncle Hal would have liked that about him.

The way the Wolf said *enjoy* made the back of my neck tingle, but the rest of it—*we'll forget it as soon as it's over*—wasn't true at all. I would obsess, I would be frightened, I would be ill, if I actually went through with it. The octopus would take up permanent residence in my chest; I imagined my entire insides like an aquarium, or maybe a shipwreck, with my ribs coated in barnacles eating at the bone. I could feel a sharp pain there, actually—perhaps they were already there, putting down spiny little roots.

"We just can't," I said. "I'm committed to my husband."

Or at least, I'm too terrified of what will happen if I'm not, I didn't say.

The Wolf made a sound of disgust in the back of his throat and said, "David? David doesn't deserve you. You should be wearing furs and drinking champagne with presidents, with movie stars, not following that paper-shuffler around."

Obviously, a part of me agreed with this assessment, but another part wanted to defend David, my David, who, even though he was critical of me, and even though he was often absent, I sometimes felt needed some type of protection. My David, who shyly tried to make fun of me on that first date, which I had understood even then was because he felt slighted by my lateness and inferior to my upbringing. He had a chip on his shoulder: he'd grown up poor, the first in his family to go to college, and he'd worked his way into an industry populated by Ivy Leaguers and government legacies. He did it through sheer smarts, too, not by befriending the right people or glad-handing; if anything, as far as I could tell, he'd made it as far as he had in spite of his personality, not because of it.

There were other things, too—his father was a drinker; his mother had left him as a little boy. The sorts of things that might make a man turn out like David, I suppose.

And now I'd done something unforgivable to him, to my poor

David, who was so worried that he had taken something precious from me that first night we spent together that he had decided the only way to make up for it was to marry me. He tried so hard to take care of me, despite my difficulties. He tried so hard to love me, even if it didn't come naturally to him, and what had I done in return?

I know now that I underestimated David from the beginning, but that day in the New Wing, I was picturing him in Milan alone in an office at the consulate, pushing his glasses back up his nose with one sweaty hand while he paged through boring trade documents with the other, while back in Rome his boss, the movie star, was trying to seduce his wife. I imagined him smiling shyly, a real smile, on Monday when he came home, once I had fixed everything and the only thing he would find in his apartment was his beautiful wife, the day before her birthday. It was a smile I craved, the real, sweet David smile—the one I saw every now and then, and had seen more lately, when he'd come back from a trip or a late day at the office and I was ready for him. I imagined his soft pink ears, and the way he got bewildered, sometimes, in expensive restaurants.

Once, at Le Coq d'Or, he ordered a dessert wine for the main course without realizing, and the sommelier was too polite to ask if he was sure. We were out with Barb and Jim, and Barb started laughing and made a joke about David's sweet tooth, and I wanted to kiss him right there in the red-papered dining room of that old cardinal's villa when his cheeks and ears went pink with embarrassment, and anger.

That was when I finally started to cry.

"Oh, Christ," the Wolf said, and let go of my hands. "All right, then. I'll leave you alone."

I couldn't speak. The photograph was burning a hole in my purse. I imagined atomic clouds coming off it; I envisioned it glowing with an evil violet light. I grabbed my purse from the table where

I'd left it, took the photo out, and handed it to him. I didn't know what else to do. I didn't want it to be mine, anymore.

"What am I looking at? Very romantic. But why—"

I pointed to the figures' faces, and the Wolf exhaled sharply through his nose.

"Son of a bitch."

Until that moment, I think I had held out hope that he might look at it and say, "Who's that?" or "There's nothing there." It seemed possible, as I handed him the photo, that I had blown this all out of proportion, or even imagined the entire thing.

At the very least, I was hoping he would see it and know immediately what needed to be done. A seasoned politician, an old-school film star, he should have dealt with scandals before. I wanted this to be his problem now. I wanted him to make it all better. But he was upset, which meant there was something worth being upset about, and, more than that, he was angry.

"Teddy, where did you get this?"

He spoke slowly to me, the way you might to a child, or to someone you weren't certain understood English.

"From the photographer. The one you hired for the party. He took our picture in the garden. I saw him but you had already walked away."

This last part came out like an accusation; it was one.

"How did you get it, though? How did you get the photo he took?"

The Wolf's voice was calm, but I knew better than to be soothed. He was gathering information, deciding how to react. Nobody in my family ever raised their voices. They didn't need to.

"I followed him home."

"You followed him? You went to a strange man's home by yourself in the middle of the night? What were you thinking?"

I hated when people asked me this. As if I ever knew what I was doing before I did it, and as if knowing had ever stopped me. I wasn't thinking, most of the time. I was running. I was hiding.

"I was trying to fix it," I said. "And I can. We can. He just wants money, then he'll give me the negative and we can destroy it, and it'll all be fine."

"And while you were thinking whatever you were thinking," the Wolf continued, as if he hadn't heard me, "did you stop to also think that perhaps—*perhaps*—you following the man home clued him in to the fact that he had something he might be able to sell? And that maybe otherwise, this never would have been a problem, at all?"

He had a hand up by his forehead, pinching the bridge of his nose with his long, dry-skinned fingers. It hadn't occurred to me, actually, that I might have made things worse, but now it was all I could think about. I had done this to myself. It wasn't much of a leap from there to the thought that everything bad that had ever happened to me, I had more or less done to myself, and a little purple octopus tentacle unfurled toward my heart.

I shook my head, a few leftover tears trickling softly, silently from my eyes—I was always a beautiful crier, which is one of the better things to be—and the Wolf sighed. This was a reaction I counted on more than I'd like to admit. Resignation; the recognition that you may as well be nice to me, because I wasn't worth the kill. If I'd been a fish, he would have unhooked me and thrown me back into the lake for being too small.

"How much money does he want?" the Wolf asked.

"A million," I said.

"Motherfucker!" the Wolf shouted.

"Not dollars," I said quickly. "Lira."

"Jesus, Teddy. Tell me in dollars. That's what—two thousand?"

"Sixteen hundred."

"Okay, fine. Not great, but that's fine. We can manage that. So, what's the plan? You're going to meet him, give him the money, he'll give you the negative? And how can you be sure he hasn't made more copies?"

I shook my head again.

"No, you can't, I suppose," he answered for me. He seemed almost happy, now, and I could see the politician, the brawler, under the tanned movie star. The man I had hoped for, the one I had wanted to come out swinging. To tell me what to do.

"You're a formidable woman, Teddy," he said, his soothing tone back in place. "You can handle this."

I wanted *him* to handle it, but the way he spoke made me think that maybe he was right. Maybe I was capable of staying calm, of fixing this.

"I can give you the money, Teddy," he went on, "but I can't be running around Rome paying off paparazzi. I can't have anything tying the money back to me."

"What if he did make copies, though? What if he won't give me the negative?"

The Wolf exhaled, almost a laugh. "Tell him something bad will happen if he goes back on his word. Tell him we'll have him killed."

"Really?" I had visions of the Wolf sending spies in, sending soldiers, to raid Mauro's stinking red apartment and take the negative back.

He shrugged. "No, but why not tell him that? It's worth a shot. I doubt he has the stomach for a longer game. It's a small enough amount; this is probably just a quick payday for him. They're all the same, these stupid jackals."

I wanted to object to that characterization of Mauro, for some reason. I suppose it was because he'd been kind enough, after all, and I thought I understood him. Or at least, I couldn't fault him: who could pass up an opportunity like this, when it dropped into your lap? If you needed the money?

It was always easy for me to understand people who did things to hurt me. I always thought, well, who could blame them?

The Wolf left me alone in the New Wing to go get cash from his office, and I tried to keep my mind as blank and still as marble in his absence. I didn't want to think about everything that could still go wrong. I didn't want to think about what was left to do, and how I would have to be the one to do it.

When he returned, the Wolf took his wallet out of his pocket and handed me the bills, one after the other. It was a lot of cash to keep in your office, I thought, but then again, he was the Wolf. Why wouldn't he keep thousands of dollars around?

"Are you sure?" I asked.

I couldn't believe, after all my worrying, that this would be resolved so easily. I wanted it to be true, but if wishes were horses, beggars would ride.

"Of course I'm sure. Something like this could abort a campaign before it's even grown fins. Fix it, Teddy. And call me as soon as you do."

"So you're running? In '76?"

I don't know why I asked him that. It seemed like a natural question, after what he'd said about a campaign. But I can see, now, how it might look like I knew more than I let on. I can see how someone might misunderstand that, later.

The Wolf didn't answer, just put a hand on my waist again, let it drift down to my hip, and said, "Teddy, it's going to be fine. Just don't falter. You don't need to cry anymore, okay? And don't let anyone see you're upset. Business as usual, okay?"

Again, I thought of a horse and how you would soothe one. A gentle touch to the flanks, a warm and reassuring hand.

"You're lucky you look so beautiful when you cry," he said, and he leaned in so close that I thought he might try to kiss me again, but he didn't.

Should I tell you how, when he touched me, I wanted to fall into his arms? I wanted to let him finish what he'd started the night before, what he'd tried to start just now. I wanted to burn through the climbing-up-the-walls feeling, that fear I'd had since I'd seen that flash in the garden the night before—no, earlier. Since I'd seen my old Eugene the first night at the Villa Taverna. Even with the money in my purse, knowing everything might be settled soon, or at least that this particular crisis might be, the feeling wasn't fully gone.

If you've ever seen a horse panic, you might know that unless you stop them, they'll run until they die. Around and around in a pen until they expire from exhaustion, eyes rolling white in their heads, foaming at the mouth, impossible to reach. I wanted to let the Wolf stop me in my tracks.

I wanted it more than anything, but I'm proud to say I didn't even lean into his hand. I still had something to hold on to, I thought, with David. I had a future I thought was still within my reach.

"And don't you go running to tell your Uncle Hal," the Wolf said, when he took his hand from me and turned back toward the door to leave. "We're perfectly capable of handling this ourselves."

"Oh God," I said, nearly retching at the thought of it. Of how Uncle Hal would decide to handle such a thing. "No, never."

The Wolf went back to his office with my promise to keep it between the two of us—as if he needed that vow, as if I wouldn't do everything in my power to keep even a single other person from finding out about the photograph, about Yevgeny Larin, about everything I'd ever done—and he told me to call him on Sunday night as soon as I'd done it. Made the handoff—it was hard not to think about it in those terms, like I was Philip Marlowe or Perry Mason. Tailing the suspect, making the handoff. Hard-boiled.

You might think I would have felt lighter after that, with the money in my purse, but there was still so much that could go wrong. There was still so much to do before it was finished.

And I may as well admit that it wasn't just the photo burning a hole in my purse, now. There was the money, too. I needed it out of there; I couldn't stop thinking about it.

I thought of everything I could buy with that extra sixteen hundred. I wouldn't spend it, of course I wouldn't, but I couldn't help the thought. There was a shop on the via Condotti that sold Venetian glass, and in the window they had an entire miniature symphony orchestra blown from the most delicate spun glass. Every position was there: the first chair violin, the French horns, the oboist. The tiny conductor in his glass tails, his baton thinner than a toothpick and raised like a wizard's wand casting a spell.

It frightened me that I would even consider it. I had been handed a solution to my problem, and here I was thinking of how to throw it away. I didn't end up spending all the money on the little orchestra, but depending on how you look at what happened next, you could say I still threw it all away—every single chance I was offered to make things right.

17. Trastevere, Testaccio

Saturday and Sunday, July 5–6, 1969

I went home alone from the embassy, and the apartment without David in it felt dangerous, to me.

The sitting room looked like a stage set. Like a room designed to mimic the real thing, one where something bad was about to happen. The rust-red velveteen sofa, the dark wooden chairs, the grandfather clock, the worn Turkish carpet—none of it was mine.

Teresa had left before she'd had a chance to open the curtains in the sitting room, which were made of a haunted-looking worn blue brocade that I never would have chosen, so I went to the windows and opened them all the way, though it was dark out. I wanted to let the night air in. I put a record on, one of David's old jazz albums.

The Huntley Foundation's holdings stopped at the Gilded Age, but I'd been to a traveling retrospective of Edward Hopper's work down in Houston just after he died in '67, and even someone who didn't study the form could've told you his paintings were about loneliness. There was one called *Night Windows*, a view from the outside of three windows into a city apartment at night. You couldn't see all the way in, just enough to catch a glimpse of green carpet and something red—an ottoman, perhaps, or a love seat. And the back of a woman, bending down. Something is happening in that apartment, the painting tells you, but you'll never know what it is.

I didn't need to imagine someone outside our little flat looking in; I already saw it that way. As a stranger. There's a woman, alone in her apartment, and something is about to happen. Something is about to go wrong.

There was an air of dread about the place, to me. But if someone had been staring up at our windows from the street outside, that night, they would have only seen me, and no hint of disaster. Just a woman sitting at the edge of the sofa, unmoving, with all the lights on in the apartment and David's jazz on the record player.

The man I imagined looking in from the street—perhaps one of the same shadowy figures who gathered information for the Russians, or for us—would have seen me sitting there for minutes more, maybe almost an hour, before I abruptly jumped to my feet.

He wouldn't have known what had moved me, though: the sudden revelation that I could solve the issue of the photograph immediately, now, today.

I had the money, didn't I? And David was gone, so there was no reason I couldn't go to Mauro tonight and get the negatives, and then call the Wolf and tell him it was done. The rest of it—the feeling like I wasn't myself, the empty apartment, the life I was cramming myself into like dirty clothes in a hamper stuffed to bursting—could be dealt with later, or not at all.

I called the number on the piece of paper Mauro had given me—had given me just that morning, I could hardly believe. Time had changed, or stopped, and it seemed impossible, when I considered it, that the days would keep coming and eventually the photo would be gone, and by Tuesday I would be thirty-five and, theoretically, an heiress, and then later, after that, I suppose, I thought of David's comment just before he'd left and the idea that there might one day be a house with two children and a Labrador, and I would take up gardening, or maybe piano.

I called the number, and a man answered.

"*Pronto*," he said.

I told him in my lazy, unconvincing Italian that I was trying to reach Mauro, the photographer—I realized I didn't know his surname. I told the man it was urgent.

I half expected him to say he'd never heard of any Mauro, but he said sure, he would get a message to Mauro, and Mauro would call me back.

So there was nothing to do but wait. I thought of pouring myself a drink but decided to make espresso, instead. It didn't matter that it was already late; I knew I wouldn't sleep, anyway.

As I waited for Mauro, I went digging through my purse to find the photo and take it out and stare at it, and then to count the bills from the Wolf again, just to be sure that I really did have them all. That I hadn't somehow lost or accidentally spent them. I clawed through the debris in my purse—chewing-gum wrappers; loose, tarnished coins; a Max Factor Pure Magic lipstick in Tangerine that was missing its top—and there it was. The photo. I wanted to allow myself to see what Mauro saw, two figures embracing. Passion, uninhibited. But I couldn't. All I saw was a threat.

Below the photo, a wad of cash. It was still there. I hadn't spent it; I was safe.

I really did have everything I needed to fix my situation. I wasn't going to take several of my calming pills at once and stare at the ceiling and miss Mauro's call. I wasn't going to get into David's bourbon and drink until I was sick. I wasn't going to pace around the room thinking about my situation and sipping shot after shot of espresso, my heart beating faster and faster until it finally went off like an atom bomb. I wasn't going to break down and call my mother and ask for help. I knew what would happen after that.

I was going to take my destiny into my own hands, and this time I was going to get it right.

The phone rang, eventually. It was Mauro, of course, and when

I told him I had the money, he said, "You have my address? Come now, and come alone," and then a click on the end of the line to indicate he had hung up.

I wanted to laugh; my life felt unreal to me, and it didn't help that everyone insisted on talking like it was the movies. The Wolf with his cowboy swagger; Mauro setting up assignations like some spy.

I changed into a dress, something fitted and black that I'd bought at La Rinascente a few weeks earlier. I still had my makeup on, but I added a little more liner around my eyes, a little more mascara. I tousled my hair and let it fall. I put on flat shoes, taking care around the raw remnants of my blisters. I wanted to walk.

I probably should have been more worried, going alone to Mauro's apartment like that, carrying over a thousand dollars around Rome late at night, but I was so close to the end that I felt untouchable. Nobody would dare to stop me on my journey through the city; they would know, just from looking at me, that I was on my way to a better, stronger Teddy.

Testaccio was charming, that night. The mountain of shards rose in the dark like a monument, and the yellow light of the street-lamps, their warm cast on the paving stones of the little streets, welcomed me. Even Mauro's apartment building had a certain appeal, with its orange stucco exterior, its brown shuttered windows. It had been a grand building, once.

Even Mauro's flat seemed less forbidding than before. When I knocked on the door and he opened it, I could see the lamps were on and it smelled, if not fresh, certainly less chemical, less hellish. Without the dim red light, it seemed almost cozy. I could live somewhere like this, I thought. All my possessions in one room, my piles of clothing and shelves of trinkets pared down to just what was actually needed.

I loved my dresses and purses and jewelry, my gold-topped nail polishes, my compact mirrors, but I did feel, sometimes, that they had lied to me. Each time I bought something new I'd think of how much better it was going to make everything. Who I was going to be once I had it. The lipstick shade I would wear out to dinner on a particular night, and how sophisticated it would make me look. The earrings that would be perfect for this or that party, and how I would look like Veruschka at tomorrow's luncheon if I bought and wore that Pucci dress. But then after the initial rush, the initial triumph of the compliments I received, the sensation of having the right thing at the right time, like finding the perfect, last piece to a jigsaw puzzle, I was left with the skin of the dress, the bones of the earrings. The carcass of the thing as I'd dreamed it, now that the moment was gone. And they piled up, these remnants, until I was living in a midden of my imagined past selves. I'd read in a magazine about archaeologists in England studying ancient rubbish heaps and finding layer on layer of the detritus of feasts. You could see when Christmas was celebrated, when Easter, based on the animal bones in each stratum. In my wardrobe, in the heap of my clothes, you could see my honeymoon, my wedding. The red chiffon of my ill-fated Fourth of July dress, the silver and gold and white sequins, already balding, of that first Valentino gown.

Mauro didn't smile when he opened the door. He hadn't shaved since I'd seen him that morning, and the scruff on his chin made him look older, tired. Well, I supposed neither of us had had much time to sleep the night before.

He didn't even grin when I sat down at the table and unfurled a million lire in bills, fanning it out across the linoleum tabletop like a hand of cards. I was giddy—I was almost free.

"Teddy," he said, lighting a cigarette for himself, and then one for me, "I need to talk to you."

If a man never said this particular phrase to me again, I wouldn't miss it. "I need to talk to you" always means a surprise. It always means you're in trouble.

Mauro took a newspaper clipping out of his pocket and set it on the table. A picture of Uncle Hal in black and white, frowning in front of the Capitol. The same one I'd seen just that morning in George's paper.

"Teddy," Mauro said, "I know this is your relative. I know your family has money."

"My family?" I hadn't told him my full name, just as I didn't know his.

"I don't have money, really. I don't. My husband is just a bureaucrat; we hardly have anything."

"No, Teddy. Your family. The Huntleys. This man, here, is a senator."

"But my name—"

"I saw your name on your checkbook, last night. And I don't think there are so many Huntleys who work for the American government, are there? It makes more sense to me that this is the same family. I asked around, too. I know you're rich. And so it's worth more to you than I thought, this photo."

"But I don't have any money! And I can't ask them; please don't ask me to ask them."

I could feel tears in my eyes, hear them in my throat. I was good at faking most things, but I could never stop myself from crying. And I didn't even want to; let Mauro see it, I thought. He was the one who was doing this to me, who was threatening my life, even if he had done it mostly by accident. Even if, as the Wolf had pointed out, he might never have bothered with the photo if I hadn't followed him home and let him know, in my panic, that it was valuable.

"Teddy," he sighed, "*porca puttana*," and put his head in his hands. "You want a drink?"

I nodded. I couldn't speak. I knew my voice would sound like a rusted hinge if I tried.

He went to the sink with its little cabinet and came back with

209

a bottle of Sangiovese. Poured each of us a water glass filled to the brim with red wine.

"Just relax," he said. "Breathe a moment. *Inspira, espira.*" He motioned with his hands in front of his chest.

Men were always telling me to relax when something terrible was about to happen. The Wolf, telling me to handle things myself. Now Mauro. David, to his credit, had never told me to relax. I think if anything, he mostly wished the opposite for me.

I gulped my wine, which burned my throat but also managed to scorch the rising panic out of my chest for the moment. Mauro was moving around the room, putting a record on. Miles Davis, I realized, only recognizing it because it was one of David's favorites, too. *My Funny Valentine.*

I had the strange idea that they would probably get along, these two men who tormented me mostly by accident.

He said he wanted ten million lire, now, and I said okay. It didn't matter whether it was ten million or one million, it didn't matter if he wanted the moon, which soon would have American boots upon it, according to the newspaper. I would try to get it for him, because the only other option, as far as I could see, was death, and so I might as well take the moonshot.

I would have to ask the Wolf, again, and this time it was more money than he could possibly have in his office. This time, I doubted that he would tell me to handle it myself. And I imagined he would look more closely at me, at this fox in his henhouse, and then he would find out about Yevgeny Larin, and they would all decide I wasn't just out of control, but actually criminal, and I would end up dying in a different way than I'd expected—in the electric chair, for treason, or maybe in prison, of old age—but this one was only a maybe, whereas if my family found out about what I'd been up to in Rome, my demise was certain.

"Tell me about the women," I said, when I could speak again.

I needed to talk about something else for a while. I pointed to Mauro's enormous nude ladies. "Why these? Why so big?"

I meant, why are the photographs printed at such a great size, but Mauro seemed to interpret it as a comment on their bodies. They were voluptuous, it was true. And the photos were cropped closely to them, so that a woman bent at the waist seemed to be almost a landscape, the folds of her flesh like the shadows of sand dunes, the hollow between her legs a cavern.

There was a sea of dunes near the ranch in West Texas, almost an ocean. Aunt Sister and I used to take trays from the kitchen out there when it wasn't too hot and slide down the dunes like we were sledding. Then return home with our shoes full of sand and the trays scratched to hell by the grit, and everyone would be angry, but we wouldn't care because, as Sister always said, who knew how long the dunes would be there. Who knew how many more times we could do this.

"Smoke 'em if you got 'em," she used to say.

"It's about fullness," Mauro said. "It's about having enough. Enough body, enough to eat, enough life to give. You don't know, because you weren't here during the war, but we were starving. You can drive on the highways down the coast now and see trees hanging heavy with fruit, and vineyards on the cliffs. During the war, those were picked clean. There was nothing; the land was dry. Infertile. So I don't want pictures of fashion models with their little legs. I want goddesses. Like the old statues, you know. Aphrodite. Venus."

I wondered what he would think of the Venus on the stairs at the embassy. She had the body of a typical Renaissance statue, soft through the hips, round arms, small chest—"Hardly bigger than mosquito bites," the Wolf had said. I wondered what Mauro would think of that.

"So," Mauro said, still watching me. "You're here, and we have a million lire."

We, he said. That's probably another thing that could be used against me. We got along sometimes, my blackmailer and I.

"We'll go out?" he asked, standing from the table, brushing his hair back from his forehead with his fingers.

It occurred to me that he might be lonely. Moving silently through parties he wasn't invited to, or standing on the street all day taking photographs of strangers, then coming home to this apartment full of frozen women. An outsider by profession. I felt that perhaps we had a kind of bond.

I suppose we did—me and Mauro, me and the Wolf. People who knew my secret. I still thought of it as my secret, though all these men were involved, too.

I had hardly slept in two days, and I still wasn't free of the photo yet, and David wasn't around to drive me safely home at the end of the night, but still I thought, why not? Why not dive all the way down?

"All right," I said. "We'll go out."

It was after nine already, but restaurants stayed open late in Rome. We went to dinner in an old cellar dug into the side of Monte Testaccio that took its menu from the local butchers' offerings, and from which you could see stacked terra-cotta shards in the wall, and Mauro ordered calf's head, liver with onions, fried testicles, stewed chicory. Peasant food, offal—he watched me the entire time, waiting to see if I objected to any of it.

I didn't. I ate everything, messily, gluttonously, and Mauro delighted in that, laughing in particular when I speared one of the testicles on my fork and ripped into it with my teeth. I'd hardly eaten anything at all that day, and I was starving, despite all the stay-awakes I'd taken, which usually kept me too agitated to eat. I could've eaten more; I could have kept eating and drinking forever. We had wine from a jug and we talked about the movies and it worried me, when I thought about it, that the most relaxed I'd felt in ages was with the man holding the rope attached to the sword hanging over my head.

"What are you so afraid of, Teddy?" Mauro asked, halfway through the second jug of wine. I rolled my eyes; he'd been talking about philosophy, and I understood that he was trying to ask a Big Question.

"Spiders," I said. "Snakes."

"The photo," he said. "Why are you so afraid of the photo? It's just something that happened. It's just the truth. That's all the camera shows you."

"You're a man," I said. "You wouldn't understand."

He didn't understand that you put on makeup for photos, you wear your best pearls. You tilt your head; you show them who you want to be. It's not the truth, at all.

"You know," he said, "I used to work with the man who took pictures of Ingrid Bergman when she was in Rome with Rossellini. The ones they published when everyone learned of the affair."

"So?"

"So, don't you think she was happier, after? When it all came out, and she could live with him in the open, instead of pretending she loved her husband?"

"She was exiled for years. She couldn't go back to the US at all! They hated her. They tore her apart."

Mauro shrugged. "Is that such a bad thing?"

I didn't bother responding.

After dinner, we took a taxi north, past the embassy and the Borghese park all the way to the via Tagliamento. As soon as I saw the neon sign over the awning and the men in suits standing outside, guarding the door, I knew what Mauro had in mind.

I had never been to the Piper Club—David hated loud music, and I was too scared of what I might get up to if I went by myself— but I'd heard all about it. The club had been built into the shell of an old cinema, with a dance floor where the seats had been and a

213

stage for live music in front of what used to be the silver screen. The Who had played there, and Jimi Hendrix, and Pink Floyd. There were all kinds of stories about what went on there, about the kinds of people who could be found within its walls.

One of the men at the door began shouting at Mauro as soon as he saw him. He employed a stream of Italian slang words I'd never heard before—apparently they hadn't, in Signora Falasca's estimation, been relevant to my particular needs—but I understood the general sentiment: he was calling Mauro scum, saying he didn't belong, telling him to hit the road. I did catch the phrase "like a fly on shit," and so I gathered that Mauro must have been here for work, before, stalking starlets and musicians as they reveled in the club below or stumbled out the door just before dawn.

Mauro as I had known him so far was impassive, unemotional; even my tears seemed to have irritated and exhausted him more than they'd genuinely distressed him. But for a moment, as the doorman shouted at him, calling him trash, telling him to get lost—just a moment—I saw the set of his jaw change, a twitching at the mandibles as if he'd clenched and shifted his teeth, and he looked almost like a little boy just before he throws a tantrum, or dissolves into tears.

It was gone, that stubborn, tearful look, in the blink, or maybe two, of an eye, and the indifferent, marble-carved Mauro was back, leaning in toward the doorman as if in confidence, speaking in a low, calming tone until the man ceased his shouting.

Mauro whispered something to the man, then pointed and beckoned me over. The Piper Club's guardian looked me up and down, glanced sideways at the other doorman, and finally nodded. He unhooked the velvet rope in front of the door and waved us forward, and as we passed through the mouth of the club and descended the darkened staircase of its throat, I couldn't help thinking that we had been welcomed through the entrance of the underworld.

Virgil said that outside the door to Hades, evil spirits hang around: Grief, Anxiety, Old Age, Fear, Guilty Pleasures, and Need. By that logic, if you think about it, it's safer to go inside.

As Mauro and I descended the stairs, I asked him what he'd said to the man. I had to shout, my voice nearly overpowered by the sound of drums and an electric guitar flooding up from the club below.

"I told him you were an American actress on vacation in Rome. I said you starred in the latest Hitchcock film."

"What? There hasn't been one in years. The last was *Torn Curtain* and I don't think anyone would believe I'm Julie Andrews."

Mauro shrugged. "He doesn't know. You're a blonde. You could be anyone. I said you hired me to show you around Rome."

The thought made me sad, and I realized it was because I wished it was true. I wished I was her: Teddy Carlyle, the Paramount blonde, the one who travels on her own to new places and hires handsome men to take her dancing. I imagined that she had booked herself into a suite at the Hotel Locarno, and the concierge made sure there were flowers waiting in her room every evening. She was in Rome to take meetings with an Italian director, maybe Fellini himself, because she wasn't just beautiful, you see, she wanted to make real art. She went shopping on the via Condotti and she paid for shoes from Ferragamo, and a belted coatdress in violet Agnona wool—no shrinking violet, our Teddy Carlyle—from Mila Schön, and a pocketbook for her beautiful Nile blue checks in embossed camel-colored leather from Gucci, all with money she earned herself, because she was so engaging, so beautiful, that people paid just to see her projected on a screen like a painting in the dark.

We pushed through a set of velvet curtains—another door on the way to Hades—and emerged into a cavernous room with walls painted white and illuminated in colored spotlights so that the crowds of people heaving along to the music or sitting at tables circling the dance floor were cast in a pink and green glow. Behind the stage, enormous photographs were pasted along the wall. A close-up image of a woman's face, heavily lined eyes glancing to the side. A laughing mouth. A field of green.

I was relieved when Mauro led me past the dance floor to a table near the back. The revelers were all a decade younger than me or more, I guessed, the women slender and lithe in short dresses and platform shoes, shaking their long glossy hair, batting eyes with spider-leg lashes under blunt-cut bangs. I was heavy, and old, and out of date; the young girls weren't wearing their hair so big anymore, I noticed. They weren't wearing powder or lipstick like mine, and some of them weren't even lining their eyes. I had seen the looks changing, obviously, in the magazines, but it didn't matter if I knew what I was supposed to be wearing or not—that easy, minimal style was never going to work on me. Not with my figure; not with my face.

Mauro took me by the hand to a table where a man with long hair and a mustache sat alone.

"Alan, this is Teddy," Mauro said to the man, in English. "Got anything for us?"

"Mauro, you dog," the man said in an American accent, and clapped him on the back. Then, leering at me, "Teddy. What a beauty. You should really keep better company."

I laughed; why not? Mauro gave Alan some of the money from the Wolf, and Alan gave Mauro a little paper bag, and then Mauro took me over to another table where a couple of girls in their twenties sat, and he kissed each of them on their cheeks and introduced me, but I've never been able to remember their names. One of them had enormous black eyes with long lashes like a cow's, and the other was impossibly thin, and for a few hours, at least, they were the best people I'd ever met. Mauro handed me two pills from Alan's plastic bag and I swallowed them dry, without even asking what they were. I was never especially picky about such things on a good day, and I hadn't had a good day in what felt like years.

It took me a while to realize that the chemicals were kicking in, and that I was well on my way to the moon. Time that day had already collapsed and expanded like a dying star, stretching and then racing along until I couldn't keep up, but now it came unmoored entirely. I couldn't tell you much about the next few hours, except that everything was pink, and green, and I did dance, even though I'm no good at it, and the cow-eyed woman kissed me on the mouth.

And I saw *him*, again, at the end of the bar. Or on the other side of the club, rather.

"It's you?" he asked, when he was close enough that I could hear him over the music.

"It's me," I answered, and he hugged me, and they felt the same, his long, awkward arms. I reached up to touch his beautiful golden hair. And he blinked at me with his rabbit eyes, his sweet puppy's eyes, and he wanted to know how I'd been, and if I was all right, and he promised not to say anything to anyone, and I believed him.

"I'm happy for you," Eugene told me, "that things turned out so well."

I didn't know how to tell him they hadn't, so I smiled and said thank you, and he clasped my hand in one of his, and then brought it to his lips to kiss.

"Your husband, he's good to you?" he asked.

"Oh, yes," I said, "he's just gone a lot. He's in Milan, right now. I don't know why."

He looked satisfied, and kissed my hand again. I don't know what else we talked about, but I remember thinking we understood each other. I wasn't worried, anymore—at least not then, in the nightclub—about our history. That he would tell anyone. It didn't occur to me, for example, that he might have already told someone. That I might be the reason he was in Rome.

I remember staring at the ceiling and feeling completely calm. I recall understanding, finally, that I was destined for great things. I was an important piece of the puzzle, and angels were coming to tell me so.

I remember standing on the shore of the little beach below the cliffs in the painting at the Villa Taverna, listening to the sound of the waves, far away from the rest of the world and yet still, somehow, connected. The seas turning, and shifting, and also not changing. Everything around me dulled and softened, a skin over the raw nerve of my mind.

It didn't last.

Eventually, the music stopped, the smoke cleared, and people began to leave, traipsing out through the velvet curtains and up the stairs, ascending to the world of the living like Orpheus leading Eurydice, and eventually, I realized that I had to be one of them. Mauro was nowhere to be found, but it didn't worry me. Everything was going to be fine. There was a solution, though in the bowels of the club, as I made my way toward the stairs, I couldn't quite remember what it was.

When I surfaced, it was almost morning again. I didn't know exactly where I was in Rome, but I knew that as soon as I found the river, I would be able to get home all right.

I was always walking home just as the sun came up, it seemed. And now that I was on my own again in streets just coming to life, and now that the drugs were wearing off, I remembered how empty it feels, how frightening, to be going home alone. In your party dress, in your fancy shoes, last night's makeup revealing who you thought you were going to be, who you saw in the mirror as you got ready, and now here you are, yourself, on the other side of the evening, and it wasn't magical after all, and everything you left behind is still waiting for you.

18. Dallas

1953

The last party of my debut season in 1953 was the Terpsichorean Ball. We had all paraded in our white dresses, and I had on Aunt Sister's pearls. The party was at the Belo Mansion, the stately old home that had once been a funeral parlor and at which the bullet-riddled bodies of Bonnie and Clyde were famously displayed after that final shoot-out. They used to lease it out for parties.

The pearls had been a gift from Aunt Sister the week before my sixteenth birthday, just before she died. When they were only saying what are we going to do about Sissie and sighing, and I didn't know there was any more to it than that. You can understand how I still didn't realize. How I thought she was just incorrigible, one of those wild Fitzgerald or Hemingway women who simply couldn't be tamed. She had spent some time in Spain and spoke of it often, so I liked to imagine her as Brett Ashley. She was always telling stories about this man or that, and she never said so, not in so many words, but you could tell she meant lovers, the way she talked about them. The way my mother would press her lips together if one of those stories came up at dinner.

When I look back now and try to remember Aunt Sister the last time I saw her, the day she came up to my room to give me the pearls—"Your present, our little secret," she'd said. "Don't show your mother or she'll try to take them for herself"—it seems to me that her eyeshadow is uneven, her lipstick smeared. Loose threads on her clothes, scuffed shoes. But I don't know; I don't know if I've added those details after the fact, knowing what I know now.

That day, she presented me with an intricately decorated bone inlay box (from the Souk Semmarine in Marrakech, she said) and watched hungrily as I opened it, as I gasped with delight. The pearls resting on purple velvet, shimmering and perfect. She told me a wild story about how she had come by them, that she'd won them in a card game with an SAS hero and a minor White Russian prince. Men who had never been bested by a woman before, but she said they took it like true gentlemen.

That was the life I wanted. Beating men at their own games, winning my place at the table, traveling the world alone, staying afloat—not weighed down with the newest Frigidaire washer or a set of matching ice cream bowls in the Autumn Harvest pattern, with pumpkins and pears painted all along the rim. I would be independent and sophisticated like the women in the magazines; I imagined the men I would collect but never keep, like butterflies or lightning bugs I could admire and then release. A bullfighter, a brilliant but troubled writer, a baron, a prince. Had it been a few years later I might have imagined the president himself, but at the time it was Truman, who was much less inspiring to a young woman than Kennedy would later be.

Just after my birthday, my mother woke me up one morning to tell me Aunt Sister had been killed in an unfortunate accident; a head injury, and there was nothing that could be done about it.

I don't remember the days and weeks after that so well. I'm sure I must have been sad. We all were, I'm sure. I do recall Daddy crying at the funeral—something I'd never seen him do before. But I don't remember the rest of it: how it felt. I suppose that's a good thing.

Two years later, I wore Aunt Sister's pearls in her memory for my debut portrait, and then again that last night to Terpsichorean. I wanted them to mean something.

I had done all of it, everything I was supposed to do—the luncheons and the parties, the charity events, the formal presentation where I bowed low, all the way to the floor, in my white dress, in front of all my friends and family. The Texas dip, they called it—Aunt Sister had stumbled at her own debut, I'd heard, and tumbled forward, flat on her face. Her hands were behind her back the way they're supposed to be when you do the dip, like the wings of a swan settling itself on the water, so she couldn't even catch herself to break the fall. She ended up with a bloody nose and laughed about it for the rest of the night.

They seized on that, later, as proof that there had always been something wrong with her.

That last night of the season, I wanted the pearls to mean that it was my turn, now. I'd done everything perfectly, I had fulfilled all the obligations that came with the dubious honor of making your debut, and now I was going to show them who I would really be. Not just eligible, but magnificent.

Buddy Belmont was my date that night, and I really was brilliant. I was beautiful. Everyone laughed all night at the stories I told, and all eyes were on me as I danced with Buddy, and I thought I heard people whispering in corners, saying Teddy Carlyle is really going to be someone. Teddy is different; Teddy is special.

Buddy drove me to a parking lot out by Love Field after the dance, where we could sit in the back of his brand-new Corvette— his father, Buddy Senior, owned the Chevy dealership—and watch the planes taking off while we drank sloe gin out of paper cups. There isn't much to say about the fumbling we did in the backseat; it wasn't particularly enjoyable, but it felt like something I should do. It was part of being sophisticated, and so when Buddy touched me, I responded. I remember my back sticking to the vinyl seat of the car where he lay me down. He dropped me home just as the sky was turning the paler blue of morning.

I felt like I had joined the ranks of daring, adventurous women as I walked up the driveway. I had a grown-up secret.

The toads croaked from the grass as I stepped onto the front porch, and I suppose I should have listened to them and known it was a warning.

The house seemed to be asleep as I slipped inside, tiptoeing barefoot up the stairs with my dancing shoes in my hand, but then there was my mother, in her housecoat in a chair on the landing. She stood when she saw me, waiting silently for me to approach her. I didn't think she would be angry; it was the end of my season, after all. Everyone had stayed out all night—it was tradition. I thought she might ask where I'd been, or say she wanted a word with Buddy Belmont's mother, but instead she held me at arm's length and whispered, finally, "Where did you get those pearls? Have you been wearing them all night?"

I was desperately tired and wanted to go to bed, and I was drunk for the first time in my life. I didn't understand why we were talking about the pearls.

"Aunt Sister gave them to me."

"Aunt Sis—oh, Teddy. They look ridiculous. It's costume jewelry. The pearls are fake."

"No, she got them in London, she said. She won them playing chemin de fer at a secret casino run by a wartime spy."

I didn't know what half those words meant, but they tasted like the life I wanted.

"Oh, Teddy," my mother said again. "Look at you."

She reached over and traced a finger over my collarbone, then held it up for me to see. It was covered in a pearlescent sheen.

"They've come off all over you," she said. "And you had them on all night? Everyone must have seen. Oh, Janet will have something to say about that, I'm sure. And the other chaperones—was Abigail's mother there? I wonder if I should call her. What if you can see it in the photos? And look—you've ruined your dress!"

I had been sweating all night as I danced, as I ran around the room thinking I was the belle of the ball. It must have pulled the paint off the pearls. And then with Buddy, in his car. Had he seen it? Had I been glowing like this, shining all night with my fake pearls, with the paint across my chest? I had thought I was so magnificent, so sophisticated, and everyone was watching me because they could see that I was destined for great things. And instead, I'd been covered in glitter, "Like you're at Mardi Gras," my mother said, pursing her lips.

I wanted more than anything now to go to my room, to wash off the shine and shame, to go to sleep. Instead, my mother told me to sit.

"There's something you should know about your Aunt Sister."

I settled into the other chair on the landing, taking care not to get any glitter on it. Mama's navy blue brocade Chippendale chairs; she would've been angry—angrier—if I'd gotten the sheen of the fake pearls on them.

And then I listened as Mama explained to me that Aunt Sister was not exactly dead, after all.

Apparently, Sister had blown through her inheritance pretty quickly after the war, and so the fact that she was living free of material things, unencumbered by houses and cars and sterling flatware, was not entirely the result of a philosophical choice. She spent about a decade bouncing from man to man, place to place, and somehow managed to end up pregnant, only you needed a lot of money, in those days, to get it properly taken care of—and more than that, you needed connections; you needed a family that could appeal to the medical board to allow an emergency abortion, and while Sister had the family, she wasn't about to go to them for help.

I recalled with a wave of nausea the night I had seen Aunt Sister asking Daddy for money. I wondered why she hadn't gone to him for help this time, and then I landed on a possible answer and didn't want to wonder about it anymore.

Mama said Aunt Sister had a friend, an actress, who claimed to have terminated her own pregnancy by drinking an entire bottle of gin in a scalding hot bath, and then throwing herself over the back of a chair, and so Sister—never one to be outdone—drank a bottle and a half of gin, plus three-quarters of a thing of crème de menthe, and took an even hotter bath, and threw herself down the stairs. She ended up in the hospital, where Hal and Mama were called to come see her.

So Hal and Mama had gone to get her from the hospital and told her they would help her, and took her to see a doctor, and the doctor drove an ice pick through her eye socket to try to take out the part of her brain, I suppose, that made her want to take off running around the world getting into trouble, but unfortunately he managed to take out some of the rest, too. So Aunt Sister disappeared, and ended up drooling in her chair, in her diaper, at the card table in the visitation room at the home. Where my mother eventually took me to see her. So no, Sister was not, technically speaking, dead.

The version my mother told me was missing many of the details, but I was able to fill more of them in myself, later on. I found an interview in a magazine with one of the surgeons who'd done it—he was famous, the best in his field, even, because only the best, of course, for the Huntley family—in which he described his usual procedure. He would give something to his patients, just a mild tranquilizer to help them relax, because he needed them to stay awake the entire time. He wanted them to speak to him, sing childhood songs or recite the Lord's Prayer, something from deep in their memory, while he inserted a metal pick through the corner of their eye socket so that he would know to stop cutting away at their brain tissue when they became incoherent.

I wondered what Sister had sung, what she had said. She wouldn't have wanted to do anything as ordinary as recite the Lord's Prayer or sing the national anthem. I could picture her laughing and joking and putting on a brave face, with her red lipstick and her eye makeup on until the end, insisting they let her sing "Rags to Riches" while they operated until her voice warped and slurred like a broken record.

"So you see," Mama said, "it diminishes you. Going out with boys like that. Every man you give yourself to, you lose a part of yourself. And you never get it back, and eventually, you're gone altogether."

I was silent, so Mama went on.

"What I'm saying, Theodora," and here she narrowed her eyes at me, "is that you are already on thin ice. If you aren't more careful, you could slip and fall, and I don't want you coming crying to me like Cecilia used to do, wondering where you went wrong.

"Now go to your room," she said, "and wash off all that paint. We'll start fresh when you wake up."

I went to my room and did as I was told, and I spent the rest of that year staying in, going to bed early. I didn't want to be brilliant, anymore; I wanted to be safe. I wanted to remain whole.

I lived at home all through college, even while my friends at SMU joined sororities and lived in dormitories or shared houses and went on dates to dinner, to the movies. I stopped answering Buddy Belmont's calls. I made it all the way to my early twenties, to when I moved out into my own little apartment on Turtle Creek, before I started to lose control. I would go out late at night, drink too much, sleep too much, stay awake for days—it would happen every few weeks or so, and then I would tighten things up again, even more than before: I would wear nothing but long skirts and sweaters to my office at the Huntley Foundation and I would be in bed by nine every night reading Dickens or Victor Hugo. I would eat nothing but stuffed tomatoes and chicken broth, just as long as I could stand such abnegation until inevitably, I lost control once again.

And here I was years later in Rome, and everything was different, but it was all exactly the same. Walking home as the sun rises, knowing you're in trouble. Knowing that you're taking yourself apart.

I crossed the Tiber, lined with plane trees. With its many bridges, the water dappled with the golden light of the streetlamps.

I crossed the medieval Ponte Sisto, built on ancient Roman foundations in that slow-moving water. I stopped to peer over the edge. I'd heard recently that dolphins had been spotted in the Arno, over in Pisa. Barb came back from a weekend trip claiming it was true, she had seen them herself.

But there was only empty water, as far as I could see. So I lifted my head up and crossed the rest of the bridge, and then I walked all the way home.

Beppo wasn't outside, but he'd gone missing for a day here and there before. He was probably fine.

When I got back inside the apartment, I should have felt all right. I'd remembered that Mauro had asked for more money, but I thought I could ask the Wolf again. It was too much money, really, but it was a burden I couldn't bear on my own, and I didn't worry, anymore, that the Wolf might think less of me. I only wanted to survive.

I still had time to get a few hours' sleep before I went back to the embassy to plead my case again, but instead I lay awake in the empty bed, feeling my heart flutter around in my chest, drifting out to sea and then back in again.

Now that the drugs had worn off completely, I understood that I wasn't destined for greatness. I knew that actually, there was something wrong, deep inside. That everything that plagued me was a product of my own character, was the result of something internal that had grown in crooked, like a bucked tooth. You can understand how they would think it was only a matter of cutting it out. You could see how someone might imagine it was like scraping barnacles off a ship, or rust from an old nail. Like hacking and chipping away at a block of marble until it takes on a more perfect form, becomes a more perfect woman.

Now

Early Morning, Wednesday, July 9, 1969

The men are silent. Even Reggie, who loves to interrupt, stares down at his hands.

Arthur Hildebrand can't be moved for very long, though, it seems, because he clears his throat after a few interminable seconds.

"Mrs. Shepard. Can you please recall, to the best of your knowledge, exactly what you told Yevgeny Larin about your husband's whereabouts?"

"Pardon?" I'm still thinking about Aunt Sister and the dolphins, or their absence, in the Tiber; I'm far away.

"You say you told the Russian attaché that your husband was out of town, in Milan, during your encounter at the Piper Club three days ago. Do you remember telling him anything else about David Shepard, or his business?"

"I'm not sure I understand—what business?"

If I really wanted to sell it, I'd put a hand to my breast in shock, but my nails are all chewed up, so I don't. Anyway, Arthur Hildebrand is a wily old fox, and I think he might have my number. Just a little bit, at least.

"You also said," Hildebrand continues, "that you didn't think Yevgeny Larin had told anyone else about your . . . dalliance. That you didn't think this was the reason he was in Rome."

"Right," I say. "I said I *didn't* think that."

228

Hildebrand smiles at me, which is somehow more chilling than his blank, distracted expression. And he says, in a calm, quiet voice, "I think you do understand, Mrs. Shepard. I think you understand much more than you let on.

"When," he asks, studying my face, "did you first learn the nature of your husband's work?"

19. Palazzo Margherita

Sunday, July 6, 1969

The sun came through the bedroom window inch by inch until I could no longer ignore it. I hadn't slept, but I emerged from my trance with a jolt and the thought that I needed to tell the Wolf the plan hadn't worked. Mauro had asked for more.

I wasn't even tired, anymore, but I took a stay-awake just to be sure. I had a bath—I was going to skip it, but I smelled like smoke and sweat and a few other things, I realized, including the pungent scent of marijuana, which reminded me of nothing so much as the clouds of skunk scent you drive through on the highway in Texas whenever someone before you has come too close to hitting one with their car, scaring the stink out of it.

My skin was glowing. I hadn't done anything to it since Friday, hadn't put on any of my serums or creams, but somehow it had taken on an almost inhuman patina. I couldn't see my pores; my cheek looked as smooth as the marble Venus's.

I put some talcum powder in my hair to give it just a little more life, then sprayed it up into something like a chignon. Found a baby blue poly-blend dress the color of a robin's egg that was clean and unwrinkled and hanging in the wardrobe. Polyester wouldn't have been my first choice, but everything else was dirty.

I took a few cans of tuna from the cupboard to pack in my

purse, just in case Beppo was hungry—I couldn't remember the last time I'd fed him—but he wasn't around, so I left an open can at the bottom of the palazzina's front steps for whenever he decided to come back.

I was already ill over how mortifying it would be to tell the Wolf we needed more money, and how pathetic I would look—how childish, how weak—but I walked all the way to the embassy, even so, and left a message with the Wolf's secretary, who was in the office on a Sunday evidently against her will, that I would be in the New Wing whenever the ambassador needed me. He would know what that meant, I figured.

I went back to the New Wing, to the third floor, past the Pointdexters, who inexplicably with all of their watching did not seem to have seen me for what I really was, past their room of whirring machines and running printouts and crackling fluorescent lights, down the hall to 33-B, to the empty office where my stacks of paper and boxes of files waited, as always, for me.

I had lied to the Wolf and let him think that it would all be fine. I had told him I could handle it, and sixteen hundred dollars was such a small amount to him that he had taken me at my word. He thought I was a formidable woman, someone courageous. But I wasn't. I was scared the whole time; I was a coward. I was a child, but I didn't want to let the photo come out, and I still couldn't go to my parents, or David, and so my only option was to ask the Wolf again for help, and to prostrate myself at his feet.

I paced around the room for a while, and when the Wolf didn't come after a couple of hours, I lay on my back on one of the massive metal desks along the wall, trying to think about nothing.

I must have managed to doze off despite the power of my precious stay-awake pills, because the next thing I knew, someone was tapping on the doorframe, saying, "Knock knock!" in a bright and bubbly woman's voice, and of course it had to be Margot, and she walked into the room before I was able to stand up from my coated-metal bower and straighten my dress.

"What are you doing here on a weekend, Teddy?" she asked cheerfully, as if that, and not, "Why are you sleeping here?" was the obvious question.

"I'm just going through these boxes," I lied to Margot, gesturing somewhat wildly around the room, "and the papers. It looks messier than it is; I have a system."

"Okay," Margot said, with no inflection, and then, moving on, "I'm here preparing for the party."

"The what?" I asked dumbly.

Hadn't we had enough parties? Why were there so many parties?

"On Tuesday!" she said. "Your birthday, silly! Well, and the ambassador was planning to host some guests anyway . . . but I suppose since it's your birthday, we have to do something special for you, too. It's going to be here, at the embassy, not at the Villa Taverna. It's for those Hollywood people, the ones at Cinecittà. David has the invitation, I think. He knows all the details."

"David?" I asked dully. "David isn't here. He's never here. He's always in Milan."

"Well, he's got a lot of work to do there," Margot said, and her tone was still cheerful, but her eyes were narrowed a bit, like a cat's.

I actually laughed. "Sure," I said, "a lot of work. Selling American calculators to Italian primary schools."

I don't know why I had suddenly decided to air all my grievances about David, but I suppose I had finally just reached the end of my rope. None of this would have happened if he had been in Rome; I wouldn't have been alone, so the Wolf wouldn't have kissed me, so I wouldn't have gone dashing through the park after the photographer, letting him blackmail me . . . and on, and on. Though I suppose I still would have had to deal with Yevgeny.

Margot stared at me. It was a look that approximated to "you stupid, stupid child."

"Teddy," she asked slowly, "what do you think David does for a living?"

"He's an economic officer," I said, though I knew from her expression that this wasn't the answer, anymore.

"Teddy," she said again, after a long pause. "I really can't tell, sometimes—are you actually this stupid, or just pretending to be?"

She wasn't trying to start a fight, exactly. From her tone, I don't even think she was trying to be mean. I think she was just being honest with me, and frankly, I didn't disagree. I'd been waiting for someone to ask me that all my life. I felt that way, too, when David asked me if I just didn't understand how money worked, if I just didn't know how to clean up after myself, if I really couldn't figure out how to get out of bed in the morning. I always thought, well, yes. Why didn't you notice sooner?

"What do you mean?" I asked.

"David isn't in Milan all the time selling car parts to Fiat, Teddy," Margot said. "He works for the Central Intelligence Agency."

I didn't even know what that meant. I only had the vaguest notion of these things, though I know nobody believes me when I say that.

Margot believed it, though. "You have no idea," she said, "what your husband is sacrificing. You don't understand—you don't deserve . . ."

She was getting agitated, and it occurred to me that Margot might, in some strange way, love my husband. David—the subject of a schoolgirl crush?

I shouldn't have, but I laughed, which only further incensed her.

"He's out there risking his life for his country," she said, in a shaky voice, "and you're here in Rome sleeping all day, throwing his hard-earned money away on . . . baubles and beads!"

I realized then that David must have been talking about me,

about the things I did that troubled him. He had been confiding in Margot, and who knew whom else. It was embarrassing, obviously. But what I really wanted to know was, if everyone was talking about me all along, if everyone was watching me, why didn't anyone ever try to help? Why didn't anyone ask if I was okay?

David must have been a bad spy, if he couldn't see any of it. I didn't even know what it meant, that he worked for the Agency, but I imagined David embedded with radicals in Milan, learning their secrets and reporting them back. Perhaps he was having an affair with one of his informants—a lovely young anarchist named Elena who wore a beret and felt things more deeply, just because she grew up in the middle of the war, just because she was fighting for something.

I could picture it: David bent over a table in an *appartamento* with Elena the Italian anarchist informant in her black turtleneck, her narrow face warmed by candlelight. She was probably slender, the passion for her cause no doubt having burned away every extra ounce of fat. David would like that. He would like that she had struggled, that she was serious. He would like it if she had been orphaned in the war.

I suppose, given my situation, I should have been concerned that David, armed with the special knowledge of a spy, would figure me out. Would learn how I'd misled him—not just about the photo, but about everything. My entire past. Yevgeny Larin. The others— there had been others. Every little indulgence, every little lie, every piece of proof that I was soiled goods. Aunt Sister, and the madness that I was certain was also in me.

But I wasn't afraid. In that moment, I felt only relief.

Firstly, because that meant he truly wasn't paying attention to me at all. He would never find out about the photo: if it was his job to learn secrets and he had no idea how damaged I was, he must either not be looking at me, or he could see it all and simply didn't care.

Teddy

And then, too, I was relieved because I realized, finally, that we were the same. Yes, I was a liar, but so was he. It didn't matter to me that his deceptions were in support of a greater cause—were patriotic, were part of the fight on the checkerboard battlefield against Communism. Weren't my lies for a cause, as well? Hadn't I lied, didn't I continue to lie, for the most important cause of all—my own life?

I even felt a hint, just a hint, of superiority. At least I was trying to end my lies. At least I had a plan to become real.

I laughed again.

"Oh, of course," I said. "Of course he is."

Margot stared at me again, and then said, "He told me you were like this."

I didn't have anything to say to that.

Margot left after that little barb; she was on her way out for the evening, I guessed, based on her lipstick—the wrong shade for her complexion, not that she would have known that—and the little Bakelite barrette in her plain brown hair. I thought how nice it must be, to be a Serious Person. Someone who thinks they understand it all.

She was probably going to meet her beau for dinner, some older Italian schoolteacher, maybe. I entertained the idea for a moment that she was going to meet David, that her defense of him was evidence of a passionate love affair, but I couldn't manage to care about that idea very much, and besides, David would never have done it. He believed wholly and completely in the rules, I thought, which was one of the things that so troubled him about me. I knew that even Elena the anarchist probably wasn't real.

I imagined that Margot and her boyfriend would go somewhere cozy for dinner and have the veal and the house wine, and then they would return to her little studio flat near the river to make love, and everything would be on the table when they spoke to each other, and they would only expect to be happy in one another's

235

company. He would be patient with her occasional brusqueness, her youthful belief in forcing her way through, and she would love the little lines at the corners of his eyes, and the gentle way he approached the world, so different from the confidence, sometimes arrogance, of the men she worked with. The Italian schoolteacher didn't try to shape the world in his own image; he observed, and absorbed, and admired, and understood.

I imagined everything added up in Margot's life, I imagined she had five blouses and three skirts, I imagined she had a tidy little sum stashed away for a rainy day. I imagined she ate when she was hungry and stopped when she was full. I could picture her on nights when her Italian lover was away, propped up in bed with a lamp on the nightstand, reading calmly for half an hour, something sharp like Joan Didion or Virginia Woolf, before she turned out the light and slept soundly, maybe dreamlessly. I doubted she ever woke up with mascara staining her pillowcases in black smudges, with an incriminating photo of herself in the previous night's purse.

I remember her saying once, at one of the parties or luncheons at which we crossed paths, that she didn't believe in messing about; her father, she explained, had a saying he had imparted to his children: "If you don't like something the way it is, go change it."

It sounded so simple when you put it like that. It sounded like the easiest thing in the world, to do what you needed to do. To set the objects of your life in motion and expect that you could determine where they would land.

The Wolf's secretary had said she thought he would be free after five thirty, and as the minutes ticked past and it grew closer to the moment I would have to tell him about Mauro, about the photo, about how our arrangement had fallen through, I began to think I might die. There was a sharp pain in my chest that was getting more persistent, and no matter how much I gulped from the glass of water I'd taken from the kitchenette downstairs, my throat felt dry and full, like someone had stuffed cotton down it. Like I was the taxidermy wolf on the wall of the ambassador's office. I thought I tasted blood in my mouth, too, like the wolf's own red snarl, but that was just my imagination, I think.

The Wolf—the man—came in at five forty-five. He didn't try to touch me, just closed the door behind him.

"So," he said. "Is everything ready? You'll meet the bastard tonight, with the money? Go straight to Bar Rosati, after; I'll be waiting there with a box of matches and we can finish this thing."

It took me a moment to understand that he was living in an entirely different timeline. In his mind, nothing had changed since yesterday. He thought I was just here at the embassy getting a day of work in; he didn't know I'd gone to see Mauro last night. He thought I still had his million lire; he still thought that would be enough.

When I spoke, my voice was hoarse. The words ended in a whisper.

"He wants more money. He found out my name."

The Wolf watched me without reacting, and I thought he looked like David, just then. These government men, how calm they are when things fall apart.

When he spoke, it was his usual soft, dry drawl. No hint that anything had changed, at all.

"How much?"

I'd expected him to shout. I'd assumed he would ask how Mauro had found out my name, and I'd have to tell him about the checkbook, and he'd say how stupid I was, with my monogrammed checks and my fancy pens. Stupid Teddy, who wants everything to be special and throws her whole life away to flash her custom checks in Nile blue and silver.

"Ten million."

The words sounded like a door on rusted hinges, slowly falling shut.

The Wolf didn't even curse, this time. He just absorbed it. I thought I could see the cowboy in him, again. The man whose only concern is how to keep going. How to dodge bullets.

I started to speak—I don't know what I was going to say; maybe an apology. Maybe just wordless noises. He held up a hand, though, to stop me.

"Let me think, Teddy."

We stood there, the Wolf and I, in silence, until finally he said, "Do you have that much in your bank account? Surely you do—from your family, at least?"

"Yes, but David—"

"David!" The Wolf laughed. "David doesn't make that kind of money. Whatever you have, it's yours."

"His name is on the account, though. It's from my uncle—he wrote a check—"

The Wolf talked past me.

"David will never know. I can wire you the money, you just need to be the one to write the check. I can't have my name on this. Write the check, give it to this damn photographer, do it now, do it today. I'll call my guy; the money will be back in your account by the end of the week. Before David even notices."

It all seemed so simple. It was, actually. It would have been.

"Are you sure?"

I sounded small, and scared, and I was.

"Don't ask me that," the Wolf said. "We'll make this go away, and we'll never speak of it again."

I'd thought I was going to go to the Wolf and surrender myself to his care, and *he* would make it all go away. It would be humiliating, but he would do it, and I would be able to sleep again, finally. And now, instead, there was still more for me to do; in fact, it all seemed to rest on my shoulders. I'd wanted him to go to Mauro's flat and break down the door; I'd wanted him to sock the photographer right in the eye, the way his character had hit a cowardly accomplice in *One Week on the Rio Grande* during a brawl in the Sagebrush Saloon. I'd wanted it to be over.

"Courage, Teddy," the Wolf said, and he seemed sweeter, suddenly. "Hold the line. You won't believe it, but I've handled things like this before. You can't blink. You can't falter. I've been shot at—"

Here it was; I wanted the famous line. I wanted the movie cowboy to rescue me.

"—And do you think I flinched and hid and cried? No. I kept my mind empty and calm; I kept moving. That's how you go on living. That's how you keep them from bringing you down."

I realized he was speaking literally; he was talking about the war, not his movies. Every threat to his grand destiny had blended together, for him, into one amorphous company of enemies: Japanese soldiers, gray wolves, political enemies, paparazzi. Debutantes from Texas named Teddy.

He spoke as if it was something you could learn—to be like him, and I wanted it. I wanted to be untouchable; I wanted to be so polished that things slid off my surface. I wanted to live without consequences instead of looking back over my shoulder and then down the road, knowing I'd end up like Aunt Sister, knowing that with every late night, with every reckless purchase, with every time I laughed too loudly or slept too late or took too many stay-awake pills, I was building the mountain of evidence they would use to put me away. I wanted to be the Wolf, who didn't worry about what he'd done wrong, but only how to cover it up.

"You've handled things like this before?" I asked.

I wanted proof that it would be fine. I believed him, because I had no choice, but I wanted to know it, too.

"Come down to my office," he said. "The floor is empty, now.

My girl has gone home. I need to call someone to get this done, and I want to watch you write the check. And I'll tell you all about it, the last time they tried to bring me down."

In his office, the Wolf poured me a glass of whiskey and a double for himself. I was running on stay-awake pills and coffee and whatever I had eaten, whatever animals' organs, last night, and my stomach rolled at the thought of the bitter, burning drink, but I knew I would feel better in the end, so I took my medicine. My hands stopped shaking after the second sip.

I sat on the couch, the ornate, carved walnut monstrosity upholstered in cream brocade that had come with the embassy building, and watched while the Wolf picked up the receiver of one of the phones on his desk—there were two—and asked for someone called Gilchrist.

"Fifteen from slush," he said to Gilchrist, or whoever was on the other end of the line. Then repeated it and read out the account number I'd given him. He laughed, too, at something the other person said, and it angered me to hear him. What was there to laugh about?

When he'd hung up the phone, he came to sit by me, and watched as I took my beautiful checkbook, Nile blue and silver, out of my bag, and my precious silver pen, and I wrote out the amount. Ten million lire from the account I shared with David. They wouldn't call him, but he would notice when he looked at the statement, if the transfer didn't come through fast enough. But I had no choice, and I was out of time, so I did it. I wrote the check.

"When I first ran for California State Senate," the Wolf explained, on his second double, "some photographs of Lina surfaced. Pictures she'd taken in the early days. It was something plenty of young girls did at the beginning, when they were trying to get established. Not a big deal, certainly not to me. Art, really—like that statue in the stairwell. Like a painting."

Art, like the Venus. Like the women on Mauro's wall. It was

strange to think of polished Lina, so strong and capable in her films, with her femme fatale's purr and a jawline you could use to cut glass, posing naked for a photographer at the beginning of her career. I tried to imagine how she had felt when the photos came up. How guilty, how ashamed. But I wondered, too, if she'd been a little bit proud of them. So lovely and young. So hopeful.

"It was just a matter of payment," the Wolf continued, "and some carefully chosen words to discourage any future contact."

"A threat," I said, and he shrugged.

"Someone will need to have a word with your photographer," he said, "at some point. It's trickier, this time. Not my home turf, of course, and people are watching. I have to be careful."

"Watching?"

I thought of the Pointdexters in their room upstairs. I thought of David.

"Oh, it's all part of the game," the Wolf said, "but yes. Don't you think, if I show up at a photographer's apartment in Rome making threats, that the Russians will hear about it? Wouldn't they love to have a little nugget of information like that to squirrel away, for when I'm president?"

When I'm president, he said. Not if.

I believed him, too—nothing could stop the Wolf. Certainly not me.

"So, you go pay him," the Wolf continued, "and you bring me that negative, and you hand it to me and watch me burn it. And make it clear, when you talk to him, that this is the end. There won't be a third chance, for him."

I didn't know how I was supposed to convey that convincingly. What did I have that I could threaten anyone with?

"Teddy," he continued, and his blue eyes were on fire; it was my own personal close-up from one of his films. I could see him standing in a dusty street outside the saloon, staring me down, drawing his gun. "I'm not going out like this. They've tried to bring me down before, but look at them now."

He gestured toward the wall, to the stuffed wolf and the dead man's gun.

"Go straight to your *paparazzo*," the Wolf said, spitting the Italian word. "Give him the check. Tell him to come to you as soon as it clears, to give you the negative. All of this will be done by tomorrow, Teddy. Hold the line; we're almost there."

I did feel braver, after his speech. We were almost there, and we would make it, as long as I didn't blink. As long as I didn't flinch. I took my bag and stood up; I'd finished my whiskey. I was on my way to the door when the Wolf spoke again from where he sat on that hideous brocade couch.

"One other thing, Teddy."

I stopped and turned to look at him, and he wasn't smiling at me the way he had been, exactly. He didn't seem quite so enchanted. He seemed, actually, a little angry.

"I'm not spending that much money on an affair I haven't had yet," he said.

There was something cruel around his mouth, his perfect movie star lips, when he walked over to me, when he led me back to the couch.

But he was tender, too; he said how beautiful I was as he kissed my neck, my breasts; he said how much he wanted me. Not to keep, of course; I understood that much. He wasn't asking if he could take care of me. He was getting reimbursed.

I wish I could say it was hard for me. I wish I could say I hated every second of it, his hands on me, the way he turned me away from him on all fours there on the antique sofa in his office, facing the dead wolf on the wall. But it felt right. It felt like something I deserved.

It was the feeling I used to get when I would go out at night with strange men, or take a few days' worth of pills all at once, or drink until I was sick, or eat everything in sight, or spend all my money for the month in just a few days.

It was relief. Instead of waiting for the slow rot I knew was inside me to take over, I was burning the whole house down. I was taking myself apart. I wanted to give a piece of myself to every man that asked, until there was nothing left to worry about. Until I was completely gone.

The Wolf smelled clean. Not like he had bathed, and not the warm skin scent I'd grown used to on David in the mornings, but like cologne, though there was just a hint of something else—sweat, perhaps—underneath.

He gave me money for a taxi and walked me down the grand staircase, past the marble statues sleeping in their alcoves, past the modest Venus, to the embassy's front door.

They were always very polite to me, these men.

It was perfect outside when I left the Palazzo Margherita, plush pink clouds drifting across the sky with golden light shining through them from behind. It looked like the sun was holding the clouds in his fist, squeezing the light out of them; it looked like the sky in a Renaissance painting. Like God himself was coming down to say something—an annunciation, word from on high, some kind of sign that things were about to change. That maybe they were about to be better.

That was wrong, of course.

In the backseat of the cab, already sore, sweaty and sticky and badly in need of a bath, I felt a peace I hadn't known in days, maybe longer. I had suffered for my sins, I thought. I had earned my keep. Now came my reward, and it wasn't so much to ask, was it? I didn't want to be happy. I just wanted everything to go back to the way it was.

I wanted to wake up before my husband every morning and make him coffee, even if I had to take a few little pills to do it. I wanted to putter around the apartment and then go to lunch, go shopping, come home and make dinner, make love to my husband, get in bed and read a book and turn the light out and then do it all again the next day, and the next. I wanted it to come naturally, but if I had to force myself into it like a bloodied, blistered foot into a too-small Dior shoe, that was fine, too. I would do it.

I took the taxi to Testaccio. There it was, my mountain of trash. There were the butchers' shops, the ones that supplied brains and balls and gallbladders to the restaurants of the neighborhood. I went to Mauro's apartment and knocked on the door. I hadn't called ahead to see if he would be there, but I knew he would. There was too much on the line, now.

He answered frowning, the room all red behind him.

"Turn off the lights," I told him. "I can't look at this."

The evil red glow, the photos on the wall, the women with their heavy bodies out for anyone to see. I felt nauseous again, like I had that first night in his room. I dropped the check on the table and went over to one of the little windows, opened it wide to get some fresh air.

I could see the sun finally setting. See the blue of dusk, that powdery, sad color. It's the same one as early morning; of my Nile blue checks, of Aunt Sister's perfume.

"You know what they call this time of day, in France?" Mauro asked idly from behind me, waving his cigarette over my shoulder as he spoke.

"*L'heure bleue*," I said. I knew this one.

"No," he said. "*L'heure entre chien et loup.*"

"What does it mean?"

"The time between the dog and the wolf. Twilight. When the dog of the day becomes dangerous, like a wolf, at night."

I turned to look at him.

Cold blue illuminated the angles of his face, casting his lips—soft, full like a woman's—in a color as purple as the suckers of my octopus. He was gorgeous, and sensitive, and I couldn't stand him. He knew what he was doing to me, and he did it reluctantly, but he did it anyway. He would have been a better person, I think, if I hadn't liked him as much as I did; he should have at least had the dignity to let me hate him. He should have been a better villain.

David, too—he made me love him, at least a little, and he really didn't want to hurt me, at least not very much, and I could never forgive that, because I needed an enemy. I wanted the Red Russians that everyone feared, I wanted shadowy figures trying to destroy me, stabbing at me from corners, dropping nuclear bombs on my head. I wanted Eugene to be what he was supposed to be, the spy; I wanted to be threatened and interrogated by nameless, faceless men—I wanted inquisitors.

And instead, I had the Wolf, who said I was beautiful while he used me, and I had David, who cried when he thought he had hurt me, but who—well, we're still coming to that. And I had my family, who loved me, who gave me everything, so how could I say they were against me? How could I say they had harmed me? The only person I could think of to truly hate, the only real villain in all of this, was me.

As if you need more proof:

Mauro said I could make the amount nine million, not ten, if I'd hand over the rest of the cash from the night before, whatever was left over from our dinner and dancing at Piper. Just so he would have something in hand, in case there was an issue with the check.

I dug around in my purse for a bit, trying to find it, but there was nothing there.

"I don't have it," I told him.

"You spent it all," he said flatly, and I shrugged.

The gesture was meant to be one of resignation; the money was gone, now, so what did it matter whether I'd spent it or been robbed of it or dropped it in the Tiber? I couldn't remember, and it was all too, too late.

But he must have taken me to mean that it was only a million lire, no big deal, because he exhaled loudly through his nose and made a little speech, right there at the table.

"You're so careless, you Americans," he said. "With your expensive clothes and your hair and your little purse. My mother sold herself to American GIs for four dollars on the via Toledo in Naples after the war, and you spend thousands like it's nothing. And then you cry over a picture, just a photo, when you will still be rich. Even if it goes in *Gente*, you will still be rich."

I could tell Mauro had been working on this, that he'd been wanting to say something like this to me for a while, so I didn't bother arguing with him. He was mostly right, anyway, and it wasn't his fault that he didn't understand what would actually happen to me if the picture came out.

It was almost funny, how easy the whole mess would have been to fix, and yet how impossible it was. David and I had more than ten million in the account—though keep in mind that was about fifteen thousand dollars, so really not such an inconceivable amount—left over from the check Uncle Hal had written to us at the wedding. But there was no way for me to withdraw it without David's knowledge, and so somehow, I was rich and yet I might as well have had nothing, for all the good it did me. For all the use it was. And even when my inheritance came through, David would be the one to decide what we did with it. To keep track of it, to see what I was spending and where, and why. If I hadn't been married, I would have been able to spend my own money, but I wouldn't have been given the money if I hadn't been married, and, of course, none of this would have mattered anyway if I wasn't married, because then letting the Wolf kiss me wouldn't have been so bad.

I don't know, though—I think I still wouldn't have wanted that picture in the papers. The lustful look on my face, the way my leg was exposed. I wouldn't have wanted people to see her, the Teddy I'd been trying all my life to hide away. I'd wanted to smother her until she suffocated, under sweaters and sturdy dresses, under pills that put a pep in your step, under clean hair and fresh makeup and a bright, shiny smile. But she was always poking her stupid blond head back up, saying, "Here I am." Saying, "Feed me."

"I'm sorry," I said to Mauro, and I didn't bother specifying what for. For all of it—for his mother, for all of us, we stupid, rich Americans, for my expensive purses, for my expensive hair.

"There it is," I said, and pointed out the check to him, where it rested on the table.

Mauro looked at me like I was stupid, like he was Margot, like he was watching me say yes, here it is, I'm good for it, but he didn't believe me, and what's more, he pitied and scorned me; but he didn't say any of that, and he didn't stop me from making promises he didn't believe I could keep. Writing checks he didn't think I could cash.

He said he would take it to the bank Monday morning and call me as soon as it went through, and he would bring the negatives to my apartment. I gave him my address.

He also said if it didn't work, he was going to the papers.

For a moment I wanted to say, do it. I wanted to say, please.

I could feel fatigue coming for me, creeping toward me, and I still had to clean the apartment before David returned tomorrow, if I truly wanted to convince him that nothing was wrong, that I was better, now, and then Margot had reminded me of my birthday party on Tuesday, too, and I would have to get dressed and ready for that, and then there would be the inheritance and all the paperwork, and there would always be something, some other thing coming, and—

Just for a moment, one small second, I thought maybe I should let Mauro sell the photo. Let them print it, and let myself disappear. I could hear the sound of waves crashing in my mind, and breathed easier for a moment.

Only for a second, though, did I let myself think it, and then I left Mauro sitting at the table in his apartment with his check, and I walked all the way home on my bloody, broken feet.

Beppo wasn't hanging around the door when I got home, and his tuna was still untouched, now spoiled and covered in flies. I hoped he had found somewhere better to live. I hoped nothing bad had happened to him—I thought of David and how he joked, sometimes, about poisoning the cats in our neighborhood. I knew he wouldn't do it, it was only his way of saying he found them to be pests, but I couldn't help thinking that perhaps something awful had happened, imagining Beppo's fuzzy little body all stiff, racked with pain to the end, and his sweet little face in a frozen scream.

The apartment was empty, the air stale again, but the former world was the same as the new one, I understood now. Or rather, there was no new world, just the poisonous miasma, the old, fetid air of secrets I thought I had closed the door on.

I went to the kitchen and found a bottle of David's wine. Opened it, poured a glass to the brim, and gulped it like water. I went to my wardrobe and looked through my dresses. Found a little black cocktail sheath and put that on, with stockings and high heels. Painted fresh black lines over the ones already flaking off my lids, glopped more mascara onto my lashes. Traced my limited-edition Revlon Lanolite lipstick in Sphinx Pink over my mouth; the dry flecks and lines on my lips picked up the frosted pink and made me look older, and ill. I sprayed my hair high again and pinned it, letting soft pieces fall around my face. I finished the bottle of wine while I did this, then brushed my teeth and spat into the sink, the dark, clotted purple from my mouth the same color once again as the veins and suckers of the octopus. I wiped my lips, leaving smudges of pale pinky-peach and deep purple on the towel, and when I checked my face in the mirror, it all looked right.

I wasn't going anywhere. I don't know why I did all that.

I knew I wouldn't sleep that night, not until I heard from Mauro in the morning that the money had come through. Not until I had the photograph and its negative in my hand, and then in ashes. Not until the Wolf told me the wire had gone through, not until I knew David would never sniff me out.

I still didn't fully comprehend, I think, that it would never be over; that once I'd gotten rid of the photo, I would have to worry about Yevgeny Larin, and then whatever came next, whatever secret reappeared after that, and after that.

I didn't understand it, because even after everything Margot had told me, I still thought it was possible that David could be a good spy at work and a terrible one at home. Why else did he always leave me there alone in the apartment? How else was he so easily fooled that I was happy, that I was fine?

I still refused, at that stage, to believe that he knew exactly how I spent my days and nights and simply didn't care. That I had really, in the end, a single purpose to serve.

I also knew I would probably die if I didn't get at least a few hours of rest, so I went to my nightstand and opened the drawer. Found the little Limoges box shaped like a dachshund—how charming, I'd thought, when I saw it on the shelf at an antique shop over by the Pantheon—where I kept the other pills, the ones for sleeping. They were speckled green and small, like lizards' eggs.

I only took one, at first, but when it didn't work after a few minutes, I took a second. I think I slept for three hours, total, on top of the covers, in my black dress and stockings, and I don't remember if I dreamed.

2O. Trastevere

Monday, July 7, 1969

I stayed in bed after I woke until the sun began to rise, not quite sleeping but lacking the will to rise and shine, or even to rise and hunt down the bottle of pills that would help me to shine artificially.

After I finally dragged myself out of bed, after I managed to brush my teeth and get dressed in something that wasn't evening-wear and prepare a pot of coffee to put on the stove, I sat down on the sofa closest to the telephone, to wait.

Why hadn't Mauro called yet? What time did banks open in Italy? He'd said he would make the deposit first thing in the morning and then call me to arrange the exchange of the negative; I could tell he wanted it to be over, too.

David was already on the train, no doubt. He would be sitting in the business cabin in his pressed white shirt—not damp, because I hadn't been there to ruin it—and his black trousers, his shoes shined to perfection. He would have his newspaper spread out in front of his face—a paper without my picture in it, still, I hoped—and a disposable cup of coffee. He would be on his way home to see his beautiful wife, expecting the new, improved Teddy with her hair all done and her nails all polished, waiting happily for him in a pretty, clean dress. Well, I'd tried to fix my hair, at least. And my nails were still manicured, long and shiny, petal pink.

Maybe Mauro would call soon to let me know that it was finished, and he could bring me the negative to destroy before David got home in the afternoon, and maybe I could be waiting flawlessly for my husband, and kiss him when he arrived, and we could go out to dinner at Giggi Fazi or Cesarina for my birthday, and toast to us, and talk about our future together the way he had promised.

I suppose I must have fallen asleep there on the sofa to these fantasies, because I was startled awake by the sound of a key in the lock. The heavy wooden door from the stairwell opening slowly into the sitting room.

David in the doorway, a bouquet of roses in his hand. Crisp, white shirt—not damp. Eyes blinking behind his horn-rimmed glasses, smiling with his mouth open, ears pink with pleasure as he handed the roses over to me, along with a long, thin box wrapped in white paper.

I know all of the containers that jewelry comes in. The little square box of a ring, the larger square for a bracelet or watch, the cube of a pair of earrings.

The flat, rectangular package of a necklace.

"From Milan," he said. "For you."

I slid a finger under the edge of the paper and lifted the tape. Undid the paper and flattened and folded it, unripped. Set it aside.

"You're so careful," David observed, and rested a hand at my back. "You'll make a wonderful mother."

And I could see he was smiling and that it was intended to be meaningful—he was telegraphing something about a decision he'd made, about me—but I couldn't enjoy it because I was beginning to suspect something, and when I peeled the paper away, I was right.

It was a champagne-coloured leather box. Bulgari. I had known it would be jewelry, but even so, I gasped when I lifted the lid.

A double strand of pearls, glowing softly on a bed of velvet. A diamond clasp. Pearls that were real, that contained their own light. Diamonds so bright it made my teeth hurt to look at them.

David mistook my gasp for delight and reached over to take my hand.

"Happy early birthday, Teddy Bear," he said.

He came to stand behind me and lifted the pearls from their case. Undid the clasp, then joined it around my neck.

"Thank you, David," I said.

It sounded like the real thing. It didn't sound like I was drowning, at all.

The pearls were warm on my skin, and toothy, like velvet. I knew, now, the difference between fake and real. I wouldn't make that mistake again.

"It was your mother's idea for me to go ahead and get them," he said. "Since the money from your grandparents will be coming soon. She wanted me to tell you she's proud of you."

There wasn't time, really, to take in this proof of the fact I had always guessed at, which was that David had been reporting back on me to Mama, and probably to Uncle Hal.

Because I knew how much these pearls cost. I had pointed them out to David in the window, that time, when we walked down the via Condotti. I had gone back to see them.

And I knew he didn't have the money for them, at least not until we got my inheritance, unless he'd used what was left of Uncle Hal's gift.

Which meant there wasn't enough in the account for the check I'd written the night before, which meant that Mauro, no doubt, had been scorned at the bank and was already on his way to the flat, would appear at any moment like an avenging angel, like a fury, following me, cursing me to my grave.

I kissed David for a long moment, tenderly, on the mouth.

"Thank you, baby," I said. I think it sounded real.

I excused myself and went to the bathroom; I still hadn't finished my makeup, I said.

I thought David gave me a strange look just then, but perhaps I was being paranoid.

As soon as I was through the door of the little bathroom I locked it and leaned against the countertop, willing my legs to stop shaking, trying to stop my entire body from vibrating into oblivion.

My hands were trembling so visibly that I didn't know how I would get my eye makeup on to maintain the lie, but then when I looked in the mirror, I realized I still had some on from last night.

My heart felt like a pigeon. They used to build their nests in the eaves of the porch at the house on Beverly, and Mama would knock them down with a broom to keep the birds from shitting all over the slate tiles. The pigeons wouldn't leave, though, because they could see the remnants of their broken nests, their babies, in the bushes or at the edge of the patio where they'd fallen, and then Daddy would trap them in cages and cart them out to the ranch to set them free, taking aim and shooting them in their flight, one after the other, heavy limp bird bodies falling unceremoniously to the ground.

I remember the way they would beat their wings against the wires of the cages, all stacked on top of each other in the back of Daddy's truck.

Once, a nest Mama knocked down had two eggs in it. One of them broke, cracked yellow and running in lines through the grooves between tiles on the floor. The other egg was still sitting there, perfect, pristine, among the twigs and tinfoil.

I took it to my room when she wasn't looking and made a new nest for it in an old cigar box and hid it in the top of my closet. I would hold it for hours at a time, keeping it warm, waiting for it to hatch. It was so smooth, but somehow not shiny. It was a matte white color that absorbed light like a fingernail, like a seashell. Like the chalky color of a stay-awake pill. Eventually it began to rot, and smell, and my mother found it in my closet and threw it away. I didn't understand why it never hatched, at least not until I was older.

I took a stay-awake pill, pigeon-egg white, with a swallow of water from the tap, and gagged over it. I could taste the bitter powder; the sugar coating came off on my tongue, on the ridges at the back of my throat, when I tried to swallow it the first time. I took another sip of water and forced it the rest of the way down.

I tried to think of what was left for me to do, to save myself—could I run outside without David noticing, or on some pretext, to find a phone? Call Mauro, call the Wolf, call anyone?

I'm pleased, looking back, that I kept going. Or tried to. That I was still trying to think of solutions, that I still thought somehow I could save myself. If I'm honest, I'd say I sort of knew it wasn't possible, but even so, I didn't stop.

There's a painting in the gallery at Royal Holloway in London that I learned about in school. I remember seeing it cast large in a darkened classroom, an illumination on the wall from the slide projector. Two polar bears among the wreckage of a ship in the Arctic, devouring human remains with mouths full of flesh, in oil on canvas. *Man Proposes, God Disposes*, it was called. It was meant to be a commentary on the futility of human attempts to manage nature, on the foolishness of thinking you can ever fully be in control. The teacher had explained that it was painted after the Franklin expedition to find the Northwest Passage went missing, and I remember going to the library to learn all I could about it.

And I recall reading, in an old leatherbound book riddled with red rot, that the Franklin expedition had become icebound, and the men of the ships had stayed trapped in the far north for two years before finally setting out across the snow in search of help, at which point they all perished of exposure and starvation—after first eating their deceased shipmates. Years later, the local tribes found cracked human bones in cooking kettles bearing the stamp of the Royal Navy, buried under the ice.

I couldn't understand why the men of the expedition had done this—they must have known they didn't have a chance, so why didn't they simply lie down in their bunks on their icebound ships and wait to die in relative comfort? What makes a man set out walking in his London winter clothes across a field of pure ice, without even seabirds or lichens to eat? What makes him keep moving toward a mirage until he dies in the attempt?

I always thought I would give up; I would make an assessment and decide it was better to die quietly and calmly than to go out into the cold and walk until my feet were bloodied and my hands were frostbitten.

But here I was with this pain in my chest, with my heart pounding away like a pigeon in a wire cage, hands shaking, hardly having slept in three days, running on coffee and pills and, I suppose, the deep-fried organs of sheep and cows from a few days earlier, and when I drank water it tasted like batteries in my mouth, but I was still walking, and I understood. I would've snapped the sinews of my compatriots with my teeth, I would have cracked their bones and eaten the marrow, if I'd had to. I would have cried, and wailed, and shaken my fist, and I definitely would have vomited all over the pristine Arctic ice, but I would have done it.

It may sound strange, but when I look back, I'm proudest of this: that I hadn't given up yet.

I understood something about Aunt Sister, too. Why she kept coming to visit at the Beverly house and the Hill Country ranch, even though she knew Mama and Uncle Hal were closing in on her. Why she brought make-believe gifts, even though she'd run out of money and she knew it would all have to end, soon. I understood that she had to keep dancing. She had to put her lipstick on and find pearls to give me for my birthday, and even though she knew they were fake, she had to give me a story to go with them. She wanted to be out in the world for as long as she could; she wanted to push the day of reckoning to the very end. Every minute more, every cocktail hour or nice meal or day in the sun, every story she could tell while people still believed her—she wanted all of it, as much as she could have, before the end.

I was eyeing the fat little tub of Pond's cold cream on the bathroom counter, thinking about taking my makeup off—so that if David asked what I had been doing in there I could say he'd misheard me, I hadn't said I was going to put my makeup *on*, but take it *off*; you see, I was still coming up with plans and lies and obfuscations—when I decided I couldn't stand it. I couldn't stand the idea that David might be sitting out there wondering where I was. Starting to think something was wrong, and starting to consider what might be the cause. If he was as sharp as everyone said he was—as sharp as I knew him to be—he'd figure it out, soon enough.

So I rushed back out to the sitting room, and when I got there, David was staring off into space, and he seemed mostly tired rather than like someone who was tallying all my possible misdeeds—his eyes were glassy under their heavy lids—and so I went and sat beside him and kissed his cheek. Rubbed his back, dragged my fingernails down the nape of his neck.

"Teddy Bear," he said, lifting me onto his lap and taking off his glasses, "what's gotten into you?"

His eyes were puffy, so sweet and sleepy without his glasses on. This was my favorite David. Not the cold fish, not the diplomat. Not David who wakes up at the same time every day and makes coffee, not David who hates a mess. David who makes a sound deep in his throat when he's with me, David who tells me he loves me, David who shivers when I touch him. David who wants me.

Whatever else, he always wanted me, and that was when I felt safest. The only minutes I knew I was perfect, the moment there was no other way I needed to be, when it was guaranteed he wouldn't send me away, at least not for a little while.

I just wanted a moment. One more moment.

We did it right there on the couch, and then I went to the bathroom again to clean myself up. I never cared about that, personally, and would have been happy to stay there on the sofa in his arms, in our sweat, twined together, at least a few minutes more—as long as I could—but I knew it would bother David if I didn't rinse off right away.

When I came back out into the living room, Mauro was there.

21. Trastevere

Mauro and David were sitting side by side on the sofa, as if this was simply a normal social call.

And I had no way of knowing how much had been said in my absence, or, really, how long I'd been out of the room—I was losing track of large swaths of time, by then.

I wondered if David would finally use his fists and hit Mauro; I wondered how he would misinterpret—or, worse, correctly interpret—what was happening. I wanted to say something, but I couldn't think what, and that octopus had clogged my throat again with his purple-suckered arms.

Mauro looked worried when I walked in the room. He had probably wanted to be angry, but when he saw me, he said, "Just let me sell it, Teddy. It won't be so bad."

"Teddy," David began, and I knew he wanted to ask me what the man meant, but I walked past them both and into the kitchen, where I had, I remembered, set a pot of coffee on the stove a while—a few hours?—earlier. It would probably be burned, by now.

That was cowardly of me. Of all the things I did, leaving the room—letting the men discuss me without me, letting the knife drop where I couldn't see it—was the most childish, I think.

I returned to the living room, because I knew I had to, and pressed a cup of burned coffee into each man's hands. I was the

258

hostess, after all. I knew the right things to do when company was over, even if I didn't always do them.

Mauro had a copy of the photo out on the table, and he tried to smile at me.

"It's not so bad," he said again.

Then, in Italian, and I realized he probably didn't know that David would understand him, he added, "You look beautiful, see?"

My hands were shaking when I picked up the photograph. There she was, Teddy or the thing inside her, that bottomless pit of wanting, consuming, collecting.

"I don't understand it, Teddy," David had said once, when he was fed up with the mess around the apartment early on. "Why do you need so many *things*, Teddy?"

When I was little, Aunt Sister gave me a doll. Not just a doll, though: she came with an entire miniature upholstered travel trunk, full of things like Doll Hair Powder and a tiny real boar-bristle brush. Miniature pink glass coupes to hold her plaster ice cream, doll dresses made of taffeta and gingham. There was a whole catalogue, too, of other things you could purchase for her. A gold-plated comb for her hair. A tiny diary with a miniature working pen. How could I not want it all?

And then when you grew up and couldn't play with dolls anymore, you could buy the adult versions of those doll things. Crystal flutes for your champagne, a handmade boar-bristle brush for your hair. Lipsticks in every possible shade of pink and orange and coral and red, and shoes so delicate they had to be repaired every time you wore them. And the bag you saw in a magazine, new for this season, with the lacquered bamboo handle, the leather inlay.

You could have a doll's house, and you could live in it. You could be in control of your own little world; you could play pretend. Pretend to do the dishes, pretend to be happy about it, pretend to have a drink ready for your husband when he walked in the door after work. You could brush your hair until it shone, you could dress yourself for dinner in your gingham frock, in your taffeta gown, and everything could be perfect, for a while.

Teddy in the photo wasn't the perfect woman she was supposed to be; she was in motion. *Figura serpentinata*, the sinuous snakelike slut, the movement captured in celluloid of a woman losing control of herself. I had wanted to hide the photo because it wasn't fair: it wasn't the truth. I wasn't having an affair with the Wolf when the picture was taken—I wasn't actually the Teddy you could see there on film. Or at least I was trying not to be.

But sitting with Mauro and David in the living room, looking at it once again, I realized that it was all true, every bit of it, and that it was the only honest photo ever taken of me.

Why not let Mauro sell the photo? Why not let the world see what I was really like? They say it's good to be honest; in church, they teach you not to lie. I fantasized once more about letting Mauro publish the picture, but it was already too late, because now David knew, and he wasn't going to let it happen that way.

I sat beside Mauro with the photo in my hand, clutching my coffee cup in the other. I stared at David; my mouth wouldn't move to form words. That was all right, though, at least; it really was too late. There was no need to tell any of the lies I might have tried if I had been able to remember them, or think fast enough to find a new one. If my hands hadn't been visibly shaking, if there hadn't been dark hollows under my eyes. If I wasn't clenching my teeth to keep them from chattering.

I can't remember exactly what was said on my behalf, except that Mauro told David the whole story, at least what he knew of it. It's strange to hear the last few days as you've lived them described from someone else's viewpoint, start to finish. Mauro didn't know everything, though—he didn't know about the Wolf's money or what it had cost me. And he didn't know about Yevgeny Larin. As far as he knew, I'd been handling the situation alone the entire time. What a woman I would have been, if that had been true!

David didn't ask me about the affair, and I didn't bother protesting that it had never happened, because now, after all, it had.

"You didn't think I would notice, Teddy? That fifteen thousand dollars was gone?"

"The Wolf was going to wire it back," I said, speaking for the first time in a while. "He made a call and asked them to send it from slush, and he said it would be there by the end of the week, and you'd never notice. But the check bounced."

"Could you excuse us, please?" David asked Mauro, not looking at me. "I need to speak with my wife."

Mauro hesitated, and David put a hand out toward him. "And could you leave the photo? You'll get your money, don't worry. I'll be in touch."

Mauro must have believed him; anyone would, really, David was so calm and collected. Mauro set the photo in David's open palm and stood to go. He stopped for just a moment longer, trying to catch my eye, but I looked down at my long, pink fingernails.

"*In bocca al lupo*, Teddy," he said. "*Coraggio*."

Men were always telling me to be brave.

The door closed behind Mauro, and David and I sat for a while in silence.

And then David asked me to tell him everything, and I did, though of course I didn't tell him *everything*, because I've never told anyone everything in my life. But I told him enough.

I began babbling about what had happened, my version of it, anyway, unburdening myself of almost the whole story, and I finally felt relief watching the weight of it settle over David. I felt it lifting off me the more rooted he became to his seat.

I'm editorializing, actually—he was mostly unmoved, as usual. His face was blank, his mouth a straight line. The only sign that anything was different was a slight slump to his shoulders that might have been there before, and a flush over his cheeks and ears that happened to him sometimes, anyway.

"We can fix this," he said, when my rambling finally tailed off into shamed, uncertain silence.

I didn't want to, anymore. I was finished. I wanted to sleep. I wanted my brain to stop moving. That was the only moment I ever truly envied Aunt Sister. I thought maybe it wouldn't be so bad. To not know, anymore.

I didn't want to fix it, and I didn't think I should have to, now that I had decided I would just let them take me, but David made me run through it again.

"The ambassador said he made the transfer? And where did he say it came from?"

When I repeated the Wolf's words, "Fifteen from slush," David sat silent for at least a full minute, and then said, to himself more than to me, "Okay. We can definitely fix this." Then, "I need to make some calls."

He stood and walked toward the kitchen, then looked back at me as if he'd just remembered I was there too, and said, "Wait in the bedroom."

I nodded, but first I took the roses from where he'd left them on the entrance table. Fresh flowers in scarlet red, petals softer than skin. I took them into the kitchen and sawed at the stems with a bread knife, diagonal cuts with the serrated edge. It absorbs the water better, supposedly, to do that to them. The stems had thorns, but I worked around them. I didn't even prick myself, not once.

I put the shorn roses in a jug of water filled from the tap and left it on the dining table, and then I went to the bedroom.

I was in there for over two hours, and I felt strangely calm. It was out of my hands, now. It was over.

I took a bath and removed my makeup. I washed and dried my hair. I painted on new mascara and a coral lipstick, like the woman in the portrait at the Barberini. The perfect, motionless woman I'd thought I could be, deludedly, for a moment. Before I remembered what I was really like; what I had always been like.

I knew early that there was something wrong. Nobody told me outright, but I could tell. The way they watched me eat, the way my mother hid sweets from me, the way she talked about it, about me. I heard her worrying to Uncle Hal that I didn't know how to stop myself, and that it was a disgusting quality in a woman. She said I would get myself into trouble.

On my thirteenth birthday, a girl from my class gave me a box of chocolates, and they locked it in the pantry.

"We don't need any more little piggies," my mother said, which was a reference to some hogs we'd been keeping, lately, on the ranch.

But I figured out how to pick the lock to the pantry, and I ate them all at once, sitting down in the bottom of that closet between the tins of tomatoes and sacks of flour, and I cleaned up all of my debris and put it in the garbage. I don't know what I thought would happen, after that—if I really believed that nobody would notice, or that they would see the chocolates were gone and simply shrug and decide there was no point in crying over spilled milk.

That was a Saturday night, my secret pantry feast, and I remember sitting in church the next morning with the choir, singing "He Leadeth Me" and not even feeling guilty, just glad I'd gotten away with it. Until halfway through the hymn, when I began to feel an aching, gnawing pain in the bottom of my belly, and I realized God was punishing me for stealing. For lying. I sat sweating through the rest of the service, feeling with every cramp and stabbing pain that I was getting exactly what I deserved. My ill-gotten gains had made me sick; I was certain.

In the bathroom at home, afterward, I found the rust-colored stains in my underwear and realized what had happened. Aunt Sister had told me all about it, before, and what to expect, and that really, it was no big deal, but she was in Switzerland at the time, so I went to my mother. She handed me a stack of sanitary napkins and showed me how to use them, and that evening after the laundry had been done, Mama brought my underpants up to my room to show me how the blood still hadn't washed out, how it had stained the white cotton a watery brown.

"Boys will start to bother you," she said, "now that you're a woman. But just know that when you give yourself to them, it leaves a stain. And see how ugly it looks? And don't you think a man would rather marry someone clean?"

Most of the time, I managed to stop myself from taking everything I wanted. I managed to keep myself in line, not because I enjoyed a sense of order, but because I was afraid of the alternative. I made sure I was always reducing, only having coffee and the occasional cracker, and maybe a bit of chicken broth, most days, at least when anyone was watching; I stayed awake from four in the morning so I could be shining, glowing in the kitchen by seven; I wore long dresses with sweaters to hide my body; I bathed every day, or almost, or close enough, spending hours either washing off my makeup or reapplying it, rinsing out my hair and drying and styling it, curling it with hot tongs that burned my ears and neck and scalp. I watched my tongue, because I knew they were taking stock and keeping track of me. I was sensible and clean and good, or at least I pretended to be.

When David finally let me leave the bedroom again, he brought me over to the kitchen table. The amputated roses were where I'd left them in their vase, and there was a little flat, pearl-gray box that looked like a tape recorder, and a tangle of wires, there, too.

"Teddy, have a seat," David said.

I didn't ask him about the thing. The wires. He could have been building a bomb and it would have been all the same to me, at that point. I thought of David's imaginary anarchist girlfriend. I envied her—Elena, I had called her—not because I was jealous of David's attentions, but because I thought she must be full of purpose, if she existed, working late into the night on her leaflets and letter bombs with the conviction that the only solution to making the world better was to create more chaos.

"This," David said, holding the little metal box up for me to see it more clearly, "is a recording device."

He seemed a little drunk, struggling with the "r" in "recording," and the sharp, herbal scent of his breath as he spoke informed me that the glass of clear liquid next to him did not contain water, but rather gin. He didn't usually drink it, and I'd never seen him this drunk before. I was happy to see him in such a state, actually— it was the most he had ever let me know he cared. That he was hurt, or at least perturbed, by my affair with the ambassador.

"Like the Thing?" I asked, and David jerked his head back in surprise.

"Where did you hear that?" he asked, apparently forgetting that he'd been present when the West German attaché had told me the story at our first party together in Rome.

Then, before I could explain, he said, "You know what? Never mind. Just listen: you have to take it to the embassy, Teddy. You have to record the Wolf saying he paid you to handle the picture, and admitting to the affair."

"What? Why?"

The words were thick in my mouth, like I had just woken from sleep. It was too much—I had wanted this to be finished.

"He committed a crime, and we're going to catch him."

"A crime?"

The only person I could think of who had committed a crime was Mauro. I didn't know the ins and outs of the Italian legal system, then or now, but I knew blackmail was not allowed in most places. I supposed I might have committed a crime, too, if you counted writing bad checks. Even though I hadn't meant to—which was often the case, with my crimes.

"He paid you off."

"It's his money, though," I said, and David made a sound of frustration.

"Well, maybe not a crime—I'm not sure yet. But at the very least it's something we can use against him."

"So, what?" I was still struggling with the idea that my story wasn't over. That there was more left to do. "I go see him, tell him the payment went through, get him to say again what happened, into the little box?"

"That's about the shape of it," David said, "though it needs to be into the microphone."

He waggled one of the wires, and I could see a little bubble at the end of it.

I had thought David would fix everything, even if it would be at the expense of my freedom. I had thought that I could stop dancing, finally, and they would send me away, and I could finally sleep. The very idea of more was exhausting.

I suppose I must have said something along those lines out loud, because then David said, and I'll never forget this, "Oh, it'll all be over after this. Just this one thing, and the rest of it won't matter. Nobody will ever ask you about the Russian, or any of the other men—we'll bury all of it, if you can just do this one thing for us."

He knew.

David knew about Yevgeny, and about the others, about the way I'd spent so many desperate nights, and in the end, he hardly seemed to care.

He registered my shock, my slack jaw.

"Your uncle heard about your little peccadilloes, Teddy," he explained.

"Well, I suppose I should clarify . . ." David went on. "I told him."

It had started with Yevgeny Larin, he explained: they'd tailed him for the first few weeks after his arrival in Washington in '63, long before he was posted to Rome, because there had been rumors that he was someone worth watching. His family connections alone were enough to merit twenty-four-hour surveillance, so David's team wasted weeks of manpower on him before they finally realized that the poor man was exactly as the West German attaché had described him at that first embassy party—a buffoon. He'd been given a cushy job as a favor to his father and because he wouldn't have managed well anywhere else.

They called off the watch after that, but they did, unfortunately, manage to capture one detail of note before the end: David, on his shift as a young grunt in the Agency, happened to notice a woman returning with Larin to his hotel room one evening, in February of 1963.

He decided to look into her, on a hunch, to see if she might be a potential future informant, and imagine his surprise when he discovered this blond bimbo was the niece of a highly influential senator, one with sensitive committee appointments.

And here's where David's crimes begin, though unfortunately not where mine end:

Instead of raising any of this with the rest of the surveillance team, or his superiors at the Agency, as he was supposed—in fact, required—to do, David went directly to the senator in question. The senator, as David had suspected he might be, was so grateful for this heads-up that he took David under his wing. Brought him into the fold, which was the only way someone like David would ever be able to skip a few squares on the board. Rungs on the ladder. Whichever you prefer.

After that, Uncle Hal became concerned that I was a loose thread, a soft spot, and over the years following that fateful trip to DC, as

David became ever more embedded with Hal, doing his dirty work, a plan began to reveal itself. Hal could kill two, maybe more, birds with one stone: David was obviously expecting some kind of payout, some kind of advancement, and I was spoiling in the sun. Why not arrange a match?

They knew I would be easy enough; hell, based on the reports David had taken back to Hal, I'd sleep with a man as soon as I met him, and David, despite all he had seen of my character, seemed to find something about me compelling. He couldn't quite put his finger on it, he told me, there in our living room. But he found himself wanting to help me.

As if I was supposed to be grateful.

But do you know what? I actually was.

And David was getting something out of it too, of course—the money, but also access to Hal's connections. An association with a family of Party kingmakers. As Hal had said at our wedding, they could make him a congressman in five years, or less.

David hated all of this; I'll say that in his defense. He didn't like playing dirty. But he'd been dealt a bad hand, and all the other players were cheating anyway, so he thought, fine, I'll do it.

My cousin Marcia hadn't known what she was doing when she set up that date, as far as I understand. Apparently, David really had gone to school with her husband, in a stunning coincidence. That's what David said, anyway—I think he was trying to soften the blow. Leave me at least a few family members who didn't think I was a whore, and who hadn't betrayed me in some arcane way.

So. The money from Uncle Hal, at our wedding—it wasn't just because he wanted us to have a nice time in Italy. It wasn't a generous gift to a new couple starting out. It was for a service. It wasn't a coincidence that David had been appointed to the embassy in Rome; Hal had pulled a few of his little strings here and there to get David the assignment as soon as he found out that the Wolf was at the top of the list of appointees for ambassador.

Hal played chess, remember? He was always thinking several moves ahead.

In the course of revealing all of this, David did not mention, but I quickly understood, that it even made sense, now, why David was so insistent on using protection when we were intimate—he probably thought I was unclean, after everything he'd seen.

I suppose for a time, at least, David was able to enjoy the feeling that he'd been right and good in trying to rescue me, and that all I'd needed was a steady hand. It must have seemed that way when, after my disastrous first few weeks in Rome, I'd turned it all around—with my allowance and my stay-awake pills and my demure office wardrobe, my dedication.

The photo of me with the ambassador had dashed those particular hopes, but had still turned out to be a golden opportunity for David, and for Hal. A chance to catch the Wolf at something red-handed.

I don't know much about boats, but a naval officer I met once in a bar explained to me that if part of your ship takes on water, it tilts and is more likely to sink. But if you add more water to the rest of it, it balances out and rights itself again.

Of course, it doesn't work if you add so much that you're in over your head, but it can be a successful stopgap.

Which is to say, I didn't think I could be shocked and surprised and appalled, anymore. I was overloaded, but it was at least pretty evenly distributed, so I felt strangely calm through all of this. Through each new revelation as it sank in; as it sank me.

So we sat in silence for only a moment or two once the whole story was out there on the table, and then I focused my attention on the other thing on the table; or rather, on the Thing on the table.

"Isn't it illegal?" I asked, once David's instructions for me had become clear. "To record the Wolf, without him knowing?"

I was just guessing, trying to find a way out of having to do anything, ever again.

"Oh, suddenly Teddy is an expert in the law?" David said, with a mean little laugh. "Stop asking questions. I'm throwing you a life raft, here. Take it."

Sometimes it's better to let yourself sink, I thought, but even then, I couldn't let go.

"Okay," I said. "I'll do it."

The Paco Rabanne bag that I'd felt so guilty about buying turned out to be a lifesaver—David asked me if I had any purses big enough to carry the recorder, because I needed to take it to the party tomorrow and get the Wolf alone, and before I'd bought the chainmail bag I wouldn't have had something appropriate for evening that would fit it.

So really, if you think about it, I was doing him a favor, buying that bag.

But when I brought it out, he said, "Jesus Christ, Teddy, that's the noisiest bag you could possibly have picked for this! You might as well try to record from inside a laundromat!"

But the only other purses I had that were big enough were for daytime, and David got annoyed when I told him that and said it didn't matter, but it did matter, because everyone would know something was wrong if I took a straw shoulder bag to my black-tie birthday party where Charles Bronson and Telly Savalas and who knows who else would potentially be in attendance.

David couldn't argue with that, so in the end he had to help me fit the box and its wires into the bottom of the bag, hidden under all of the other things I would need with me on a night out, the powder compacts and lipstick cases and tissues. He showed me how to slot the little cassettes into it, which were where the Wolf's confession, ideally, would be stored. He showed me how to angle the wire with the microphone out the side of the bag to collect all the sounds—this was important, he said, because the jingling of the bag would drown out any recording if the bulb of the microphone wasn't out in open air.

I didn't know what I was going to do about a dress—I'd planned to find something new over the weekend, when I'd thought it was going to be a normal party, and I wasn't going to be blackmailed by an Italian photographer. Or, no—before that. Before I spent all my money on the red Valentino, because after that, I wouldn't have had enough, anyway.

I was starting to have trouble with my timeline, I'll admit. I kept forgetting it was just a few hours, now, until my birthday.

David made me call the Wolf at his office that evening to say, "It's done," and held the microphone up to the phone's receiver to record his response. David was hoping he would say something incriminating, but the wily old Wolf only said, "Good girl, Teddy. Come to find me as soon as you get to the party tomorrow."

"And bring the negative?" I tried. "And has the payment gone through?"

David watched me, nodding.

The Wolf just laughed, and said, "I'll see you tomorrow, Teddy," and hung up the phone.

Neither of us was sure what to do after that, alone in the apartment together, so we decided to get ready for bed.

"Do you think she'll find out about the photo?" I asked David, sitting at my dressing table, applying all my essences and creams.

He knew who I meant.

"Don't worry about the photo now, Teddy," he said, catching my eyes in the mirror. "I'm going to take care of everything. I'm going to take care of you."

And then his eyes flicked downward and to the left.

"You're lying," I said. "You're lying. You looked away when you said it. It won't be all right, at all."

"What does that mean?" he asked, his eyes on mine again in the bathroom mirror.

"It's something I heard once," I said. "That people look away when they lie."

He laughed.

"Oh, Teddy," he said. "There's no trick for that. No giveaway. You can't tell if someone's lying or not. You can only know. You have to know the truth, to catch someone in a lie."

He helped me unclasp the pearls he had given me only hours earlier, and which I was still, somehow, wearing, and just for a moment he touched the baby hairs at the nape of my neck. Softly, the way you might pet a kitten behind its ear.

I wanted to tell him I was sorry, I wanted to say, "Please forgive me." I wanted to explain myself, but I thought, in the end, that it would only make me sound worse, to tell him what I'd been thinking the whole time, how I'd been feeling. What had moved me.

I put the pearls back in their box for the night. Took my dress off and put on one of my nightgowns. The silky slips with matching robes I'd bought in full sets, in seafoam green and pretty peach and dusky blue, at Neiman Marcus, for our honeymoon. Took my makeup off again, let my hair down.

Just before he turned out the light, I rolled over to face David and asked him, "And what about the baby?"

But he just pulled the cord on the lamp and the room went dark, and he said, from his side of the bed, "Get some sleep, Teddy. You have a big day tomorrow."

So I rolled over and closed my eyes.

What else was I going to do? What next but lie there together, lie to each other? What else but wake up in the morning and bathe and dress, go to the salon, go to lunch, eat something small, talk about nothing with all of your friends, pretend to wash the dishes, make coffee, buy the face cream you've had your eye on, make yourself a drink, put a record on, wait for your husband to come home, move slowly and stay calm, go home and go to sleep, and do it all again?

Somehow, David began to snore almost as soon as he turned out the light. But not me. I took one of the lizard pills. The doctor on the leafy street had said I wouldn't dream, but what did he know?

I dreamed of my baby.

22. Dallas

1958

When I was twenty-three, I got pregnant.

I'd been living in my Turtle Creek apartment, paid for by my parents, for less than a year. I'd only just begun my forays into staying out all night, into quietly doing the things I had to do to stop feeling like a horse running wild in a pen. Aunt Sister was long gone, and I knew they were watching me, waiting for me to spoil.

I don't know if I was sick from the baby or sick with fear, but I couldn't keep any food down for weeks. I was the thinnest I've ever been, and my mother complimented me on my trim figure. Daddy pinched the tops of my arms and said, you look like a little bird, you look like Audrey damn Hepburn. I wore girdles and loose skirts, and nobody could see the beginnings of a bloat.

It was only in there for a few weeks, anyway, so it never got that big.

I'm not completely sure whose it was, but I thought it might have come from Brian Gordon, a salesman I'd met at the Rubaiyat one night. And also, and maybe more importantly, I had a business card I'd taken from his wallet when he went to the bathroom, so I had a way to contact him, and I didn't have the money for the procedure.

I couldn't go to the hospital, though I knew Eleanor's mother had arranged one for her legally, somehow, through the hospital

274

board, probably because her brother was a surgeon at Southwestern. Eleanor never talked about it, but we all knew.

I'd heard of a clinic in Snider Plaza that would do it for five hundred dollars, so that's where I wanted to go, but I didn't have the money. So I called Brian Gordon and met him at the Rubaiyat again—his idea; he liked jazz, which I suppose was something he and David, who I didn't know yet at the time, had in common— and he handed me an envelope of cash with Texas Instruments on it and his office's address in the return spot, and he told me to call him when it was done, just so he could stop sweating.

I made it all the way to the office building that housed the clinic, the first time.

I went inside and the girl behind the desk handed me the intake form and asked, "Are you here for Dr. Ryan?" which I'd been told was the code they used for the procedure. It smelled like a scab in there, and there was a dead fly on the windowsill, and I didn't want to be in that dim room with its closed blinds anymore, so I gave the paper back to her and I left, and I walked in circles around Snider Plaza, past Kuby's German Restaurant and Jack's Burgers, where SMU students in sweaters and loafers sat and laughed together, past the doughnut shop and the dry cleaner's and the grocery store, past the tailor's and the fur storage facility and the optician's, until I came to De Graaf's jewelry, and then I went inside.

Mr. De Graaf was in there and waved hello; he knew me. He'd sized my class ring, and I always came in with Mama when she brought her diamonds to be cleaned. He gave me a coffee with two sugar cubes and left me to wander the store and look in all the cases, only coming over when I called on him to ask for a price.

I'd found a case of gold jewelry, bracelets and earrings and neck-laces all shaped like animals; they were made by an artist back in Holland, Mr. De Graaf said. There was a pair of gold filigree hoop earrings, each in the shape of an outstretched hare, the front paws and hind legs touching at the pin. They looked like William Morris rabbits, those medieval-style creatures prancing through his woodland floral wallpapers. I loved them.

I paid for the rabbit earrings with Brian Gordon's money, and I took the three dollars I had left to get a burger and fries at Jack's and a taxi back to Turtle Creek, and it was another week before I realized that nothing had changed, actually, and I couldn't wait much longer, and I didn't have the money for the procedure, anymore.

I told Mama at the Zodiac Room because I knew she wouldn't shout. Not that she ever shouted, but she might have slapped me. She couldn't, though, over Maryland crab cakes and tomato martinis in front of all of the other lunching ladies in Dallas.

She surprised me. I'd been sure she would say it was time to talk to Uncle Hal, it was time to talk to Daddy, and that they would decide what to do with me. But instead, she said, "You're lucky, Teddy," and "We can fix this," and she took me back to the clinic in Snider Plaza that smelled like a scab, for the surgery.

She came into the room with me and waited while I changed into the worn white gown with its little blue polka dots; I think it was the softest fabric I've ever touched. It felt like it had been worn and washed a thousand times before me. I didn't fool myself that Mama was in the room to offer me support; she was there to make sure I went through with it.

"You're lucky," she told me again, just before they put me under. "Not everyone gets a choice."

The only painting I could think of was *Saturn Devouring His Son*. Red; ugly. They gave me something so I would sleep, and the charcoal darkness at the edges of the Goya painting crept in and covered my eyes.

"It'll be like it was never there," the nurse said, with a reassuring hand on my knee. But when I woke up, I was on my side, and when I looked down I saw drops of blood on the tile floor; one, two, three, still wet.

Carmine. Cochineal. The color made from crushed beetle shells.

I never wore those earrings; I still have them, though.

Mama sent me to the ranch after that, to rest. I felt for a few days like there was something inside of me, gnawing at the bottom of my belly, trying to claw its way out, and I worried that they had left it in there, somehow. I remembered reading a story about Ancient Greece, or Sparta, I think it was, when I was a child, about a boy who had stolen a fox cub from a rich man and hidden it under his shirt. When people questioned him, he refused to admit that he'd taken the pup, and the animal grew hungry and frightened and gnawed all the way through his belly, the boy continuing to deny all the while that he'd ever done anything wrong, until he fell down dead. That's how it felt, for the first few days. A lie gnawing you to the bone.

The pain went away, eventually, but I kept telling Mama that I wasn't feeling better, yet, even when I really was, and I spent a few weeks riding horses and sitting quietly by myself on the porch swing at sunset, and it was probably one of the happier times of my life, all told.

I used to think if they'd just let me stay there like that, I might have been happy, although at night, out there, you could hear the foxes calling from down by the riverbed. If you've never heard it, I don't recommend it—it sounds like a woman screaming.

Now

Early Morning, Wednesday, July 9, 1969

"Mrs. Shepard," Hildebrand says, and for the first time I think he seems a little worried. "Are you telling me that your husband gave you a piece of classified Agency equipment—classified doesn't even begin to describe this—in order to perform domestic espionage on a political rival of your uncle, a high-ranking United States official?"

I make a sort of sheepish, Charlie Brown kind of a face.

"Yeah. I guess that's right."

He closes his eyes for a moment.

"Mrs. Shepard. Could you please retrieve that item, if it is still in your possession, and bring it to me?"

"No problem," I say, and excuse myself to the bedroom, where I dig up the Paco Rabanne bag with the recorder still inside, and then return to the sitting room to deposit it on Arthur Hildebrand's lap. He peers inside and grimaces. Hands the bag to Archie, and says, "Get this to Eastman. Now!"

He takes a moment to rearrange his facial expression into something like composure, then says, "And that brings us to the events of this evening?"

The sun will be up soon, I think. I can already see the sky getting light through the window—see the cold, blue color of morning.

"Almost," I say. "There's just a little bit left to tell."

23. Palazzo Margherita

Tuesday, July 8, 1969

I woke up before David, and thank God. I don't know what I would have done if I'd come back into the world with him watching me, leaning over me and looking at me as I lay there.

But I woke first, by some miracle, or maybe I never really slept, and I bathed and dressed myself as quietly as I could.

It was still summer, beautiful, sweltering Italian summer, so I wore a sleeveless white shirtdress with lace edges, and I put on leather sandals I'd bought on our honeymoon in Capri. I wore the coral necklace I'd bought then, too. I doubted David would remember what fun we had that day, going into the shops, looking at all the fine work from local craftsmen; it didn't matter, anyway.

I took another pigeon's-egg pill in the kitchen and made coffee on the stove to wash it down. The sharp pain was still there in my chest, but it went away when I ignored it.

The little recorder, all tucked away inside my Paco Rabanne purse, was waiting for me on the table with the roses dying in their vase.

Once David woke up, he dressed for work and had a cup of the coffee I'd brewed and a prairie oyster from the fridge. He was a little hungover, I think, though he wouldn't admit to it.

"I'll see you later, Teddy," David said, as he walked out the door.

What he meant was, I'll come back to get you, so don't go anywhere.

He did trust me enough, apparently, to be alone in the apartment—he didn't seem to be worried I would run. And he was right: where would I go? I was like a housecat, or a little lapdog. It wasn't safe for me, outside.

I wanted to go to the embassy with David that morning, even though I risked seeing the Wolf; I didn't want to be alone in the apartment. I wanted to go walking in Rome. I wanted to do anything other than stay by myself in our empty flat.

I waited, though. I did as I was told.

When I was little, everyone commented on how good I was, how obedient. I've always done well when I've had instructions.

I tried to organize my wardrobe, but it didn't make any sense to me. Where had all the clothes come from? Who could possibly have so many dresses?

At some point, around midafternoon, I think, I remembered Beppo, and that I hadn't seen him in days. I slumped down the worn stone stairs to the building entrance and sat on the step just above the street, but Beppo was nowhere to be found. The can of tuna I'd set out for him earlier was gone; perhaps David had thrown it away when he left for work.

I don't know why, but for the first time in a day or two, I felt like I would cry. I thought maybe Beppo had been hit by one of the mad Roman motorists who pelted like furies down the city's ancient side streets with no regard for the fact that they were built thousands of years before cars were even invented. I thought maybe another cat had attacked him—he was small, for a tom. He might've gotten into a fight that he couldn't get out of with some bigger, scrappier alley cat. He was lively, and I'd always thought he had a particular glint in his eyes; I could see him trying to punch above his weight.

I sat there and wanted to cry, and thought surely I would, but then couldn't, just breathed in little gasps as I opened another can of tuna I'd brought down with me to set beside the steps, just in case.

And then suddenly there he was, pattering down the gutter on his dirty little feet toward me, rubbing his fuzzy apple head against my knee. And it isn't such a miracle, that a stray cat should appear on the street when there's food, at the creaking, metallic sound of the lid popped from a can of tuna, but to me it felt important, and, as stupid as it sounds, it made me want to keep going. It made me want to do whatever I needed to do to stick around, no matter how tired I was, no matter how much I wanted to lie down and stay there.

It should have been something bigger, I guess. The reason for what happened next.

David came home at six, and I was still getting ready.

I'd chosen a dress from the ones I already had; it wouldn't quite go with the chainmail bag, but it was the only nice dress I'd brought from Dallas that I hadn't worn yet. A blue, pleated cocktail-length chiffon from Balmain with yellow beads at the wrist and neck. Blousy and drapey and not too revealing, which David would like, if he would ever like anything about me, again. I had a matching three-quarter-sleeve jacket, too, for good measure.

I made my hair as big as I could get it on top, spraying and teasing it while I sat on the vanity stool before the mirror in the bathroom. I let it fall, soft and full, like pale gold or straw, to my shoulders. I took a makeup brush and wet it in my mouth, just touching it to my tongue. Dabbed it across the powdery surface of my eyeliner compact, the color a burnt, soft brown that always made me think of the tip of a Siamese cat's ear, and drew a line over my eye, corner to corner. Perfect. I colored it in. I glued the lashes on.

"You look nice, Teddy Bear," David said, coming into the bathroom behind me holding the pearls in their leather box.

"Thank you, darling," I said.

I never used to talk like that, but suddenly there we were, playing our parts. I tilted my head backward, craning my neck to smile up at him.

And he leaned down to kiss me on the mouth, so suddenly that I jumped and stiffened on my little dressing-table stool like a startled cat.

He reached down over my shoulders, tracing his finger across my collarbone and its hollows. Down through the neckline of my dress to let a hand drift over, and then cup, a breast. It felt foreign, strange. My body responded the way it always did, though, and I heard David exhale behind me. As if this was all he had ever wanted. To feel me answer him.

I was still looking up at him, and I thought he might lean down to kiss me again, more deeply this time.

"How much longer?" he asked, instead, and slid his hand from my breast as if pulling it from a dirty glove. Turned at the wrist like he needed to hold it separate until he could wash it.

"Until you're ready, I mean," he added, straightening his tie. He looked good in his suit; he always cleaned up well.

"Just fifteen minutes," I said. I was almost done.

He took the pearls from their case and clasped them around my neck. They were heavy, like a collar. Aunt Sister's fake pearls had been light, and cold, and I should have known at the time that it meant they weren't real. The Bulgari pearls, the real thing—you could feel the weight of them.

It wasn't a good outfit—the pearls with that dress and the chain-mail bag. None of it matched. But I needed each of these things, my strange symbols. My weapons and charms; a patchwork of the objects that plagued me.

David drove us to the embassy in silence and parked on the street. The paparazzi were clustered around the entrance, which was no surprise, but it was even clearer why they were there when we reached the gallery on the second floor, where the party—my birthday party, supposedly—was already underway.

Margot had been right—it wasn't really about me. The honor I thought the ambassador was doing me was just an afterthought.

The Wolf was nowhere to be seen, but there were, in addition to the moneymen, the directors and producers, some of the most famous actors and actresses in the world in attendance. I won't say which ones, if you don't mind—I don't want to bring them into this. Just know that I saw a true Paramount blonde, and a lantern-jawed young man from a famous gladiator film, and an actor who'd made his name in movie musicals decades ago until he lost his voice to cigarettes and whiskey.

David took one look around and said, "I forgot, I have something to do in my office."

He hated those gorgeous, glossy people. He hated what they stood for, and I think he also hated how much power they had, and that he was never, ultimately, going to be one of them. I knew what he did for a living, finally, and I'm sure it wasn't lost on him that he wasn't anything like the men in the films. He wasn't James Bond; he wasn't even close.

"Sure, darling," I said, and kissed him on the cheek.

And then he was gone, and I was alone in the room with all the Hollywood people, who eyed me with interest. I assume they could see that I was something of an actress, myself.

It was a small gathering, compared to the Wolf's previous parties, and there was a self-service bar set up along one wall. No waiters serving drinks or passing trays of canapés; I suppose this was meant to be a small get-together of friends.

I went to make myself something, I didn't really care what, and was standing at the bar deciding between vodka and gin when an older man in a linen suit approached.

"Tom Pfander," he said, holding out one hand and swirling a highball glass around with the other.

"Teddy Shepard," I said. "And what do you do, Mr. Pfander?"

I was just making conversation; I didn't really care. I was killing time until the Wolf finally showed up at his own party and I could get him alone. Until all of this could finally, finally be over.

"Oh, call me Tom," the man said. He had a mustache that must have been devastating when he was young, after the First World War or so. "Screenwriter. Did you see *Cleopatra*?"

"Of course! That was you?" I was impressed, in spite of myself. Even though I didn't really care.

"No, that was garbage. All shine, no substance. I write dramas. I write *real human stories*."

"Ah. And are you enjoying Rome?"

These conversations weren't that difficult to get through; I assumed Tom Pfander was familiar with the script. It was his job, after all.

"No," he said. "I hate this city."

Apparently, he didn't know his lines. I'd have to pay attention to this one, it seemed. He wasn't following the rules.

"And why is that, Tom?"

He grinned; he'd been working on his answer to the question, probably waiting all night to be asked.

I knew a girl at SMU who used to say you had to have one strange answer to a common question in your back pocket, just to show them you weren't a doll. Whenever someone brought up the ocean, as in "I love to go to the beach and swim in the ocean," she would say, "I never go in the sea. I wouldn't want a fish coming into my house without knocking on the door, so I won't go in theirs." She always got a lot of laughs with that one. She married a boy from the basketball team and moved to Oklahoma after graduation, I think, which is about as far as you can get from the sea.

"It's old," Tom said, of Rome. "Moldy. Rot of the old world, all the history builds up like barnacles. Give me something new, a city I can work with. Untarnished."

"That's interesting," I said, "because a lot of people would say new and untarnished means fake. Like a movie set, for example."

He laughed. "And where are you from, that you're so wise?"

"Dallas," I said, and he laughed again.

"A new, fake city if there ever was one. The Hollywood of the Wild West—not because they make movies, but because it's all new money and shiny cars. Somebody gave a bunch of cowboys credit, and they built a temple to gloss."

"My mother would hate to hear you say that. She would agree with you about the old world, though. She thinks Dallas is better than New York or London or Rome; she thinks it's newer. Cleaner."

"And who is your mother?"

"Alice Huntley," I said.

The way he asked, like he assumed she would be no one, made me want to prove him wrong, so I let him have the name.

I'm not sure what I expected, but he looked thoughtful for a moment, and then exclaimed, "Alice Huntley! I knew an Alice Huntley, forty years ago or more, if you can believe it." He shook his head. "I always wondered what happened to her. You must be—"

Then he stopped and peered at me. "But you can't be, you're far too young. Forgive me for breaking the one sacred rule, but I must ask the lady her age."

"I'm thirty-four," I said. Then remembered, "Thirty-five."

"So you couldn't be, then. Must have been a brother. Sister?"

"What must have been?"

He had his free hand under his chin, a caricature of recollection.

"Alice Huntley, quite the gal!" he eventually exclaimed, not answering, exactly, my question. "She was *something*—I remember

285

she wore an entirely gold-sequined dress, once, to Archer Darrow's Precious Metals party at the Waldorf."

"Are you sure you're thinking of my mother? You might mean my aunt, Cecilia."

"I don't recall a Cecilia. This was 1920, I believe. Maybe '21."

It couldn't have been Aunt Sister; she wasn't even born until '21. It was strange to think of my mother at wild parties in New York—I knew she'd gone off to school at Barnard, but I'd assumed she was always as conservative, as staid and elegant, as she was now. She hated New York, she'd told me. It was no place for good people, she'd said.

"I don't mind saying this to you, though, because I'm sure you know," Pfander went on, "but she disappeared after that. Back to Dallas, I think someone said, when she got into trouble."

"Trouble?"

"You know," he motioned with a hand over his belly, "with child. Immaculate conception, as it always is when the woman is unmarried. Your brother, I assume, or perhaps sister, as I said."

I believe I must have opened my mouth to speak, but I don't know what I could possibly have been planning to say, because at that moment the Wolf appeared, tanned and handsome as always, meetings, apparently, finished.

"Tom Philanderer!" he cried, walking over to us from across the gallery. "There you are. How are you liking our little home away from home? Good? Good. Mind if I borrow the lady for a moment? I'm sure she's told you all about her work here—I just need to ask her a quick question about one of the paintings. For an audit; dull, daily government stuff."

All in one movement, he clapped Tom Pfander on the back, put another hand on my shoulder, pulled me back toward him, and pointed me to the exit.

I moved dumbly along with the Wolf as he frog-marched me

over toward the offices. I couldn't see what was in front of me; I couldn't hear a word he said.

They had called her Sister for Sissie, for Cecilia. And it was fitting that I called her Aunt Sister, I'd heard my father say once, because she was so young that she was more like my sister.

I wondered if he knew.

I wondered if Sister had known, when she was still capable of knowing anything at all. If anyone besides my mother, her parents, and Hal had known.

My mother, who sent her own daughter to be rendered dumb and helpless, an infant once again—no, less than that, even. Who sacrificed her own child because Hal was running for Senate and Sissie had gotten into trouble. Who worried all the time that I would get into trouble, too, when she herself had been the first to fall.

I could see it clearly, in my mind: my mother, confident and stunning at nineteen, imagining herself to be worldly and clever, set free in New York. Shining in gold sequins at parties, at dinner at the Ritz, all summer in East Hampton. Parties in uptown apartments with writers and artists, thinking she was unstoppable.

That's how I had wanted to feel, before I got frightened. That was the life I had wanted until they took Sister away and I saw how dangerous it could be, to be a woman alone in the world, and decided instead to settle for sweater sets and the Huntley Foundation and furtive nights in dingy bars and hotel rooms with strangers, and then the weeks of fear and guilt, afterward.

Mama must have looked forward, in her youth, and seen the future that Sister later described to me, whether it was real or not—a week on a prince's yacht, a private sitting for Picasso, a hot-air balloon ride, a safari. Adventure, and independence, and being important.

She gambled everything on it, and got pregnant, and Grandpop would have been running for governor at the time, and the scandal—Dallas's favorite daughter gone to New York and living a life of sin—would have been impossible to withstand. I was sure they had threatened her with money; that was always how it worked. With Sister, too, and with me.

And we were like lapdogs, overbred, with no idea how to do it on our own. Useless but charming, well groomed. Unable to clean up our own messes.

So my mother had handed the baby over to Grandma and pretended it never happened, counting on the chaos of the decade and the distance between Dallas and New York to keep it quiet.

Then she met Daddy, and had me, and went along as if her life had been entirely orderly the whole time, entirely contained and in control, so much so that she dared to act horrified by Sister's indiscretions, and eventually sent her to doctors who effectively killed her.

I was far away, but the Wolf brought me back with a shake, once we were in his office.

"Well, Teddy? Where is it? We'll put the negatives in the bin and light them on fire, and then we can finally be done with this godforsaken mess. I'm sure you'll want to keep one of the prints for a souvenir," he winked, "but please don't."

How could he be so lighthearted? How could any of this be funny, or fine? I wanted to scream at him; I wanted to hit him, make him feel it.

I remembered the recorder. I needed to turn it on before he said any more about what we'd done. David said to get it all. To ask him about the money.

I fumbled with my purse, the metal rings of the chain mail jangling as I dug around in it. Found the device; found its little button and pressed it. I hoisted the purse up a bit, trying to get the microphone closer to our faces, but the bag was heavy, and I wasn't any good at this. Or at least, I'd never done it before.

"I wrote him a check," I said, trying not to speak so slowly and loudly as to be obvious. "But when will the money you sent arrive? It needs to get there before David notices."

"It'll be fine, Teddy, someone called the bank for me two days ago. Should be there before the weekend."

"Where did you send it from, though? How do you know Lina won't notice?"

He laughed. "Lina! As long as her credit's still good in Baden-Baden, she doesn't give a shit what's happening at the bank. I told you, I sent it."

"From where, though? What account?"

"Why are you—What's that you're fiddling with in your purse?"

I pulled my hand out, dropped the microphone back into the bottom of the bag. It rattled a bit on impact, giving me away.

"Nothing," I said.

As if anyone ever believes that answer.

The Wolf reached for the bag, and even at fifty, he was so much stronger than me. He ripped it from my hands and dumped it out, pushing a long finger through its ejected contents on his desk: peppermints. Bobby pins. A powder compact. A few loose coins. A lipstick. All of the artifacts of my life. Helpless, simple Teddy, with her useless, costly detritus.

And then, of course, the little thing. The recording device, and its microphone.

"What's this, Teddy?" he asked.

I had edged away from him and stood on the other side of his desk, by the wall with the wolf and the gun. I wanted to be far away from him; he wasn't laughing or winking anymore. He looked dangerous.

"I don't know," I said.

"Bullshit," he said.

He was advancing on me, saying, "Who gave this to you, Teddy? Who are you working for?"

I kept moving away from him until my back hit the wall, knocking the wind out of me, and then the Wolf was close, far too close, clutching my shoulders, questioning me, faster and faster, "Who gave this to you, Teddy? Who are you?"

He was stronger than he should have been, for his age, and then he pressed an arm against my throat.

"I don't know, I don't know," I heard myself saying. I was babbling, then only gasping, croaking, as he pressed his arm harder into my throat.

"Who do you work for?"

I looked up into his eyes, thinking that something of the movie star might be left in there. The jovial politician, the laughing man who chased women around Rome and hosted perfect parties. But the political appointee, the person David had insisted all along was just a dilettante, was nowhere to be seen. Before me was the man who'd made a career throwing his competition to the wolves. This was a man who could do real harm. A true cowboy; a man with no allegiances, at all.

"I don't know what you mean," I tried to say, but I was finding it harder to speak. Harder to breathe.

The Wolf was pressing his arm deeper; I couldn't even hear what he was saying anymore, and for the first time it really felt real. The animal fear, deep down, that I always had at the back of my mind: that I would die.

And not in the general way I imagined my heart might stop or I might be taken home and sent away, subjected to the same surgeon's knives as Aunt Sister, but I could see it happening, now, because I could already begin to feel it. He was crushing, I felt, whatever little delicate fish bones held up my throat. I imagined I could feel them popping, crunching, and soon they would fold and crack and my neck would collapse like a Christmas cracker pulled to snapping after dinner.

The bones of my throat. The throat of the wolf on the wall ending in its bloody, red mouth. The wall. And on the wall, below the wolf—

My free hand closed around the little handle of the Nambu pistol and ripped it from its nails before I completed the thought.

I didn't know what I would do with the gun, I only wanted to have it. I only wanted to even the scales, to restore the balance in the room between myself and the Wolf.

I would say, "I've got a gun," and he would let go, and I would be able to breathe, and think, and I would point it at him so he had to let me leave, and then—

No need to think that far ahead, I just needed air. Needed the Wolf to know that I had the gun and let me breathe.

I was clutching it so tightly in my hand, trying to bring it around to where he would see it. There were stars in my eyes, spots of light dancing, blinding flashes of light. He just needed to see it. Then he would know.

There was a sound like a door slamming shut, and something wet on my hand, and suddenly I could breathe again.

Now

Early Morning, Wednesday, July 9, 1969

"I didn't mean to do it," I say.

"We've heard that one before," Reggie retorts.

I really don't care for him.

"And correct me if I'm wrong, Mrs. Shepard," Reggie goes on, "but didn't you mention earlier that your father taught you to shoot as a child? Didn't you say you were as good a shot as he was, by the time you were—ah, twelve? I believe it was?"

"That's very interesting, Evans," Arthur Hildebrand says, and Reggie smiles triumphantly.

"Well, fine," I snap, "I do know how to use a gun. So if I was trying to actually kill the Wolf, I would've done it, wouldn't I? I wouldn't have just grazed him. The problem was that stupid pistol, that war souvenir. If you've ever seen a Nambu pistol, you'll understand: it looks like something from *The Jetsons*. The long, thin muzzle, and that fat little grip. The trigger was higher than I'm used to, and too far forward, and I must've just brushed it. I really didn't mean to, but I had those long nails, and they got in the way."

"Hmm," is all Arthur says, and I can tell he doesn't entirely believe me.

"And then?" he asks.

24. Rome

Tuesday, July 8, 1969

So. The gun went off, obviously, and it hit the Wolf, but it was only a scratch, really.

Of course, I didn't know that right away. The first thing I saw after the sound was the Wolf sitting on his desk with a red rose of blood on his shirtsleeve, clutching it with his good arm and cursing. But he wasn't dead, at least, and he wasn't even on the floor.

I rushed to him and tried to help—I'm not sure exactly what I thought I was doing, but I managed, in my efforts, to get the Wolf's blood all over my dress, and even more on my hands, and then I suppose at some point I must have put my hands over my face in panic or despair and the blood there mixed with my makeup. It must have been quite frightening, really—I don't think the Wolf found my presence to be particularly comforting, in that moment.

It was so loud that I thought the whole embassy would come running, everyone at the party, but for some reason they didn't. I learned later that Tom Pfander had found some brass band records from his youth and put them on at full volume. I suppose I could have thanked him for that.

David must have heard the shot over in his office, even if all the Hollywood people at the party didn't, or maybe he was listening at the door, but either way, he came bursting in soon after.

"What the fuck is going on?" the Wolf shouted. "What the *fuck* is this?"

David remained calm, nearly motionless, even as he took in the scene: the Wolf's arm bleeding through his white shirt, the bullet hole in the wall, the gun where I'd dropped it. Me standing there, staring. Blood on my dress, hands, face, though I didn't know about that—my face—at the time.

"Let me see the wound," he said to the Wolf. "How bad is it?"

I couldn't understand how he'd put it all together so quickly, and I didn't see why they weren't calling the police, or at least an ambulance. I was certain I was going to jail. I was looking forward to it, actually—at least I would be able to rest.

But the Wolf just took his shirt off and showed David. It was really only a little cut. I don't mean to minimize my crime, but it wasn't such a bad wound, after all.

"Just the surface," David said, dabbing at the scratch with the Wolf's bloodied shirt. "You'll be fine."

"What did Teddy tell you?" the Wolf asked, now holding the shirt over the wound himself.

"Everything," David said, and I realized that was true. It was strange to think, after all the hiding, that David knew it all, now.

"So I think you'll agree," David continued, "that we probably shouldn't call anyone, if we don't have to. That we can find a way to settle this ourselves."

"What about the photo?" the Wolf asked.

"I'll take care of it," David said.

"And Teddy? Can you keep her quiet?"

They were talking over me and around me. These two men understood something that I did not; I'd thought they were rivals, and now suddenly they were on the same side, and I was over here on the other, alone.

"Don't worry about Teddy," David said. "She just got in over her head."

I was thinking of the Signorini painting from the Villa Taverna, the town on the coast at the edge of a cliff, and of a series that Claude Monet painted from Étretat, a beach town in Normandy surrounded by great chalk cliffs. The sea in his paintings was sometimes turquoise, sometimes a deep green, sometimes Nile blue or champagne-colored, reflecting the sunset sky or early-morning mists, depending on the time of day and season.

Teddy in over her head. I imagined myself walking on the beach while the tide was out, so far past the shoreline that I saw fish flopping on the sand, saw barnacles and anemones and strands of seaweed draped like tangled jewelry, saw the strange foams and gelatins of the ocean left on land. And then the tide coming in, and the water pale green and still like in the paintings, the cold salt sea sliding in up to my ankles, my knees, my waist, and then over my head. It wasn't violent; they weren't rough waves that I fought against and then lost to. It was something that I allowed to happen.

"Who hired you?" the Wolf asked David. "This isn't Agency business."

David just shrugged.

"Huntley, then," the Wolf said. "The whole time? Since I got here?"

David shrugged again, and the Wolf kept talking.

"They were paying you to watch me, see if I slipped up? See what they could get on me?"

Again, David said nothing.

It would have been the perfect way to sink the Wolf's ship, or to blackmail him into dropping out of the race, if it came down to it. And now they'd have to call it even, because I had accidentally shot the Wolf, and he'd discovered that David was spying on him, and I was pretty sure that both of those things were not allowed.

"And what about you?" David asked the Wolf, after a pause.

"What do you mean, what about me?"

" 'Keep your enemies close,' right? Don't tell me you really wanted to spend so much time with my wife because you're so damn interested in art. We're all adults here, Warren. Teddy's just another trump card you could play if it came down to it. 'Hal, here's a story I know about your pretty little niece.' "

We're not all adults! I wanted to cry, Not me! Because I hadn't figured that part out. I hadn't even suspected it. That Lina and the Wolf had invited me to work at the embassy and the residence to keep an eye on me; to see how I might become useful to them.

The Wolf shrugged and winked at me—he actually *winked* at me—and I was suddenly not so sad that I'd accidentally shot him.

"Sorry, babe," he said.

"What about Aunt Sister?" I asked him. "Cecilia. Was any of it true?"

"Oh, it was all true. That's why I kept bringing her up—I thought you might give me something interesting. Tell me, Teddy, where is she really? I know something must have happened; I know Hal's got her squirreled away somewhere."

"What?" I asked dumbly. "How do you know that?"

"I always figured something would happen to her," the Wolf said, like it was no big deal. "She always shone a little *too* bright, if you know what I mean. If you did something, she would want to do the same thing two times over. She was always someone who was going to get into trouble; even what I saw in California would be enough to sink Hal, if I wanted to tell it—only problem is, I was at those parties, too."

"Teddy," David said. "Why don't you go home? Get cleaned up. Wait for me there; the ambassador and I have a few things to discuss."

It was strange to have been so close to the center of everything and yet not to matter at all, in the end.

"Okay," I said.

I packed everything up from the desk where the Wolf had dumped it, all my peppermints and pins, my powder, my lipstick. Just before I left the room, David took a handkerchief he'd found somewhere and wiped the blood off my face, and I thought the gesture was very tender, all things considered. And he handed me my jacket as I walked out the door—he really could be very polite, my David—and said, "Teddy, don't forget to cover up, or they'll see the blood."

I had to walk back through the gallery on my way to the exit. Tom Pfander grabbed my arm as I passed by.

"Come on, Huntley, let's dance! Your mother used to dance on the piano at the 300 Club, I saw her; it's in your blood!"

The Hollywood crowd had somehow gotten exponentially drunker in the few minutes we'd been in the Wolf's office; the actor from the gladiator film was standing in front of the piano, trying to play it with his—well, you know.

I smiled at Tom and pulled my arm away and said, "Sure, Tom, I'll be right back."

Nobody stopped me on my way out the front door of the embassy, even though I'd shot the ambassador. The beautiful Marines in their bright uniforms waved me onward.

David and the Wolf would come to an understanding, it would all be painted over and polished, like a simple scratch on the fender of your white Thunderbird with the custom red interior, and I was going home, the way I'd been told.

Go to your room, Teddy. Go to bed. Wake up early and put the coffee on. Be dressed with your hair freshly washed, your makeup on, your cardigan over your shoulders. Keep dancing and spinning and standing there prettily, the most important statue in the collection. The loveliest woman in all of Rome, the masterwork, the modest Venus.

But I didn't put my jacket on and button it tight like a good girl; not out of any intentional rebellion on my part, but because, in the moment, I couldn't think straight, and I remember I didn't want to get blood on my jacket, too, not when it was already all over my favorite Balmain.

So I walked through the party covered in blood—Tom Pfander didn't notice, nor did the lantern-jawed gladiator at the piano, but some of them certainly did, I'm sure. They might not have put it together immediately—might've thought it was a bloody nose for some fun, wild reason, perhaps a narcotic one, but once they started to think about it, and remembered that they'd heard a loud crack that was almost, but not quite, muffled by the sound of the brass band music . . . well, even the Paramount blonde might have been able to put two and two together.

Now

Early Morning, Wednesday, July 9, 1969

"And I suppose someone saw the blood, and said something, or called someone else, and that's how you gentlemen heard there was an incident? And that's why you're here? And you've already spoken to David, I assume, and to the ambassador."

"Your husband," Reggie says, "is not terribly pleased with you."

"Well," I answer, in the same tone, "it seems like *you're* not terribly pleased with *him*."

This is directed at Arthur Hildebrand, who says nothing.

"Anyway," I say, "that's all she wrote. I left the embassy, and then I came straight here."

"Thank you, Mrs. Shepard," Hildebrand says. "That's all we need, for now."

The men rise in unison from my ugly sofa.

"Your husband will be home soon, I'm sure," Reggie says, as if it's a threat.

"But," he adds, "we may need to speak to you again, at some point, in the course of the investigation. Don't worry, though. It's strictly an internal matter. We'll handle this in-house."

"Great," I say, and follow them to the front door. "Thanks for coming. Bye now."

"Mrs. Shepard," Arthur Hildebrand says from the doorway, just before he turns to go. "I hope you've been completely honest with us. Because if you haven't, we'll find out."

Oh, I'm sure they will—in fact, I'm counting on it.

25. Via Veneto

Tuesday, July 8, 1969

What I didn't tell them: I didn't go straight home, that night.

I walked out the front entrance to the embassy past the Marines, who didn't see the blood in time to stop me, past the packs of paparazzi gathered at the gate.

There was a moment, only a moment, when the men in their suits with their silver cameras just watched me, with no flashes. They didn't take photos right away, even with their predator's instincts, or call out to me. They understood, maybe, that something had happened. Something more than a drunk crooner or a lecherous director caught with his starlet.

It didn't last. They began snapping seconds later, as I walked on.

At some point I must have passed Mauro—it was a side gig of his, this street photography, when he couldn't get paid to take photos inside the parties. He called out and I didn't answer, so he began to trail after me.

This time he was the one chasing me through the streets of the city at night. This time, he was the one who was afraid.

I have to imagine he feared I'd killed a man, knowing as much as he did about my situation, though which of them it was, he likely couldn't venture to guess.

It was early enough in the evening that people were still seated at cafés and restaurants and tavernas on that famous street, at outdoor tables, perhaps hoping to catch a glimpse of someone famous.

And instead they saw me, wandering in a daze in my bloodied dress, past the car lights and neon signs, which glittered in the corners of my eyes like fireworks or shooting stars, but really, they reminded me of nothing so much as those Christmas lights that come on a string, the hot, bright lights in blue and red and green and orange, and if you touch them the bulbs burn your hand.

I understood now that I would always be afraid. If I accepted their help, if I kept trying to hide, I would spend the rest of my life slicing away at myself, trying to fit, trying to become smooth and polished and perfect, and one day I would find a fatal flaw in the marble and a crack would open up, and that would be the end of me.

And I didn't want it to be. I wanted to live.

I walked all the way down the via Veneto, past gaping diners and shoppers and tourists, to Anna's flat, and when she buzzed me up, Mauro came in behind me.

That was a good thing, because it took me a moment to sort myself out, and I couldn't yet explain it all to Anna, the reason I had appeared bloodied at her door on a Tuesday night, and so Mauro began telling her about the blackmail, or his version of it at least, as much as he knew, and by the time he was done I was ready to speak.

But first, Anna asked if we had any proof besides the photograph, said we might need it if we wanted to go any further—if we wanted to publish—so I offered her the recording device in my purse, but when we played the tape it was only muffled voices and jangling metal, so David had been right about the Paco Rabanne after all, I suppose.

On the other hand, this meant that there wasn't any hard evidence of what had happened in the Wolf's office. This meant, I realized, that the story could be whatever I wanted it to be.

So I told them.

When I finished, Mauro whistled low.

"Teddy," he said. "*Che cazzo fai?*"

Anna didn't say anything for a while. She looked at her papers, with her frantic notes scribbled across them, and then up at me. She repeated this process a few times, and then finally asked, "Are you sure you want to do this, Ted?"

"I am," I said.

Anna and Mauro wanted me to stay with them—they worried what would happen to me if I went home—but I told them I needed to see it through. There were a few loose ends to tie up before I could make my escape.

I was expecting Archie and his friends, for one thing.

But first I went with Anna and Mauro to Testaccio, to Mauro's apartment, so they could set about gathering their evidence. And when I left Mauro's after a while to return home, to await my inquisitors, I stopped first at the mountain of shards, the ancient spoil heap. Two thousand years ago the Romans threw their broken pottery here, layers and layers of cracked and damaged amphorae, so many that it became a mountain. And the grass grew over it and you could climb to the top of it, and anyone could easily forget that you stood on the garbage of civilization.

It was hot, that night, and I was the only person on the hill. I walked, struggling over the uneven terrain, to the top of the mountain. It was a clear night, and the moon looked like a hole punched in the sky, and I knew that brave men were leaving the earth soon, to walk on it; and I knew, too, that soon, someone would be looking for me, so I stood only a moment longer there, on that mountain of refuse, that heap of trash. All the things discarded in the process of building Rome. What is used until it is no longer needed; what is disposable to the empire. Pots and pans and jugs and dishes; half-formed Venuses left in broken blocks of flawed marble.

Epilogue

After

The sheets are thin, almost threadbare, but in a pleasing way. Like they've been washed a thousand times. I wake to the soft sound of the ceiling fan, turning lazily above me.

Many people have been here before me, and each time the room is cleaned, bleached, and scrubbed, made ready for the next. A woman comes to take my sheets every week; there's not enough water around here to do it more often than that, the hotel manager has told me.

There probably is in the nicer hotels in town—I'm sure they manage to find enough water for their paying guests—but I like this place better. It's simpler.

There's no man in bed beside me. The other side is still tucked in, crisp and flat against the mattress. And I don't mind it.

I do miss David sometimes, if I'm honest. But I'm happy, now. Things have become so simple.

I've been here for a long time; I'm not even keeping track. I wake up in the morning when I'm not tired anymore, and I do whatever I feel like doing all day. Read a book or a magazine, though by the time the magazines reach us, they're often out of date, and they're rarely in English. Lie on the beach, listening to the waves.

Sometimes I go into the town to tutor children from the wealthier

304

families in English—it's not much money, but it's all I really need. And I sleep so well, every night, on these threadbare sheets.

I don't have any of my things. No Bulgari pearls, no negligees, no drawer of gold-topped nail polishes. No cocktail dresses or designer purses.

I sit up in bed, stretch, swing my feet to the floor. I've been napping all evening, and it's dark out. It's late. I pad across the linoleum floor, slightly sticky, out to the hallway. Put on my sandals and walk down the stairwell and out to the hotel's garden.

"Garden"—it's mostly a patch of sand, with a few palm trees and some fading bougainvillea. Three plastic lawn chairs are arranged together in a cluster, and I lean back in one with my feet on another. Take out a pack of cigarettes I bought at the kiosk in town, and a half-used book of matches.

One of the local stray cats weaves a figure eight around the legs of my chair; another one dozes in the sand nearby.

And in the distance, over the guesthouse's crumbling stone gate, I can see long lines of container ships on the water, moving toward some distant port. They're beautiful, to me. Their lights glowing, drifting steadily across the horizon. Knowing there are people out there on them working the night shift; there are people out there awake with me. Probably far from home like me, maybe without a particular home like me, and I feel like we're part of the same family, and so I'm never lonely; not here.

David came home, eventually, and we spent the night together.

He didn't know it was our last. He thought everything had been resolved. I didn't say anything to him about the investigators, though I knew he would find out what I'd told them soon enough. Archie and Reggie and Arthur were probably already preparing a deeper investigation into David's conduct. Taking payoffs, domestic espionage—I believe that sort of thing is generally frowned upon.

In the morning, I made David's coffee and toast, and helped him to put on his tie. I wished him a good day at work—he still thought, at that point, that we could pretend everything was fine.

I spent all day packing my things, all my party dresses and designer shoes, and then as the sun began to set, and the time David would return drew nearer, I realized that I didn't really need that stuff, and in the end, I took one of my larger purses filled with just a few key items.

I did take the pearls; I knew I could sell them, and I was going to need that money, eventually.

I stopped at the front step to feed Beppo, then changed my mind and put him in a basket I snagged from a grocery store down the street. He curled up right away, like he'd been waiting for this moment. He never complained, not even once, even though we walked all the way to Testaccio that evening.

Mauro answered the door in his undershirt, in a halo of red cellophane light. His apartment didn't feel like hell to me anymore. It was warm and red in there like a womb, and the women on the walls looked soft and full and, though headless, seemed content.

He let me stay the night with him, though he wasn't so happy I'd brought a street cat with me, and then Anna came by with cash the next day—one of the scandal sheets had bought the story and the photo, and there was enough money there for me to pay for a room in a *pensione*, at least for a few days, until I made my way farther down the coast.

I rented a place a few blocks away from Mauro, under a fake name. It was mostly too late for David or Arthur Hildebrand or Archie or Reggie or the Wolf to do anything to stop me, but not quite, and I knew they would be looking.

The room was one I had imagined in my fantasies. Empty of all but a few of my things, simple furniture, paint slightly peeling on the walls, sun coming in through the windows and falling in angles across the bed. The street was tree lined; I was content. I waited there with Beppo for my world to fall apart.

I waited all weekend in my little room, eating bread and cheese and pieces of a cake topped with sour cherries that Mauro had brought me, petting Beppo, watching people out the window, reading magazines. I slept a lot, too. I was pretty happy.

There's a painting by Edward Hopper called *Morning Sun*, another of his images of women alone in city rooms. In this one, a woman sits at the edge of her bed facing the window as the sun rises through it, casting rays of warmth across her form. You might see her face and think she looks thoughtful, or lonely. But I've always thought she looks hopeful, watching the sun come up in the early morning and maybe, for once, not feeling afraid.

Monday morning, it began. Mauro came to my door with *Gente*, and by Tuesday we were on the front page of *La Stampa*: the photo of me in the arms of the Wolf, and the story of the gunshot, and hints of a debauched Hollywood party that had gotten out of hand.

We'd made it to the *New York Times* by Wednesday, and that's when I called Mama. She didn't want to speak to me, Daddy said, so I just told him I was alive and in Europe and I wouldn't be coming home any time soon.

I packed up my pearls, and Beppo in his basket, and moved on; I traveled south and kept going.

My story was everywhere until July 20, when men finally walked on the moon, and then everyone seemed to forget about it for a while, at least until the hearings. I'm pretty sure they were looking for me, too, to testify, or maybe to go on trial myself—I don't know. They didn't find me, or maybe they didn't look too hard. I'm not so sure they wanted to hear everything I might have to say.

So I only had two weeks of it, of being the most hated person in America. I wasn't even really *in* America, so as long as I stayed out of the big cities on my journey down the coast, I figured people would mostly leave me alone.

It would've been bad, if I'd been back in Dallas, or if I'd been in DC. They found a lot of different ways to call me a whore, over there, I believe. Uncle Hal refused to speak about me when reporters followed him through the halls of the Capitol building.

It hurt at first, to feel alone in the world, and to be hated, but eventually—pretty quickly, actually—it felt better. Like diving into a swimming pool in Texas in the winter, or any of the things they say will only hurt for a second, like getting your ears pierced or taking your medicine.

I sold David's pearls, which gave me plenty to live on for a long time. Free of things, no longer weighed down by all the little decorative objects I'd been using to line my tomb. It would've been more meaningful if I'd thrown the pearls away, probably, or sent them back to him, or maybe left them symbolically on the bed in the flat on the via della Scala, or even sent them home to my parents, but I needed the money. And I suppose I had earned them, in a way.

I sold David's pearls—my family's pearls, my mother's pearls—but I kept Aunt Sister's fake ones. I wear them out to dinner in the town, to the movies, around my room. The shine has come off almost entirely, and now they're little more than misty glass beads, but I prefer them that way.

The Wolf resigned his post, and Lina left him—for all her talk about how tolerant the Italians were on affairs of the heart, she wouldn't stand for public humiliation. He returned to California to wield his power in other ways. He went back to Hollywood, this time as a producer, and made a series of films about dangerous women. He cast Tuesday Weld as Mata Hari—as, indirectly, me, I suppose, which was actually very flattering. I sent her a letter, but I don't know if she ever received it.

I have no idea what happened to David after I left him. Whatever disciplinary measures he faced were kept quiet. Handled by the Foreign Buildings Office, no doubt.

I fantasized for a while that he'd managed to make things work with Elena the anarchist, but she didn't exist, and David wouldn't have been romantic enough to pursue her, anyway. He's the one I miss most of all, though I wonder about Yevgeny, who was Eugene to me, sometimes, too. But David—well, if love is knowing someone, is attention, then David loved me best. He knew all my secrets, he saw my worst moments, and still he tried to care for me, in his way.

I walk down to the beach and there's a silence like there was in Capri, like I imagined in the painting on the wall of the Wolf's house, a loud silence with the night breeze off the water and the turning of the waves, and even after everything that has happened, nothing feels final to me. Nothing feels permanent.

And I like it. I've learned not to hold on to things so tightly, not to wear myself out with grasping and clinging. I've learned to let things drift away.

To let myself enjoy the muffled sound of the waves, of a ceiling fan, and the sight of the ships moving past, back and forth, in the distance.

And what used to frighten me—that I would be eternally tripping over my own past, and that one day I would be called upon to explain it all—now seems so far below me. I always wanted to be polished to perfection, buffed and shined and bleached, so that any errant flaw or error would glance right off my silver skin. But now I know that you can be the one to cut your own moorings. Now I know it's not so bad, to float away.

Acknowledgments

This book simply would not exist without my agent, Katie Greenstreet, who understood Teddy from the very beginning and who has been a source of endless support and instrumental advice ever since. I am grateful to everyone at Paper Literary as well, and particularly to Catherine Cho and Melissa Pimentel for their immense support.

This book would also not exist without my incredible editors at HarperCollins and 4th Estate, Sara Nelson and Katie Bowden, whose joint efforts brought the book forth in its final form and whose encouragement has meant everything. I am grateful as well to Katy Archer, Edie Astley, and Lola Downes, and to Amber Burlinson for her exceptional copyediting and for very tolerantly allowing certain Texas-isms into the final manuscript. Thank you to Niriksha Bharadia and Naomi Mantin at 4th Estate, and Katie O'Callaghan and Bel Banta at HarperCollins, for ushering *Teddy* out into the world in such a wonderful way.

While Teddy's Rome is necessarily invented to a certain extent, and her experience exploring the city on foot is largely based on my own wandering, I have tried my best to put everything where it would have been in 1969. Several sources were of great help to me: Shawn Levy's *Dolce Vita Confidential: Fellini, Loren, Pucci, Paparazzi, and the Swinging High Life of 1950s Rome* was an excellent introduction to the factors that made Rome the center of fashion, film, and fame in the 1950s and '60s. *Valentino: Themes and Variations*, by Pamela Golbin, was also helpful, as was the

Acknowledgments

Metropolitan Museum of Art, which is host to the real-life version of Teddy's sequined party dress. For near-contemporary details about the American Embassy, Sylvia Jukes Morris's biography of Ambassador Clare Boothe Luce was very helpful, as were the memoirs of the extraordinary Letitia Baldrige. The U.S. National Archives were indispensable to my research, and in particular their extensive photographic documentation of the Villa Taverna. I should also mention the iconic photographs of Slim Aarons, which helped me to set the scene for Teddy's time in Capri. Teddy's shopping map of Rome is a real item produced by L'Associazione via Condotti in the 1960s, a copy of which I managed to find on eBay.

Teddy's Dallas is based largely on my own knowledge, plus plenty of fact-checking by my family, but I am grateful to a *D Magazine* article, "The Mad Men of Dallas" by David Ritz, for certain details about the city at midcentury.

For information on some of the major political scandals of the 1960s to early '70s, I read *An English Affair: Sex, Class and Power in the Age of Profumo*, by Richard Davenport-Hines, as well as several accounts of Martha Mitchell's involvement in Watergate. Winzola McLendon's biography, *Martha*, is the standout on that subject for any readers interested in learning more.

I am grateful to my writing professors at Princeton for always encouraging me, and to Curtis Brown Creative for the opportunity to continue working on my writing from afar—in particular to my tutor Suzannah Dunn, my fellow students in her three-month novel course, and my mentor Cathi Unsworth, all of whom saw Teddy in her earliest iteration.

The support of my family and friends is instrumental to everything I have ever done. I am grateful to my Abu Dhabi family, and in particular to Kelsey Warner for being an early champion of Teddy's and an even earlier champion of mine. To Ksenia Camacho, thank you for advising on all things DC, and sorry if I fudged it a little.

Acknowledgments

I'm grateful to Ameera Samy and Sara Silverstein for a lot, but especially for finally going on that Dubai weekend. Thank you to Greg Harris for the opportunity of a lifetime, and for being a true friend.

Thank you to Lauren Christensen, for the wisest advice on everything, but especially book things, and to Devin Walsh, Veena Putcha, Kate Adamson, and Kate Mangels, for constant support and great jokes despite being in various time zones.

I'm grateful to Margaret for being the most supportive sister I could ask for, and to Aaron for being not only a great brother-in-law but also excellent legal counsel. To Will and Louise, for being hilarious and perfect and for traveling all the way to Abu Dhabi to see me.

To Grandma (Betty Louise), this is for you; I wish you were here.

To Boo and Miss H, thank you for keeping me company while I write, and no thank you for scratching up my drafts and vomiting on my laptop.

To Mom and Dad, for reading so many drafts of so many other novels. And for encouraging me to keep going, to do everything, and to take chances.

And to Jimmy. For perfect timing.